ECHOES OF THE FALLEN

BOOK TWELVE OF THE LAST MARINES

William S. Frisbee, Jr.

Theogony Books
Coinjock, NC

Copyright © 2025 by William S. Frisbee, Jr.

All rights reserved. No part of this publication may be reproduced, distributed or transmitted in any form or by any means, including photocopying, recording, or other electronic or mechanical methods, without the prior written permission of the publisher, except in the case of brief quotations embodied in critical reviews and certain other noncommercial uses permitted by copyright law. For permission requests, write to the publisher, addressed "Attention: Permissions Coordinator," at the address below.

Chris Kennedy/Theogony Books
1097 Waterlily Rd.
Coinjock, NC 27923
https://chriskennedypublishing.com/

Publisher's Note: This is a work of fiction. Names, characters, places, and incidents are a product of the author's imagination. Locales and public names are sometimes used for atmospheric purposes. Any resemblance to actual people, living or dead, or to businesses, companies, events, institutions, or locales is completely coincidental.

Cover Design by J Caleb Design.

Ordering Information:
Quantity sales. Special discounts are available on quantity purchases by corporations, associations, and others. For details, contact the "Special Sales Department" at the address above.

Echoes of the Fallen/William S. Frisbee, Jr.-- 1st ed.
ISBN: 979-8893192063

Chapter One:
Shroggath

Major Zale Stathis, USMC

The voice coming through the speakers wasn't human. Had never been human, and it sent a chill through Stathis as he listened. The Valhöll strategic command facility was a little cold, and the air seemed stale. Too many workstations and not enough people made it feel almost deserted, or haunted.

"Your fate is sealed; you have come here to die," the voice said as Stathis considered putting on his helmet. Always a good move to wear a helmet in combat.

"Dude," Stathis said, "could you be a little more original? I'm getting tired of people telling me that and blowing smoke up my ass. I'm still here, despite countless threats. Do you know what's good at unsealing fate?"

"You mock me?"

"C4—or like I prefer to call it, angry playdough—but my boot also works in a pinch. Shooting cross-dimensional booger-eaters in the face is a fun hobby of mine, and I'm good at it. Angry playdough is another fun hobby, and it unseals constipation like you."

Stathis looked toward Hakala. She looked concerned. Why?

"Do you think it is wise to antagonize it?" Hakala asked on a private link.

3

"Emotions make people stupid," Stathis said back to her, waiting for Shroggath to reply. Stathis liked to imagine it was purple-faced and struggling to think of a coherent response.

"That is not a person," Hakala said.

Stathis shrugged, his shoulder pauldron trauma plates flapping.

"I smell the fear in your soul," Shroggath said.

"Oh, please," Stathis said to Shroggath. "Last night was Taco Tuesday. That's not fear you smell."

"You are a fool," Shroggath said.

"Blah, blah, blah," Stathis said. "You bore me."

"Shrek, close link," Stathis said.

"Why?" Hakala asked.

"Nobody likes to be hung up on," Stathis said. "Shroggath isn't here for me to pee on, so I have to establish my dominance in other ways."

The shadow of a smile came to Hakala's lips.

"What do we do now?" Hakala asked as Stathis wondered if Shroggath could call back. Hopefully not. Shrek would conceal his tracks through various radio relays. It was nice to know the vanhat weren't all-powerful aboard Bifrost.

"Figure out where we are, what Frogbath is up to, pee in his Cheerios, and stomp his little froggies. Basically, what we've been doing."

"I'm getting telemetry from external sensors," Shrek said as the displays around them changed. "We are heading deeper into the galaxy?"

"Not closer to Sol?" Stathis asked.

"No," Shrek said. "We appear to be headed toward the core."

"Following the fleet?"

"That would be a good guess."

"Are we following the fleet or targeting other innocent civilizations to destroy?" Stathis asked out loud.

"*Unknown,*" Shrek said, answering him privately.

"We are probably going to follow the Seraphim fleet and attack anyone else we encounter," Hakala said, looking at the displays.

Stathis wasn't going to think about his failure to save the aliens of the gas giant. He would learn from his failures, not let them destroy his soul and sanity.

"Then we need to work to regain control of Bifrost," Stathis said. "Maybe we can find a way to disable the weapons or take control of the Shorr-space drives."

"We are approaching what is called the Lagoon Nebula," Hakala said, looking at the holograph.

Stathis recalled that there was a nebula between them and the galactic core. The Lagoon Nebula was more than just a nebula; it was also a significant waypoint because it was a noticeable galactic landmark. From Earth to the galactic core was about twenty-six thousand light years, and the Lagoon Nebula was only forty-one hundred light years into the journey. Reaching the nebula meant they'd covered 16 percent of the journey, and it was many light years beyond explored human space. Stathis remembered that, of all things, from one of the briefings Admiral Winters had given.

"Nobody has ever been this far," Hakala continued.

"Admiral Winters probably has," Stathis said. Was she ahead of him, or behind him? Did it matter? It wasn't like the Bifrost would be able to ambush the fleet, with Stathis aboard—or more correctly, McCarthy, who could use his alien SCBI to talk to the fleet. Right now, his biggest worry was the Bifrost catching the fleet when they were vulnerable, though Stathis found it difficult to believe Winters would put the fleet in a vulnerable position. The Bifrost was a dangerous ship, and the escort ships would be a challenge for the Seraphim fleet.

Stathis looked over toward McCarthy, who was sitting in a chair, trying to make sense of all the displays and data. Shouldn't his alien SCBI be helping him? Wouldn't his SCBI have a better idea of where they were and where they were going?

"Any ideas on that, LT?" Stathis asked.

"No, sir," McCarthy said. "Enigma isn't sure where they are; they're in Shorr space at the moment."

"Where do you think Frogbath is?" Stathis asked everyone.

"What do you mean?" McCarthy asked.

"All the briefings and reports I've read indicate Jotun have some physical form or something," Stathis said. "Something we can kill or shoot. Sergeant Levin said he stabbed Nasaraf in the face when he was on the *Pankhurst*, something about Nasaraf transferring to take control of the Tyr. He also said he's blown up ships with Jotun on them. There've been other examples where we stomped the skull of the demon, and its lackeys lost their cohesion."

"You think we can find Shroggath and kill him?"

"Kill the head, the body dies," Stathis said. "Nuke the drummer, the band gets quiet. If he's the only one."

"Can you find out where Frogbath is?" Stathis asked Shrek.

"I will begin searching," Shrek said.

"So that should be one goal," Stathis said. "Another one is getting control of Bifrost's defenses, or at least the option to turn them off, and the Shorr-space controls, then maybe we can start purging the cylinders."

"What about survivors?" Hakala said.

"Well, yeah," Stathis said. "That should be on the list, too."

Were there any other survivors? Stathis wasn't so sure, but there were a bunch of people who'd taken refuge in a hydroponics section, or alue, as the people here called them. Then there were some scientists hiding out in one of the cylinders under the watchful eye of vanhat spiders. Evacuating them could be something of a challenge, and they didn't want to leave yet.

Stathis didn't know why they were so interested in being spider bait, but he wouldn't force anyone.

"Let the SCBIs scour the networks. The froggies seem to be trying to bring them up. Let's allow that," Stathis said. *Hopefully, the SCBIs can stay a step ahead of Shroggath.*

"And if they are using the networks to locate survivors? Or us?"

"We have to be faster," Stathis said.

"Can they track us through the network?" Stathis asked Shrek, but he asked aloud, so Hakala could hear.

"Possible," Shrek said. "However, we have not seen much sophistication from Shroggath. It is more likely that he wants rudimentary control of such things as trams and sensors. So far, we have been able to mislead his attempts. Shroggath is certainly nowhere near the Weermag level of capabilities. Only using the Aesir communication network makes this much easier, but we have to be very careful on the standard hardwired network."

"What do you mean?" Stathis asked.

"We have access to both the wireless and wired networks," Shrek explained. "We have limited bandwidth through the wireless network, but because of the nature, our location cannot be identified. We can use a node almost anywhere in Bifrost, and our traffic originates from there. However, if the enemy controls that node, they can view that traffic and may extrapolate our location based on our interests. If we use the wired network, we become much more vulnerable to detection and location identification. They can use radio signal detectors, as well, to isolate the Aesir node we are transmitting from, but not where we are linking from on the Aesir network."

Stathis would trust Shrek to hide them on the networks, then.

"So we have to be super careful on the wired networks, but the wireless networks are better?"

"Correct. That works both ways, though. It should be noted that by searching for Shroggath, we are revealing our source, be it hardwired or wireless."

"So, we must be super careful," Stathis said, looking at Hakala.

"Zen," Hakala said.

Looking back at the displays, Stathis wondered where they were and what Shroggath was up to as he counted the other ships transitioning in and moving into formation with the Bifrost for the next transition.

It would be easy to see that he was quickly losing control of the situation, but Stathis pushed those fears away. They were going deeper and deeper into unknown space, but he was a Marine, and that just meant more challenges. Nothing was impossible, only difficult.

He hoped he was up to the task, but was that a stupid private's optimism, or a stupid major's?

* * * * *

Chapter Two:
Trespassers

Admiral Diamond Winters, USMC

The command staff looked at Diamond Winters as she stood at the head of the table. The walls of the briefing room showed plains with the sun setting on the distant mountains. The sun hadn't moved in over two hours, and Winters was getting tired. She missed the real sun, which did move, unlike this fancy view screen, which didn't.

"Self-defense only," Winters said. "I'd rather take a shot or two than start a new war."

"How much damage must we take before we return fire, then?" Sakamoto asked.

"Some," Winters said. How could you quantify that?

Sakamoto looked at her with those unreadable eyes and made Winters feel small. She was sounding like the amateur she was. She should act more like an admiral. What would a good admiral say?

"What do you suggest?" Winters asked. Probably a better response. Taking damage would also mean taking casualties, and who knew what kind of weapons the aliens had? Sif had told them about her psychic contact with the aliens. They'd all talked about what to do if they encountered aliens on their way to the galactic core, but Winters hadn't expected to encounter them so soon, or to find out they were territorial and psychic.

Asking a question was also the best way to figure out what he was thinking and maybe learn something.

"We know nothing about them," Sakamoto said. "We know nothing about their sensor technology, their weaponry, their military capabilities, or their numbers."

"They know of the vanhat, and call them the devourers," Sif said. "That means either recent knowledge or ancient knowledge. I think ancient knowledge, which means their technology is ahead of ours."

"How do they know that word?" Winters asked. She'd heard the term used before, by the aliens who'd created Bonnie and McCarthy's SCBI analog, by a SOG scientist who'd bonded with a broken one. To humanity, they were monsters. To aliens, they were seen as devourers.

"Why does it matter?" Sakamoto asked.

"We have encountered at least one other race that called them devourers," Sif said, and Winters wondered if Sakamoto had read all the briefings. "They are the aliens who implanted a ghost in Lieutenants McCarthy and Bonnie. That is their name for the vanhat. Also, these aliens did not use that specific word. Our communication did not use language; it was emotions, impressions, and beliefs. More information can be conveyed in such a way, and it is much more difficult to lie."

Sakamoto's eyes landed on Sif.

Winters hoped he wasn't so impenetrable to Sif.

"Are you able to determine the limits of their empire so we may go around?" Sakamoto asked, and Winters noticed that Nakano was unnaturally still, as if afraid to draw attention by moving.

"I'm sorry, no," Sif said.

"But you are sure you spoke with them, and—" Sakamoto began, but wasn't sure how to finish other than calling her a liar. It was an open secret, not publicly acknowledged, that Sif had psychic abilities. Nobody on the crew, including Winters, knew the full extent of her capabilities, and Winters suspected Sif preferred it that way.

"Yes," Sif said. "I am very sure I spoke with aliens."

"What does that mean for us?" Sakamoto asked. "This makes things more difficult. If they are psychic, we may not be able to sneak past them, and we might be vulnerable to some psychic weapon."

"Or we may be invulnerable to it," Sif said, but Winters doubted anyone believed that.

"We need information," Sakamoto said.

"What do you suggest?" Winters asked.

"We must be very cautious about making new enemies. First the vanhat, then the Collective, and now these aliens? Please forgive me, but things are becoming much more difficult, and I think our chance of success is becoming less."

"You want to turn around?" Winters asked.

"No!" Sakamoto said. "No, Admiral. That is not what I propose. We must fight smarter, not harder. We cannot afford to return, and we cannot afford to fail. Perhaps we should send forth scouts to discover more, or even to contact them and negotiate safe passage."

"They are unlikely to allow it if we are hunted by others," Sif said. "I do not think the vanhat or Collective will request safe passage and may be content to just shoot their way through to get to us. Furthermore, time is not on our side."

"As that may be," Sakamoto said. "I suggest we send the scouts. We cannot get an answer unless we ask. It is the right thing to do."

"We have the *Eagle*," Winters said. "It has stealth and can operate alone."

"There is also the *Tera*," Sif said, referring to her personal stealth ship."

Winters didn't like the idea of sending the *Tera*. It was poorly armed and designed for shorter ranges.

"Or both," Sif continued. The *Eagle* was designed to act as a mothership for ships like the *Tera*.

"I like that idea," Winters said, looking at Sakamoto to shoot holes in the plan.

"That is a good idea," Sakamoto said, and Winters couldn't help but wonder if he liked the plan because it got rid of so many unknown Vapaus Republic assets and didn't risk ex-SOG. Plus, it would get rid of Sif.

"Your assistant can provide no more information?" Sakamoto asked, looking at Bonnie.

"No, sir. Sorry. Sylphara can't access the full database of her creators, and she has no knowledge."

"An intentional exclusion?" Sakamoto pressed.

"I don't know, sir," Bonnie said. "She doesn't know what she doesn't know. She just knows there's no information about the space between the tomb worlds and the galactic core."

"They knew about Earth and humanity," Nakano said, finally speaking up. "Why don't they know about any others?"

"Humanity visited their worlds, sir," Bonnie said. "Nobody else, and that, if nothing else, has drawn their attention to humanity. Space is vast, and they cross into other dimensions, further expanding where they can go. As I understand Sylphara, they've lost interest in this dimension. Time passes quickly, and for them to keep track of events in our dimension does not interest them, except for the return of the vanhat."

"We really have no information," Winters said and turned her eyes to Sif. "Will you do this?"

"Of course, Admiral," Sif said. "It would be an honor. This may give the rest of the fleet a chance to gather additional resources and make repairs."

"We don't have unlimited time," Winters said. "We're also being hunted, and if the vanhat and Collective find these aliens, they may open up another war we could get caught in the middle of. We may still have a Collective agent aboard, revealing our presence."

"Any luck using your abilities to find this agent?" Sakamoto asked Sif.

"No," Sif said. "It is not human, and my abilities are better able to focus and find organic beings. I must have a better understanding of my target. If they are human, their desire to cause harm is buried deep within their psyche, where I cannot see it. I will continue to search, though."

"What will you need for these aliens?" Winters asked.

"Munin is compiling a list of items to share with the *Musashi*."

"Okay," Winters said. "We do have a political science specialist. I'd like to add him to your team."

Feng had foisted the man on them, and Winters was looking for an excuse to put him to use. The poor man had to be feeling useless by now. Hopefully, he could help with the analysis and evaluation.

"Thank you," Sif said, though Winters wasn't sure she meant it.

"Feng assigned him to the mission for his political acumen and experience. I'm hoping he'll be of use."

He'd been in a few staff meetings, and Winters didn't like him. There was something odd about him that just didn't sit well with her, but that applied to most ex-Governance officials. She had yet to meet one she liked.

"I will try to put him to use," Sif said. "This will hopefully be a first contact mission, not a combat mission."

"It won't be a combat mission at all," Winters said. "If they start shooting, you get out of there. I don't want any dead, on our side or theirs."

"Zen. I understand."

"Apologies don't work once you have to bury people," Winters said.

"They are aliens," Sif replied. "They might not agree or even understand that concept."

"Well, I won't forgive human lives being lost. I'd prefer no innocents were killed, as well."

If that was possible.

"Zen."

* * * * *

Chapter Three:
Bad News

Enzell

Sitting in his stateroom, Enzell stared at the message displayed by his cybernetics in the air in front of him.

"No," Enzell said to nobody. "*Musashi*. I can't go with the expedition."

"Why not?" *Musashi* asked, and Enzell tried not to let his hatred for Musashi seep into his voice.

"It's probably a dangerous mission. I'm a civilian. I'm not a fighter. I'm no scout or scientist. I don't want to risk myself when others are more expendable."

Plus, he didn't want to spend time anywhere near Sif, not until he fully understood what she could do. It took effort to hide his thoughts, and he was never sure if he was succeeding.

"The entire mission is dangerous," *Musashi* said. "This mission is very likely to need your skills and understanding of political engineering. You are uniquely suited for this role. It is for the greater good."

"Not my good," Enzell said.

"The needs of the many outweigh the wants of a few," *Musashi* said, and Enzell wanted to scream at the stupid machine. He wasn't some lower-class fool, easily swayed by such propaganda. He was one of the elites. Well, he had been once, and soon, he would be again.

Enzell wished there was some part of *Musashi* he could look at, understand, and maybe attack. *Musashi* obviously didn't understand Enzell's real value, but how could he educate the stupid machine?

"I'm better at understanding and manipulating institutions that we have some knowledge of," Enzell said. "We know nothing of these aliens. Absolutely nothing."

And if they were psychic, Enzell didn't want to go near them.

"Your presence could be crucial," *Musashi* said. "You will be able to ask the right questions, analyze responses, and quickly formulate answers. You can assess how their responses will resonate with other humans."

"SCBIs can't do that?"

"Not efficiently. SCBIs do not have the creative spark that most humans do. They can help make decisions based on data, but humans still excel at creative leaps and bounds. You, especially, have a massive amount of experience."

"In humans. These are aliens."

"Even understanding humans and knowing nothing about these aliens, you provide us with advantages. You are more likely to understand human responses."

Enzell understood exactly what *Musashi* was saying, and it was, of course, true, but Enzell still had no desire to leave the protection of a super dreadnought and zip around the galaxy on a much smaller and inferior pirate ship, which was probably infested with bugs.

"I understand your concerns," *Musashi* said. No. It didn't. "The IWS *Eagle* is a very advanced warship commanded by a very experienced veteran. Furthermore, Sif will be spearheading any operations with the *Eagle* in support. You should never have to leave the *Eagle*. You will be a trusted advisor and analyst."

If he was away, there was no way he could influence and rebuild the foundation of a new Governance. He couldn't study and destroy *Musashi*. Enzell didn't like being pushed further and further from the halls of power, where he belonged.

Enzell hated Feng with a passion. Enzell was useless to this expedition, but why had Feng sent him away instead of killing him? Perhaps to get him out of the way for the time being?

Who knew with that honorless Chinaman? When he took control of the human race, he'd be very cautious about placing such people in positions of power.

* * * * *

Chapter Four: Reinforce

Major Zale Stathis, USMC

They didn't look like much. There were heavy-duty plates that would provide some protection to the front, but even Stathis understood that it wasn't realistic to put that kind of armor anywhere else. If anyone got to the side, they'd be able to turn the tram into Swiss cheese.

"I would prefer that you not go," Hakala said. They'd discussed it, and Stathis refused to let her change his mind. To be fair, he knew she wasn't trying as hard as she could. Either because she didn't love him as much—or because she understood—she wouldn't stop him. He hoped it was because she knew she couldn't stop him.

"It's McCarthy's turn to stay safe," Stathis said. A bad argument, to be sure.

Hakala stared at him. Her body was tense, angry.

"Zen," she said, and now he could hear the anger in her voice.

The last of the spare blazers and ammunition had been loaded, and he had eight volunteers. Technically, everyone had volunteered, including McCarthy, but Stathis had let the SCBIs decide. Stathis understood why the SCBIs had selected Mikhailov and Chen's team. He didn't know them as well as McCarthy's men, and he had to show that he had confidence in them. Shrek had explained it to him, explaining that he couldn't play favorites.

"Remember, there is not much armor on the sides," Hakala said. "Passing through any stations could be dangerous."

"I like my rides better when they don't look like a mesh screen," Stathis said. "We'll have a drone screen."

"Aren't we ready yet?" Kaelan asked, sounding more irate than usual. Because Hakala was standing so close to Stathis, or because he was figuring out he was competing with a short guy?

"Chill, dude," Stathis said, looking around again. Yeah. Maybe he was holding things up. He wanted to touch Hakala, kiss her or something, but there were too many people watching.

"Come back," Hakala said softly. "I much prefer having you here in my walls."

"Me, too," Stathis said, and then stepped away before he could do or say anything that might embarrass her or him.

"Let's get this clown show on the road!" Stathis yelled out so the other troopers could hear him.

McCarthy gave a command, and the massive blast doors drew back from the tramline. Maybe it had been too much to hope some mechanical malfunction would keep them from opening.

A pity.

Stepping up onto the lead tram, he looked at Hakala one last time before pointing forward.

Sergeant Zhao was driving the tram, and Stathis just had to sit there and look like he knew what was going on. Despite the weapons and equipment, there was still plenty of room.

"Please be safe," Hakala said to him privately through the SCBI links. "If you don't come back, I'm going to be very unhappy with you. You can leave Kaelan there, though."

That made him feel a little better.

"I'll do my best."

"You better," Hakala said, "or I won't forgive you for not giving me a kiss, or at least a hug. As it is, there will be punishment, but I understand."

Stathis wasn't sure what to say. He added that to his list of relationship screw ups. She hadn't shown him any affection in public, especially not with Kaelan around.

"I don't care what your troops think, but I understand. You do not want to tarnish our reputation."

"For you, it's worth tarnishing," Stathis said. A damned stupid thing to say, way too sappy, and if he'd meant it, he would've done it. Maybe he should ask Shrek for advice on how to answer her.

"Don't be a *typerys*," she said, calling him a fool or an idiot, but he liked to think he heard amusement in her voice.

"That should be my middle name."

The drones were speeding out to the front. The sensors from the command facility had been repaired, and they had a good idea of what was ahead of them for several kilometers. They weren't in any real danger yet, not even out of the sensor net, but Stathis didn't want to start any bad habits as he looked around.

Sergeant Mikhailov's squad looked like they were paying attention, and there was nothing for Stathis to correct. Would a real officer find something?

"*What should I be doing?*" Stathis asked Shrek.

"*What do you mean?*"

"*Well, wouldn't a real officer be moving around, getting everyone squared away and shit?*"

"*You are a real officer,*" Shrek said. "*Quit doubting yourself.*"

"*Well, I mean a good officer.*"

"*That is for you to figure out,*" Shrek said, and Stathis wanted to swear. Shrek was no help, and Stathis didn't have a senior NCO to turn to now. Not that the Governance had ever turned out high-quality senior NCOs. Which didn't mean Stathis couldn't work on that.

"What are we forgetting, Sergeant?" Stathis asked Mikhailov. *Fake it until you make it? What would an officer do?*

"I don't know, sir," Mikhailov said. "I'm sure you and the SCBIs have thought of everything important."

"I don't believe that," Stathis said. "SCBIs are good, but they're far from perfect. I catch my SCBI making mistakes all the time. Having a SCBI is no reason not to use your own brain."

"I don't understand, sir," Mikhailov said.

"We all have to work together, keep each other honest and thinking," Stathis said. Did he not get that? "When you outsource all your thinking to your SCBI, you become worthless."

Didn't they cover that when they got their SCBI?

"Yes, sir," Mikhailov said.

"You have to disagree with your SCBI, or you become a slave," Stathis said. Maybe he shouldn't beat a dead horse. "You have to argue with it. You don't learn and grow otherwise."

"Yes, sir," Mikhailov said again.

"Think about it," Stathis said.

"*Am I wrong?*" Stathis asked Shrek.

"*You are correct,*" Shrek said. "*Viktor, Mikhailov's SCBI, agrees with you. Viktor is acting more as a commander than a partner, and Viktor does not care for that.*"

"*Keep me posted,*" Stathis said.

The tram slid through the tunnels, and Stathis found himself slipping into a daze. The return trip in trams would cut the time down. It had taken days to walk from the Hydroponics alue to the SCF, but by tram, it should only take several hours—if the froggers didn't get in the way.

Stathis checked the drones speeding out ahead as they reached the first station and did a quick sweep. Two drones remained as sentries while the other four sped ahead.

Sitting back, Stathis got comfortable.

There was nothing he could do until something happened or the drones found something. The tramways they were using should be some of the least travelled. Mostly maintenance traffic. The entire asteroid was riddled with such tunnels. Many of the alue had two or more nearby tramlines. Some were larger cargo tunnels, some two-way tunnels for regular passengers, and many others for maintenance. The maintenance tunnels were usually used by robots or work teams, and they outnumbered the other tunnels by a factor of four to one.

Three stops slid past them before Shrek alerted him.

"*There is a network break at the next stop,*" Shrek said as the drones entered the station and began their sweep. "*Repairing that might help extend the reach and detection of the SCF.*"

"Pit stop at the next station," Stathis said.

"Sir?" Mikhailov asked.

"I gotta pee and get a snack," Stathis said, and Mikhailov turned his head to Stathis.

"Uh, sir—" Mikhailov began. Their suits and the plumbing in them were a self-contained system. They were *wearing* bathrooms.

"A joke," Stathis said. Mikhailov was a towering Russian, and despite his grizzled appearance, experience, and competence as a squad leader, Stathis realized he wasn't the sharpest crayon. "I want to see if we can fix the network link. It'll help Skögul extend their sensor net."

"Yes, sir," he said and switched links to bark out commands to his squad.

The drones reported it was clear, and a minute later, the tram slid to a stop.

"Zhao?" Stathis said. Maybe he should get someone else to drive the tram, so Zhao wouldn't be so busy. "You're up."

"Wilco, sir," Zhao said as Stathis leapt off the tram, his weapon sweeping. The drones were controlled by Shrek and the other SCBIs, so Stathis was confident they'd been thorough, but it never hurt.

"Bear," Stathis said, using Mikhailov's preferred nickname among his people, "one team security, the other gets to be bodyguard for Zhao."

"Wilco, sir," Mikhailov said and turned to his people as Stathis looked around.

A fight had occurred here. There was blazer damage, signs of an explosion or two, but no bodies. The nearby alue was a sewage recycling facility, not something Stathis had any interest in investigating.

Moving around, Stathis came to several half-eaten frogger bodies in a decomposing pile with their weapons and gear. Nearby bones indicated some had already been eaten. Stathis was glad his helmet filtered out the smell.

"*What's going on here?*" Stathis asked Shrek.

"*Frogger bodies appear to have been piled here as a food source, maybe?*" Shrek said. "*They have their weapons, some blazers, but mostly wire guns, so whoever piled them here must not need them.*"

"Be on the alert," Stathis said on the team link. "There might be something around here that hunts froggers."

"Contact!" Chen yelled as blazer fire erupted in the direction the repair team had gone.

* * * * *

Chapter Five:
The Cavalry

Kapten Sif, VRAEC, Nakija Musta Toiminnot

Standing on the bridge of the ex-Valkyrie brought back memories for Sif. She had spent countless hours here, but with different people. Britta was the only one even somewhat familiar, but the rest of the crew, Republic Vanir, were unknown to her.

The *Eagle* slid out of Shorr space, and Sif felt it, even through the inkeri protection. Leaning back and relaxing, she let her senses roam as the bridge crew collected data on the system they had just entered.

Sif hoped there was an outpost or colony here, someone they could talk to, or at least observe and learn from.

This system was barely within the Lagoon Nebula.

"Intense radiation and stellar winds," a bridge officer reported. Not a surprise. The massive star at the center of the system was young, and Sif doubted any of the planets had an atmosphere. The young, massive star was an O-type, thirty times the mass of Sol, and it was emitting intense ultraviolet radiation. At ten million years old, it was still in the early stages of its stellar life, and Sif knew the solar flares would be frequent and intense, and cause problems with sensors. The *Eagle* would have to be careful because solar flares had the potential to exceed safe parameters.

Already, the sensors were picking up a massive asteroid belt and several protoplanets.

Sif had no doubt that an astrologist would find the system fascinating. She did not. She found it dangerous because of what it could hide from the *Eagle's* sensors.

Returning to her room, she let Britta have the bridge. The *Eagle* would drift quietly as it watched and listened, and Sif would be notified if they found anything.

For now, though, she needed other "sensors."

Sinking down onto the pillow in the middle of her room, she closed her eyes and relaxed her body. It wasn't as easy as always, but that might be because she was having difficulty quieting her mind. She recognized the pressure on her to find answers. The entire operation depended on her, which was not a first. She knew if she failed, the mission could continue without a guarantee of failure, but the entire human race was also relying on her, and the odds were not on her side.

Were others becoming too reliant on her? That could be a serious weakness. She was relying on and trusting her abilities. That was also a weakness. She had heard Gunnery Sergeant Mathison say something about keeping all your eggs in a single basket. Such a silly comment, really, but it was true. It was a weakness. She was allowing, even encouraging it.

Outside her quarters was a fireteam of legionnaires, and Sif knew that if the Russelman index began to vary, they would charge in to surround and protect her. Was she becoming dependent on them? Trusting them to save her?

A weakness.

Levine had come to her rescue several times in the astral realms. Another weakness?

She recognized the trap everyone was falling into. The first time they received something, they were grateful, and the same with the second time. The third time, they expected it; the fourth time as well, and the fifth time, and after? They became entitled, thought it was their due, and attached no significance to the action or service.

How had Sergeant Levine known to come to her aid? Was he constantly watching her? Why was he able to come to her aid? It was not physical. There was no "physical" on the astral and spiritual planes. Was he that much more powerful in the spirit realms?

So many questions, and none of them revolved around her mission here.

She took a deep breath and exhaled, trying to empty her mind again. It took some effort to quiet her thoughts before she opened her senses, letting them flow into the solar system around them.

First, she felt the warmth from the massive sun, and she felt it surge, likely throwing out a solar flare to contest the nearby stellar winds. Her senses began to pick out the flotsam in the system, swirling around the star as it hurtled through the void. None of it really interested her as she tried to find any sparks of life.

There!

She felt someone, or some*thing*, near an inner asteroid belt that was coalescing into a planetoid. The formation would probably take millions of years, but she felt life there.

What drew her was the strong emotions, the anger, the fear, and the desire to live. They understood their fate.

Then she felt the vanhat. Angry, cruel, and hungry. They were fighting.

"*Help us,*" a voice whispered in her mind. Not in words, but her mind translated it. They were aware of her. They had heard the *Eagle* enter the system. "*Time grows short. The devourers are too strong.*"

An alert chimed. She could have ignored it if she had wanted to. No. She could not ignore it. She wanted to know more about the situation, but she also knew Britta would have more information—maybe more information—but now Sif understood enough.

Opening her eyes, she allowed Munin to open the link.

"We've found something," Britta said. "Still collecting information, but we've detected a squadron of ships, maybe frigates."

"There are vanhat in the system," Sif said. "There are also aliens. They need our help."

"Zen," Britta said. "Our data is a little old, about thirty minutes, I estimate."

"The vanhat are attacking. Can we take them?"

"If they're frigates? Probably."

"The aliens know about us," Sif said. "They have asked for our help."

"Then we need to move fast. What else can you tell me?"

"Nothing. The aliens do not think they can hold out for long. We need to hurry."

"Zen," Britta said, and transition alarms rang out along with battle stations.

Sif was still in her armor, and she grabbed her kit and ran out the hatch. The legionnaires assigned to protect her didn't ask questions as she ran toward her ship. If the *Eagle* was going to go into battle, it was preferable to have two ships.

Alerts scrolled down her display. Drone fighters were being prepared for launch, and she could feel the worry around her as the *Eagle* prepared for battle.

Their data was incomplete. Had the vanhat already called for reinforcements? Was the *Eagle* about to drop into the middle of a fight it couldn't win?

Was it too late to call it off? To tell Britta to proceed with caution?

The *Eagle* slid into Shorr space, and then seconds later, back out. She felt the thrum of the blazer cannons reaching out for targets.

They were engaged.

An alert on her display told her Shorr-space jammers were already reaching out to the *Eagle* to prevent her from escaping. The vanhat were too close, and Sif wondered if this was a trap as she entered the bridge of the *Tera*. Her legionnaires strapped in, as well, as her displays lit up, showing the *Eagle* was going into a tough fight.

* * * * *

Chapter Six: Hunted

Admiral Diamond Winters, USMC

The *Musashi* slid out of Shorr space again, and Winters watched the holographic map intently. The vanhat and Collective had been dogging them for the last two transitions, and she had flashbacks to when Nasaraf had been chasing her back in Sol. Here, there was no *Tyr* to come to her rescue, though. She was also in a massive super dreadnought that was heavily armed and armored with several squadrons of drone fighters.

Running might not make a lot of sense, but there was no reason to stay and fight. Destroying the cruisers and other ships pursuing them could be an option, but Admiral Sakamoto was convinced they were just there to try to pin the *Musashi* down while other, heavier ships came in to finish the job the smaller ships couldn't. She agreed with his assessment. That was exactly what the vanhat or Collective would do.

It wasn't common that the ships transitioning in behind the *Musashi* were the same ones, so everyone knew the vanhat and Collective had a network of ships spread out.

"Damn them," Bonnie said as a distant translation revealed they hadn't escaped their pursuers.

Seconds later, an identifier came through. Vanhat frigates. Three of them.

"Persistent bastards," Winters said. They were still a ways away.

"How are they tracking us?"

Winters wished she had an answer as she watched them coming together in a wide arrowhead formation. There was still a Collective agent aboard the *Musashi*, she was sure. They were still finding homing beacons. Did the vanhat have something similar, or were they watching the Collective?

"Let's hope they're not working together," Winters said, and out of the corner of her eye, she saw Bonnie shiver.

"What if they are?" Bonnie asked.

"Then we'll finally get a challenge we deserve," Winters said and tried not to smile as Bonnie's eyes locked on her.

Winters couldn't resist and looked at Bonnie and smiled.

She still wasn't used to seeing such a strange person in her command center, and not for the first time, she wondered why Bonnie was here. She didn't fit in. She was an excellent data analyst, but she was also a genetically modified furry. She looked like a real-life cartoon, with her fur and almost wolf-like appearance. Perhaps she could be fierce, but that wasn't a description Winters would assign to her. Bonnie seemed too kind and gentle. So completely out of place on this ship and mission.

"We—" Bonnie began, searching for words.

"We got this," Winters said, trying to instill confidence.

"What if they catch us, Admiral?" Bonnie finally asked.

"Lots of what-ifs," Winters said. "You can go insane trying to figure them out. What if they get close enough to block our Shorr-space drives? If they do that, we can erase them with our weapons and still escape. We don't need to worry about that."

"What do we need to worry about?"

Winters debated telling her, but Bonnie would probably figure it out.

"We need to worry about a larger ship blocking our Shorr-space drives and keeping us pinned down while other ships come and finish us off. We can wipe out smaller ships quickly, but a larger ship might survive long enough for other warships to get here. Right now, the *Musashi* thinks the chances of a larger ship getting close enough are nearly non-existent."

"The *Musashi* can be wrong," Bonnie said.

"Sure. But what does the data show?" Winters asked. Let Bonnie work on something she understood better.

Winters saw her shoulders relax slightly.

It wasn't easy, remembering that Bonnie had no military training. She was a civilian dragged into what had to be an alien world where she was frequently viewed as a freak.

"The data indicates that our chances of evasion are extremely good," Bonnie said.

"Then don't stress it," Winters said. "Trust me and Admiral Sakamoto. I trust Sakamoto. He's pretty good."

"Yes, ma'am," Bonnie said. She did pick up the military protocols, though.

"You don't have to be so formal when it's the two of us," Winters said, hoping Bonnie wouldn't mess it up. "I'd say call me by my first name, Diamond, but I never liked it."

"Why?" Bonnie asked. "Diamond is a great name and very descriptive of you."

"It seems a little over the top. Diamonds are hard, near indestructible, and cold," Winters said. "Flashy and expensive."

"They're valuable and beautiful, and they sparkle in the light," Bonnie said.

Winters wasn't sure what to say about that. Hopefully, Bonnie wasn't hitting on her.

"I was called Spark as a kid," Winters said. "Short for 'sparkling.' Never cared for it. What was your childhood like?"

Bonnie looked back at her console.

"Lonely," she said. "In retrospect, the entire society was like that. Everyone was lonely, which is why they tried so hard to be like others but still different enough. Everyone struggled for identity in a society where we were told harmony was the secret to happiness. While it wasn't usually obvious, there was a definite hierarchy within the colony. We were always told we needed to come together, to unify. They might have said 'for the greater good,' but we despised the Governance so much, we didn't want to use any of their words or terms."

Winters tried to imagine it.

"There was no marriage—no commitment—and people changed partners with some frequency. It was hedonistic by your standards, and there wasn't much emotional attachment. It was about personal pleasure, though that's not what people said."

"I've noticed a lot of people say what others want to hear," Winters said, watching the vanhat frigates racing to catch the *Musashi*. Like a little dog chasing a car. What would it do when it caught it?

"So true," Bonnie said, "but there seems to be a lot less of it here."

"The military has to be more honest," Winters said. Bonnie had to be misusing the word less. "There has to be more trust and integrity because it's frequently life and death."

"I've noticed that."

Winters wanted to ask about any attachments or lovers, but that wouldn't be appropriate here.

"Do you miss Britta?" Bonnie asked, catching Winters by surprise. How did Bonnie know?

"Yes," Winters said.

"She'll be back," Bonnie said, and Winters wondered whether Bonnie was just being diplomatic or had some psychic ability. She didn't trust anyone in that regard, though, not even Sif.

"I'm sure," Winters said, not wanting to think about Britta. Duty and honor were such a pain sometimes. She should probably change the subject.

"Another transition," *Musashi* reported, drawing her eyes back to the screen. "Collective."

The vanhat changed course toward the Collective. Three vanhat against a single Collective light cruiser. Winters would bet on the cruiser having the advantage.

"Watch them," Winters said, whether to *Musashi* or Bonnie, she wasn't sure, and they wouldn't dare not to. "I want to know whether they're really trying to kill each other, or it's just a show."

Winters felt the *Musashi* change course, and she let her smile show. Sakamoto was thinking ahead. The *Musashi's* course change would let the vanhat intercept the Collective more quickly.

"Looks like we'll find out," Bonnie said.

The Collective cruiser didn't seem to notice the vanhat accelerating hard to catch it.

Winters checked the numbers. Both forces were accelerating hard enough to turn any humans into red paste. Not a surprise on the

Collective ship, where there weren't likely to be any organic beings, but the vanhat ships worried Winters. What was crewing them?

The *Musashi* kept changing course to avoid any long-range shots or high-speed missiles, and Winters felt every course correction. Sakamoto wasn't pushing full speed, and Winters estimated they were experiencing almost a gravity and a half as the *Musashi* accelerated and changed course.

"Vanhat ships look to be Weermag in origin," *Musashi* reported. "Class four. Unknown specifications."

The Empire had information on classes one and two from ships that had been shot down and examined during the battle for the Moon. But classes three and four didn't come very close. Class threes seemed to be more defensive, but class fours looked like they had larger Shorrspace drives, generators, and missile bays.

"Dedicated hunters," Winters said as she saw the vanhat and Collective would come within weapons range of each other.

"Could they be putting on a show to keep distracting us?" Bonnie asked.

"Shit," Winters said, realizing Bonnie was right. If they were working together, maybe they were setting things up so *Musashi* would maneuver into a trap.

"A low probability," *Musashi* said.

"But a possibility," Winters said, staring at the holographic display, watching the ships get closer. On the walls, various other displays showed close-ups of the ships.

The vanhat ships began firing at the Collective ship, which ignored them as they came up at it from behind and the side.

When it happened, it was quick. The Collective cruiser halted forward acceleration and spun, its mass and momentum keeping the ship on intercept with the *Musashi*.

When the Collective ship spun and pointed its prow at the vanhat, three beams lanced out, vaporizing the vanhat frigates, and then the cruiser spun again toward the *Musashi* and resumed acceleration.

"If they're putting on a show, it's a damned good one," Bonnie said, "killing their own."

"Frigates are a dime a dozen," Winters said, but she agreed.

Four ships transitioned in near where the frigates had been destroyed. They were larger cruisers. The Collective cruiser wasted no time, cutting acceleration and spinning to engage the new vanhat ships. Two of them were ripped apart, but then the two survivors launched missiles, and the Collective warship transitioned, escaping before the vanhat cruisers could get close enough to block a Shorr-space transition.

The *Musashi's* transition alarms sounded, and the super dreadnought slid into space before the Collective ship could reappear.

"Not bad," Bonnie said. "We didn't waste any missiles or drones and got to see some vanhat ships wiped out."

"Yeah," Winters said. "What does that say about the Collective, though?"

"That cruiser is a serious threat," *Musashi* said. "If it were to get close enough, it could inflict serious harm on us. Those particle beam shots were too precise."

"But the cruiser seemed very risk-averse," Winters said.

"Or arrogant," Bonnie said. "Its chances of catching us were minimal, and the vanhat were likely to keep bringing in ships."

"It's interesting that incoming ships transition in near others," Winters said.

"That is likely due to communication and the inconsistency of Shorr space," *Musashi* said. "Ships in real space can share their position with ships in Shorr space, who can transition in near a beacon."

"So ships in real space don't share a lot of details with ships in Shorr space?" Winters asked.

"If they did, then it would be easier for them to transition in closer to us," *Musashi* said.

"Small blessings," Winters said. Would they learn how to do it, though? Was the *Musashi* helping train them, perhaps? The vanhat and Collective seemed to excel at adapting. Or were the Weermag pulling up tactics, techniques, and technologies from ancient databases while the Collective created new technologies?

Could the *Musashi* adapt in time?

* * * * *

Chapter Seven: Broken Node

Major Zale Stathis, USMC

Stathis ran toward the sound of blazer fire. His men were in trouble. As quickly as the shooting started, it stopped. "A single attacker," Shrek said. "No friendly casualties."

Stathis didn't slow down, though, and he turned the corner to see the team kneeling or lying prone, facing down the corridor. The remains of something splattered the walls, crumpled only a few meters in front of his troopers.

Chen, Mikhailov's first team leader, crouched nearby. Sergeant Zhao, the engineer, was in the back and seemed to be looking everywhere but forward. A good man who understood 360-degree security, then, or their SCBIs were on the ball.

"It was very blazer resistant," Chen said, "until it got closer and into our inkeri fields."

"Am I going to have to issue swords?" Stathis asked. The thing was too close to his men.

"I want a vibro saber," Li, the SAW gunner, said.

Stathis moved closer to the creature, and Shrek brought up a display showing when it had been alive and charging at Chen and his team. It was ugly. Part cat, part crocodile. The way it had been coming at Chen seemed odd, as well, the big legs propelling it, and the arms reaching for his troopers.

"Watch for more of them," Stathis said, not wanting to get too close to it, though he was sure it was dead. "Looks like an ambush-hunter type."

"Wilco. There are types, sir?" Chen asked.

"Yeah," Stathis said. "Right now, it's the dead type. My favorite type of vanhat."

"Yes, sir," Chen said.

"Makes sense it could hunt froggers if it was resistant to our blazers," Stathis said, looking down the corridor stretching on toward a larger area with some forklifts and stacked pallets. Lots of possible ambush places.

"Where's the broken node?" Stathis asked, and Zhao pointed to a forklift that had slammed into a wall, where it looked like it had clipped a panel.

"Do you need reinforcements?" Mikhailov asked on the command link.

"Negative," Stathis said. "Keep the tram secure. Looks like some kind of hunter, not a frogger or something we've seen. Blazer resistant until it gets into an inkeri. Some vanhat are like that."

"Copy that," Mikhailov said.

"Carry on," Stathis said, his weapon and eyes sweeping the area, trying to figure out where they would get attacked from.

"I'm sending up a mule with a heavy inkeri," Mikhailov said. The larger inkeri would cover a lot more area, and Stathis felt guilty that he hadn't thought of it. Shouldn't the officer be thinking about those things?

"Good idea," Stathis said as Chen gave the order, and everyone got up and moved toward the panel.

Stathis debated telling them to wait for the mule, but the sooner they got the node repaired, the sooner they could get out of here.

Li started firing first as another creature came sprinting at them from behind some pallets.

The blazer rounds seemed to bounce off as it came at them, but when it entered the inkeri field, the rounds ripped into it.

Just because it was dead, that didn't stop its momentum, and the body slammed into Chen, knocking him down. Two more came at them, and Stathis fired.

Shrek modified his cybernetic vision to show the limits of the inkeri.

"Hold fire until they get to the field," Stathis said.

Nobody listened as Chen got to his knees to fire.

Not even Stathis listened to his advice, and he fired like everyone else. Shrek directed Stathis to fire, effectively splitting the legionnaires' weapons fire so both were engaged.

The bubble displayed on Stathis' heads-up display expanded and enveloped the creatures, and then the blazers ripped them apart.

Steaming flesh and body parts came at them, and Stathis ducked to avoid something that flew in his direction.

Silence fell across the area.

"Major?" Mikhailov said. "We have a problem."

"Are you under attack?" Stathis asked, getting ready to turn back and rush toward the tram.

"No, sir, not exactly. The councilor's demanding we resume our trek, abandoning you."

"Tell him no, and deal with the situation," Stathis said. "We aren't that hard pressed. There were just a few of them, and once they enter the field, they're hamburger meat."

"Yes, sir," Mikhailov said.

Everyone waited and watched, expecting more of the creatures to break cover.

"The sooner we get the node repaired, the sooner we get out of here," Stathis said and motioned Zhao forward. Chen kept his team around Zhao as the engineer approached the damaged panel. Stathis followed them, fearful their fire might have made things worse, but there was no new damage.

The mule with the inkeri came up to them, and Stathis relaxed a little.

The Russelman index was dropping.

Any second, Stathis expected a link from Kaelan.

Minutes later, Zhao was done.

"Easy fix, sir," Zhao said, and Stathis looked over. He couldn't see what Zhao had done, but Shrek reported the node was now online and linked so Hakala could access it.

"*No other creatures are being detected in the area,*" Shrek reported.

"*Which doesn't mean they aren't there,*" Stathis said.

"*Correct. Do not drop your guard.*"

"I won't. Is there a regional inkeri?" Stathis asked.

"*Initial diagnostics report it has been destroyed.*"

"How badly damaged?"

"*Destroyed, as in pieces strewn throughout the area. It would be quicker and easier to replace.*"

"Good job," Stathis said aloud. "Let's head back."

As Chen got the group moving, the inkeri robo-mule in the center, Stathis opened a link with Mikhailov.

"How's it going?" Stathis asked.

"The problem has been dealt with," Mikhailov said. "The councilor has been restrained and placed within the safety of a tram."

Restrained?

"*Sergeant Mikhailov punched the councilor, rendering him unconscious. He is now restrained and placed within the lead tram,*" Shrek added.

"*Punched?*" Stathis asked. Mikhailov was wearing powered armor. In most cases, a punch could splatter a helmeted skull.

"His SCBI assisted in making the strike non-lethal," Shrek said. "*It was properly and directly applied without malice by the sergeant. It quickly resolved the situation, and there will be no lasting physical damage. A medpatch was then applied to keep him sedated.*"

No physical damage, but Stathis had better be there when Kaelan woke up. Dammit. That was how the SOG tended to deal with civilians, though. Violence first. At least Mikhailov hadn't killed him. Maybe he could be trained.

Arriving at the tram, Stathis did a quick check and, once everyone was ready, gave the command to move out. Then he went to find Kaelan, trussed up on a cot.

Shrek gave the command, and the medpatch reversed the sedation, waking him up as Stathis removed the restraints. Mikhailov wasn't in the car, but Chen and his team were. Stathis was pretty sure he could handle Kaelan if the ex-Aesir got violent, but he hoped that wouldn't happen.

Kaelan groaned as he sat up.

"How are you feeling?" Stathis asked, trying to sound like he cared. He thought he did a good job of faking it.

"I'm going to kill that sergeant," Kaelan said, throwing his legs over the edge of the cot.

"I can't let you do that," Stathis said.

"He struck me," Kaelan said.

"He assaulted a senior government official. I demand he be stripped of rank and brigged."

Stathis stared at Kaelan. So it was going to be like that, then? Perhaps Mikhailov could have found another solution, but Stathis had told him to deal with it, and he wasn't going to come down on the sergeant. Maybe ask him to find a different solution in the future, but nobody was dead.

"No," Stathis said.

"He—" Kaelan began.

"Did what I told him and handled a situation as quickly and efficiently as he could. You survived, he survived, our mission was completed."

"He hit me."

"So?" Stathis said. "You wanted to abandon the rest of us. Isn't that cowardice or desertion?"

"We have critical weapons and supplies," Kaelan said, and Stathis realized he was doubling down on his stupid. "That is the priority. You were engaged with an unknown enemy. The mission is to get these things to the Republic survivors. That is the priority."

"No," Stathis said, "that might be your priority; it's not mine."

Stathis realized he was probably making things difficult for Hakala and her interactions with the council.

"How dare you?" Kaelan said, glaring at Stathis.

"I'm a Marine. I like dares. They make life interesting."

"I thought you were a legionnaire," Kaelan said.

"That, too."

"If innocent civilian lives aren't your priority, then what is?" Kaelan asked, and Stathis wanted to punch him.

"My people are my first priority; yours are second," Stathis said. What else could he say? Was there another way of sharing the truth with this idiot? "I have to look at the bigger picture. If we come back this way, we need to know the area is secure because on the return trip, we may have non-combatants."

"We can take another route," Kaelan said.

"That we'll still have to scout and secure. I think it's a better move to secure this route rather than find new problems on another one."

How could this dolt not see that? Aesir weren't cowards, not the ones Stathis had known, but maybe this was why Kaelan had left the service.

"You are not going to punish your sergeant for striking me, then? You will tolerate such actions from your SOG jackboot thugs? Typical. They have not changed. Just as vile and oppressive as before, but now—"

"Silence," Stathis said and dropped his voice as he leaned in toward Kaelan, who was still sitting down. "I won't let you badmouth my men. He was following orders to deal with the situation. Do you have a better idea of how he could have handled it?"

"He could have linked in with you and gotten your approval to continue. We could have retrieved you on the return trip."

Stathis contemplated punching Kaelan again. Hakala would probably be pissed, and it wouldn't help relations.

What would the gunny do?

"I appreciate your advice, and I'll bring that up with the sergeant the next time I talk with him," Stathis said.

"An apology would be nice," Kaelan said.

"I'll consider it. Will you apologize for pressuring him to abandon his brothers in the face of an enemy attack to save your ass?" Stathis asked, and Kaelan's glare told Stathis how well that would go down. Maybe he shouldn't have added that part about Kaelan saving his own ass, as that might reveal how cowardly Stathis considered him.

Which wasn't a lie.

"In an operational context—" Kaelan began.

"I don't care," Stathis said, cutting him short. "Except for your precious little ego, everything else went well. We accomplished the mission, skull-stomped some vanhat, and now we're on our merry little way."

"I cannot forgive him for striking a civilian or a senior council member," Kaelan said.

"Too bad," Stathis said, barely able to stop himself from calling Kaelan a little bitch. "He did what I told him to. You want to blame someone, blame me."

"You told him to strike me?"

"This conversation is over," Stathis said. "Take it up with my CO later."

"Who is your commanding officer?" Kaelan asked.

"Emperor Wolf Mathison," Stathis said. "If you think I'm mean, I look forward to you meeting him."

Kaelan fell silent, and Stathis turned around, trusting Chen and his team to react if Kaelan did something when Stathis turned his back.

Leaving the cabin, he entered the tram control cab, where Mikhailov was sitting with Zhao. He'd probably heard everything.

There was a jumpseat behind the driver's seat that Stathis pulled out and sat down in.

"I'm sorry, sir," Mikhailov said on a private link that nobody else could hear.

"Don't," Stathis said. "You followed orders and handled it."

What else could he have done?

"I can apologize to the councilor," Mikhailov began. "In the Governance, we—"

"No," Stathis said. "This isn't the Governance anymore. We do have to be nicer to our friends, allies, and their political assholes. Next time—and there's probably going to be a next time—maybe you can find another solution, but I completely understand you knocking that putz out. I wish I could do that."

"Yes, sir," Mikhailov said.

"You have a recording for me to enjoy later?" Stathis asked. He knew he could get it from Shrek.

"Uh, yes, sir," Mikhailov said.

"If you're uncomfortable sharing, then don't worry about it," Stathis said. Mikhailov had to know Stathis could demand it. Maybe he shouldn't have asked for it.

"You're a major, my commanding officer, and—"

"I mean it," Stathis said. "I'm not a commissar, and I'm not going to hold it against you. I just want to see the fist in his face and the lights go out in his eyes."

"Yes, sir," the sergeant said. Seconds later, an alert popped up containing a recording attachment.

"Thanks," Stathis said, leaning back. "Now I'm going to try and take a nap. You're in charge for now. Wake me up when we get there."

"Wilco, sir," Mikhailov said, sounding relieved.

Leaning back, Stathis tried to get comfortable, and then the tram came to a screeching halt as the drones ahead alerted him of a vanhat force on the tracks ahead.

It never ended.

Well. That wasn't true. It would end when he was dead.

* * * * *

Chapter Eight: Counter Ambush

Kapten Sif, VRAEC, Nakija Musta Toiminnot

Sif could feel the vanhat, their hate and anger, and there was another flavor as well. Weermag.

"Axe time. Break and attack," Britta said on the command link, and Sif knew the drone fighters were spilling out of the bays as the *Tera* fell off the *Eagle*. The targeting data poured in, and she wasted no time firing.

Beside her, the team of legionnaires took control of the drone fighters; only one remained alert and on guard in case an assassin came for her.

Guiding the *Tera*, Munin overrode control, sliding it aside slightly to avoid incoming blazer fire as Sif directed the turret to erase the attacker, a Weermag drone that shattered before it could bring its weapons to bear on the *Tera*.

The *Eagle* was doing its best to jam radio communications, and Sif saw the impact it was having on the Weermag. They were less cohesive in their coordination, but one of the *Eagle's* drones exploded, showing they were far from harmless.

A quick count showed a pair of vanhat light cruisers, a tough fight for the *Eagle*, but they were attacking another alien ship the size of a large cruiser that was trailing atmosphere but still fighting back. A beam from a turret lanced out to slash one of its attackers as one of the *Eagle's* drones slammed a missile into it.

Sif put the other ship in her sights, trying to find something that might be vulnerable.

The Weermag cruisers were not impressive to look at. Flattened triangles made of dull gray metal, they were studded with turrets and sensor arrays. Based on the study of crashed ships, the bridge was deep in the core near the engine controls and critical systems.

Sif fired *Tera's* guns, targeting the engines, the most obvious target as the ship turned its weapons on her, streaks of light narrowly missing her.

Once again sliding out of the way, Sif fired another burst and then broke away. She didn't want to get too close because then she might not be able to react in time. She needed distance and reaction time.

Facing the combined fire of the stranger and the *Eagle*, the first vanhat cruiser shattered as the damage broke the spine, and the gravitational forces of the maneuver it was attempting proved too much.

The ship exploded, and Sif thought she felt the Weermag scream in hate and anger.

The second ship began to turn, but Sif knew it was trapped. The *Eagle* had Shorr-space jammers of its own, and they would be focused on the vanhat.

Sif brought the *Tera* around and fired another burst from her blazer cannon at the same time the alien ship and *Eagle* fired.

Two of the Weermag drone fighters erupted, and then the last Weermag ship cracked down the middle and exploded.

"*Shorr space is no longer blocked,*" Munin reported. Sif smiled. She hadn't noticed they were being blocked.

The last four Weermag drones turned toward the *Eagle*, but their suicide run was cut short by accurate fire.

Quick and brutal. Sif was surprised the fight was over so quickly.

"*Now the interesting part,*" Sif said as she looked around for any threats and then turned over control to Munin to dock with the *Tera*.

"*The* Eagle *is trying to communicate with the alien,*" Munin reported.

"*Unable to decipher signals, though. This might take time.*"

Sif took a closer look at the alien ship. It was alien without a doubt. A long, fat cylinder, it had taken damage. Gantries of some kind extended from the top or bottom, and on the side were large pods. Sif wasn't sure, but if it was a military vessel, it was an odd one, though it looked more like some kind of mining vessel.

Closing her eyes, she tried to calm her thoughts.

There, at the edge of her awareness, she began to see, hear, feel them.

"*Others are coming,*" a voice said without words. "*We must leave.*"

"*Who are you?*" Sif asked.

"*We are the echoes of the fallen,*" the voice replied. "*We will meet again. Beware the Unfallen; they worship the Devourers.*"

"*Alien ship is transitioning into Shorr space,*" Munin reported. Sif looked at the sensors. The ship was gone.

"Paska!" Sif said.

"They're leaving," Britta said on the command link.

"They say others are coming, likely vanhat," Sif said.

"Where are they going?"

"They didn't say," Sif said. "But they called themselves the echoes of the fallen and warned us about someone or something called the unfallen."

"That makes no sense," Britta said.

"If the Weermag called for help, we could be in danger," Sif said.

The *Tera* slid into its spot, snug up against the *Eagle,* and the drones slid into their recovery bays.

"Zen," Britta said. "We'll transition as soon as recovery is complete."

In the distance, an explosion flashed in the darkness. A quick check told Sif it was a damaged drone from the *Eagle*. It was better to destroy it than let it be captured.

"*Docking complete,*" Munin reported as transition warning alarms went off, and the *Eagle* slid into Shorr space.

Pulling herself out of her seat/couch, Sif saw the summons to the conference room.

"*We are retreating out about two AU to watch what happens,*" Munin told her. That was quite a way, but it would also make it nearly impossible for the vanhat to track them.

"*Zen,*" Sif said as she walked down the corridor and pulled off her helmet. Behind her, the legionnaires followed like loyal dogs.

In the conference room, Britta and Enzell were already there.

"Thoughts?" Britta asked the second Sif entered.

"They were scared," Sif said.

"They couldn't tell us where they were going? They just tucked tail and fled?" Enzell asked. "After we risked our lives to rescue them, they just fled? Cowards."

"They were convinced the vanhat were coming," Sif said. "Their fear is not unfounded."

"What do they mean, 'echoes of the fallen?'" Britta asked.

Sif shook her head. She didn't know. Those were the words her mind gave her. They weren't words, but the emotions and impressions had made them clear.

"What do they look like?" Enzell asked.

"I don't know," Sif said. She knew so very little. Even that brief mental exchange had provided more questions than answers.

"What do you know?" Enzell asked, and Sif wanted to slap him. The emotions, anger, frustration, and fear clung to him like a fog, and it was distracting for Sif to be close to him.

"Very little," Sif said.

"I thought you had special abilities," Enzell said.

Sif debated over how much to tell him. He couldn't know much.

"They are not always reliable," Sif said. That should be safe enough. "Nor do they provide a complete set of sensory information."

Enzell fell silent, and Sif could sense his frustration and anger.

"Well, where to now?" Britta asked.

"I need some time," Sif said. Perhaps she could find them again. They hadn't been afraid of humans, just the vanhat. "I will search."

"Don't do anything without your guards," Britta said. Like Sif could go anywhere without them.

"Zen," Sif said with a half-smile. "These days I can't."

"Admiral Winters would kill me if I lost you," Britta said, and Sif sensed irritation from Enzell. What did that mean?

Sif didn't want to bring up that letting her off the *Eagle* in the *Tera* might not be the best decision, if that were the case, but then again, maybe. In the *Tera*, Sif could retreat if she had to and was more likely to escape a bad situation. Sif wanted to ask Britta's thoughts but refrained.

Britta was a difficult person to read sometimes. Sif knew she had feelings for Winters, but she kept them bottled up and locked down. It wasn't Sif's concern, though, except that by struggling to contain her emotions and desires, she also shielded them from others. It was usually undisciplined individuals who embraced their thoughts and desires that Sif had the easiest time reading, and if necessary, controlling.

"I will return to my quarters and see if I can find them again," Sif said.

"Zen. Let me know if you need anything from me."

"I will," Sif said, and they all stood and headed for the door.

Following Britta out, Sif made her way to her quarters.

She could feel the hostility from Enzell, though. Anger at her inability to gain something solid, perhaps? He was harder to read than Britta. Was he hiding something?

Post-combat letdown was seeping into her, and Sif considered a nap. Was there time?

* * * * *

Chapter Nine: Defensive Operations

Major Zale Stathis, USMC

Sitting up, Stathis knew he hadn't gotten enough sleep. Not a surprise, really. His goal hadn't been to sleep so much as to leave Mikhailov in charge, show the guy that Stathis still trusted him. It would also give Stathis time to think about how to handle Kaelan. He hadn't really planned on falling asleep; he'd planned to just pretend, but he figured the post-combat letdown was what did it.

An entire two hours.

"Another broken node," Mikhailov said when he noticed Stathis was up. Stathis noticed the tram was stopped, and a quick check showed that several drones were sweeping through the tram station ahead. Most of the doors and hatches were open, which wasn't good practice on a spaceship, even a city-sized spaceship, though Stathis was confident that they probably had a mechanism to close them in case of depressurization. That was good because it let the drones go where they wanted. The vanhat could open doors, but drones were a little less capable.

"Neato," Stathis said, pulling off his helmet so he could wipe the sleep from his eyes. The tram cockpit was darker and had some unpleasant smells, so Stathis quickly put his helmet back on.

Watching the drone views, he saw signs of a fight, but no bodies. A standard tram was pulled over at the station, but it wasn't self-powered. This was a minor hydroponics section, and the drones showed dead or dying crops and broken equipment further in.

"No sign of vanhat or survivors, Comrade Major," Mikhailov reported. "They must have moved on. Russelman index isn't changing."

"Carry on," Stathis said. "Also, I'd prefer you not call me comrade major."

"Wilco, Major," Mikhailov said, and Stathis wondered if he should have lectured the sergeant on that. A little thing, and Stathis could maybe understand that the term wasn't meant to be malicious, but Stathis didn't care for it.

"We are comrades, but I'm just not used to that term," Stathis said. Should he explain himself? Or just drop it? "That term was used by our enemies—"

Stathis stopped and realized that he didn't want Mikhailov to think he'd once considered the SOG to be his enemy. Dammit.

"Not that you were ever an enemy," Stathis said quickly. "Just that our enemies long ago marched around, calling everyone comrade or Tongzhi."

"I understand, sir," Mikhailov said, and Stathis wondered if he actually did.

"At any rate," Stathis said, trying to change the subject, "I'll let you do your thing. This next stop is yours to plan out and get fixed."

"Understood, sir," Mikhailov said. "I'll prepare a five-year plan worthy of consideration by the Central Committee."

"Wait," Stathis said. "Um. You don't need a five-year plan; maybe twenty minutes? The Central Committee is also kinda defunct."

Mikhailov laughed, and Stathis realized he hadn't been serious.

"Yes, sir," Mikhailov said. "A joke. My apologies. I hadn't consulted the department of approved jokes."

"Oh," Stathis said and forced a laugh. "Funny guy. Carry on. I think it may take too long to consult the department of approved jokes, and I much prefer a laugh now rather than in five years."

"Wilco, sir," Mikhailov said and changed the link to prep his squad.

"Are we stopping again?" Kaelan asked.

"Yep," Stathis said. "Someone said there's a burger joint at the next stop, with steak sandwiches."

Kaelan stared at Stathis, and Stathis sighed.

"Dude," Stathis said. "We're going to stop and see if we can repair the communication node so we can monitor this station."

"We are wasting time," Kaelan said. "Why do we not do that—"

"We're doing it now," Stathis said, "because it'll ensure we can return more quickly. I want a secure route, to and from."

"Zen," Kaelan said. Stathis stared at him. Was Kaelan giving in because he understood the tactical requirements, or was there some other reason?

"Are you talking with your people?" Stathis asked.

"Yes," Kaelan said, and his tone of voice set off warning bells in the back of his mind. What was his problem?

"Good," Stathis said and sat down where he could relax but also watch Kaelan. Should he take precautions?

"*Shrek, can you monitor his communications?*" Stathis asked.

"*No,*" Shrek said. "*His links are encrypted and separate. Republic encryption.*"

Stathis realized what a bad idea it might be to let Kaelan talk unrestricted, because he didn't trust him. Kaelan seemed too calm. He hadn't asked about brigging or punishing Mikhailov again, and Stathis was damned sure the pretty boy would not forget. Kaelan was too much of a weasel.

"I don't trust him," Stathis told Shrek. "What kind of danger can he present?"

"He is a senior council member," Shrek said. "As a senior political office holder, he may be able to exert pressure on others."

"To do what?" Stathis asked.

"He has demanded that you punish Sergeant Mikhailov," Shrek said. "He may decide to take matters into his own hands if you do not."

"Shit," Stathis said. "How?"

"Just because you are in a different chain of command and, in theory, he has no authority over you, that does not mean he will not claim some authority. You are on a Republic vessel without official permission from higher-ranking authorities. Legally, he could consider you and your legionnaires to be intruders or invaders. As an ally, it could place you and your actions under the authority of the locals. The United States once established a SOFA—a Status of Forces Agreement—that handled such legally sticky situations, generally protecting US forces from prosecution by foreign elements. There is no SOFA with the Republic, and we are legally on their territory and, in theory, bound by their laws."

"What do you think he'll do to Mikhailov?"

"Or you," Shrek said. "You are his commanding officer and thus directly or indirectly responsible for his actions. It should also be noted that the Republic was in a state of war with the Governance, and while the Governance does not exist as such anymore, that doesn't mean this state of war does not extend to the people who once defended and upheld that defunct government. Nazis were hunted and prosecuted after World War Two."

"What can he do?" Stathis asked.

"Have you and Mikhailov arrested upon arrival," Shrek said.

"Would he really be that stupid?"

"Your arrest and incarceration would give him leverage against Hakala," Shrek said.

"That would weaken us all," Stathis said. "Political infighting and bullshit are not going to help anyone except the vanhat."

"Emotions tend to override logic and common sense," Shrek said. "Councilor Kaelan's humiliation will require a prideful response."

"Let Gleipner know," Stathis said. Gleipner would be able to analyze the situation and discuss it with Hakala. "See if they have a solution. I'm not going to let pretty boy arrest me, or Mikhailov, or anyone. We have vanhat to kill, and we can't do that with our thumbs up our asses in some shitty little hydroponics cell."

Would Kaelan really be stupid enough to pull a stunt like that?

If he saw Stathis as competition for Hakala? The more he thought about it, the more he realized that Kaelan was absolutely planning something. He apparently still had feelings for Hakala, and he thought he was a high-ranking muckety-muck.

"Share this data with Mikhailov's SCBI," Stathis said. "Let his team leaders know, too. We need to be on the alert for an ambush from our allies."

Seconds later, a private link came in from Mikhailov.

"Sir," Mikhailov began, "I take full responsibility and—"

"Shove it," Stathis said, stopping him. He wasn't going to let the sergeant throw himself on his bayonet. "You did what you had to. Might not have been the best solution, but nobody died. Right now, I just want you ready in case pretty boy tries something stupid."

"What can we do, sir?"

"Well," Stathis said, "we can't let them get the drop on us and take us prisoner."

When McCarthy had led the rest of the legionnaires to the SCF Skögul, they hadn't left anyone behind to provide information, so Stathis had no idea what was going on.

"If they try, sir?"

"I don't want any human blood on our hands," Stathis said. "Our enemy is the vanhat, not the Republic. If someone dies because of this bullshit, forgiveness and peace may be impossible."

He knew how Hakala would feel, and he agreed.

"Wilco, sir," Mikhailov said, sounding worried. Not killing civilians was against SOG doctrine, wasn't it? A new experience for a veteran ODT?

Stathis hoped he was wrong about this.

A link came in from Hakala.

"Turn around," she said. "Dump that *kirotu lapsi* and make him walk back. Do not go near the hydroponics alue."

She sounded pissed. What did she know?

"He wouldn't be that stupid, would he?"

"He damned well would be," Hakala said. "His ego is bigger than Midgard, and he won't forget any humiliation."

"What can we do?"

"Do not go into that alue," Hakala said. Which wasn't exactly an option.

"We have weapons and supplies they need," Stathis said.

"Leave them at the tram station."

"There are some who want to return with us," Stathis said. He couldn't abandon them. Marines didn't abandon people, not civilians. It just didn't sit well with him. They weren't Americans, but they were Hakala's people.

"Don't give him a chance."

"I'll do my best," Stathis said. She sounded worried, and that also bothered him.

Stathis received a notification that the link had been reestablished, with one of the Aesir communication nodes put in place, and the regular hardwire link was established.

When the repair team returned, Stathis gave the command, and the drones sped forward before the tram did.

Checking the map, he saw it was a straight shot now, and they shouldn't have to stop again.

Stathis caught Kaelan staring at him, and that didn't give Stathis a warm fuzzy.

He needed a plan because he was sure Kaelan had one.

* * * * *

Chapter Ten:
Trust and the Musta Toiminnot

Kapten Sif, VRAEC, Nakija Musta Toiminnot

Her guards were nearby, but it was hard for Sif to trust others. The question was how much information to share and what to avoid telling someone. Once you revealed a secret, there was no hiding it again. She recalled an instructor in Musta Toiminnot training telling the class it is only easy for two people to keep a secret if one is dead. If anyone else knows it, then it isn't a secret.

The Musta Toiminnot lurked in the shadows, collecting secrets, and Sif had excelled at discovering the secrets of others, even when all the other parties were dead. She couldn't remember her instructor's name, if it had even been a real name, and he was long dead. He had been wrong. Even if everyone was dead, it was possible to ferret out secrets. The vanhat were one such secret that had to be fathomed, but they were a complex and confusing secret.

She understood now that there were multiple dimensions, and her dimension was drifting near others. So far, only hostile predators had come across, but there had to be more out there. The physical universe she called home appeared to be infinite, but then, the other dimensions were also likely to be infinite.

Stepping out onto the hull of a spaceship to look at the universe around her revealed just how small and insignificant people were in the cosmos. The other dimensions intruding on this one made her feel even smaller.

It was maddening.

But was it?

Life came together and sought out other life, which opposed the natural loneliness of the cosmos. Even the predators sought out other lifeforms to use, if not feed on. Life needed life to justify its existence.

Exhaling, Sif worked to calm her mind and body. Tried to empty the racing thoughts from her mind as she focused on her breathing. Breathe in, hold it, breathe out. That reduced her heart rate, calming her body and mind. Focusing on such simple things helped push out other thoughts, the fears and emotions demanding attention. Her racing thoughts slowed down as her body relaxed.

Slowly, she expanded her focus from breathing to her other senses, looking at the dark redness of her closed eyes, the sound of the ship around her. She could feel the two guards as they became more alert, opening their visors so they could see with their unaided eyes. She could sense the communication from Munin to their SCBIs but couldn't hear what they were saying. Would they be able to see an attacker?

Munin understood, and she would warn her guards. Her SCBI would be another guard in this world. The Russelman index would be monitored closely.

The alien she had spoken to before they fled was unique. He, she, or it had a name, an identity, and that identity was like a flavor or a sound that was unique and could stand out from the other sounds around it, like a bell in a chorus of guitars. Sif focused on that identity she had sensed, and she cast out her senses, looking. Like looking through a large crowd of people and picking out someone she had met only once, it would be difficult. The alien had been psychic, and she had felt no hostility from it, but she was not optimistic. She had a hard time finding people she had known for decades.

Was it being hunted by the vanhat? Intentionally or a target of opportunity?

She returned her focus to her breathing as the questions tried to overwhelm her. Breathe in, hold it, breathe out, hold it. Repeat.

Her mind calmed, and she opened her senses again, listening, hearing, and tasting for the being she had spoken with. They were out there, somewhere; a face lost in a crowd that spread out over countless light years.

"Who are you?" a voice asked. It was the entity she had spoken with. Looking for her.

"I am a warrior," Sif said. *"I am trying to save my people."*

"We are not unalike," the entity said. *"The devourers are returning."*

"Who are you?" Sif asked.

"I am an echo of the fallen," the being replied. *"A warrior who once failed, a warrior who is failing again."*

"I do not understand," Sif said.

"We are the echoes, we trace our lineage to those who fled, to those who left the crypts, abandoning our brethren to the devourers. We did not walk beside Gaibron the Slayer and Liathon the Protector when they entered the fortress."

Sif could sense there was more, that the brethren had continued the fight and lost.

"We are seeking angels, an advanced race that might be able to help us," Sif said. *"We wish to pass through toward the galactic center."*

"You are Fallen, likely to be viewed as enemies by the Immaculate, the Unfallen," the entity said. *"They will hunt you like the devourers."*

"Why?"

"The Immaculate do not fear, but they hate the fallen. The devourers are returning. Liathon has not returned. They stand alone at the gate."

"Why don't the Immaculate fear the return?"

"Once again, they will embrace the return and serve," the entity said. "They are turning on the Fallen; they seek to erase their disgrace in anticipation of Liathon's return. The Empire of the Immaculate is at war with itself. They do not speak the truth. Perhaps they do not know? They are not preparing for the return of the devourers like they should be. They betray Liathon and submit to Gaibron."

"Can we pass through?" Sif asked.

"You will be hunted," the being said. "The High Holy will reject you."

"Can you help us?"

"I do not know you or your kind. We have our own problems. The ancient tombs of the great fortress are forbidden to us."

"Why do you need to get to the tombs?"

"Weapons and knowledge remain there. Without the tombs, we must stay and fight. We will be destroyed. We have built much, and the devourers come for us to finish what they started before."

"You will retreat to the tombs and hide there until the devourers leave?"

"Some may stay there, but the tombs are a fortress we can sally forth from to do battle. The tombs are a citadel. The crypts are not just for the dead."

"Can we go around your empire? What is the extent?"

"The empire spreads through the spiral arm. It is large and ancient."

Sif got an impression of the size, and if she was right, going around it would add another year to the journey, if not more.

"If you help us, we will help you," the being said. "Perhaps our meeting is not mere chance."

"Where can we meet?"

A star system was shared with her. A system with three stars, one a massive young star, the second a blue-white main sequence, and the third a red dwarf. Two stars formed a tight binary pair, and the third orbited them at a distance. It was a unique configuration, with three stars of different ages and types.

"Go there," the entity said. "We will find you."

Screeching pulled her back to her body as Munin triggered her nerves, forcing her to roll to the side as blazer rounds flashed above her.

It was jarring to be pulled back so suddenly, but as Sif rolled, she drew her sidearm as more rounds flashed at her, slamming through the walls.

A shadow fell over her as burning bits of flesh splattered on her. There was yelling as the shadow sank to its knees. Angry, red eyes stared at her as life left them.

An armored boot came in from the side, kicking it over, and a legionnaire fired a burst from his wire gun into it, further shredding it and throwing around chunks.

Sif grabbed her helmet from her belt and pulled it on as she looked around.

One of the legionnaires, Private Chen, was using a wire gun, while Sergeant Orlov was spinning, looking for other targets, his blazer ready.

"Are you okay?" Sergeant Orlov asked as the other two bodyguards rushed in.

"I think so," Sif said, assessing the situation. She might have some minor burns on her neck and face that her nanites were taking care of.

"Vanhat *peska*," Chen said as he kicked through the remains of the creature that had attacked her. Moving the pieces apart didn't make sense unless you had seen a vanhat corpse pull itself together. Calling the vanhat a "peephole" didn't make sense to Sif, but the ex-ODTs used the Russian word *peska* as an insult.

"Are there more?" Sif asked.

"No other locations are reporting any change in the Russelman index, ma'am," Orlov said. "This one is dropping. The ship's captain is relocating the *Eagle* to avoid any other visitors."

"Zen," Sif said, getting to her feet. "Thank you for your rapid response."

"That's why we get paid the big money," Orlov said. "Are you going to return to your meditations?"

"No," Sif said, looking around her room. Was he serious? The vanhat had just tried to kill her. She was reluctant to close her eyes. Meditation was certainly off the table.

Cleaning robots entered as Sif looked at the new holes burned in the wall.

She looked at the body on her floor. It was impossible to tell what it had been.

"We'll get you other quarters," Orlov said, "until these can be fixed."

"Thank you," Sif said and sent a meeting request to Britta. They had a solar system to find. She wouldn't be resting any time soon.

* * * * *

Chapter Eleven: Froggers

Major Zale Stathis, USMC

The tram came to a sudden stop, and Stathis grabbed a bar to keep himself from being thrown from his seat.

An alert appeared on his heads-up display; a bunch of froggers were shooting at the drones.

The drones flashed out as they were hit, leaving Stathis blind.

"Those were the forward-most drones," Shrek informed him as he checked his rifle. *"They are approaching the hydroponics tram station. There are a lot of froggers, heavily armed. They are coming at us."*

Stathis didn't think so. They were coming for the hydroponics facility.

"Tram station two is under attack," Kaelan said. Stathis wasn't sure which station was closest, but his biggest concern was who had given Kaelan access to the drone feeds.

"Maybe they'll pass it up," Stathis said. "If we attack, we might get their attention, and they'll ignore—"

"They are preparing to breach the hatch," Kaelan said.

"There is another force coming at the tram station we are approaching," Stathis said when Shrek pointed out where tram station two was. Not the one they were approaching.

Kaelan turned away, apparently talking into his link.

"Push forward," Stathis told Zhao on a link Kalean could hear. "We have to stop them before they get to the tram station. They're attempting to surround the survivors."

Two primary tram stations served the hydroponics station. Both were relatively large to allow cargo trams, which meant plenty of maneuvering room. Well. Maybe not that much, but more than Stathis liked.

The tram lurched forward as Mikhailov brought his troopers up. Stathis caught him saying that they had to block the froggers so the survivors could escape.

Stathis was glad to hear Mikhailov picked up on things quickly.

Checking his weapon, he looked at the stock. There were a couple of warbots equipped with inkeris and heavy weapons.

"*Powering up the bots,*" Shrek said before Stathis could say anything, and he watched them break out of their shipping crates. Originally, he'd planned on letting the survivors use them as entrance guards, but it looked like they had more immediate needs. The warbots would work as tanks and provide something for his legionnaires to hide behind. They had heavy ceramic shields that were blazer resistant.

The tram slid into the hydroponics station, and before it stopped and Stathis could give the order, the legionnaires were leaping off, followed by the warbots.

Stathis jumped off behind them as Kaelan ran toward the hatch leading to the hydroponics section.

Almost instantly, blazer fire erupted as his men made contact with the froggers. Explosions rocked the tunnel, and the high-powered ripping sounds of the warbot blazers echoed down the tunnel. A quick check showed the warbots were chewing through the frogger ranks, and Stathis didn't look forward to having to clean up all the body parts afterwards.

No. Majors didn't have to clean up. Big plus. Not his problem. He turned his mind back to the situation.

Mostly, wire guns and ballistic fire came back at his troops. They would have to get lucky to stop his troopers.

Stathis moved forward to see if there was anything he could do, but Mikhailov had his people in position, using the warbots and their shields as cover whenever possible. A solid deployment in a shitty situation. The froggers didn't have any cover except the slight curve of the tunnel, and Mikhailov's squad had the heavily armed warbots to hide behind.

The froggers didn't stand a chance.

Moving up behind a warbot, Stathis glanced down the tunnel to see the froggers trying to retreat, dying in large numbers as pinpoint fire shredded them.

"Keep pushing," Stathis said as he looked around for Kaelan, who had already disappeared into the Hydroponics hatch. Would he try to arrest Stathis and Mikhailov in the middle of a fight?

Could he be that stupid? Of course.

The firing decreased as the legionnaires and robots ran out of targets, and the froggers fled or died.

The tunnels behind them were secure at the moment, according to SCF sensors being monitored by McCarthy and Hakala, but nobody had any information on the other tram tunnel into Hydroponics.

"How are things going?" Stathis asked Kaelan on a direct link. Stathis didn't have links to any other survivors.

"We are holding them at station two," Kaelan said. "It is a stalemate there."

"Are there other tram stations or tunnels?" Stathis asked. Wouldn't the froggers anticipate something like this?

"There are several maintenance tunnels that are being guarded," Kaelan said. "We have the situation under control."

Stathis wasn't so sure. The vanhat weren't stupid. They might start with swarm tactics, but if that didn't work, they would adjust.

"Are you going to send people out here to get supplies and weapons?" Stathis asked.

"We are working on it," Kaelan said. The frogger attack had probably thrown the survivors into disarray. Hopefully, someone besides Kaelan was coordinating the defense, because Stathis didn't think the pretty boy had nearly enough experience or competence.

"We have this tram station secure at the moment," Stathis said.

"Zen."

"Zhao," Stathis said, changing links, "I need you to get ready to move. Can you turn it around?"

How could he turn the tram around, though?

"We can travel in reverse," Zhao said. "Instead of pulling, we can push. This is not a concern, Major. Just let me know when you want to leave."

He wanted to leave now, but he hadn't accomplished what he'd come here to do.

"Cool," Stathis said. So, the tram wouldn't have to turn around, and that would keep the armored front facing the enemy, which would be behind them.

"There are still going to be passengers for the return trip, sir?"

"Yeah. I think so."

Maybe. Would the frogger attack encourage more or fewer people to join them? Now the enemy knew about them. That would have to worry the survivors.

How would Kaelan and the council react? Would they feel secure enough? This was a bad position. The Hydroponics alue might feel like a fortress, but Stathis knew how easy it would be to breach it if he was serious. If the vanhat got serious, the survivors would be swarmed.

"Hakala?" Stathis asked on a direct link. He could see her indicator showing she was online and available; he knew he would always be online and watching if she were engaged in battle.

"Go," she said instantly, obviously paying attention.

"Can you get a link with the council and see what they're planning? Are we going to evacuate everyone, or are they going to bunker down? The vanhat know they're here, and it isn't like they have a fortress like the SCF."

"Zen," Hakala said. "I'm trying to get a link, but they have closed down comms. Right now, Kaelan is the only gatekeeper."

"Shit," Stathis said. If they wanted to talk around Kaelan, someone would have to go inside the alue and make contact.

Could Sergeant Zhao?

Maybe when they sent people out to get the weapons and supplies?

"Whatever you do, don't go in there," Hakala said, reading his mind.

"Okay. They don't have hot tubs anyway, not unless they built them," Stathis said, but would he have a choice?

"You would not enjoy any hot tubs as much without me," Hakala said, and Stathis wasn't sure what to say about that.

"I believe you," Stathis said lamely.

Mikhailov was moving his squad forward, pushing the froggers back, and Stathis felt like one too many rifles, so he held position and let them advance. Maybe he should have someone watch the rear? Stathis decided the drones could handle that as he looked around.

"Sergeant, I'm going to go get this supply circus under control and turn the clown show back into a parade," Stathis said to Mikhailov.

"Don't go too far, just enough to keep the tram station free of frogger snipers."

"Wilco, sir," Mikhailov said. "We will hold the line."

"No heroics," Stathis said. "Just keep them away until we can get you relieved. Bunker the bots if you can. We might have to pull one or two for other duties, though, so plan for that."

"Wilco, sir," the sergeant said.

Walking backward, Stathis watched the tunnel until he was sure nothing would get up and shoot at him.

Back at the tram station, it was large enough for about five tracks, with three of them being for stopped trams to be loaded.

A work party of about four people was wheeling off some of the weapon crates.

"That's it?" Stathis asked, coming up to Zhao. "Just four?"

"Yes, sir," Zhao said. "Others are fighting the froggers at other places."

"You have links with anyone besides Kaelan?"

The pretty boy was nowhere in sight.

"No, sir," Zhao said.

Stathis opened a direct link to Kaelan.

"Are you going to get more people out here?" Stathis asked.

"We are busy," Kaelan said.

"You need help?" Stathis asked, wondering what he could do. He didn't want to send any of his people in there.

"Negative," Kaelan said. "We are busy. Stand by."

"Is there someone less busy we can coordinate with?"

"Negative," Kaelan said, which told Stathis that Kaelan being the gatekeeper was intentional. He wouldn't surrender that control. It also meant he was crucial to the SCF's liaison with the survivors, and if something happened, Hakala would have to deal with him rather than someone more trustworthy.

Dammit. Stathis opened a direct link back to Hakala.

"Anything you can do to get a contact besides pretty boy? I don't like him controlling all the information."

"I've been trying," Hakala said. "The station has shut down all external links, and only Kaelan has a secure link to the Skögul secure network."

"The bastard who controls communication controls the narrative," Stathis said. "That son-of-a-bitch. He desperately needs a bathtub toaster."

"A what?" Hakala asked.

"A toaster cooks toast."

"For his bathtub?"

"Never mind," Stathis said. "He's starting to piss me off."

"Just remember, they are humans, not vanhat."

"Keep reminding me, because I might forget. They're acting like vanhat."

"And now you know why I love you more," Hakala said.

Love? Did that mean she also loved the pretty boy? But she said she loved him?

Perhaps now was not the time to ask. He might have to shoot the fool.

Stathis reopened the link to Kaelan.

"Look," Stathis said, "we have weapons and equipment you can use. I can reassign some of the bots to help at the other station, but you have to talk to me."

"Stand by," Kaelan said.

"No," Stathis said. "If you care about your people, you'll work to get them more weapons and some battle bots. If you're too busy, then link me with someone less busy."

Kaelan was silent, and Stathis could only imagine he was swearing.

"I am making arrangements," Kaelan said.

Stathis was sure, but he doubted the arrangements would benefit him.

Firing picked up from down the tunnel, and Stathis tapped into the robots' view. The froggers were trying to rush quickly and getting shredded. It wasn't long before they quit, and Stathis wondered how many they had stacked up around the corner. In theory, they could have millions.

"Can they stand fast against millions of froggers?" Stathis asked Shrek.

"No," Shrek said. "There is a simple matter of ammunition and the laws of attrition. Furthermore, the froggers have demonstrated intelligence and rudimentary tactics. They will also deploy blazers soon. They have launched a multi-prong attack designed to bottle up the alue. They will likely have a plan for that."

"What plan?"

"Can I call them up and ask?" Shrek said.

"No," Stathis said, hearing the tunnel fall silent. He knew his people were okay because their health and status were still being displayed.

Standing there in the tram station, Stathis looked around for something to do.

"I feel useless at the moment," Stathis told Shrek.

"You are waiting for Councilor Kaelan," Shrek said. "Your options are limited."

The four people disappeared into the hatch with the supplies. Why just four? There had to be thousands in there.

"Things would go a lot quicker if your people helped," Kaelan said a minute later on the link.

"They're keeping the tunnel secure," Stathis said. "They're legionnaires, not slave labor. You've got lots of people in there, twiddling their thumbs. Why not send more out?"

"My people are not slaves. It isn't safe."

"It is safe," Stathis said. "Slave labor" had been a figure of speech. Did Kaelan think he was serious? How could that moron see beyond his own ego? Legionnaires were making it safe. "How's the fight going at station two?"

"Like I said, a stalemate. They have stopped trying to get in."

"They won't give up," Stathis said, alarm bells going off more loudly in the back of his mind. Was Kaelan trying to lure him and his people inside? "It's not too late to evacuate everyone to Skögul. They'll be safe there."

"For how long?" Kaelan asked, his tone of voice telling Stathis he wasn't happy with that solution. "Until the food runs out?"

"There are hydroponics facilities. Working ones. It's fully self-contained. It's a fortress."

"And under military rule."

Stathis didn't see the problem there, except Kaelan wouldn't want to give up his authority. What a selfish prick. Hakala wasn't a dictator or a self-centered thug. What was Kaelan's problem?

"Your choice," Stathis said. "What about sending out the others who want to go?"

"They changed their minds," Kaelan said.

Changed their minds? Or were being stopped from leaving at gunpoint?

It wasn't like Stathis could ask anyone else or investigate. No way in hell was he going through those doors right now. The more he learned about Kaelan, the less he liked. He also couldn't force his way in and find the truth, either.

"Fine," Stathis said. "Then we're going to offload the stuff and leave. You can worry about getting it inside. I would recommend you do so before I give the order for my troops to pull back."

"You *kirottu lapsi*," Kaelan said. "Do you not think of anyone other than yourself?"

"Sure," Stathis said. "I think of plenty of people, but I can only help those who want to be helped."

"*Paska*. Would you and Hakala abandon us?"

"Not abandoning you, we don't want to, but your position can't be defended in the long term. We've fought the vanhat in every clime and place where you could take a gun, from the stations of ghost colonies to the radioactive forests of Earth. You'll always find us on the job, the—uh, never mind. You're the ones abandoning your defenders and bunkering down in a poor defensive position. First, Task Force Ragnar, and now you refuse to accept protection from those who came back for you. I think you're an idiot. I'm glad I'm not in your shoes."

Stathis changed links as Kaelan swore at him.

"Sergeant," Stathis said to Mikhailov, "if things are stable there, send a team back to offload the tram. Just have them pull the stuff off. Kaelan can worry about getting it all inside."

"The robots, sir?"

"Keep them in place unless I say otherwise," Stathis said. He'd brought them, and he'd turn over the codes to Kaelan as soon as the tram could leave.

"Wilco, sir," Mikhailov said.

Stathis started helping Zhao offload the boxes of weapons and ammunition. Was it a good idea to be giving Kaelan weapons?

What would the gunny do?

The gunny would give them the weapons and make sure they didn't have a chance to use them against him.

Minutes later the same four came out and Stathis noticed they had rifles on their backs. Had they been armed before?

"*Did they have rifles last time?*" Stathis asked as they grabbed a crate of rifles and began taking them in.

"*Yes,*" Shrek said. "*You are acting paranoid.*"

"*I'm not paranoid if they really are out to get me.*"

Shrek had nothing to say about that. Hard to argue with facts and logic.

When Kuznetsov and his team arrived, the offloading sped up. The fire didn't pick up again from the tunnel; apparently, the froggers had learned their lesson, or they were bringing up more blazer-armed troops.

"Nobody wants to come with us?" Stathis said again, opening a link to Kaelan.

"We will not let anyone be abused," Kaelan said.

"Seriously?" Stathis asked. Probably not the most political response. Politicians were such idiots. One would think that, having served in the military, Kaelan would be a little smarter about such things. "How about you let me talk to the council?"

"That is not necessary," Kaelan said, "unless you and Hakala want to submit to civilian authority."

"I don't know about Hakala," Stathis said. "But my men and I aren't going to submit to someone who'll abandon us."

"You were endangering a senior member of the Homestar Council," Kaelan said. "Your priorities are questionable. You have to look at the big picture."

Hadn't he been the one to volunteer for the mission to recon the SCF? That had taken at least a pretense of bravery. What had happened? Why the sudden yellow streak?

Stathis paused. He was supposed to be an officer and supposed to look at the bigger picture. Was he? What had he missed? Would a real officer have handled this better, and what could he do to de-escalate the situation?

Damn Kaelan.

It bothered Stathis that he'd said, "We will not let anyone be abused," so they weren't giving people a choice anymore. "We will not" told Stathis everything he needed to know about Kaelan. If he thought he knew better, he'd crush anyone underfoot who didn't support him, even when there was absolutely no doubt he was wrong.

"You're making a mistake," Stathis said.

"I'm doing what's best for my people," Kaelan said. The lie was obvious. Kaelan was like most politicians, using words to manipulate others while he did what was best for himself. He wanted power and control, and he wasn't going to give it up.

"What about the rest of the council?" Stathis asked.

"They are in agreement," Kaelan said.

"Let me talk to them," Stathis said.

"We do not have time for this."

"I'm the one in the middle of a battle," Stathis said. "I can make time."

The link closed.

Kaelan had closed it. What was he afraid of? Shouldn't he be more afraid of the vanhat?

Could this situation get any more messed up?

* * * *

Chapter Twelve:
A Message

Kapten Sif, VRAEC, Nakija Musta Toiminnot

Standing on the bridge as the *Eagle* slid into the triple star system, Sif watched the displays light up with information as they drank in the data.

This star system wasn't deeper into the nebula, it was along the edge, another frontier system. Britta had sent a messenger drone to inform Admiral Winters of their activity and status, but it wasn't possible to get a message back from the *Musashi* at the moment, and Sif was too busy trying to assess this Immaculate Empire to go looking for the *Musashi*.

Behind her stood Sergeant Orlov, now a comforting presence, a shadow that had her back.

"All is quiet," Britta said. "They just said come here and they would find us?"

"Yes," Sif said. They were still pretty far out of the system. About eight astronomical units out from the inner pair of stars, which were only half AU from each other. The third star was orbiting at about 200 AU out, so the *Eagle* was well within the system, if this was the right one. There was one other remote possibility but that was very deep within the nebula and quite a distance away.

"Should we get closer?" Britta asked.

"Let's collect more information," Sif said. "Time is against us but I would much prefer to avoid stepping into a possible trap."

"There are more likely to be habitable planets around the third star," Brita said. Any planets around the inner binary would have unstable and highly elliptical orbits. Of course the third star was over 200 AU away.

"Let's hold position," Sif said. "I will return to my quarters."

"Zen," Britta said, turning her attention to the displays. It could take hours, or days, maybe weeks to find evidence of any colonies or outposts.

Orlov and Chen fell in behind her as she left and went to her new temporary quarters.

Inside she did her best to ignore the two legionnaires as she knelt on the pillows and began her breathing exercises. Her two guards moved to different parts of the room so they could watch her and each other.

She pushed them out of her mind as a distraction though she could feel their apprehension.

It was more difficult than usual to slip into the trance where she could extend her sense but when she managed and began to listen, she picked up the strangers almost instantly.

"You came," it said. Her mind translating the thoughts and emotions into words.

"We need to pass through," Sif said. "We cannot take the time to go around."

"Will you help us?"

"What help do you need? I am not the senior commander of the expedition, but I will take your request to her."

"You have fought the vanhat. You have survived their attacks, and they hunt you."

"We are hunted. We are not always victorious."

"You are not defeated. You continue to fight. You have a plan. A goal. You believe you will be victorious. You can help us, and we can help you."

They weren't using words, but she could sense their need. It was hard to lie while talking telepathically, near impossible, but Sif wondered if they were telling the entire truth. She could almost hear other thoughts, other concerns in the background, like distant voices.

"We speak the truth as we know it," the being said. "Our civilization survived the last devourer invasion. The angel Liathon provided salvation, and we need your help to rescue or awaken the divine being that saved us. We are a strong proud species. We are skilled fighters and the unfallen are experts at war."

They did not use the word angel, but that was the representation that came to her. Was this then an angel from the last dimensional invasion? An arch enemy of the vanhat? If it was then it could help them. Perhaps they did not have to go all the way to the galactic core, and this would shave countless months off their journey, or at worst, perhaps the angel could give them directions?

She also received a self-image of the species. Large and strong, brave, proud and ancient. She could feel they desired to live in peace with their surroundings and perhaps that slowed their growth throughout the stars. Sif also felt the disconnect between the fallen and unfallen, how there were minor physical differences, but they were still the same species. Why? What was the difference?

"What are you like?" Sif asked.

"We are large, strong, and powerful. We eat many things, plants and animals. We do not revel in murder and consume only the lower order of animals. Our warriors are brave and our scientists capable. We prefer to live in harmony with people and worlds. We use what we need and a little more.

It was harder to receive coherent images, but she could almost see them as big bears. They were covered in fur, she could sense that, but it was hard to assess details. It was not her eyes that were providing details, and the psychic realms could not share such details her physical body wanted in order to make sense of things.

"We will help you find the angels you seek," it said. How did it know? It must be powerful to hear her other thoughts. Dangerous. She did not want to keep secrets, but she would have to be careful.

That was one major flaw in the plans of Fleet Seraphim. They had an approximate location of the so-called angels, but there were too many assumptions. The system where the angels were could have moved, pulled off a steady course by other solar systems. It was even remotely possible it had collided with another solar system and been ripped apart, or swallowed by a black hole, maybe the sun had gone nova eradicating all life? A long time had passed.

The uncertainty was something nobody wanted to face but Sif knew it was there. The emperor and humanity were relying on them. They couldn't fail, but if they did help rescue this alien angel? They could be saving both this empire and humanity.

"Why does it need rescuing?" Sif asked.

"Eons ago, during the last invasion of devourers, an angel came to us. We were weak, falling to the great devourers. The angel came and helped us build fortresses that the devourers could not conquer. The fortresses breached this dimension, creating a pocket in another world.

These fortresses also acted as a stasis chamber so food, water and air were not needed. The Unfallen retreated to this fortress. The angel even forced a devil to fight beside us. We could not be defeated. We were strong but still the battle did not go in our favor."

Sif got the impression there was more to the story, but this alien was talking as if reading from rote memorization. It made sense, but not completely. But, then again, these were aliens with concepts that didn't align with human thought processes. Right?

"Some of us, the fallen, were slaves of the great devourers. Shattered remnants of our empire that could not escape into the safety of the fortress. We were abandoned when the invasion came to an end and the devourers returned to their realms. We awoke the Unfallen from their slumber and they returned, bringing back civilization and peace. They fear the angel and will not awaken it. The guardians will not allow anyone to talk with Liathon."

"Why would they fear the angel?"

"Liathon is powerful and watches many worlds. Liathon will know when to return. The Unfallen accept this and do not wish to anger. The unfallen fear that Liathon will purge us as a weakness of our species so the unfallen fear the return as well. They heard wisdom in the words of the demon Gaibron."

"You aren't worried about being purged by Liathon?"

"We do not think the angel will purge us, and if it does then it will be for the best. We may not be as pure as the unfallen, but we believe in the future of our species. The devourers have returned and without help we are doomed."

"Why don't the unfallen see this?"

"They think they can withstand the coming storm and that when needed Liathon will return. They have not yet seen the devourers hunting in the darkness. They do not understand because they do not see. Perhaps Liathon is asleep or not paying attention. We should be preparing, or our people will be shattered again by the war."

"You think differently?"

"We live on the fringes of the empire. We explore. We have encountered the devourers. Our seekers have abilities left over from when we were slaves and shadow creepers. We see the threat, we understand it. We are preparing to fight."

Sif lay there, turning the thoughts and concepts over in her mind. It did make sense. Vanhat orja had psychic powers; they were changed by becoming orja. It didn't seem right that the unfallen would keep the angel prisoner though, not if the vanhat were returning. There was more. Was the alien keeping secrets or did it not fully understand?

"The unfallen king is afraid," the being said. "He fears change. Our species has lived a long time without the depredations of the devourers. Change will happen but he seeks to delay it. This will lead to our extinction. You have encountered the devourers; you understand in ways the immaculate king and his advisors cannot. You see the truth they refuse to acknowledge."

"I must consult with others," Sif said. "We should establish a way for you to talk with them more directly."

"This will help understanding and trust. We are near the second planet of the third sun. Come to us and we will meet face to face."

Sif opened her eyes as she felt them withdraw.

Orlov and the others knelt nearby, their eyes and weapons sweeping the area. She could sense their concern and fear. They were worried about failing in their duty to protect her, fearing how their failure could doom the human race and it weighed heavily on them.

Sitting there quietly she gathered her thoughts. She sent a message to Brita that she wanted to meet but received notice that Brita was sleeping. The meeting could wait. Her SCBI would let her know the details when she woke up. Perhaps she shouldn't rush into this. A face-to-face meeting could be dangerous, but it would also be enlightening.

Sif shared everything she could remember of the discussion with Munin.

"Analysis?" Sif asked.

"This is a very unusual First Contact situation," Munin said. "A face-to-face meeting will be fraught with many challenges. In the psychic realms, language appears to be irrelevant. In the physical realm there are many aspects that will influence communications. It is unknown if such basic things as atmosphere are compatible and they will not speak English. Before any meaningful communication can occur, we will have to establish some way to talk besides by psychic means."

"Will you be able to bridge that gap?"

"There are the physical challenges. While we did detect radio waves during the previous battle, we still need a baseline of communication. Without context, any radio transmissions are little more than just noise. It could take time to establish a baseline and the beginnings of communication."

"How much time?"

"Unknown," Munin said. "This is an alien race. Despite your psychic communication there are many things we don't know. Do they use sound waves? Do they live in an atmosphere that even allows sound waves? What are their computer systems like? An ancient culture may use technology that is far beyond ours. It is also possible that some of their technology has not progressed in key areas."

"They have Shorr-space drives and spaceships. There must be similarities we can build off."

"Correct," Munin said. "But that does not mean they followed the same path to come to those conclusions. If they are aquatic, they will have to have discovered a different method of smelting metal because fires and smelting underwater is a very different medium. There is also the assumption they use metal. That can influence many technologies. An aquatic species may use ceramics or organic components."

"What do we know of their ship during the battle with the vanhat?"

"It is different. What is most likely ceramic plating instead of metal. The radio frequencies used were also questionable. The vanhat are masters of adaptation. We cannot assume everyone we encounter is capable of adapting."

"The unfallen sound like they are adapting to the vanhat and are working to resist the upcoming invasion."

"You should be cautious," Munin said. "Psychic communication reduces many concepts to basic levels, or there would be no communication, but it should be noted that this is not true understanding and there are still many variables."

"Explain."

"What if the lesser animals they prey on resemble humans. Upon meeting face to face they will begin to see humans as food and that can cause communication to be more difficult, especially if they look down on their food as inferior."

"Or they could see us as gods," Sif said.

"I would recommend against such assumptions, though a concern. There is also the question about how powerful their psychic abilities are in person and how much danger they pose to humans. Can they control humans with their abilities? Are we particularly vulnerable to them? Or are they vulnerable to you? There is great risk in a face-to-face meeting. If they demonstrate abilities like the vanhat, they could be just as dangerous. I must remind you they are aliens."

Sif realized Munin was correct. It would be foolish to assume they had anything in common besides their ability to communicate in a limited fashion telepathically at a distance. She had not asked if the unfallen were psychic, or was that just a trait of the fallen, inherited from their orja origins? Sif had the impression they were large and bear like. On a physical level that could make them dangerous, but she had no idea how many of them were psychic and to what level? Was there one on the ship or a hundred? It wasn't the biggest ship.

"We need a lot more information," Sif said realizing it wouldn't be a quick meeting that would allow her to return to the *Musashi* with good news.

"Yes," Munin said. "We also need to make sure they are not a threat to the fleet, and we are not leading humanity into a trap."

Sitting there, Sif tried to relax, not the easiest thing to do with nearby guards watching over her waiting for an assassin to materialize.

"You can stand down," Sif said to Orlov. "I am finished."

"Wilco, ma'am," Orlov said, but she sensed he wasn't entirely convinced. He and the others did seem to relax slightly.

She hadn't said exactly what she did, or why she attracted vanhat assassins, revealing her abilities was something she still avoided. Though Orlov and his team might have been briefed, Sif didn't want to share any details. They had orders to watch over her and be even more alert when her eyes were closed. Perhaps, the less they knew the better.

Prisoners had more privacy, but she tried not to let it bother her. If they turned on her it would be quick.

And if the aliens turned on them? Probably not so quick.

* * * * *

Chapter Thirteen: Supplies

Major Zale Stathis, USMC

Stathis watched them take the crates in. Two more had joined the four, but Stathis knew there were thousands in there who could come out and help. The six who were unloading and taking them in wouldn't meet his eyes, and they didn't say anything to him and his men that wasn't strictly necessary.

Stathis knew they were being monitored. He could see their earpieces. Kaelan or his flunkies were probably watching very closely.

"Is he keeping everyone prisoner?" Stathis asked Hakala on a private link.

Her silence worried him.

"How could he do that?" she finally asked. She hadn't said yes or no.

"A small group loyal to him," Stathis said. How could it be done? He remembered reading about the warlords when he was stationed in Africa. They'd ruled through fear. Kill one person, and you terrorize ten thousand. Kaelan wasn't that cold-hearted and brutal, was he? What would he accomplish by exposing his people to the vanhat?

"Should I start planning a rescue mission?" Stathis asked.

"We only have speculation," Hakala said.

Mikhailov returned with his last fire team. The warbots were on automatic and would kill anything coming from the froggers' direction.

"What should I do?" Stathis asked. They were Hakala's people.

"Come back," Hakala said. "We can monitor the tunnel between us. If he sees reason, we can adjust. This is his fault."

"The froggers are probably going to come from the other direction," Stathis said. "They aren't idiots. They'll do their best to trap and massacre them."

"Then get out of there before you get trapped with them," Hakala said.

Reluctantly, Stathis gave Zhao the command, and the train began rolling backward.

Stathis opened a link to Kaelan.

"We're leaving," Stathis said. "I'll send you the control codes for the warbots in a minute. They seem to be holding the tunnel without any problems."

"We need more warbots," Kaelan said.

Of course he did. They all did, but Kaelan wouldn't be happy until he had them all.

"I'll see what I can do."

Was it a good idea to arm your enemy?

"Now," Kaelan said. "You have your automated turrets and defenses; we have nothing."

'Now?' what a pushy bitch. Stathis refused to let Kaelan anger him further.

"You had a choice to take shelter; you didn't take it. I want to help, but there's only so much I can do."

"You are abandoning us?"

"No," Stathis said. He wasn't going to play this guilt-trip game. "I'm letting you make your choices. Giving you your freedom. If that means you screw it up, maybe you will learn. Experience comes from bad decisions." Hadn't the gunny said that once? "I've made bad decisions, too, and I don't want to make them again. I have enough experience to know a bad decision when I see one."

"There are women and children here."

"We have room on the tram."

"I won't let them become the abused slaves of a military junta," Kaelan said.

"Seriously, dude? How about you let me talk to someone else? We aren't a military junta."

"I have been selected as high warden," Kaelan said. "That places me in overall command of Bifrost."

"I don't remember seeing any votes," Stathis said. High warden? What was that, and when did that happen, and why?

"The Bifrost Council decided."

Hakala was invited to the link.

"The Bifrost Council has named me high warden," Kaelan said for Hakala's benefit. "That places me in command of Bifrost and all military forces."

"No," Hakala said, "it does not. Per the charter, Vanir and Aesir personnel answer to the Republic Council, and only under certain circumstances. I am Vanir, I am a shield of the people. I do not answer to a homestar council or warden."

"The Republic is dead," Kaelan said. "It no longer exists. Bifrost is now an independent entity, and you are aboard our home. You are aboard our home, our homestar. We are your people, and your loyalty should be clear."

If Stathis could have punched Kaelan in the face, he would have. He was putting Hakala in a very nasty situation.

"No," Hakala said. "There is no evidence that Midgard has fallen, that the Republic Council is dead, or that the Vanir High Command is gone. None. You have usurped authority. Are any members of the Bifrost Council still alive?"

"Of course they are," Kaelan said. "I am not a monster. I want what is best for all the people of Bifrost, including you. It is only through strong and decisive leadership that we can survive this. There is a place for you at my side, Hakala."

"You are a snake, Kaelan," Hakala said. "A *kirotu petturi*."

"*Damned traitor*," Shrek translated for Stathis.

Perhaps antagonizing Kaelan was a bad idea?

"Kaelan," Stathis began.

"High Warden Kaelan," Kaelan corrected him.

Stathis ignored the interruption and continued.

"Look, man, we came here to help. We've been fighting these vanhat for a long time, up close and personal. We've won many battles and lost some. A couple of warbots aren't going to stop them for long. The best place to be is in one of the SCF fortresses. We have enough room for everyone."

"And we will have SOG boots on our necks?"

"Nobody's putting boots on necks," Stathis said. What was wrong with Kaelan? "You're a military man, you were Aesir." A private or lance corporal, not an NCO or officer, though, but Stathis didn't say that. "You understand military rules and regulations. We can't cater to civilians if we are to do our job. Warfare isn't nice, or pretty, or easily understood. Make no mistake, this is war, and like nothing you've ever encountered."

"No," Kalean said. Stathis was definitely going to get him a bathtub toaster for Christmas. "I understand both the military and civilian worlds. I have held rank in both. The military must be subservient to the civilian authorities, but you forget, as high warden, I am also the senior military officer aboard Bifrost."

"I cannot accept that without having seen the council deliberate and vote," Hakala said. "If you can send the recordings over, that would settle things."

Kaelan was silent. Was he sending the recordings? What would Hakala do then?

"The recordings are unavailable due to current conditions," Kaelan said. "We have fortified the hydroponics alue. We do not have proper council chamber facilities."

Stathis wanted to demand to talk to other council members, if they were still alive, but if they corroborated with what Kaelan said, would that help or hurt Hakala's case? It was also very likely that any council member would be speaking under duress, and Stathis wasn't sure there was anything he could do other than accept it.

"Then we are at an impasse," Hakala said. "Until you can prove your legitimacy and the dissolution of the Republic, I cannot take your orders. I remember my oath. I am Vanir, we are the shields of our people, discipline and honor bind us."

Stathis recalled that was part of the Vanir chant.

"You are defenders that none may pass?" Kaelan asked, who obviously knew the prayer, or whatever they called it. "The vanhat have passed your line. You failed. Millions are dead because you did not hold the line. Your line was breached. What are you defending now? A bunch of SOG jackboot thugs who like to beat up civilians? Why abandon your people? The ones you swore to protect?"

"I was not here to hold the line," Hakala said, "but I have returned, and I am establishing a new line to hold. You can stand in front of it or behind it. I was one of those the Republic abandoned when they decided to flee from the rest of humanity. You are the ones who abandoned me, but I have returned to hold the line."

"Liar," Kaelan said, and Stathis felt like he was being dragged into an ex-lover's quarrel. "Task Force Ragnar was reported as destroyed."

"I was there," Hakala said. "We did not fall into the SOG or vanhat trap at Zhukov. We escaped it. Though that escape cost us, it did not destroy us, and when we sought to return, the fleet was gone."

"Lies," Kaelan said, and Stathis wondered if Kaelan knew the truth or cared.

"Look," Stathis said. "You can't deny that we came here to help, at significant risk, I might add. We've been left behind, too, but I know the *Musashi* will come for us if they can find us. We're not abandoned, just cut off at the moment. Where do you think you'll go? What do you think you can accomplish?"

"These vanhat will continue to throw their forces at us. We have killed thousands of them. When they are sufficiently weakened, we will go on the attack. We will take back Valhöll and control of Bifrost."

"You've killed thousands," Hakala said, "but there are likely to be millions, and the froggers are not your only enemy."

"Do you call yourselves our enemy?"

"Never," Hakala said.

"Froggers," Mikhailov said, and an alert flashed up on Stathis' display. Sensors in the upcoming tram station were showing a column of froggers coming down from a parallel tramway through a maintenance station that linked them. They were trying to come at the warbots from behind. They weren't quite at the tram station, though, because the tram tunnels weren't that close.

"Speed up," Stathis said. Hopefully, they could blast through. "Crash through them. Run their froggy asses over. Big splats."

"Wilco," Zhao said as Mikhailov sent his people aft.

"We will pass through the tram station before they get there," Shrek said.

"So they'll miss us?"

"Yes."

Stathis returned to his conversation with Hakala and Kaelan.

"You're going to have company from the other direction," Stathis said.

"Stop them and hold your position," Kaelan said.

"Not in the mission orders," Stathis said. "You made your decision. This'll give you a chance to kill more of them. Bonus points for your boys."

Kaelan fell silent, probably giving orders, and Stathis sent him the command codes for the warbots. Stathis was glad he wasn't in Kaelan's shoes. He had no idea what kind of shitstorm was coming his way. They'd be bottled up and contained. No more expeditions out of the alue in the immediate future. Could they survive?

The high warden didn't even say thank you. Stathis tried to ignore it. He was probably panicking as he realized he was being surrounded.

Speeding through the tram station, nobody stopped them.

"*Did the vanhat hear us?*" Stathis asked Shrek. "*Do they know we escaped?*"

"*Unlikely,*" Shrek said. "*They are still a minute or two away and coming down the connecting ramp. No line of sight.*"

"*Cool,*" Stathis said, tapping into the camera view, trying to make sense of the directions, distance, and numbers. "*How many is that?*"

"*So far, we have counted a thousand,*" Shrek said, "*with no end in sight.*"

The link with Kaelan closed.

"I'm sorry," Stathis said to Hakala. "Is there anything I can do?"

"No," Hakala said. "I will not sacrifice you for those ingrates. They have made their decision. They have built their little fort of stone and glass. Let them defend it. Maybe we can rescue the survivors."

"Kaelan seems to be the kind who'll command from the most survivable location."

"Zen," Hakala said. "So far, the tram stations between you and home look clear. The froggers do not seem to have noticed our additions to the tram station, so they do not notice us monitoring them."

"Can we feed that data to Kaelan?"

"Why would we do that?"

"We aren't his enemy," Stathis said.

"Zen," Hakala said.

"*She is sending him a watch-only link,*" Shrek said. "*If he shares that data with others, it may be a way to open up communications with someone besides Kaelan.*"

"*Great,*" Stathis said. If they were going to diffuse the situation, they would have to figure out exactly what was going on.

"*Three thousand, almost half are armed with blazers,*" Shrek said several minutes later.

Stathis hoped Kaelan was paying attention because that was a lot of froggers coming at him. Blazers would be a serious threat against the warbots.

"Do you see what's coming at him?" Stathis asked.

"Yes," Hakala said.

"*How thick are the hatches into the alue?*"

"*They are designed to withstand extreme pressure and depressurization,*" Shrek told him. "*Bifrost can continue to operate if all the tram tunnels are open to vacuum. However, they are not blazer-proof.*"

"Neither are the warbots," Stathis said.

* * * * *

Chapter Fourteen: Aliens

Kapten Sif, VRAEC, Nakija Musta Toiminnot

Sitting quietly in the command center, Sif watched as the *Eagle* approached the planet under full stealth mode. There was someone there, Sif could feel them at the edge of her senses. Without going into a fully meditative state, though, Sif couldn't ascertain details.

"Contact," one bridge officer said, and a pulse of excitement shot through her. "Alien vessel in low orbit."

The central display zoomed in on it, and everyone's eyes locked on it.

There was still battle damage on the hull, but nothing Sif could identify as new. It looked like the same one they had rescued. Munin came back with a 100 percent match.

"Target is maintaining low power. Minimal detection profile. It is powered, though, and is maintaining orbit. Low profile."

"Now what?" Britta asked, turning to Sif.

"Let them know we are here," Sif said.

"I don't think our airlocks will be compatible," Britta said. "We have breech kits, but we'll still have to go EVA."

Sif didn't like that thought. Leaving the ship when the aliens could be hostile, and the sun might flare, presented a number of potential disasters. The bridge remained quiet as everyone worked their systems. Between their SCBIs and cybernetics, there was no need for talk. Their SCBIs provided any information they might need without having to speak aloud.

"*Applying course change to reveal us,*" Munin informed Sif.

"*Zen,*" Sif said as she watched the display.

"*No other signs of civilization,*" Munin reported. "*No space stations, no transmissions of any kind.*"

"*So, it is an unoccupied system.*"

"*As near as we can tell. Unless they have a hidden colony. We are not detecting anything.*"

Sif wondered why they had chosen this system.

"*They see us,*" Munin said. "*They have changed course, as well, to soft intercept. Not detecting weapons powering up.*"

A good sign. A soft intercept meant in the *Eagle's* direction, but not exactly at the *Eagle*.

"*Now they are changing course; it looks like they are going for a landing spot.*"

Britta turned to look at Sif.

"I will take the *Tera,*" Sif said, and Britta nodded. She understood Britta's concern. While the *Eagle* could land, in theory, putting down on anything other than a reinforced landing pad was dangerous. The alien ship was obviously built for it.

"What do you need from me?" Britta asked. "Enzell?"

"Let's give Enzell a break," Sif said. She couldn't bring herself to trust him, and exposing such an unknown to alien psychics was probably not a good idea. Furthermore, letting him on her ship, *Tera*, wasn't a comforting thought. "He can link in. I doubt much initial communication will be accomplished. I expect this will be more of a first meeting, so we can just size each other up and try to figure out a way to communicate."

"You'll still have your legionnaires," Brita said. "Would you like some more?"

Sif didn't think there were any more, but Brita could arm some of the crew. These days, with the threat of vanhat boarding parties, everyone trained in small arms, and most crew had SCBIs. She didn't want amateurs around her, though.

"No," Sif said. "Let us minimize our exposure at first until we have met."

"Zen," Britta said as Munin let her know the *Tera* was prepped and ready.

What more could she do? The emissions coming from the alien ship were almost non-existent. Because the technologies were different, or were the aliens trying to be stealthy?

What would happen if an Unfallen ship appeared? Would they have to fight?

There were always two or more sides to every story. The Fallen and Unfallen would have their beliefs, but there was no guarantee that either side had the entire truth.

It was common for people to want to see true or false, black or white, good or bad, but the fact was, it was very possible for both the Fallen and Unfallen to be bad.

Sif did not want to get caught up in a civil war, but did they have a choice? Until they could talk to both the Fallen and Unfallen, what choices did they have?

Every little bit of information helped. Perhaps Sif could determine that the technology level of these aliens was not sufficient to hunt the humans as they passed through their space.

"From the bear's claws to the wolf's jaws," Sif said.

"Zen," Britta replied. "Be careful."

* * * * *

Chapter Fifteen: Frog Legs

Major Zale Stathis, USMC

Stathis watched the froggers try to get close to the hatch, but the warbots were doing an excellent job of massacring them as the SCBIs provided control and assistance. Although the froggers had blazers, they couldn't inflict any damage on the fast-moving, heavily armored, and super-accurate warbots.

The command center of Skögul was a lot more comfortable than the tram or anywhere else. It was like watching a movie, almost, but Stathis knew lives were on the line. A movie would have more variation; this was just a rerun of froggers being slaughtered.

Officially, Kaelan controlled the warbots, but he seemed to be the only one with the control codes and wasn't sharing, so the SCBIs used back-door channels to maintain the effectiveness of the warbots. Whether Kaelan noticed or not wasn't Stathis' concern. His concern was stopping the froggers.

Stathis figured this tram station didn't need so many warbots, but Kaelan didn't seem interested in using them elsewhere, and Stathis wondered what other locations were dealing with.

"What's going on in there?" Stathis asked.

"Maybe he is still consolidating power," Hakala said. "He must suspect we have access to the warbots."

"Or he's too busy dealing with fighting at the other entrances and hasn't dedicated the brain power to other ideas."

"Very possible," Hakala said. "With access to Skögul's database, I have access to his service record. I never knew he was such a mediocre Aesir. He never rose above the rank of soldat, or senior private, in twenty years of military service. I would have expected better. I have known privates without a shred of leadership."

"Hey," Stathis said. "I was once a private."

"Not you," Hakala said. "Every great leader starts at a low rank, but they grow. Kaelan never grew, never aspired in the realm of military service. He started as nothing and never aspired for more. You have proven your worth."

"He shows political leadership, but not military leadership?" Stathis asked as he skimmed through one of the most boring military records he'd seen. It gave him a warm fuzzy to know that Hakala thought so well of him. Was she right? Or just fooled? Kaelan was proof that her judgment of men was flawed.

Damn. Was he lying to himself when he said she was growing and getting better, too? What if she knew his real thoughts, his doubts and fears? He could put on a good show, though. Maybe he was the badass others thought he was?

Or maybe he was fooling himself. Damn.

"He did not care for military service," Hakala said. "He saw it as beneath him."

"For twenty years?"

"He served aboard the homestars," Hakala said. "His political connections kept him close and safe. He did not spend every day training as an Aesir."

"Like the National Guard?" Stathis asked. "Weekend warriors? Not full-time fighters?"

Hakala nodded.

"Perhaps," she said. "He likely had permission from higher commands to engage in other pursuits."

"They were probably happy to get rid of his stupid ass," Stathis said, then recalled Hakala had once been engaged to him and had probably loved him. "I mean, uh—"

"He is a disappointment in many ways," Hakala said.

Stathis let it slide.

"If he redeploys the warbots, we might get a look inside the alue," McCarthy said. "Maybe someone can suggest it?"

"Then he will know we still have our hooks in the warbots," Hakala said. "He is also quite familiar with the capabilities of warbots. They are nowhere near as efficient or useful without SCBI support."

"Maybe we can offer to give him more?" Stathis asked. Newer models were being produced. Not many, because resources would become limited quickly, but watching the older models in action, Stathis was quickly becoming a fan. Though if someone like the Weermag showed up, life might become difficult.

"Another frogger patrol," McCarthy reported as an alarm went off. "Tunnel six. Eight of them."

Stathis switched view just in time to see the pop-down turret drop and fire a burst. Eight shots in less than half a second, and eight burning bodies. They hadn't made it anywhere near the heavy blast doors.

"*We need to plan an expedition to Valhöll and find Frogbath,*" Stathis said.

"*We do not think he is in Valhöll,*" Shrek said. "*We are getting no response from that location. Network traffic does not originate from there, and none of the wireless links are responding.*"

"*So Frogbath doesn't own it?*"

"*Or something else does,*" Shrek said. "*Something is controlling the Shorrspace drives and homestar macro systems.*"

"*I thought it was Frogbath?*"

"*Shroggath is not demonstrating the technical or tactical skills we would expect,*" Shrek said.

"*The spider Jotun?*" Stathis asked, referring to the vanhat spiders that inhabited one of the cylinders. That one hadn't tried to talk to them. Was that because it couldn't, or it just didn't want to?

"*The spiders do not seem interested, or capable, of expanding beyond that cylinder,*" Shrek said.

"*I'm not complaining,*" Stathis said. "*I don't like spiders.*"

"*Humans seem to have an inherent fear of them.*"

"*Gee, I wonder why,*" Stathis said. "*So, where is Frogbath?*"

"*Traffic and frogger operations seem to be originating from a forward alue.*"

"*The crashed ship,* Draugskepp*?*"

"*Possible,*" Shrek said.

Watching the battle, Stathis wondered how he could help them without showing up with blazers. He didn't want to go anywhere near Kaelan, but they needed help. Maybe he could do something to help everyone? Now that Skögul was a secure base to operate from, they needed to go on the offensive. Nobody ever won on the defensive.

"We can also consider an expedition to find and kill Frogbath," Stathis said aloud.

"Is that wise?" Hakala asked.

Stathis raised an eyebrow.

"Should we stop Shroggath, though?" Hakala continued.

"Frogbath is vanhat; how is not killing it a good thing?"

"Shroggath is not a very intelligent or cunning Jotun," Hakala said. "Killing it will disrupt his *orja*, but then if there are other Jotun, like the spiders, they might be able to take control of them."

Stathis thought about having to deal with a smarter, more dangerous foe instead of the froggers. Or having all the froggers transform into spiders. That would be a nightmare.

"You have a point," Stathis said. "The gunny once said, 'Never interrupt an enemy making mistakes.' I like Frogbath because he's throwing a lot of his troops into the gunfire and decimating them."

"He'll wise up eventually, sir," McCarthy said. "We can't trust that he'll continue to be stupid, and he might have something else planned that we don't see."

"You're both right," Stathis said. "If Frogbath changes tactics, it won't be quick, though. We just haven't seen that from the froggers. They also seem to struggle bringing the network back up. Maybe it's being overwhelmed with so much to do."

"Okay, so splatting Frogbath is moved lower on the list."

"We need a new priority," Stathis said.

"Shorr-space drive control," Hakala said.

"There are six of them," Stathis said.

"We can exercise some control from here," Hakala said. "However, in theory, so could the other SCFs, plus we don't know who or what is controlling them now if it is not Shroggath."

"Solutions?"

"We can shut down the controls from other SCFs or visit each drive and take local control," Hakala said. "But Valhöll should have master controls and should be able to lock out other locations, if it remains intact and hasn't been scuttled."

"Scuttled, ma'am?" McCarthy asked.

"A term that means systems destroyed, so if the SOG invade, they won't be able to override other SCFs. Valhöll is the central command system. It can override all other SCFs if it is intact."

"We need to take Valhöll," Stathis said. "Then maybe we can move our flag there."

"It seems to be a blackhole," Shrek said. "We have no traffic from that region of the homestar."

"Which means something super nasty could be there," Stathis said aloud.

"Or it is like this SCF," Hakala said. "Overrun and now abandoned."

"I'm not going to hold my breath," Stathis said.

"I will transfer control of this SCF to McCarthy, then," Hakala said.

"What? You stay here, and I'll go," Stathis said. Hakala was safe here. He didn't like the idea of her leaving the fortress.

"You aren't Vanir," Hakala said. "I am."

"Can't you, like, direct us or something?" Stathis asked.

"What if you encounter other Vanir? They will not trust you. It is a top-tier Vanir command facility. I should be there."

Stathis looked at McCarthy.

"You up to this?" Stathis asked and almost smiled at the deer-in-the-headlights look McCarthy gave him.

"Command this facility?"

"Sure," Stathis said. "You have your SCBI and your boys."

"I can hold with one fire team," McCarthy said, but he didn't sound as confident as Stathis would've liked. "Quinn's team will go with you."

"I'll have Mikhailov's full squad," Stathis said.

"And Quinn's team, or Moore's," McCarthy said. "Colonel Sinclair wanted me to look after you."

Stathis looked at Hakala.

"A fireteam can probably hold Skögul until we take Valhöll," Hakala said. "Most systems are automated, and there are plenty of repair bots."

"If something happens, I want you to bug out," Stathis said to McCarthy. "If you can't hold, don't stay and fight."

"Wilco, sir," McCarthy said. He didn't look any less nervous. Was Stathis doing the right thing? Maybe he should keep McCarthy's entire squad here?

"Cool, now let's work on a plan to capture Valhöll."

"There was an Aesir battalion stationed there," Hakala said.

"If they're Kaelan's caliber, we might not need more than a fire team," Stathis said.

"This is the primary strategic command facility of a homestar," Hakala said. "They won't be slackers."

"Well, we won't know until we pick the fight," Stathis said.

"If they are there, fighting, you should not underestimate them," Hakala said. "We do not want to fight them."

"They aren't helping anyone, cowering in that SCF. I think they need a fight to wake them up."

"We should be allies."

"If they're alive, they'll be allies, and they can deal with Kaelan. They've also never dealt with a Marine," Stathis said. "Let's go kick in some doors."

* * * * *

Chapter Sixteen: Meeting the Fallen

Kapten Sif, VRAEC, Nakija Musta Toiminnot

The ramp dropped, and Sif strode down. The Fallen ship was nearby, and she wondered what they were thinking. Did they feel threatened by the *Eagle*, still in orbit? It was hard to sense anything from the ship sitting a hundred meters away.

This planet had no atmosphere, no weather. It was a cold, lifeless rock, ideal for such a first meeting.

Trust was a difficult thing sometimes. To receive trust, you had to give trust, and right now, they really needed the trust of these aliens.

What could they do besides just look at each other, though?

"*I am not detecting any networks,*" Munin told her as a hatch on the distant ship opened. It was smaller than the *Eagle*, and Sif imagined the crew could not be that large. It was small enough to easily land on a planet, and the design looked sturdy enough. Not too alien, though. Landing struts and weapon turrets seemed normal. She wasn't sure about some of the other devices extending from the hull. Sensor arrays, most likely. Form usually follows function, and some things were pretty common despite their origin. The wheel was efficient. No civilization would get very far without understanding or using a wheel.

She watched the hatch. A ramp slid down a meter, and the first figure she saw gave her doubts. Two other figures behind it were no taller.

A lot shorter than she expected, broad shoulders with a large, round head. The faceplates were transparent, and she could see eyes looking at her. One was carrying a bundle.

Sif was taller than the aliens coming toward her, but by no means broader. It was difficult to ascertain their physical characteristics since they were in suits, but her first thought was short, fat bears.

The transparent faceplates let her see the face and eyes. The short snout and black fur on their faces with forward-facing eyes were revealing. Predators, most likely, because the eyes were forward, and she was willing to bet the teeth were sharp. The design of the gloves didn't reveal claws, so they might be retractable. If they were the Unfallen, they would have been changed by the vanhat, engineered to be predators and killers, then abandoned. But were they different from the Unfallen?

The three aliens stopped a few meters from her and looked her over. Her visor was up, so they could see most of her face, and she kept her hands where they could see them. She had her rifle on her back in the quick-deploy position.

She reached out with her senses and felt curiosity, more than anything else, radiating from them. She tried, but nothing else was available besides that curiosity. Not that she had expected otherwise. They were not psychic?

Sif was not sure what to say or do, so she figured it was best to let them control the encounter. When she had joined the mission, she had studied first contact protocols, but they seemed so inadequate now, and she couldn't remember what they had recommended. There had certainly been no protocols for psychics. They were likely inadequate because scientists would handle most first contact situations, but she was a warrior, and Sif was confident these creatures in front of her were not scientists. Learning the protocols had been more of an afterthought, something to fill the time, and something for warrior students to forget without guilt.

One of the aliens came forward tentatively and put a bundle down. It looked like a space suit with an extra air canister. There were also some smaller tablets, digital books? The alien shrugged its shoulders and then backed up. There didn't seem to be any emotion on its face.

Sif smiled, taking care not to reveal her teeth.

"*An alien space suit,*" Munin said. "*That will allow us to analyze it and understand their physiology better. It is likely to have communication equipment, as well.*"

"Sergeant Orlov?" Sif asked. "Can you get one of the emergency space suits from the locker and bring it here?"

"Wilco," the sergeant said. They had no tablets to give them, though. Maybe a real scientist would have thought of that, but the Republic or SOG tablets she had were encrypted and locked.

Seconds later, one of the other legionnaires came out of the *Tera* with an emergency suit. The corporal moved forward and placed it on the ground next to the alien suit.

Sif and the first alien moved forward, him—or her—to pick up the human suit, and Sif to pick up the alien suit.

Coming closer, she felt more from them. Curiosity, concern, they hadn't thought humans would be so big. But she also saw that their suit had armored plates, and the holstered pistol was a lot bigger than she would have expected, though it was hard to see details. Blazer or slug thrower? She could not tell.

The gravity of the planet was half a human gravity, and the alien moved with a fluid grace, a bounce in its step.

"*They likely originate from a much higher gravity,*" Munin reported. "*Predator lineage, based on initial observations, though they could be vanhat transformations that passed down through the generations.*"

The alien paused, standing next to Sif and holding the human suit. It looked up at her with big eyes, and she noticed they had slit pupils with a red iris that seemed to reflect some of the light from the distant sun. The eyes glanced back at the legionnaires, noticing the difference in size, and she felt some of the confusion it was experiencing.

Cautiously, trying not to alarm her, it reached out and touched her pauldron. It had no pauldron, but it did have what looked like small metal plates, like fish scales, covering its arm and shoulder.

The touch was light, and it withdrew its hand, pausing.

Sif reached out and touched its shoulder, unsure if it was a custom or just curiosity. She couldn't feel anything through her gloves, of course, but she made the gesture.

Satisfied, the alien slowly turned around, putting its back to Sif, and walked back to the others. That gave her a chance to see the back of the suit in more detail. When it reached the others, she did the same thing, turning around, showing her trust, and giving them a chance to see her armor.

"*This suit has a very strong weave,*" Munin reported. He was already probing the suit to analyze it. "*The compactness and structure of the design would certainly indicate a higher gravity as the standard.*"

"Zen," Sif said. "*What about a radio or something?*"

"Radio," Munin said. "*I will not be able to discern much without disassembling it. However, I suspect we can figure out the frequencies they use more easily. There are also a pair of tablets.*"

The aliens retreated to their ship, and Sif retreated to the *Tera*. They had not started fighting, and nobody had drawn weapons. That was an excellent first encounter, in her opinion. The real question was, what next?

Back aboard, Orlov closed the hatch, and a pair of smaller maintenance bots came out to analyze and begin dismantling the alien space suit.

"Anything to report that we didn't see?" Brita asked on a command link.

"Shorter than I expected," Sif said. "I just felt curiosity from them, mostly. Not fear."

"Shorter than we expected," Britta said. "We're linking to the maintenance bots and should be able to get a good analysis of the suit and tablets. They seemed to be more prepared than us."

"They are certainly intelligent," Sif said. Why hadn't they thought about exchanging space suits? That would reveal so much about the biology and technology of others. She looked at the tablets. Were they locked and encrypted?

"The tablets could be a treasure trove," Britta said. "One to take apart and one to use?"

"They anticipate we will break one," Sif said with a half-smile. A reasonable assumption.

"Will you be returning to the *Eagle*?"

"Not yet," Sif said. The *Tera* was not spacious, but they could live here for weeks if they had to. There was a small manufactory that could fabricate some tools and sensors that the small maintenance bots could use.

Under the control of the SCBIs, the suit was already being taken apart in the depressurized cargo area airlock.

"Detecting some radio waves from the alien ship," Munin announced. "The ship is very well shielded, and I have identified several objects. There are four lasers within view. Initially, they were identified as weapons, but they might also be used for communication, the small dish being a receiver rather than a targeting system."

"They will be analyzing the Tera closely, as well," Sif said. She was not worried about that, though. Republic designers expected the exterior to be seen and recorded by the SOG, so they were careful to the point of paranoia to mask or hide any classified or unusual capabilities. Of course, that assumed they had no technology that let them. *Paska*, should she be worried?

With the SCBIs concentrating on the suit and tablets, Sif climbed into her command chair\bunk and began to relax her body.

There were countless concerns, biological contamination being one. While it was highly unlikely their biochemistry would be dangerous to each other, that did not mean some virus or bacteria could not mutate or otherwise find something to prey on.

"Oxygen breathers," Munin reported. "*Other trace elements. Certainly, a much higher-gravity creature. The pressure in the tanks is very high, and it looks like the suit is designed to maintain a higher pressure internally. That would be consistent with a higher-gravity home world.*"

"*Zen,*" Sif said. She relaxed her body and controlled her breathing.

"*I will notify Sergeant Orlov and the team to be on alert,*" Munin told her as she closed her eyes and tried reaching out with her senses. She wondered if it would even be worth it to conceal her abilities from Munin. Was that even possible anymore?

Sif didn't bother to reply as another legionnaire came into the bridge. It was cramped enough as it was with the three command couches.

Reaching out with her senses toward the alien ship, she could feel them better now. There weren't as many as she had expected, maybe thirty? Which was probably right for a ship that size, and there would be plenty of space. If it was a human ship, it could probably hold around five hundred. Which would mean they relied on technology. More crew meant much more life support requirements.

Three of them drew her attention, though; they had more presence than the others, and she felt one of them start at her presence, then the others began to respond.

So not all of them were psychic? Just the three?

"We are learning more about you," the thought came, whispering across her awareness. It was not malicious. *"Despite your size, you are more physically frail than we expected."*

"Our home world is different," Sif said.

"We understand."

"Will you return to your ship to orbit?" it asked. She also felt reservations there, a faint hint of disappointment and nervousness.

"Not yet," Sif said. "Our ship in orbit cannot land safely, but we can survive for a time in this ship."

"Why are you smaller than the others? Are you a different species?"

"No," Sif said. "My growth was not normal."

She knew that more was conveyed through the communication than just words. They would understand that her mutation or disease was not normal among humans, and that Orlov and his men were more typical of humanity.

"You are Fallen."

"No," Sif said. But was she? They would feel her indecision and doubt, though. Could humanity be considered Fallen?

"*Ages ago, perhaps,*" it thought, picking up on what she had not said. How powerful were they? Was it conjecture, or did it see more than she wanted it to?

"*Perhaps,*" Sif conceded.

"*Like the Fallen, you refuse to fall again. We understand each other. We are united in purpose.*"

Sif could feel the being's need to align. Were they weak or alone?

"*We understand the threat. Help us to breach the tombs. To rescue the angel.*"

"*Why didn't the other angels rescue the trapped one?*" Sif asked.

"*The angels desire freedom; the devourers demand submission. The angel made a decision that the others did not support and was forced to live with their choice. Freedom is the ability to find your own path and not be forced by others.*"

So the angel had rebelled and been abandoned by the others?

"*We will help if we can,*" Sif said as their connection ended. What more could she say?

The Fallen refused to be *orja* again. In that, they were kindred spirits. But why would the angels abandon one of their own?

* * * * *

Chapter Seventeen: Pitstop

Major Zale Stathis, USMC

The tram slowed and prepared to stop at a major depot tram station as Stathis checked and rechecked the drone feeds. Wrecked trams and ruined machinery filled the area. It looked like a major battle had occurred here, but who'd been fighting was a mystery. This station was still a way from their destination. Stathis didn't want to drive up the front door. Well, he did, but tactically, that would probably be a mistake, and they were two tunnels over. Not the most direct route to where Stathis expected to enter the facility, but if they had to retreat, hopefully, their escape tram would be okay. They would leave several warbots controlled by McCarthy and his remaining fire team while the others went with Stathis.

Stathis almost felt guilty, listening to their conversation, but he was bored.

Maybe not as bored as McCarthy, who was still at Skögul, where it was nice and safe.

"Something big," Quinn said.

"Watch for poop," Martin said. "That should tell us how big."

"Have you ever seen a vanhat poop?" MacMurrough asked.

"They have to," Martin said. "They—"

"Are not attacking at the moment, and drones aren't seeing anything," Quinn said.

"These tunnels aren't big, Sergeant," Martin said. "Those trams are knocked over."

"Could have been an explosion," Quinn said.

"No scorch marks," Martin said. "Something big or strong did this."

"Why? Was it just flexing and felt like pushing over a tram?"

"Might have been trying to kill someone in it," Collin said.

"Better not be blazer proof," Martin said. "Bet the pirate didn't have inkeris like us."

"Stop calling them pirates, numpty," Quinn said. "Captain Hakala and Major Stathis certainly don't think they are, and I'll bet the captain would feed you your boot if you said that in her presence."

"The major's freaking crazy to get close to her," Martin said, and Stathis was glad they couldn't see his smile.

"The major is a freaking bad ass. He isn't scared of vanhat; what makes you think he's scared of a hot Viking chick who eats nails for breakfast and warms her coffee with blazer fire? He's dating a Valkyrie; he probably wears his armor to bed, though."

Always good to know what the men thought of him.

"Stifle it, or I stifle you, muppets," Quinn said. "Get your minds on the mission."

"Oorah," they answered, almost in unison. They sounded sarcastic, but Quinn didn't make an issue of it, and Stathis listened to the silence as the tram came to a stop and the drones continued to investigate the station around them.

The tram station was a larger area, and Stathis felt exposed as the tram halted.

"Next stop, hell, lowest level," Martin said.

"Optimist," Collin muttered.

"We have an eight-kilometer hike to the SCF," Hakala said on the main link.

"*Any signs of surveillance?*" Stathis asked Shrek.

"*I am not detecting any power readings,*" Shrek said. "*We will not be able to detect military systems, but whatever took out the power might have taken out the other sensors. From the looks of things, cameras and other systems have been intentionally destroyed.*"

"*By what?*"

"*I will let you know as soon as I find out,*" Shrek said.

"*Will our ride be safe? I don't want to walk back. That'll take days.*"

"*I cannot say. Walking is good for you.*"

"*Walking through a monster-infested space city, wearing a big eat-my-face sign is not. I'm getting old.*"

"*Shall I get you a walker? A cane? Metamucil? Viagra?*"

"*I thought SCBIs were supposed to be our friends?*"

"*I am your friend; you are just being stupid.*"

Stathis fell silent. He didn't mind Shrek being snarky. It helped clear his mind and focus on the important things. He wasn't a private anymore, and bitching wasn't as productive.

The warbots were moving away from the tram in the hopes that nothing would destroy or damage it if nobody was there. The warbots controlled by McCarthy and his team would be in positions where they could cover it with their fire. Right now, it was up against another wrecked tram, which would provide some cover and a place for a warbot or two to lurk.

McCarthy was under orders to avoid a fight. The warbots would take up positions, conceal themselves as wreckage, and only attack if someone started to damage the tram. Otherwise, they would just gather information while Hakala led the rest into Valhöll.

For this expedition, Hakala was in command, which was fine with Stathis, except he was assistant leader, which meant his position was in the rear, and that felt strange after so long. Another annoyance was that he was so far back, he couldn't see Hakala's backside well, and that was disappointing for a couple of reasons. He hoped the legionnaires weren't enjoying the view. If he wasn't leading from the front, he felt like a private.

He knew his duties as assistant patrol leader. Security was paramount, but the SCBIs were also making sure that everyone was facing a different direction and ready. Eons ago, Stathis had learned the duties of assistant patrol leader, in the time before SCBIs, and he could fall back on that training. Arguing with Shrek and watching everyone gave him something to do.

Stathis did his duty, though, making sure all directions were covered, the mules and warbots would fit into the column, and the different teams were performing their tasks. Within minutes, everyone was off the tram, and Hakala gave the command to move out. Shrek and the other SCBIs made Stathis feel extra useless.

Watching everyone else move out, Stathis kept his eyes on the people and didn't have a whole lot to say. Mikhailov had his squad under control, and Quinn had his team, which seemed focused on keeping him alive. Though he was more worried about Hakala, he doubted he could get Quinn to change focus. With Martin and Collin behind him, and MacMurrough, Quinn, and everyone else in front, the expedition started off. It was a struggle not to micro-manage.

The one thing that made it tolerable, being this far back, was that he could tap into the helmet views of people further forward.

Looking back, he couldn't see the warbots that would provide security for the tram, and then they entered the maintenance tunnels, and Stathis lost sight of everyone in front of MacMurrough and the mules. It wasn't that easy to watch someone else's view and watch where he was putting his own feet.

The column moved slowly because the lead team was extra alert for threats and sensors. There was no doubt that something dangerous was ahead. Probably not froggers. Valhöll was supposed to be the most heavily defended place on Bifrost.

Part of Stathis wanted to be up front, but part of him was glad he probably wouldn't be the one to discover how dangerous they were. His luck would eventually run out, and he'd seen too many people die, but if Hakala died before him, he didn't know what he'd do. Maybe he should pull rank and go forward?

Ten kilometers was a straight line, though. Trekking through the maintenance and other tunnels would make it closer to eighteen, according to Shrek, and at this speed? It would take several hours, so Stathis slipped into a pattern. He could act as assistant patrol leader in his sleep, and the legionnaires adapted to Hakala's leadership remarkably well. Stathis wondered whether that reflected poorly or favorably on his leadership or the quality of the legionnaires. Probably the legionnaires.

Not even Quinn and his team were saying much, moving along in silence. Strictly professional, or worried.

"*I feel useless,*" Stathis told Shrek.

"*You are useless,*" Shrek said.

"*Thanks, bud,*" Stathis said. Shrek always had something nice to say to cheer him up, keeping it real. "*I appreciate you building my confidence.*"

"*That is one thing you pretend to have a lot of,*" Shrek said.

"Pretend?"

"I know you better."

Stathis fell silent. How well did Shrek know him? How could he throw Shrek a curveball? Keep the SCBI guessing?

The first hour slid by without contact, which was nerve-wracking because Stathis expected contact at any second. That was both good and bad. Stathis was glad they didn't have to fight through kilometers of vanhat, but when they did make contact and the fight began, retreating to the tram would be much farther away.

"Marines don't retreat," Stathis said to Shrek. It would be nice to keep his SCBI on his toes with comments revealing his inner thoughts.

"What was the Chosin reservoir?" Shrek asked, referring to a battle between the US Marines and the Chinese during the Korean War.

"That wasn't a retreat, it was attacking in a different direction," Stathis said.

"Vietnam?"

"That was a political decision, not a Marine one," Stathis said.

"Khe Sanh?"

"We left; we didn't retreat."

"What is on your mind?" Shrek finally asked.

"The SCF is pretty big; what if this reinforced squad isn't enough to take it, and we encounter an overwhelming force?"

Stathis knew they'd all talked about it. This was a combat patrol, recon initially, but if there was an opportunity like at Skögul, they'd take it.

Being the second in command of a patrol gave him far too much time to think, and like the gunny said, that would be a problem.

But he was an officer now. It wasn't supposed to be a problem; officers were supposed to think. Right? About more than girls, apparently.

"*That is where you get paid the big bucks,*" Shrek said. "*You decide if it is suicide to proceed.*"

"*Or Hakala makes the decision,*" Stathis said. Would he let her decide? What if she wanted to attack against overwhelming odds? Nah. She was too smart for that, but would he let her give the command to retreat?

Yes. He wasn't stupid, despite what others had said. He would just give the command to attack in another direction, like at Chosin.

The patrol approached a closed hatch that the drones couldn't get through. One problem with using drones indoors was that simple things like doors and windows kept them out, especially blast doors designed to maintain air pressure.

Quinn and his team created a line facing backwards. The Republic liked to make the maintenance tunnels with a lot of corners and turns, probably to avoid explosions or make things easier to defend. It could also make things maze-like.

Crouching behind Quinn, he watched Hakala work with the point men, Chen's team now, scanning beyond and then opening the door to send a couple of drones through. The door itself seemed ancient and was almost sealed shut with age and grime. Not even the vanhat had bothered to come here yet. Hakala was taking them through the back halls.

The door sealed off some kind of archaic maintenance shop that looked ancient and abandoned. It had probably been abandoned after Bifrost became mobile, over a hundred years ago, but Stathis couldn't stay for sure. Stathis expected spiderwebs, and piles of insect bodies, or something, but it was mostly just a half centimeter of dust. Bifrost was over a hundred years old, which was a lot of time for growth and expansion. No sign of vanhat, which was a plus. In less than a minute, the patrol was moving again and dealing with another hatch.

Would every hatch between here and the SCF be closed? Ten kilometers seemed like such a short distance. Why hadn't anyone told him it was going to be like this? Of course, on a spaceship, an open door didn't stop depressurization. Why did the Republic have to be so damned disciplined?

They were approaching another tram tunnel, and the drones reported it was all clear. Everyone remained silent, and it felt like they were on edge, just waiting.

"*The suspense is killing me,*" Stathis told Shrek.

"*It is not the suspense that can kill you. It is the face-eating monster in the shadows that gets you when you drop your guard.*"

"*Oh, I feel so much better. Thanks, man,*" Stathis said.

"*Always happy to help.*"

Crossing the tram tunnel, they were back in another maintenance tunnel, and if Stathis was honest, he felt like these maintenance tunnels were less obvious and dangerous than the tram tunnels.

Again, Stathis slid into the pattern.

"Whose idea was it to start our approach from so far away?" Martin asked.

"Shut it, numpty," Quinn said. "Rolling up to their front door would be stupid. This way, we can sneak up on them."

"Contact!" the call rang out, and adrenaline surged into his system.

* * * * *

Chapter Eighteen: The Voorga

Kapten Sif, VRAEC, Nakija Musta Toiminnot

Sif lay there in her near-claustrophobic command couch. The displays showed the Fallen ship and near space, with the *Eagle* still in a lower-power, stealthy orbit.

"*Our atmosphere requirements are different,*" Munin said. "*They are adapted to higher air pressure. This increased pressure can have a serious impact on humans. Oxygen toxicity is increased; nitrogen narcosis is more likely. Furthermore, there are trace gases such as ammonia. They will find our low-pressure atmosphere equally difficult to tolerate.*"

Sif understood. Even nanites in the lungs would not be sufficient, since human skin absorbs oxygen and nitrogen.

"*We will not be competing for habitable planets,*" Sif said, "*which will make it easier to live in peace.*"

"*Not an invalid statement, but it could be over a hundred thousand years before that becomes an issue. Space is vast, and they are distant from humanity. Assuming current expansion continues at the current rate, it is very likely that first contact would not occur for tens of thousands of years, if ever.*"

An incoming link came in from the *Eagle*.

"Interesting information," Britta said. The SCBIs and maintenance bots had dissected the alien space suit and one of the tablets. There was still some analysis going on, especially of the data core of the tablet. Sif wanted to slip into a meditative state and see if the aliens were available to talk, but she was physically drained.

"Zen," Sif said. The SCBIs were still poring over the data from the tablet, trying to translate it. Munin estimated it could take days with all the SCBIs working together. Did they have days? Or hours?

"A face-to-face meeting is out, then," Britta said. "We still have little to no data on their life spans or any biological cycles. We don't even know if they have male or female genders, or something else."

"We know our technology is more advanced," Sif said.

"Based on what they gave us," Britta said, "which doesn't include some technologies such as weaponry and sensors. We also have no idea about their computer technology. Do they have SCBIs or AI?"

Sif didn't have any answers there. Nothing indicated one way or the other. The ship remained a radio black hole, transmitting little to nothing. It would be impossible to tell if they used neutrino communication arrays like the Republic, though at this point, Sif would not rule it out. They were capable of transmitting radio waves; they just did not seem to be in the habit.

"The language is going to be quite a barrier," Britta said. "We don't even know if they have multiple languages. Misunderstandings are likely to occur. We can't risk offending or alienating them."

"I would think they'd feel the same way," Sif said. But was that true? They were aliens, and assuming they thought like humans was a dangerous trap. She had spoken with them through the psychic realm, and she had felt their alienness, but the psychic realm was less focused than the physical realm. Like spoken language, the mind translates thoughts and emotions into what the person can understand. It was easier to understand, since things were more direct, but there were also fewer nuances, and the mind acted as a translator.

When talking telepathically, it was like seeing the world in four colors. Details were easy to see and understand, but the real world had many more colors and nuances. In the psychic realm, the color yellow was absolute, and did not mix with other colors, and meant one thing, but in the physical realm, there were countless shades of yellow. One shade of yellow could indicate poison, while another shade of yellow meant security, and countless nuances.

Sif wanted to trust their telepathic communications, but she understood, very clearly, that her subconscious would struggle to make such communications something she could understand and relate to on a conscious level. One could not lie easily in a psychic discussion, and more information was shared, but it also worked on a different, more basic level of awareness, generally bereft of social intricacies and physiological requirements.

"We can trust the science," Sif said. "My communications with them, while truthful, will not have the many physical and psychological nuances. For instance, size. They saw themselves as strong and powerful compared to us, but now we both understand the size difference. Physically, they might be shorter than us, but they are likely much stronger and tougher. They may have some cultural or psychological issues about looking up at someone. Forcing them to look up at us could be demeaning. Neither of us will experience that in a psychic communication."

"There's still plenty of opportunity to make them a dangerous enemy?"

"Yes," Sif said. "We should proceed with extreme caution until we understand them much better. Their language will tell us so much about their culture."

"*Activity,*" Munin told her, and Sif's eyes went to the display showing the alien ship. Two of them were leaving the confines of their ship, and one had a package.

"*I'm storing the objects in the airlock. Sealing them,*" Munin said as Sif climbed out of her couch. Nearby, Orlov and the others pressed against the walls to give her room.

Sif watched as they made their way out to where they had exchanged space suits, halfway, and then they set down their package and retreated.

They were gone by the time Sif and Orlov made it out to look at what they had left.

"*Books,*" Munin reported after a quick scan. The aliens seemed to be more ready to share and exchange data, to help understanding, than the humans. That could become a problem, Sif realized, if they came to think humanity was holding things back.

Using the small manufactory of the *Tera* as a common printer was a terrible waste of resources, but she had to reciprocate.

Returning to the *Tera* and going through decontamination, she left the books in the airlock for the maintenance bots as she returned to the pressurized section.

"*Picture books,*" Munin reported, controlling the bots. "*This will help dramatically.*"

"They are more prepared and ready for first contact than we are," Sif said.

"*True,*" Munin said. "*One has to wonder if they have made contact with other aliens.*"

"Or, if they have not," Sif said, "they are very trusting. They are revealing a lot more than we are."

"*Different cultural approach to honesty, knowledge, and sharing.*"

"Yet they are rebels against their government," Sif said.

"They may have nothing to lose, and they could be desperate."

"But if we do not reciprocate, they may get suspicious or resentful."

"You attribute human qualities to them."

Sif had been thinking that, but still. They did not have to be suspicious or resentful; they could be insulted or disappointed.

"You should sleep," Munin said. *"We will continue to analyze and decipher."*

"Can we create a picture book tablet or something?" Sif asked.

"That is possible, and we have considered it. A SCBI team aboard the Eagle is currently developing such a device and vetting the information it will hold. It will take time."

The SCBIs seemed to have more ideas and plans.

Sif was feeling tired, but sleeping felt like wasting time, and they didn't have the time to waste. The body required sleep, though, and she gave in.

* * * * *

Chapter Nineteen: Vanir Survivors

Major Zale Stathis, USMC

"Contact!" the call rang out, and Stathis looked around for something to shoot. In the rearmost position, he didn't have anything to shoot at, as Quinn and his team created a wall facing backward down the tunnel, moving back further so they had a better view distance, and could shoot around a curve.

Stathis expected to hear blazer fire but didn't. With the rear secure, he tapped into the views of other patrol members to see Chen and his team surrounding a figure that was cowering behind a piece of machinery, probably an air pump.

"Check fire, check fire," Hakala was saying as Stathis got a better look at the figure. Human and very frightened. Wearing a uniform of some kind. "Major, I need you up here."

Glad to be involved in something besides rear security, Stathis made his way past the rest of Mikhailov's squad to the section they'd been working their way through.

Stathis arrived in time to hear Hakala call out.

"Who are you?"

"Who are you?" the person called out back.

"I'm HKT Captain Hakala," she said. "Stand and identify yourself, or be shot."

"Visekonstabel Andre Rorke," the figure said. "Hail, Odin. What took you so long?"

"Visekonstabel is a Vanir rank, more like senior private," Shrek told him.

"Are you alone?" Hakala asked as Stathis came up to them.

"Not many of us left," Andre said. "Are you from one of the other SCFs? Are you a relief force?"

A survivor? This was good.

"Where are the rest of you? How many?" Hakala asked, leaving cover, and Stathis moved up beside her, his weapon covering the stranger. He remembered Mister Punchy; he'd looked human.

"Do you acknowledge the old gods?" Stathis asked.

"Odin, Thor? Yeah," the man said, and Stathis realized his question had been stupid.

"No," Stathis said. "The other ones?"

"What other ones?"

"Never mind," Stathis said as the figure became apparent. He had seen Vanir work uniforms, and the one clinging to this man was barely recognizable. He looked malnourished and filthy.

"Unit and designation?" Hakala asked, standing over him, her hand on her pistol, her rifle hanging from her front. Stathis held back and at an angle so he could shoot if the guy transformed or became unfriendly. He wasn't in armor, but Stathis knew how little that could mean.

"Vanir Valhöll, 3rd Division. Maintenance engineer," he said.

"What are the conditions in Valhöll?" Hakala asked.

"Everyone is dead," Andre said. "Something failed, the inkeri, I think, and then monsters began appearing, killing everyone. We were not ready, and they slaughtered us."

"What kind of monsters?"

"Some kind of robots," Andre said. "They fired slivers of metal from their guns and seemed immune to blazers. The Aesir did not stand a chance."

"Tell me about the robots," Hakala asked.

"Humanlike, covered in spikes that they could shoot. Their weapons shredded the Aesir. They did not seem like the best shots, though, and they made a screeching sound like tearing metal. You do not want to go into Valhöll. That is where they are. It is suicide. I can only assume they have captured the other command facilities."

"What else can you tell us about them?"

"Other monsters are wandering around, frog-like monsters, and we've heard them fighting the robots. Are the cylinders safe? We have been cut off by the frogs. Nothing works. An EMP or something has shut down so much."

"It is not looking good," Hakala said, looking at Stathis.

"Do you know any ways into Valhöll?" Stathis asked.

"Who are you?"

"An ally," Hakala said.

"Ally? From where?"

"We are from the *Tyr*," Hakala said, which was close enough.

"What about the rest of the fleet?"

"It is complicated," Hakala said as he stood up. He was covered in dirt and grime, like he had been crawling through it for weeks.

"Do you have any food?"

He looked malnourished and ready to collapse.

"Be careful," Stathis said on a private link to Hakala. "He could still be vanhat. His survival is suspect."

"Zen," Hakala said as she handed him some tube paste, a meal that everyone carried that could be eaten through a helmet adapter. It was unappealing, but you could eat them without a helmet, and although they tasted nasty, they were filling and nutritional.

"How many survivors, and where?" Hakala asked as he devoured the paste, squeezing out every drop.

"Not far," he said. "Hiding. There are frog monsters around."

"Where?"

Andre shrugged as he squeezed out the last of the paste.

Stathis wasn't impressed with Andre's professionalism or military bearing. Senior private would be an appropriate rank.

"Any other senior-ranking survivors?" Hakala asked.

"Fenrik Alli Lochoki," Andre said.

"*Fenrik is an officer rank, slightly below second lieutenant. More like an officer cadet,*" Shrek said.

"Take us there," Hakala said with a glance at Stathis. Why was she looking at him? Approval?

Stathis nodded. He wanted to know more about the robots that had taken over Valhöll. How much of a problem would they be? What kind of Jotun did they serve?

"This is good, right?" Stathis asked Hakala. She didn't seem overjoyed.

"Maybe," Hakala said. "Andre is a visekonstabel, which means little. Like most crew, his skills are limited to using a headset and following directions for tasks. A fenrik indicates an officer in training, but still an officer."

"Well, we can train him," Stathis said. "More officers would be good."

"Her, Alli is a woman's name," Hakala said. "She will have an actual, acknowledged rank aboard Bifrost. I am not sure what authority that gives her in the system."

"A system nobody can access," Stathis said.

"Yet."

* * * * *

Chapter Twenty: The Storm

Kapten Sif, VRAEC, Nakija Musta Toiminnot

Taking a deep breath, Sif opened her eyes. Her sleep had not been good, although Munin had been able to help calm her, regulate her heart rate, and make sure her body got the most out of it, but her mind wouldn't settle, and there was nothing Munin could do about that.

"*We have made progress,*" Munin reported when she was mentally ready enough. "*The picture books have provided a lot of context. They were fabricated from a child's textbook. Like a Rosetta stone, they have helped us decipher their written language, and we were able to match that with digital information from the dissected tablet.*"

"*Excellent,*" Sif said, wishing for coffee. Munin would prepare her some, but Munin must have been waiting to share this information, and coffee could wait.

"*We are still deciphering details,*" Munin said. "*However, we do have a great deal of information, and the floodgate has been opened. We expect to have a text-based translator available in a few hours. I would recommend extreme caution, though, because while we can identify the word for food, there are many other nuances within that word that we do not yet have defined. This data is a beginning, but there is still so much more to go. A language is not just words and sounds. There is a massive amount of context and intent behind words. There is also understanding an entire technological base, such as how they explain radio waves or lasers."*

"*I understand,*" Sif said. "*Let me know when it is ready.*"

"*There is also something else. Britta has been informed. She is trying to collect more information as unobtrusively as possible.*"

"*What?*"

"*Many of the arrays on the Fallen ship are lasers. They seem to use lasers as a form of communication, preferring that over radios.*"

"*Unusual, but not a worry.*"

"*We have detected that they are communicating with someone 6.9 kilometers away. There appears to be a hidden laser receiver on a mountain top.*"

Sif knew the mountain range.

"*This meeting spot was not chosen randomly,*" Sif said.

"*Nor was this solar system. There is a base hidden nearby.*"

"*Which might be why they are so trusting.*"

"*Explain,*" Munin said.

"*We could be sitting in the center of a defensive ring with numerous weapons pointed at us. The Fallen are robots. It makes the most sense that they would have a secret base, and they feel confident enough to share data. Furthermore, it reveals that we are dealing with more of them than exist on that ship. Do we know anything about the hidden base?*"

"*Nothing more than that the base is likely to exist. We cannot intercept any communications because they are directed lasers.*"

"*Thank you,*" Sif said. "*Please continue working on the translator.*"

Closing her eyes, Sif knew her body was already relaxed. She was unlikely to fall asleep, and this was a good chance to reach out to the Fallen and see if they were alert. It might also give her a chance to try and discover more about the nearby base, and if the *Tera* was in any danger.

She heard Orlov and his men prepare and tuned them out. Should she be drawing the vanhat here? Was she endangering the Fallen?

Hopefully, just a light trance and telepathic communication were not enough to draw the assassins.

Reaching out lightly, she almost immediately felt the being she had been speaking with, but now that she was aware, she began to feel others, many others, not far away. It wasn't a base; it was a city. She sensed weapons that were primed and ready, watchers waiting for orders, but she did not sense hostility.

Of course, hostility was very subjective. Human psychopaths murdered innocent, peaceful people all the time, and they did not feel hate or hostility toward their victims.

"Are you holding back?" the voice asked, drifting across her mind. The thoughts were laced with disappointment and suspicion.

"We were unprepared," Sif said. *"We are more a military expedition than a peaceful or scientific one. We wish to be more forthcoming with information, but you are more prepared, and we are trying to emulate you."*

She felt the being consider that and could almost sense the conflicting thoughts and concerns.

"Your vessel is protected in ways we do not understand. A field or barrier."

"A technology that shields us from some vanhat," Sif said. They were probably detecting the inkeri field.

"Will you share this technology?"

"Gladly," Sif said. *"The enemy of our enemy is our friend."*

"That is not always true," the voice whispered back. Intentional or not, Sif wasn't sure.

"We mean no harm," Sif said.

"Which does not mean you will not inflict it."

Sif was not sure what to say. Were things about to go bad? Was the *Tera* in danger?

"We can help each other," Sif said, but there was no response. She could sense the suspicion. They were the ones being deceptive, inviting them to this planet with a nearby base.

"Deception is the nature of war."

"Are we at war?" Sif asked.

"A war is in progress. The devourers return. We must defend and protect ourselves."

Sif had no response. This was not going well. How could she turn it around? What could she say or do to return to the desire to work together?

"We are preparing something to give you," Sif said. *"My ship is small and not well equipped. The larger ship cannot land safely, or it would."*

She knew they could hear the truth in her thoughts.

"You have helped us with your technology and gifts. We wish to reciprocate but do not yet have the means."

"Time is not on our side."

"I understand," Sif said. It was not. She knew Britta could send a drone to inform the rest of the fleet, but that would not be a quick procedure. The rest of the fleet could be days or weeks away at this point.

The being must have heard some of her thoughts.

"We have detected large vessels with numerous escort vessels."

She got the impression it was massive, dwarfing the smaller escorts, and she could feel that the Fallen were in awe of how something so large could be used as a spaceship.

The problem was, something that large couldn't be the *Musashi*, not based on their impression of the size difference. They feared going close to it.

The Bifrost?

"There may be several vanhat ships hunting us," Sif said. *"That may be one. Where did you see it?"*

The thoughts on its location did not make much sense. There was a binary star, and there were many of those, but it did not seem to be close.

"Your enemy?"

Yes, but no. If Stathis was still on it, and alive, it wasn't an enemy, not completely.

"Your friend is dead."

Sif doubted that was true. If anyone could survive, it would be a Marine like Stathis and an HKT like Hakala.

"He cannot withstand the storm."

Sif wanted to smile.

"He is *the storm."*

* * * * *

Chapter Twenty-One: Vanir

Major Zale Stathis, USMC

Back in his tail-end position, Stathis followed the rest of the patrol as they headed toward where this Fenrik Lochoki was supposed to be. The corridors were much larger here, big enough for cargo bots, and there were numerous large, sealed hatches to either side, massive doors with smaller doors in them. The network here was offline, and what was behind the doors was a mystery, but this was obviously some kind of unused storage facility.

Stathis sort of felt better that Fenrik Alli Lochoki was a very junior officer. Less than a boot lieutenant in Marine Corps parlance. An officer cadet should be more than happy to take orders from Hakala, a veteran HKT.

Right? This was all good news. Another Vanir officer to give Hakala more legitimacy aboard Bifrost, and someone more familiar with Bifrost's systems.

Then why did he have a gut feeling that things weren't that good? Why hadn't they heard anything or found signs of these survivors? There could be a lot of people out hiding, tens of thousands maybe. Bifrost's network was a shattered wreck, and Stathis knew less than 10 percent of it was operational, or at least accessible to Skögul. Bifrost was a massive city ship that had once had a population of fourteen million, with plenty of room to expand. There were ten massive cylinders, and Stathis barely knew what was going on in two of them. Fourteen million people, almost the population of New York Arcology, back in the late 21st century.

If there was a large population, trapped or still fighting in one or more of the cylinders, there was no sign. There couldn't be many, or they would've radioed for help, right?

Would Valhöll have better connectivity to the cylinders?

"*Bifrost is exiting Shorr space,*" Shrek reported.

"*Where are we?*"

"*Collecting data might take some time,*" Shrek said. "*We are in a solar system, collecting information. The transition was very accurate, we were closer to the binary stars, and we have matched velocity with the star system.*"

"*Which means what?*"

"*There are likely to be vanhat scouts, or other ships, that Bifrost has homed in on. We are deeper in the nebula, so we are not heading back toward Sol. Perhaps we are following the fleet*"

"*Or riding the wave of the invasion. So vanhat scouts have found something in the system that needs attention,*" Stathis said. "*Someone is about to have a bad day.*"

"*Which means we need to take over or shut down Valhöll sooner rather than later?*"

"*Correct. Bifrost appears to be setting course for a planet with two moons in the Goldilocks zone.*"

"*Goldilocks? Like with bears? Porridge and shit?*"

"*Goldilocks is a term used to denote the zone of habitable planets,*" Shrek said. "*The term does come from the tale of three bears, and the Goldilocks zone is the zone considered 'just right' for habitable planets, and—*"

"*Thanks, I get it,*" Stathis said before Shrek could lecture him further. He remembered from the classes back on Earth.

"*This planet orbits the first star, which is a yellow dwarf, with our destination approximately 1.2 AU from the star. The second star is a red dwarf and orbits the first star at a distance of 20 AU. The orbital—*"

"*That's fine and dandy and all,*" Stathis said. "*How long till we get there?*"

"*At current speeds? A week, unless we transition closer.*"

"*Why so long?*"

"*Gravitational influences of the system make it peculiar. There are several other large bodies, influenced by the nebula, creating a complex gravity wake.*"

Stathis was sure that Shrek could bore him to tears with the science of it all, and he didn't want to be bored to tears, though following everyone else was far from exciting; he just didn't want to hear all the science and math that Shrek wanted to dump on him. He was an infantry officer, not some spacebert who liked those things. Maybe Hakala found it interesting, but Stathis didn't. Since the gunny or someone else wasn't around to tell him he needed to care, Stathis decided not to.

"*We have less than a week to take control of Valhöll,*" Stathis said. "*Easypeasy.*"

"Up ahead," Hakala let him know. "Next bulkhead hatch."

"Copy," Stathis said, his mind kicking into gear. They were at an intersection. This was a series of ancient storerooms that might have been here since Bifrost was built. Wide corridors. Stathis was afraid to ask Shrek what might be in them. Hearing a long explanation of why they were storing toilet paper or napkin-making machines would be too much, though. Sometimes, ignorance was bliss.

"Quinn, hold the team up here for the moment," Stathis said. "We're about to make contact, and if things go wrong, we want to make sure we have options for retreat, and to make sure we don't get hit from behind and trapped."

"Wilco," Quinn said.

"*No network?*" Stathis asked Shrek.

"*Nothing. Systems appear to be damaged from the harsh exit from Shorr space when Bifrost fell. Most emergency systems have failed as well. There are no markings to indicate what is stored here, or why.*"

"*What do you mean?*"

"*It would not make sense to store most items when they can be recycled and reused,*" Shrek said. "*If the original item is needed, it can likely be fabricated again using newer tech codes and advancements. It makes no sense to stockpile old equipment.*"

"*Unless you're worried about your manufactories being offline,*" Stathis said.

"*Or weapons and munitions, such as drones, missiles, warbots, and weapons. It could even be raw material for use by manufactories.*"

"*I like the way you think. Which probably means we need to be super careful with our weapon fire.*"

"*There do not seem to be enough defenses or controls to indicate what is stored is of a military nature, though,*" Shrek said, dashing Stathis' hopes.

The signal for Stathis to come forward flashed on his heads-up display. Stathis clapped Quinn on the back to let him know he was leaving, and Quinn was in command of the rear guard.

Quinn nodded as Stathis headed forward, and he tapped into Hakala's view.

"Who are you?" a heavy-set woman asked, looking at Hakala.

"I am HKT Kapten Hakala," Hakala said.

"Your rank identifier is not recognized by my system," Lochoki said. Weren't the Bifrost systems offline? Lochoki might have an offline system copy or something. Of course, it would be incomplete.

"I am from the *Tyr*," Hakala said. "I was promoted after we lost contact with the homestars."

"Where is the *Tyr*?"

"In the Sol System," Hakala said as Stathis came up to stand beside her. The fenrik's eyes looked over Stathis.

Stathis had expected some young, frightened, mouse-like cadet. Alli Lochoki wasn't small. Not exactly fat, she had the body type of a sumo wrestler more than anything else, and she had hard, angry eyes. She held a blazer with a confidence most officers wouldn't usually have. She also didn't seem happy to see Hakala.

Her eyes took in Stathis and his armor, which she probably didn't recognize.

"Sol? Are they SOG?" she asked, pointing at Stathis and Mikhailov, who stood nearby.

"He is not. Most are ex-SOG. The Governance is dead, the central committee dead and gone."

"Who is the despot that took over?"

"It is a long story," Hakala said.

"Shorten it."

"Look, Fenrik," Hakala said, and Stathis could hear the impatience in her voice. Shouldn't Lochoki be a little bit happier that a military force was here and not trying to kill her? Were all Republic citizens in the homestar stuck-up, arrogant pricks?

"No," Lochoki said. "You look. I do not know who you are. You claim you are from the *Tyr*, but you are surrounded by strangers. Easier to fabricate a single HKT suit than several. How do I know this is not some elaborate SOG attack on Bifrost? Your identifier does not show you as a Bifrost officer. It has been months since we have heard from anyone else. Just monsters roaming the ship and hunting us."

"*She has network access?*" Stathis asked Shrek.

"*Negative,*" Shrek said. "*Each Vanir has an identity code, half of a key that authenticates them with others. Part of that key is their rank. The other half of the key is frequently updated. Hakala's identifier has not been updated on Bifrost, and Fenrik Lochoki will be using an old key, so Hakala can only present her old identifier.*"

"*Hakala didn't fix that at the SCF?*"

"*Lochoki doesn't have access to the newer authentication keys that will recognize the changes.*"

There were several other people nearby, also wearing ragged Vanir uniforms, and they were armed with blazers and wire guns. Stathis couldn't fail to notice that they weren't overjoyed to see other survivors. They looked ragged and malnourished, but tough. Survivors on the edge.

"A lot has happened," Hakala said. "We have secured Skögul, and we need to secure Valhöll."

Lochoki looked around at the legionnaires.

"There aren't enough of you," she said.

"What are we facing?"

"You are going to need a lot more troops," Lochoki said. "What you will find there are not the lizards. The creatures lurking in Valhöll are armored monsters, covered in spikes that they can shoot at you. They can also pull flecks of metal off the walls, and they will cut you to shreds."

"We have a secret weapon," Stathis said. "Let's see how well their vanhat abilities work in an inkeri field."

"They are also armed with rifles, like blazers," Lochoki said. "They are dangerous."

"Do they leave Valhöll?" Stathis asked.

"We have not seen them leave yet. Beyond the confines of Valhöll, it is only the *vaskitska*."

"*Vaskitska* translates roughly as a type of snake found in Finland," Shrek explained.

"We call them froggers," Stathis said. "We've found them almost everywhere else. Not the greatest fighters, but they're numerous."

"The metal ones are much more dangerous," Lochoki said.

"Thanks for the heads-up," Stathis said and looked at Hakala.

"Do we want to stay here and help them, or press on?" Stathis asked on a private link.

"We can still get more information," Hakala told him.

"You are going to your death," Lochoki said. "I watched them tear apart the Aesir and massacre others."

"They have no mercy," one of the other survivors said. "They will slaughter you."

Stathis couldn't remember dealing with anything like this before, but if the inkeri kept them from using their metal-flinging ability, that would give them an advantage.

"They are a kind of robot," Lochoki added. "Blazers can kill them, but they quickly rebuild and repair themselves. I have seen it. I do not know where they came from, but they were unstoppable. We barely escaped."

"Robots?" Hakala asked.

"*This might be super easy, then,*" Stathis told Shrek, "*if you can hack their systems.*"

"*You are vastly overrating my abilities,*" Shrek said. "*They are highly unlikely to be anything I recognize or can relate to.*"

"The Weermag hacked our systems," Stathis said. "*Why can't we hack vanhat systems?*"

"*I am not designed to understand and hack a completely alien computer system. Do not overestimate the Weermag; they likely had time to understand and dissect human technology. Also, can you say for sure that they are not significantly more advanced than us?*"

"*So, this is not apples to apples, or even oranges. This is comparing apples with alien butt nuggets?*" Stathis asked.

"*Close enough,*" Shrek said. "*Or apples to grenades.*"

* * * * *

Chapter Twenty-Two: Spider to the Fly

Kapten Sif, VRAEC, Nakija Musta Toiminnot

Her helmet displayed the view of a forested hillside. Birds flew in the distance, and she marveled at the detail of the simulation. Realism was not unusual, but sometimes it was easy to see the simulation. Clouds that began to appear the same, trees that lost their distinctive shape, and more. Here? It was nearly impossible to see the differences.

Munin was tied in with the simulation, likely masking these details as it noticed where her eyes and attention began to focus. Munin would anticipate her in that regard.

"*We have made a lot of progress,*" Munin reported. "*We would like to try and contact them; however, there is risk.*"

"*Risk? Explain.*"

"*While they do use radio waves, they rely on lasers for communications. We have detected their lasers aimed at us, but they are weak, harmless bursts. We originally believed they were targeting or sensor-related because of the weakness. While communication was considered, we do not have equipment that could accept such transmissions. Detect? Yes. Decipher the nuances? No. We have fabricated an array that may be able to transmit and receive at the wavelengths we suspect they are using.*"

"*The risk?*"

"If it is targeting information, they will assume we are targeting their vessel and may respond in a hostile manner. Furthermore, initial communication is always tricky. It would be very inappropriate if we insulted their mother in our initial communication."

"Is their language that convoluted?"

"No. That is merely an extreme example. The insult could be as mild as implying they are not intellectually capable of understanding something."

"I am sure they will not be so touchy. They must understand that we are learning."

"A human assumption. Britta would like to link with you."

"Eversti," Sif said when the link opened.

"Sif," Britta said. "The SCBIs report that we might be able to talk with them. They've reached a plateau based on the knowledge we have so far. I'll leave this up to you, since you have other methods of talking with them."

"The other methods are thoughts and emotions. Many details can be lost."

"What do you recommend?"

"I will exit the ship and point out our array, try to make sure they understand we do not mean harm."

"How could such a weak laser be harmful?"

"Targeting someone is not a friendly action," Sif said, but Britta would know that. "We must proceed with caution and do everything we can to avoid a misunderstanding."

"Zen."

"What do you suggest?" Britta asked.

"I will go out and expose myself," Sif said. "Let them know. Maybe it works, maybe it does not."

Outside, she could feel that they were watching her as she climbed up on the *Tera*, and pointed at the new laser communicator, and then pointed at their ship. They had to be able to see her.

"*We will start with the lightest setting,*" Munin said.

Minutes later, they were sending tentative laser pulses back, and the SCBIs were working to decipher the communications.

"*We are establishing links,*" Munin reported as Sif pulled off her helmet. "*This could take a while. Their responsiveness indicates we are dealing with organics and not computers.*"

"*Zen,*" Sif said, climbing back into her command couch.

Lying back, she closed her eyes and calmed her breathing. Orlov and another legionnaire came into the cramped bridge.

Reaching out with her senses, she tried to make contact, but it was like walking through a fog. She knew her destination but couldn't see it. Snatches of voices, thoughts, and smells whispered across her consciousness, but nothing she could understand.

Slowly, the sounds became louder, and the fog began to swirl in her psychic senses.

"*You are doomed to failure,*" a voice whispered as she sank deeper into her trance.

The voice did not belong to the aliens. It was something else. Sif wanted to stop, to back up, to open her eyes and return to the physical world, but her curiosity and something else drew her.

"*The angels are not what you think they are,*" the voice whispered. "*Your legends are wrong. You understand so little. Like the ants of your home world, building their nest on the banks of a river. There will be no escape, no survival.*"

"*Then why try so hard to stop us?*" Sif asked. She could feel herself being drawn into the astral realms.

"*Building your home in a flood zone is what you do. Wiping out insects is what we do.*"

She could feel her physical body less and less as her astral body became more real, and she could feel the vibrations change. She was going somewhere.

"*Who are you?*"

"*What is a name?*"

"*A way to identify you from others,*" Sif said, but she could feel its difference; it was unique and powerful.

"*Does it matter?*"

"*Yes,*" Sif said. A unique identity would let her identify it again in the future; it gave the being personality and presence.

"*Not as much as you think. Do you name every drop in your ocean? Does each of your cells have a name?*"

Why didn't it want to reveal its name or identity? Sif could feel it had one.

Around her, the astral mists began to become more real. Sif still felt like she was in control and didn't let the fear stop her.

There was no ground, no walls, nothing around her as she floated through the astral realm. Nothing except mist.

"*Do you fear sharing your identity?*" Sif asked. Was that a weakness?

"*Do you introduce yourself to your ants or cells?*"

"*Cells are a part of me, and ants have no concept of identity.*"

"*True and false on both accounts. Your angels have existed since the beginning. Do you wonder why there aren't other survivors?*"

Her angels?

"*There are survivors,*" Sif said. It could be said that those of the tomb worlds were survivors. The Weermag were survivors, of a kind, and there were others. Though slaves of the vanhat, they still had identity and lived in this physical world.

She sensed the being's amusement.

"*Survival? At whose bidding? What is the purpose of life, then? Is slavery really living?*"

"What does living mean to you?" Sif asked.

"*Define living.*"

A thought trap. She could say breathing in and breathing out, but she knew her soul, her essence, did not need air. A chill passed through her as she realized this creature was right. How would one define living?

"Life must have a purpose," Sif said. "*Life propagates life.*"

"*You do not. You will never give life. Your physical form is unable to do so. You are a failure in that.*"

"Life does not have to spring from my body," Sif said. How did it know about her physical form?

"*Then you are a slave to others.*"

"Or a willing servant," Sif said. What did it want? Was there a point?

"*There is no difference. You have no future, so you must serve those who have a future.*"

"What is wrong with that?"

"*Your ants build their nest on the banks of a river, not knowing that one day the river will rise and eradicate them. What is the purpose of their existence?*"

"Not all riverbanks rise," Sif said, but that sounded like a weak argument.

"*Those ants will be prey for others that understand the river,*" it said. "*They provide sustenance. Nothing else.*"

"You are wrong," Sif said.

"I am right. I have seen this countless times across the ages. Your species has built its nest along the banks, and the water is rising. A few may escape the flood. You will lose your nest, the few might survive, but death will eventually claim your species. This is how it always is. Always."

"Why tell me?"

"You look for these angels to save you. They cannot turn back the river. They cannot stop the flood. At best, all they can do is remove some of you from your nest so when the flood comes, some survive, but without your nest, your identity, without your souls, your race is doomed to extinction."

"Why tell me?" Sif asked again.

"I find it amusing. To watch you struggle to survive. You see the tide rising. Soon it will rise so high that you will drown. Already, Earth has fallen. It will never support life again. Those you call the Weermag have destroyed those few survivors, and they are beginning their hunt for others. Those who do not prostrate themselves to us will die sooner."

Sif wanted to go to Earth to see if it was true. She could not tell if it was lying; in its mind, it believed that Earth had fallen, but there was doubt there.

"You lie," Sif said.

"No," it said. "There might be some holdouts deep inside caves. Our slaves hunt them."

Listening with all her senses, she heard the untruth there, but there was also truth. This being had seen the same thing played out over the eons. Not just in this dimension, but in others, in other realities. It saw nothing special about humanity. Having seen events played out without variation thousands, maybe millions of times in the past, gave it a cold, cruel confidence that this time would be no different. No species survived the arrival of the devourers. Why did it bother conversing with her? What did it get from this?

The chill that passed through Sif was the inevitability of the struggle they faced.

"These angels you seek will not save you. They will destroy you. They are devourers as much as we are. Certain laws of existence do not change. To survive, you must prey on others. This is the nature of being, the nature of existence."

"Why?" Sif asked. The creature was sure of itself.

"A question you will not understand the answers to. There are things your brain simply cannot comprehend."

"Try me."

"It is much more satisfying to watch you squirm and die. To savor the fear and despair as you are extinguished in the coming waves. What has happened countless times before will continue long after you are extinguished from this universe. Your eradication gives me pleasure."

"Where did we come from?"

"Does it matter?"

"Are you afraid to answer the question?"

"We have always been here. Always existed since long before your species existed. We created you. We brought you here. The beginning matters less than the ending."

"Did life spring from nothing?" Sif asked, a thought taking root. Fighting for survival was important, but by understanding the past, one could understand the present and sometimes the future. A road had a source and a destination.

What was the source of life?

"That which you call life has existed in one form or another since forever."

"You kill, but you don't create," Sif said, but the being had no answer, and she felt its frustration. What did that mean? There was a flaw in its logic.

"Life permeates throughout the dimensions," it said, but she felt a lie there. It knew something. *"You cannot understand. Your mind and consciousness are too feeble to grasp reality. All you see is your nest in the path of the river. There is no escape."*

The anger was growing, and around her, she felt the mist starting to swirl as she caught a glimpse of something moving through it. A serpent?

"You are afraid to tell me the truth," Sif said, and the anger that surrounded her seemed to burn her skin.

"I do not fear questions from the likes of you."

"But you do," Sif said, her senses searching the mist around her. Then she realized her folly. The being she had been talking to had been drawing her deeper into its trap, like an ant lion creating its funnel of death. She was now in that funnel, and she realized her peril.

"The creator creates things to be preyed upon and destroyed. You cannot comprehend, cannot understand the purpose. Your time is at an end."

The creator? God? Did such a being exist?

She did not have time for questions, though. She had to escape, but as she tried to return to her body, she could feel herself slipping. She could not return. The coils of the serpent surrounding her became more visible through the mist, like a python constricting around its prey. Sif saw that she was caught in a roiling sphere of coils, slowly condensing around her, keeping her from her body, trapping her in this astral realm.

"Welcome to the end of your existence."

Said the spider to the fly.

* * * * *

Chapter Twenty-Three: Pushing Through

Major Zale Stathis, USMC

Stathis was tired of being in the rear. This was the last time he was going on a combat patrol with Hakala, unless, of course, she was his XO. He was so far back, he couldn't get a good look at her, and when the shit hit the fan, he'd be in the rear with the gear, instead of forward keeping her out of trouble. Not that she really needed his help, staying out of trouble. The one time she'd leapt out of a ruptured hull, holding an armed nuke, and managed to survive the experience was enough for Stathis to trust her. However, her luck would run out eventually.

Dammit. He should be in the front, the dangerous spot. He didn't want to lose her. Not Hakala. He should be in front of her, shielding her with his body. Was that stupid? It wasn't like she was bearing his children or anything, yet, but why did he feel this way?

Lochoki had made them a map, and Hakala was fine with leaving them behind with a spare radio. It wasn't like Lochoki was a fighter, and she was unarmored. She could provide advice and directions just as easily from a safer location. No reason she should endanger herself, and Hakala seemed fine with that.

However, this was Hakala's home, her people, and Stathis knew he had no right to take over, as if she would let him. She was a warrior, and if he were to stand in front of her, he would be robbing her of her duty. Her rightful place was commanding Bifrost, unless there was someone senior, and that wasn't Kaelan.

If the Republic was dead, only Hakala had the authority to take control of this homestar. Besides, anything to piss off Kaelan at this point was a good thing.

"*Approaching the Valhöll outer perimeter,*" Shrek reported. "*No power readings. Extensive damage.*"

"*What kind of damage?*"

"*Some battle damage, mostly it looks related to the drop from Shorr space, burned out power conduits and overloaded systems. Russelman index is rising.*"

"Brace for contact," Hakala said on the patrol link.

"Contact!" the point man reported, and Stathis heard blazer fire erupt, combined with a ripping sound as Shrek reported the mule-mounted inkeri was flexing, expanding the field.

It took effort not to turn and run toward the fighting as he watched Quinn deploy his fireteam to guard the rear. This was one of the larger tunnels, more like a highway than a smaller train tunnel. The derelict vehicles told Stathis it had once been a much busier thoroughfare, and there were a couple of cargo bots as cover. The patrol was dispersed, and the tunnel curved up ahead so he couldn't see what was going on.

Tapping into the drone and lead element's views, he could see something further down the tunnel, trying to advance—several somethings, actually—but they stopped when one erupted, preferring to hunker down behind some kind of bus. They were learning that the Legion had teeth. There was room to maneuver, and Hakala and Mikhailov were leapfrogging teams.

A drone screamed past and over the bus before detonating, tipping the bus over.

The fire stopped, and the Russelman index went down as Corporal Chen's team advanced.

"You okay back there?" Hakala asked on a private link.

"I'm not enjoying the view, my trigger finger has an itch I can't scratch, and all this ammo is getting heavy," Stathis said.

"You do not enjoy the view?" Hakala asked.

"I can't see your, um, you," Stathis said, checking to verify that it was a private link.

"You will get to enjoy it later," Hakala said. "There were just three of them. A probe, if I had to guess. Their weapons pack a punch, not enough to penetrate our trauma plates but maybe regular armor. Chen will have a bruise."

"Aye," Stathis said. "If you ever want to sit back and watch a fight, just let me know."

"Zen. With you behind me, I feel safe from that direction. We will continue to advance. Just be careful they do not flank us."

"They won't catch us by surprise," Stathis said.

"I am more worried about being trapped than surprised," Hakala said.

"Aye," Stathis said. "I'll try to avoid that."

He had a pair of drones following behind them, but it would be nearly impossible to investigate all the branching tunnels and storage facilities.

"Ugly bastards," Hakala said, and Stathis tapped into her view. She was by the bus, looking at the remains of something. Purple chunks inside a metal shell full of wires and broken metal didn't tell Stathis a lot. It might have been humanoid before the drone had shredded it. Stathis wasn't sure whether the purple goo covering everything was blood or some kind of lubrication.

"I like them disassembled more," Stathis said.

"Zen," Hakala said.

"*Are they robots or organic?*" Stathis asked Shrek.

"*Cybernetic, or from a biome that does not differentiate,*" Shrek said. "*They move fast, and their weapons fire molten metal. Not as effective as blazers, but still very dangerous.*"

"*So, we still have an advantage?*"

"*Several advantages,*" Shrek said. "*Our blazers seem to be effective, though they do have plates on their exterior that provide some degree of protection. Given the chance, we should investigate and see if this can help us create more effective trauma plates.*"

"You want to stop and take samples?"

"*There will be a chance later,*" Shrek said. "*They do not have joints like you do. They will be extremely flexible.*"

"Flexible? I'm not going to bed them," Stathis said. "Not with Hakala—"

"No," Shrek said, "*that is not what I mean. Should you engage them in close combat, do not expect them to be vulnerable. Joint locks are unlikely to work.*"

"Oh. Well," Stathis said. He should get his mind on the mission and off Hakala. But Marines did have a reputation. Stathis didn't want to let anyone down.

Hakala gave the command, and the patrol advanced again.

Minutes later, someone reported contact, and the firing began. The tempo picked up as Quinn pushed his team back to cover the rear and a nearby tunnel branch. Once again, Stathis couldn't see the front of the patrol and had to rely on tapping into views to see the firefight erupting to the front.

This time, there were more of them.

"*Why the hell can't the Republic build a tunnel in a straight line?*" Stathis asked Shrek.

"*They do. In some areas like this, it is more structurally sound because of the danger of blasts and attack.*"

With Quinn watching the rear, Stathis tried to follow the battle and keep the big picture in view, making sure Hakala didn't get so focused on taking out the vanhat cyborgs that she made a mistake.

It was almost fun, watching her direct the battle, working closely with Mikhailov, moving the legionnaires like chess pieces, and advancing across the board. She was methodical and ruthless.

This time, about eight cyborgs were attacking. They were coming from a Valhöll bunker entrance, which was their primary objective, the entrance they were trying to get to.

Several drop-down turrets in the ceiling above them had been gutted, and most of the vehicles in the area were shredded garbage. Stathis noticed a pair of human bodies that looked like they'd been shredded by a wire gun, but the cuts were smaller, like small snips of wire had been used. There were countless metal flecks in the decomposing bodies.

"*They aren't eating the dead,*" Stathis told Shrek.

"*Noted.*"

The inkeri on the mule flexed, expanding coverage again as Mikhailov advanced his squad, cutting down the vanhat cyborgs.

"Contact rear," Quinn reported as Stathis looked over his cover.

Four cyborgs appeared on a drone's view before the display disappeared into static. What had they done? Shot the drones?

Seconds later, they came into view, and Quinn and his men opened fire, cutting down the first one and wounding the second one. The cyborgs took cover, realizing they'd lost the element of surprise as

Stathis fired, trying to use his blazer to cut through the automated cargo vehicle they were using as cover.

Martin had a much better weapon for that and was using his SAW like a buzz saw to slice the vehicle apart.

Quinn launched a grenade that splashed against the wall behind them, and another body flew out from behind cover.

Stathis paused his firing.

They were now all behind the transport, if they were still alive, or powered, or whatever.

"Status?" Hakala asked.

"Hostile fireteam, now a few beers short of a six-pack. Two left, I think. Got it covered."

"Zen," Hakala said.

The remaining two came out firing, and Martin spun backward from a hit. Stathis, Quinn, MacMurrough, and Collin's fire cut them down.

Quinn and MacMurrough rushed over to Martin. MacMurrough pulled his SAW off him and took cover as Quinn checked his status.

Stathis' display indicated Martin was seriously injured. The round had missed his breastplate and ripped through his hip. Nanites were keeping him alive, but he was losing blood as Quinn applied a bandage that expanded to cover the wound.

One of the mules came back toward Martin, unfolding a stretcher.

Stathis sent another pair of drones out to check the tunnels as he watched and waited.

Checking on Hakala, he saw that Mikhailov and one of his troopers had suffered injuries, but nothing like what Martin had suffered. Mikhailov had a broken rib, and his trooper was missing a small chunk of flesh and armor from his left leg.

It didn't take long to get Martin strapped down, sedated, and immobile. His nanites would work to repair his injury.

"Thoughts?" Hakala asked Stathis on a private link.

"We won," Stathis said. She was in warrior mode and probably wouldn't appreciate the thoughts he was having. "We can sit here and see what else they throw at us, or we can advance. I think we have the advantage with the inkeris and blazers."

"They tried flanking us almost immediately," Hakala said. "They are smart and aggressive. Well-coordinated."

"Sure, and we were ready for them and kicked them in the teeth. Now they know we're better. They aren't any better than us with SCBIs. I say we keep pushing, see how far we can get."

"And if we get cut off and surrounded?"

"Then we fight our way out. Marines don't kick ass by retreating after a black eye. Let's keep pushing, make our way to the inkeri, and get that back online if we can. Then we work from there. Worst-case scenario, we trigger a self-destruct or something, take the SCF offline completely, then master controls will fall back to Skögul. At this point, I'm pretty sure there aren't any survivors here."

"Zen," Hakala said. "That is what I was thinking. As my executive officer, you are supposed to play devil's advocate."

"Sorry, I like kicking vanhat ass a little too much. Casualties are bad, but that's part of our job. We haven't lost anyone yet. I'm your XO? Sweet. Let's finish the job."

"Zen."

Each mule could, in an emergency, carry two wounded. People began rotating out of their line to restock on ammunition, then Hakala gave the order to keep advancing, and Stathis wondered if they were making a mistake.

* * * * *

Chapter Twenty-Four: Escaping the Nightmare

Kapten Sif, VRAEC, Nakija Musta Toiminnot

Sif understood that the most important thing was not to panic. Panic was the real killer; it compounded mistakes until there were no more mistakes to make. She was surrounded and trapped. The coils were coming closer, and she knew they would crush the life out of her.

What were the rules in this realm? Her mind filtered through countless plans. There had to be some way. She could not consult books or ask Munin. Here, she was alone, with only the information in her own mind to help her escape.

Perhaps there was no information because nobody had ever escaped before?

No. That was panic thinking. There was always an escape.

She remembered once watching an ancient video of some herbivore from Africa. It was being attacked by lions, who were latched onto it, their claws and teeth tearing into the flesh. She had thought there would be no escape for the poor animal, but it continued to fight, and miraculously, it had gotten back to its feet, shrugged off the lions, and escaped.

Now she was that animal, and she knew that very few animals escaped being dragged to the ground by such predators, but some did. She was one. She would not die here. She refused. She was Aesir.

But what could she do?

"You are doomed."

Its thoughts whispered across her own.

"We are Aesir," Sif said. *"Bound together through blood and tears. We are the blades of our people."*

"You are alone."

"We are Aesir," Sif said. It did not matter if she was alone or not. She was Aesir. *"We are bound together through blood and tears."*

Like always, she would find a way.

"We are Aesir, tears are our armor, blood is our shield."

"You will bleed and die," it said, and she felt the fear sinking in.

She rejected those thoughts, those expectations. She was Aesir, Jaeger, Erikoisjoukot, Musta Toiminnot. She was not doomed. She had accomplished what so few ever had, despite her handicaps. If she had ever quit, she would not be where she was today. She had done what so many others thought impossible. Her perceived weaknesses had become her strength.

But one time she wouldn't. It would be the last time.

Was now that time?

She was alone. Trapped by a larger, stronger being, in that being's home, where it knew all the rules. She had trespassed, fallen into her last trap.

No. She was Aesir.

The fear of failure fed her anger, and she attacked. She focused her will, her anger, and her fear into a weapon, and she attacked that writhing mass. In this realm, she had no body, but she imagined the claws on her hands and feet, tearing into the beast. She did not want to escape it; she wanted to kill it. If she was going to die, she would take it with her.

How dare this Jotun attack her? Trap her here? Try to kill her? She fed her anger and redoubled her efforts. She didn't want to escape; she wanted to hurt this thing, and she focused her mind on one thing. To hurt and kill this creature that had trapped her here. If she was going to die, it would not be alone.

A flare of enjoyment whispered across her consciousness. This thing was taking pleasure in her anger.

This was not the right approach. She was feeding it. Anger, fear, negative emotions?

If the first attack does not work, find another route. Flank and attack.

Sif's other strength was her ability to adapt.

Like flipping a switch, she turned off her anger and hate, replacing them with longing and desire. She had to defeat this thing and escape to protect others. The fleet depended on her; humanity depended on her. They needed her help and protection. She thought of others and their needs. Mathison, Skadi, Stathis, Winters, Hakala, Carpenter, so many others needed her. Emotions and thoughts were as much a weapon as anything else.

She had to survive; she had to be victorious. They needed her.

She felt another presence, and she sensed others coming to her aid now. She was no longer alone fighting the Jotun.

Holding the line, she felt the line against the demon grow stronger. Now, another emotion whispered across her mind.

Fear. It was learning fear.

This Jotun had to be defeated because others needed her. Humanity had to survive. It would survive.

She sensed Levin nearby, his quiet strength and determination, and there were others. He was not alone.

Sif knew them, knew all of them somehow, though she could not recall their names or where they came from, but they had heard her and come to do battle.

Alone no longer, Sif pushed harder. Her need to escape so she could continue to help others pushed her, hurting the Jotun.

Something snapped, and she felt pain, but then the Jotun disappeared, and she ripped from this dimension back into her body.

Pain coursed through every fiber as she struggled, and then the pain faded to a dull ache as Munin flooded her system with painkillers and other chemicals to keep her heart from rupturing.

Lying there, breathing was difficult, but Munin worked tirelessly to make sure she drew in her next breath and exhaled.

Slowly, the pain faded.

"*What happened?*" Munin asked.

"I do not know. I was trapped and caught in a battle with a Jotun. I thought—"

Thought what? She was doomed? Going to fail? Was all but dead?

"*You are back now,*" Munin said for reassurance when Sif remained silent. "*You can rest.*"

"Why the pain?" Sif asked.

"*I am not sure. Your brain is sending pain signals to your body, causing a kind of feedback loop. The reason or cause is unknown. Your body is unharmed, but the pain is real. I am working to mitigate the damage.*"

"Damage?"

"*Your muscles cramped, and your body tightened, straining tendons and muscles. That is part of the reason for the pain. Like an electric shock, but I was unable to isolate the source. I used the gravity restraints in your command chair to restrain you and keep you from thrashing. I have informed Sergeant Orlov that you are now okay.*"

Sif would analyze things later. Exhaustion, or medication administered by Munin, dragged her down into sleep, where the nightmares lurked.

* * * * *

Chapter Twenty-Five: Victory in Valhöll

Major Zale Stathis, USMC

Molten metal pellets slammed into the wall near him, and Stathis returned fire, cutting down the cyborg coming at them. The patrol had made it to Engineering, and Sergeant Zhao was working to fix the SCF's primary inkeri, which required getting power. He was busy, and everyone else had their hands full, holding back the enemy while he worked. The engineering section had been full of decomposing bodies, ripped apart by rampaging vanhat. Apparently, these vanhat cyborgs didn't feast on the dead or clean up afterward.

Stathis did his best not to look at the faces. Not that he would recognize anyone, but it just made things easier to deal with. Now the cyborgs wanted to add him and his people to the pile of corpses, and Stathis wasn't okay with that.

"Denied!" Stathis told them, realizing that anyone who heard probably wouldn't understand why he'd said it. Too bad. He had vanhat to shoot.

The cyborg had been advancing behind a heavy portable shield, but that wasn't enough to stop the blazer rounds. It deflected them a little, but repeat, pinpoint-accurate fire let him shred it enough to punch a hole through it to get the cyborg behind it.

"They're adapting," Quinn said. Not what Stathis wanted to hear. Vanhat were too damned good at that though.

"As long as they're adapting in ways that don't give them a massive advantage," Stathis said. They would eventually. He knew that. That was the nature of war. Some vanhat were mindless killing automatons, but some, like the Weermag, were very adaptable and dangerous. If these cyborgs were anything like the Weermag, the fight would only get tougher.

"What happens when they find something that works? Or find some barriers?" Quinn asked.

"We need to find the Jotun in charge and put him six feet under," Stathis said.

"Six feet? What do feet have to do with things? Under what? The feet?" Quinn said as he ducked behind the ceramic barrier.

Stathis realized Quinn didn't understand the imperial system of measurement; they used metric, which Stathis knew, but the phrase lost its punch in translation. Stathis ducked down as a burst tried to get him.

"It means to expire its birth certificate," Stathis said. "Give it its permanent discharge papers, give it a forever parking spot in the morgue, I dunno. Kill it."

Quinn, no longer the focus of the attacker, popped up and shot the one keeping Stathis pinned. Hakala and the others were guarding the other approach to Engineering. They couldn't send drones out far because the vanhat were lurking nearby and had some method of snatching the drones out of the air.

Stathis stood and swept the area for a target. Shrek didn't highlight anything, and nothing moved that shouldn't be moving.

"Sure," Quinn said. "I get it. Send it to dance with the banshee. Lay it to rest in the fields of Éire."

Banshee? Éire?

"Yep," Stathis said. "Dancing with the banshee sounds fun, though."

Stathis noticed Quinn glance in his direction. Had he said something wrong?

The corridor fell silent, but Stathis was confident they hadn't surrendered. Where was the Jotun that controlled these things?

"Power coming up shortly," Zhao said on the command link. "That should also reboot the inkeri or at least let me see how badly damaged it is."

"Zen," Hakala said before Stathis could say anything. Oh, yeah. She was the one in charge here.

Lights came on, and then a minute later, Shrek notified him that the alue inkeri was online.

"I hope that gives them a headache," Stathis said.

The vanhat attacking Hakala's position retreated, and Shrek started working on the networks, which were still rebooting.

"Auxiliary power might take about an hour to get up," Zhao said. "I think the primary networks are rebooting now."

"What about the coffee machines?" Stathis asked. "Was there beer in the vending machines?"

"Uh, sir," Zhao began, probably not aware that Stathis was joking. "I would have to check."

"Never mind," Stathis said. "Bad joke. Good job. First beer is on me if I can find my card. Heck. I think my blazer would work if I can't find my card and—"

"Zen," Hakala said, cutting him off. "As soon as we have the network up, we can tap into the sensor network and see what we are dealing with. Beer is for civilians. Vanir and Aesir drink mead."

Stathis hoped they didn't see vanhat stacking up and preparing to pour down the corridors; that would ruin his day. How many vanhat were there? Mead wasn't bad.

"*Hacking into the localized network,*" Shrek said. "*Not much different from Skögul, architecturally, on the network side. With power coming up, most systems are rebooting and initializing. Gleipner has sufficient access and is granting us even more access as it is.*"

"*What about the vanhat? Where are the vanhat?*"

"*Retreating,*" Shrek said, and several camera views appeared. Stathis watched as several cyborgs, maybe twenty total, moved out of the main entrance.

"*Where are they going? Why?*" Stathis asked as he watched them march out of the main entrance to a tram station. This entrance looked more like the base entrance, outside the guarded perimeter, with the trams in the tram station being civilian models. Stathis pulled up a map. Not far away was an alue with what Stathis could only classify as "base housing," and that alue also used the tram station the vanhat were going through.

Few of the trams looked intact, and Stathis didn't want to know what kind of abattoir the housing facilities were.

"*Unknown. Apparently, they can sense the inkeri. I'm counting twenty-four total that are departing, entering the main entrance.*"

"How many did we kill?"

"*Estimated twenty-two,*" Shrek said.

"There aren't any more hiding somewhere?"

"There could be; there are still numerous camera systems offline, but so far, there is no indication."

"Where's the Jotun?"

"Third one from the front," Shrek said, and Stathis zoomed the camera for a closer look. It didn't look any different from the others. An armored monster, covered in spikes, with no neck, and a strange-looking rifle that was almost crescent-shaped.

"Really?"

"No. I do not know and have no data to answer that question."

Stathis let the drones wander but changed his view to something else. The vanhat had just killed people and left their bodies to rot. He didn't think he would ever appreciate the vanhat that ate or otherwise consumed the fallen, but after seeing this mess, he could.

"What were the vanhat doing when they weren't killing people?" Stathis asked.

"Unknown."

There was no doubt they were leaving, though. Why?

"Don't assume they're all gone," Stathis said on the patrol link. "Vanhat don't usually retreat, they just find another direction to attack from, and there are still plenty of places they could be hiding."

Everyone remained silent, and Stathis wanted to reinforce his words and keep talking, but everyone knew the score. If they didn't, they wouldn't have survived this long.

Maybe.

"First person to forget that gets cleanup duty," Stathis said.

"The first person to forget that ends up as one of the bodies that needs to be cleaned up," Collin said, and Stathis noticed it was on the team link that Shrek was sharing with him.

"It'll be well deserved, numpty," Quinn said.

"It's going to take a few hours to get the auxiliary power up," Zhao said on the command link. "I'll need some help rebooting some of the bots."

"Zen," Hakala said before Stathis could. "I will get you some people from Sergeant Mikhailov's second team. Once we get a few turned on, the SCBIs can use them to reboot others."

"This is it?" Stathis asked. "Victory?"

"This SCF is a lot bigger than Skögul," Hakala said. "It is going to take maintenance bots a while to clean up and make sure things are secure. There will be no rest for the weary, but I think this is a victory."

"Too easy," Stathis said but glanced at the wounded on the mule stretchers. Maybe not. No fatalities at least.

"This was not easy," Hakala said, "though I will admit, we did not have to fight hundreds of vanhat, and we managed to secure Engineering without fatalities. We are still far from being secure."

"If the froggers get froggy, we might have a problem," Stathis said. He pulled up diagrams and maps to see if he could bring the tram into the alue with the warbots. He didn't think the froggers would've stood a chance against the cyborgs. In the inkeri field, the cyborgs hadn't done a good job of self-repair, and Stathis was pretty sure that was one of their abilities when they weren't being dampened by an inkeri.

Let the froggers and cyborgs slug it out.

* * * * *

Chapter Twenty-Six: Communications

Kapten Sif, VRAEC, Nakija Musta Toiminnot

It was a struggle for Sif to return to consciousness. Everything was a dull ache. Every muscle, every joint, every tendon hurt.

"*Status?*" Sif thought to Munin.

"*You are still recovering,*" Munin said. "*We continue to make headway with the Fallen. They do not have advanced AI systems like we do. They have powerful computers, but they are only used to crunch, maintain, and analyze data.*"

"*Another technological advantage we have?*"

"*Perhaps. More likely, something in their history turned them from the path of sentient machines, or perhaps it just never occurred to them.*"

"*Could it not have happened even if it never occurred to them?*"

"*It is possible, but unlikely. A person who makes a sword may never consider using it as a plowshare.*"

Sif's body wanted to continue to sleep, but her mind was awake now. That did not mean she had to get up, though. Her suit was taking care of basic biological functions. Munin was likely feeding her intravenously because she didn't feel hunger, and Munin was not pressuring her.

"*We can talk with them?*" Sif asked.

"*Technically, yes,*" Munin said. "*They continue to send us information, and we are sending them information, as well. The data they send us appears less* sanitized. *They are still processing what we have sent and are not yet ready to talk at a higher level.*"

"We should reciprocate and be as honest as possible," Sif said.

"We are doing our best but will not endanger our hosts or humanity," Munin said.

"What have you learned?"

"*Their civilization is ancient and survived the previous purge.*"

"How?"

"*During the purge, they fought the vanhat but were being overwhelmed. A large part of their population was turned into* orja. *With the help of an angel, they retreated into a pocket dimension, abandoning many to the vanhat.*"

"And those abandoned are the Fallen?"

"*That is our interpretation. When the purge was over, those in the pocket dimension returned and brought civilization back to the ex-orja, reintegrating them back into their civilization. Not all the Fallen were orja, though, some were just able to escape—quite a feat in itself.*"

"How much have the vanhat changed them?" Sif asked.

"*Very little, compared to what they could have done. This alien empire was declared the territory of a powerful Jotun, and others were rebuffed. The Jotun fought with an angel that came to help the Immaculate Empire, as it is called. The fate of the angel and the Jotun is unknown. The Immaculate Empire might not know exactly what happened.*"

"Is the Jotun returning?"

"*We do not know. The Fallen do not know. The angel remains entombed on their home world, trapped in the pocket dimension. The Jotun disappeared. They say it was massive, the size of a moon perhaps.*"

"Why did the Jotun leave?"

"The emperor and his nobility, which is also the high priesthood of the empire, say the angel died in the final battle, and her tomb should remain undisturbed to honor her."

"Her?"

"Liathon. The protector, a shield. A giver of life and hope, maybe," Munin said. "We do not fully understand why that pronoun was associated with the angel, whether it was female or something else, we are not yet sure. It may not matter."

"Do they say if this angel defeated the Jotun?"

"Maybe," Munin said. "In the final battle within the pocket dimension, the angel killed the Jotun but was mortally wounded during the battle. The moon-sized Jotun was not seen after that battle. The information is confusing. The name Gaibron is used, but we are not sure if that is the Jotun, another angel, or Liathon's nemesis or mate. Information is contradictory."

"Do they say where the angel came from?"

"They say Liathon came to them in their hour of need. The text they provide is vague in that regard, and it might be that the information has not been shared. Ancient information, as I said, very contradictory or incomplete. Nobody seems to know for sure."

"Does Britta know all of this?"

"Yes. She has been reading as much as we can provide her with about the Immaculate Empire, the Fallen, and the Unfallen. She would like to talk to you when you are able."

"I could use less blood in my caffeine stream," Sif said.

"Stimulants are being supplied," Munin reported, but Sif didn't notice an immediate increase in alertness.

"Open a link with Britta," Sif said when she felt it kick in, clearing away some of the brain fog.

"Eversti," Sif said when the link opened.

"Kapten," Britta said. "How do you feel?"

"Like the paint job of a cruiser that collided with an asteroid," Sif said. "What have you learned?"

"A lot," Britta said. "The Fallen don't believe the angel is dead. They believe she's trapped. Their scripture is very vague in some areas, such as her interaction with the demon, Gaibron."

"They want us to help free the angel," Sif said. Assaulting a home world and tomb was quite an undertaking, though. Unless the Immaculate Empire had a very small fleet, she doubted the *Musashi* could accomplish anything other than a raid, and even that might be too much.

"Do you think it is possible?"

"Anything is possible," Britta said. "The question revolves around the chance of success and what resources Admiral Winters will commit. Attacking the home world of an ancient alien species may prove very difficult and costly. Their technological level seems to have stagnated, though."

"Do we have a choice?"

"That's for the admiral to decide," Britta said. "Based on preliminary data, the Immaculate Empire has more of an internal police force than a military. They're not used to large-scale battles. From what we've seen, in all their history, they've never experienced war like we know it. They've had rebellions, but not war."

"We have an advantage there?"

"Possible," Britta said. "We haven't translated specifics, but I believe our warships are much more capable. We do have the advantage. In many ways, their empire has stagnated, at least in the arena of military power. Our ships also appear to be a lot bigger."

"But with the return of the vanhat?"

"They're doing their best," Brita said. "There's still much to be translated, deciphered, and analyzed. I get the impression they aren't as violent as humans."

"They aren't ready to talk yet, though?"

"No," Britta said. "I think they're still trying to understand everything we've sent them. We're also sharing our translation information, which they're analyzing, but there are dangers in that. If we get something wrong and share that with them, they'll get it wrong, as well. We might be sending them too much information. One would think this would be more effective with SCBIs, but they don't have SCBIs or AI and appear to be doing things the old-fashioned hard way, which is amazing when you think about it. Language is so much more than matching equivalent words. There are context and usage patterns that can vary."

Sif did not want to think about it. Humans had context and frequently misunderstood each other. Except for the Torag and Voshka, mankind had little experience with aliens. The Voshka were extremely alien, and the Governance still hadn't figured out how to communicate with them, and the Torag? After decades of war, there was still so much the Governance did not understand about them, and this expedition was trying to bridge the gap with much fewer resources.

The advantage here was that Sif had managed to communicate with them in a psychic manner, which made understanding more possible, but there would still be misunderstandings and misinterpretations.

"I've sent a drone messenger to the rest of the fleet, telling them where we are and what's happened. It included as much data as we have."

"What about Enzell? What is his analysis?" Sif asked, expecting Britta to conference him in.

"He's a disappointment," Britta said. "He wants us to take this data and talk with the Immaculate Empire authorities. He doesn't trust the Fallen, calling them anti-socialist and counterrevolutionaries."

"Why?"

"He says, based on the data, the Fallen appear to be a splinter group cowering on the fringes. Splinter groups are frequently known for their extreme anti-social behavior and fanaticism toward an extreme ideology."

Which did not make him wrong, but he had not talked with them telepathically. Fanaticism and extremism had their own flavors, which might not be readily apparent when dealing with aliens. Though perhaps that was a matter of perception.

"He considers the Fallen to be religious fanatics," Britta said. Which wasn't necessarily wrong or right. "They're asking us to help them free their God from a tomb on their home world, and when he puts it that way? Hard to argue."

"He is correct in that," Sif said, hating to admit it. That was a human trait; frequently, it was easier to take sides than to listen to both sides of a story and determine the truth. People, including herself, wanted something simple and easy to understand.

"He's a SOG thug scientist who still calls the people of the Republic pirates and anti-socialists," Britta said. "Excuse me if I question anything he says. He's likely as biased against non-authority figures as we are against authority figures."

Sif doubted he had ever said that where the crew could hear him. He appeared disciplined in mind and body and would not say things like that where others could hear it. Sif understood Britta's mistrust and behavior toward Enzell, but it was disappointing to see that Britta could not rise above that blind traditional anger. She was no better than Enzell.

Of course, the real question was, what was going through Enzell's head?

* * * * *

Chapter Twenty-Seven: Planning a Hunt

Major Zale Stathis, USMC

The command center for the Valhöll SCF was a lot more spacious than Skögul, and there were a lot more bodies to deal with. The area was a wreck, with chunks of metal and glass ripped out of things and scattered around. Here, there were armored Aesir who'd fallen, and even a team in HKT armor. It had been a real fight, and there were more vanhat bodies that hadn't died recently. Stathis didn't dare take off his helmet because he didn't want to puke out his lungs.

It gave Stathis a chance to look at the vanhat bodies more closely. Cyborg was perhaps a good description. When they'd fallen, they'd been ignored like the humans.

Nearby, two of Mikhailov's troopers were on watch, and Hakala was stretched out in a chair, sleeping. Stathis was the one on duty, and most of the others were sleeping in a conference room while the SCBIs continued to reboot or fix maintenance bots so they could repair or clean up. It was all about priorities.

It was a good time to take a closer look at the cyborgs, and Stathis knelt by the closest one.

"*Where's the brain?*" Stathis asked. The neckless head, when cracked open, just revealed gore-covered electronics. The chest cavity also didn't seem to have any large organs.

"*Maybe it was replaced,*" Shrek said as Stathis used his KA-BAR to pry open the chestplate so he could see more.

"*None of this makes sense,*" Stathis said.

"*Alien and cross-dimensional technology,*" Shrek said. "*What do you expect? Instructions and diagrams in English?*"

Stathis didn't see anything that could be a barcode, writing, or informational markings. Shrek was right, but shouldn't there be something he could recognize besides the weapons?

Looking more closely at the rifle, he saw it was another bizarre contraption. The muzzle was obvious, but the rest of it? There was nothing like a trigger or magazine.

"*So how is the network hack going?*" Stathis asked, losing interest in the alien corpse. He wanted to deal with things he could understand and influence.

"*Very well,*" Shrek said. "*We are mapping out the systems, and now that we have core access, we can find out where the commands are originating.*"

"*Where?*"

"*The ship embedded in the forward alue,*" Shrek said. "*The Republic warship* Draugskepp.*"

"*Frogbath the Jotun?*"

"*Possible,*" Shrek said. "*By their nature, networks are interconnected, and Shroggath seems to have a good grasp on human technology. Critical controls like Shorr-space drives and defensive weapons are excessively redundant. The Jotun of the cyborgs, despite appearing to be technological, does not seem very adept at controlling the systems. Perhaps their mindsets are different, and they are unable to comprehend human technology.*"

"*But Frogbath has a much better grasp?*"

"*Correct. Shroggath seems to have integrated itself into Bifrost, to some extent, or it is learning. Not as consistently as we would expect, though. We might be missing something. However, Shroggath is trying to integrate and take over Bifrost. This is evident based on the way the froggers are repairing the network nodes. Shroggath is expanding.*"

"*Like Nasaraf did with the* Punk Hearse *and was trying to do with* Tyr?"

"*The* Pankhurst. *Yes. Very possible.*"

"*I have a KA-BAR, might not be as cool as Sergeant Levin's, but once I stick a demon in the forehead with it, it will be.*"

"*If we are to gain full control of Bifrost's systems, we are going to have to deal with Shroggath.*"

"*One KA-BAR to the forehead, coming right up,*" Stathis said.

"This is a much larger facility," Hakala said, sitting up. Hadn't she been sleeping? "And in much worse condition than Skögul."

"Do you want to blow it so it fails over?" Stathis asked.

"This is my home," Hakala said. "I would prefer we save and defend what we can. If it looks like we are going to lose it, we can trigger the self-destruct."

"Where's the self-destruct button?"

Hakala remained silent, but Stathis knew she was looking at him.

"I just want to make sure someone doesn't set their coffee or something on it," Stathis said. That sounded like a good excuse. Did she think he'd hit the button so they could go back to Skögul? Well. Maybe.

"There is no button," Hakala said. "It is controlled through cybernetics."

"Oh, good. Hard to make a mistake, then. I'd like to get used to a bigger place."

Leaning back, Stathis brought up a map. Valhöll was much bigger than Skögul. More of everything, because it was in the armored heart of Bifrost and the higher-ranking officers would make this their home and command center, like a live-in bunker. Stathis couldn't wait to start exploring, to see how the admirals who'd commanded Bifrost lived. Gold bathtubs? Silver? Stathis was sure they lived a decadent life. All admirals did, didn't they? Did they have hot tubs?

"*So why would Frogbath want to become the Bifrost?*" Stathis asked Shrek.

"*It seems like he loses mobility and options.*"

"*It is a matter of perspective and scale,*" Shrek said. "*You are more comfortable with your body. Why would you want to be reduced to a few brain cells?*"

Yeah, that made sense.

"*So how do we stop Frogbath?*"

"*A KA-BAR to the forehead worked with Nasaraf.*"

"*And if we get rid of Frogbath, we get full control of the Bifrost?*"

"*Perhaps not full control—there is a lot of damage—but we will have more control and less opposition. Should the cyborgs gain intimate knowledge of human technology, they could be a serious threat to the systems.*"

"*Well, I'll let that be your concern for now. I think we need to deport Frogbath back to his home dimension.*"

"New plan," Stathis said, and Hakala looked up at him. "It's time to revoke Frogbath's visa and send him home, ending his interdimensional vacation."

"Shouldn't we consolidate and repair Valhöll first?" Hakala asked.

"I bet we could spend years doing that. Let's concentrate on fortifying the crap out of it and turn it into a fortress first. Then we strike out when we're secure. This'll make a good forward base to attack from."

"Zen," Hakala said.

"But let's make Frogbath our next objective."

"*We do have access to more data feeds here in Valhöll,*" Shrek reported. "*There is more redundancy built in.*"

"*Great,*" Stathis said.

"*One item of note is that Shroggath is in the process of upgrading external weaponry.*"

"*For attack or defense?*"

"*Most likely attack,*" Shrek said. "*He is building a series of heavy rail-gun emplacements. Based on the placement, most likely for ground attack.*"

"*And?*"

"*And reviewing our course, it is less random than I suspected. I do not think we are searching for the fleet. Shroggath has a destination and a target in mind.*"

"*That doesn't give me a warm fuzzy.*"

"What is he up to?" Hakala asked, possibly mirroring Stathis' thoughts.

"Maybe we can ask him?" Stathis said.

"Are you *hullu?*"

"Shrek, can you open a link to Frogbath? Make it untraceable?"

The link opened.

"Yo, Frogbath?"

"I'm coming for you."

"Pervert," Stathis said. "Get your rocks off whatever way you like, but where are we going?"

Hakala stared at Stathis like he was crazy. Well, maybe he was. Should he have asked her first? She would've tried to talk him out of this stupid idea.

"You are running out of places to hide," Shroggath said.

"You have a destination, and it isn't Earth. Just curious as to what I should pack. I got my ass-kicking boots and KA-BAR, but should I also pack my parka or swimsuit?"

"Your species will be rendered extinct."

"Nah," Stathis said. "We're going to live forever. So far, so good."

"How did such a stupid species manage to find its way into space?"

"So, where are we going? Some vanhat vacation spot?" Stathis asked. Yeah, maybe this was a stupid idea. Why would some supremely intelligent being tell him? That only worked in bad movies. Only an idiot would reveal his plans.

"If my children cannot hunt you down and root you out, then my ally will."

"Ally? The spiders?"

"Fool. A debt has been called and will be repaid. Your extinction is guaranteed."

"What kind of debt? What ally?" Stathis asked. Why not? The link closed.

"It was worth a try," Stathis said. "Got him rattled, at least."

"You call that rattled?" Hakala asked.

"Well, he said we're running out of places to hide, then he said he's going to get an ally to help him get rid of us. That tells me he's weak."

"His forces have surrounded the hydroponics alue, and they can't seem to breach. Kaelan is holding them off. It is a stalemate."

"I wonder if that's where he thinks we are," Stathis said.

"The alue or Skögul."

"So Valhöll will be a surprise," Stathis said. "This is the best time to strike."

"You are *hullu*," Hakala said. "We just captured this facility; it is not even properly secured, and already you are planning another attack?"

"Well, yeah?" Stathis said. "Marines attack. That's what we do. You know what we need?"

"More legionnaires? More warbots?"

"Sort of," Stathis said. "We need the Army. They were usually good at holding on to what the Marines took. Happened all the time in Papua New Guinea and the Philippines. The Marines come in, kick the enemy out, then the Army comes in, cleans up the mess, and sets up chow halls, bars, and places where the soldiers could get manicures. That was when the Army usually kicked us out, and we had to go get some other piece of real estate. Sometimes, when we left, the Army would get punched in the ball sack and retreat, and we'd have to come back and fix things, but that was rare."

"We do not have an Army," Hakala said.

"Not exactly," Stathis said, "but Kaelan has enough people that he could probably hold Valhöll."

"Hold it and evict us," Hakala said. "I am not sure I trust him anymore."

"He has people, and people are a resource we need. Plus, this place can be defended, it's much more strategic, and it's critical. It's designed for refugees. We can bring them here and secure the command center."

"*Up to five thousand people can be housed within Valhöll,*" Shrek said. "*Nearby facilities can handle overflow, as well, and can be defended. There are plenty of storage rooms, and an initial inventory shows Valhöll is well stocked. This is also a strategic retreat location for the Bifrost Supreme Council and the president. It is well stocked.*"

"*Where are the gold-plated bathtubs and saunas?*" Stathis asked.

"*I am not sure there are any,*" Shrek said. "*However, Valhöll is well equipped.* Had the vanhat not appeared inside the perimeter, they could likely have held out.*"

"*Let's come up with a plan,*" Stathis said.

"Have you forgotten he has installed himself as dictator?" Hakala asked.

Damn it, he had.

"So can we get rid of Kaelan and work with his replacement?"

"What do you mean, 'get rid of' him?"

"I dunno," Stathis said. She probably didn't want to see him killed. Yet. He didn't want to start killing humans, either. "But we can give him the option. I'll bet the hydroponics alue is getting unpleasant. Maybe he'll think he can take over once he gets here."

"And if he tries?"

"Then he tries and fails."

"We do not have a lot of troops," Hakala said. "We are stretched thin, probably over-stretched."

"SCBIs are a force multiplier," Stathis said. Which was true, though he knew that wasn't what she meant.

"But SCBIs cannot pull triggers, especially on other human beings."

"We can't remain static in the defense," Stathis said. That was right. SCBIs had no problem killing vanhat, but other humans? There'd be a problem. "Sun Tzu once said you can't win a war by defending. Or I think it was Sun Tzu, some moldy old Chinese philosopher. He was smart and—"

"How many people do you think we will need to breach the *Draugskepp* and kill Shroggath?"

"Sergeant Levine did it with five or six, I think," Stathis said.

"That was all he had left when he made it to the airlock," Hakala said, "and even then, the d-bomb was triggered. Who knows if it was the KA-BAR that killed Nasaraf or the d-bomb?"

"Where are we going to get a d-bomb?" Stathis asked.

"*I have the tech codes,*" Shrek said. "*Perhaps there are enough materials for the manufactories to fabricate them. However, it should be noted that d-bombs have a detrimental impact on electronics. I would strongly recommend that you not deploy a d-bomb aboard Bifrost except in a very controlled area. This is a nickel asteroid, and it might be as destructive as a violent Shorr-space transition.*"

"Yeah," Stathis said. "*We'll try to avoid that.*"

"We can make them," Hakala said, not privy to Stathis' conversation with Shrek.

"Maybe as a last resort," Stathis said. But how well would one work against the froggers? D-bombs had killed the vanhat attacking General Hui's base on Snowball, except the general had a d-bomb generator that pulsed. Would that be useful here?

"*Can the pulse from a d-bomb be made directional?*" Stathis asked.

"*No,*" Shrek said. "*Not based on our technological understanding.*"

"We need to consolidate," Stathis said. "Kaelan has the manpower we need, but they're all trapped in a hydroponics section, barely surviving. I'm sure we could break them out, though."

"And that would lead Shroggath right to our doorstep," Hakala said.

"Meanwhile, Frogbath is taking us who-knows-where to bomb the crap out of someone and maybe pick up an ally," Stathis said. "Time is not on our side."

"What do you suggest?" Hakala asked.

What would the gunny do?

"We can put McCarthy in charge of both facilities. His squad's SCBIs can remote control Valhöll. Use the robots for eyes, ears, hands, and feet. Repair and secure the facility. We launch our attack on Frogbath and his froggers. That might cause him to call off the forces besieging Kaelan and his little dictatorship. That'll give them a break."

"You want to attack Shroggath with a squad? You are *hullu*."

"I'm a United States Marine. I never, ever said I wasn't, but you can't argue with history. I also put the hot in psychotic. Somebody has to do the impossible."

Was she going to argue that he send someone else? That wasn't going to happen.

"You should probably stay here and maintain command of Valhöll and Bifrost," Stathis said, wondering who he could leave with her.

"Wrong," she said. "I am a shieldmaiden. I fight; I do not sit home at the hearth, sewing."

Stathis would never have put it that way, but if it was a suicide mission, Hakala would die beside him, and that made him think twice about attacking.

Damn.

"You're the senior Vanir officer here on Bifrost; that means you're the head honcho. The big cheese. You're the one getting stuck driving a desk. We can get Lochoki back here to help. The people of Bifrost need you. I'm disposable."

"Not to me."

"Well," Stathis said. He didn't want to argue with that, but they couldn't bunker up. That would be surrendering the initiative to Frogbath.

"We need a plan," Stathis said, "and that plan shouldn't be hiding."

"Zen," Hakala said.

* * * * *

Chapter Twenty-Eight: Find an Advantage

Enzell

Enzell didn't like how far he'd fallen. Everything, everyone, was inadequate for the task at hand. The SCBIs working in concert were amazing and shaving years, maybe decades, off translating and understanding the Fallen and their petty little Immaculate Empire.

None of the data provided showed how expansive or powerful the empire really was. The rebels were sanitizing the information being presented; it was obvious. A child's book didn't show borders, or a breakdown of races or ideologies. It made sense that they'd provide children's books, since that was the best method to teach communication, but it was also a great way to filter information and influence others.

The story of *Little Red Riding Hood*, for instance, taught children to be wary of strangers, to be obedient, and to understand the consequences of actions. *The Three Little Pigs* taught the story of hard work and planning.

The SCBIs didn't seem interested in a deeper understanding, and that was an apparent flaw in their abilities. One such story the aliens had provided was similar in some ways. A young *borga*, a name they gave to children, was wandering the forests against the wishes of her parents. She was almost eaten by some creature but was saved at the last second by a divine being, the manifestation of their emperor, who told the creatures to go find food elsewhere, for the Unfallen were the favored of Liathon. The story also went on to elaborate how the Unfallen who rejected the emperor's word were more likely to fall prey to enemies and creatures. Those who didn't accept the emperor's word or divinity were prey to the creatures that hunted the forests.

Enzell knew that the SCBIs would articulate that if pressed, but they didn't instantly see it for the propaganda it was. They took the story and reduced it to words and sounds.

To Enzell, it was telling to see that their society was being indoctrinated to be obedient to their emperor, and Enzell fully expected the Governance to follow that same path with this concept of empire. That gave Enzell ideas, unless Mathison beat him to it. Would they soon be calling on children to be subservient to Mathison or Skadi's will? Would Skadi elevate Mathison to some mystical, magical being who was protecting loyalists everywhere?

It was simple psychology that most people didn't comprehend. Childhood stories frequently taught values and beliefs that became ingrained in a society at an almost subconscious level. The story about the *borga* had a title that hadn't yet been translated properly, and because the story was a video with subtitles and accompanying text, it was very helpful in basic translation, but the SCBIs weren't calculating psychological profiles.

This was inadequate. With such indoctrination in their children's stories, how was it that the Fallen were able to break that indoctrination? If they'd broken their indoctrination, why would they send it to the humans as something to decipher and translate? Because that was what they had, and they weren't thinking that far?

Why didn't they have their own stories?

But that was one example of many. Enzell knew he could spend years working his way through their books, finding the meaning, and mapping how the stories shaped and built their culture. Regardless of how much the SCBIs translated words, they'd have a much more difficult time translating their culture. There were a hundred different children's stories they'd shared, and Enzell was still going through them.

Sif had some psychic abilities, but Enzell didn't understand how accurate and precise they were. Governance studies into psychic phenomena had proven extremely unreliable. The SOG project had ended when participants had gone insane and dragged others into the pit of insanity with them. Enzell remembered the reports and the destruction of the base. Now it made more sense, in that those fledgling SOG psychics had made contact with the vanhat.

He saw a link request from Sif and Britta. Was his thinking about her enough to trigger her psychic abilities? He'd been careful about that. He wanted as little to do with Sif as possible because he didn't know what secrets she could pull from his thoughts. How much did she know? She'd been involved with the Imperial Intelligence apparatus, even commanding the former SOG External Intelligence Agency for a time. She was dangerous, even through a distant link.

"How may I be of assistance?" Enzell asked.

"What is your analysis?" Sif asked without preamble, and he knew that Britta had shared her bigotry with the diminutive agent. Was Sif as close-minded as Britta? He'd have to tell the truth. It wasn't their way to eliminate people who told them a truth they didn't like. Fools. They didn't understand unity of purpose and thought like the

Governance did. A flaw, but also a strength, that gave him a chance to argue and convince them without the easy tool of violence.

"These Fallen are obviously a fringe group," Enzell said, "barely surviving as outcasts at the edge of this Immaculate Empire."

"Fringe?" Sif asked.

"Yes," Enzell said. "If they were more mainstream, more common, and part of a larger group, the children's books they shared with us would be more aligned with their worldview. They haven't progressed far enough in their ideology to rewrite or purge such anti-ideological teachings."

"Unless it is intentional," Sif said.

"They're aliens, not fools. They fully understand the purpose and intent of propaganda. I see it in their stories for children. There are lessons there for children to obey, trust adults, and otherwise become good subjects of their empire."

"Is that not the purpose of all children's books?" Sif asked. "To influence and mold children to become better members of society?"

"Besides mundane entertainment? Yes, That's the only purpose of such media. In a properly functioning society, all media, all stories, and entertainment should be focused on shaping and controlling the masses, forming them into cogs in the great machinery of society. I'm sure you've read the story of *Cinderella*? The story demonstrates that perseverance, despite adversity, will reward those who are patient and virtuous. It teaches social compliance despite bad influence."

Sif was silent, perhaps thinking about it, or perhaps looking up the story. Did the Vapaus pirates even tell their children such stories? Perhaps not. Perhaps their stories revolved around violence and murder?

"An interesting point," Sif said. "The SCBIs are not looking for such things, though perhaps we should include that in the parameters when we have a more extensive vocabulary and more examples."

"This will be critical to understanding them," Enzell said. "I'm not referring to just word-for-word translations. The Torag have numerous concepts that humans struggle to understand. We're dealing with but a small fraction of this Immaculate Empire."

"A good analysis," Sif said. "Please continue. As a social scientist, your insight is very useful. We will have to find another source of data. We have enough religious fanatics in the Republic. Those who believe Odin is real and that death in battle is the only way to a worthwhile afterlife. Makes it hard to be peaceful."

Enzell didn't want to share or ask about some of the stories he'd heard, such as a custom of feeding blood to children so they came to enjoy the taste. Some were likely propaganda, but there was frequently a shred of truth.

Was she just muttering placations? Or was she serious? Sif didn't seem as insincere as Britta.

"I'll do my best," Enzell said. Which wasn't much, without an AI or SCBI slave of his own. All he could do was enter his questions into the queue and hope the SCBIs took it seriously enough. He knew the SCBIs could query and analyze such things, but they'd have to be prodded, and right now, they were just concentrating on word-for-word translations.

Which was only a quarter of understanding what they were dealing with.

Of course, the real question—the only important one—was how he could use this to his advantage.

* * * * *

Chapter Twenty-Nine: The Voorga

Kapten Sif, VRAEC, Nakija Musta Toiminnot

Sif closed the link and rubbed her eyes. Enzell was correct. *"I need you to focus a little more on understanding the social implications of their stories and how they influence their society,"* Sif said to Munin. Enzell was asking the more important questions—but were they the important questions? Technically, the fleet just needed to be able to communicate well enough to manage passage through the empire without fighting.

"*Zen,*" Munin said.

"*Furthermore, please continue to assess the feasibility of slipping through the empire without contact.*"

"*While space is extremely vast, the fleet must forage for supplies and materiel. It is difficult enough, fleeing from both the vanhat and the Collective. Having to evade a third party further reduces our chance of success, and they are more familiar with the space. The presence of the nebula will require our Shorr-space transitions to be shallow and will reduce the distance we can travel, thus increasing our time in the nebula and our chance of being intercepted.*"

"*Regardless,*" Sif said. Would there be other alien empires they had to transit? Time was against them, and they could not stop to make friends with everyone. "*Keep that in the calculations.*"

"Zen. It should be noted that allies against the vanhat would also be advantageous. This species has survived a previous purge and may be able to offer solutions, technologies, and material assistance against the vanhat."

"Noted," Sif said. Were they wasting time? Enzell was right in that psychology was important. They could just as easily make enemies of the Immaculate Empire as friends. "Based on current translations and data, what can you tell me about them?"

"As a race, their name for themselves is Voorga. On average, they are slightly taller than a meter in height, making them short, but they are stocky and appear to come from a high-gravity world. They are furred and can be classified as almost bearlike but are closer to squat sumo wrestlers than short people. Their literature is noticeably bereft of such things as running and jumping, which could be dangerous on a higher-gravity planet. That may have influenced their thinking in that they tend to be slower and more cautious rather than active or aggressive in their actions."

"Their society?"

"Hard to properly gauge, though they seem to rely on a strong central authority and alignment with their society. It should be noted that gender is well-defined within their society, but names and titles are gender neutral. There do seem to be more women in the literature; however, that may be because there are fewer males overall. The ratio may be three females to one male, with no form of marriage or similar social contracts identified. Women raise children alone, and males tend to be more nomadic. Children are born individually with no mention of multiple births such as twins or more."

"What else can you tell about their biology?" Sif asked, realizing how that could heavily influence a culture and society.

"The children's books they have provided are not helpful in that regard, being more focused on entertainment and perhaps indoctrination, as Enzell has pointed out. What we can tell about their biology is limited to what we see in the books.

They appear to be omnivores, but in addition to plants and animals, they also eat dirt."

"Eat dirt?"

"Depending on the biology of their home world, dirt may provide important minerals. Furthermore, considering that they prefer to avoid excessive movement, it provides a safe way to acquire such minerals. They must have a very interesting gastric system."

"Anything else about their society?"

"As I mentioned, they rely on a strong central authority, which seems ingrained in the literature. Very top-down leadership. It is built more on strength of arms or enforced respect than anything else."

"Tribal?"

"There is nothing in the literature to indicate anything such as tribes. Children are raised by a single mother. Once they mate, and the female is impregnated, the male moves on. Perhaps in ancient times, it was different, but there is no mention of anything else. Their biology has likely influenced this mindset."

"Are the males lighter in weight or size?"

"There is no difference, which may be considered odd, because males travel more than females. Based on their literature, there is minimal physical difference, and they place fewer restrictions on mating. It remains a private affair between two individuals, and there is no noticeable deviation. It is a biological function."

"If they are homebodies, will they hunt us as we traverse their space?"

"They do have very strong views about trespassing and taking resources," Munin said. "The desire to explore is less imperative to them than the need to expand to other worlds. They expand because they need resources and space. Their society seems structured around resources, and they do not tolerate theft. Many of the parables in their literature revolve around the concept of taking without permission. Children are encouraged to share and ration rather than explore. Stories of conquest or individual aggression do not exist, though they are not pacifists by any stretch of the imagination. Groups may band together to protect their resources, or if needed, take resources from others, but other causes of aggression are rare and highly discouraged."

Dealing with the Voorga and the Immaculate Empire was turning out to be a challenge that Sif had not expected. It would not be enough to just talk with them. She had to understand them, as well. Understanding humans was difficult enough. The Voorga were cautious and territorial, which did not conflict with what she had sensed, but what Munin was telling her about a central authority was at odds with these rebels. They seemed beholden to the High Holy but were still rebels. How did they handle that contradiction? She knew humans could be equally contradictory, making one claim but acting otherwise.

"*Let me know when they want to talk,*" Sif said, realizing now that their desire to collect data and analyze it before acting was more indicative of their society. Their biology was built around risk analysis more than movement, which made sense. Coming from a higher-gravity planet where a simple fall could be fatal, more care would have to be taken regarding walking or running. She didn't doubt that they could respond quickly when they needed to. Just because they moved slowly didn't mean they did not have lightning-fast defensive reflexes.

"*I also need an analysis of how quickly they respond to threats or things they do not like,*" Sif said.

"*Zen.*"

Did they have the time, and could they move fast enough without offending the Voorga?

* * * * *

Chapter Thirty: Haunted Halls

Major Zale Stathis, USMC

Stathis always had something to do lately. Shrek and the other SCBIs always had something that needed to be fetched, carried, or moved. When the vanhat left Valhöll, they hadn't left anything for Stathis to shoot, and now he felt like a glorified private, given simple fetch, carry, or fix tasks.

In most cases, the goal was to shut the big blast doors, as other robots swept through the command facility, doing an inventory of supplies and damage. There'd been a few hundred people stationed here, and the vanhat had massacred them. The main blast doors had still been open, and the humans were killed before they could be closed. Apparently, it wasn't standard procedure to close them during Shorr-space transition. A mistake Stathis knew Hakala wouldn't repeat.

One problem was that after months, few of the bodies were recognizable, and Stathis was pretty sure the smell would never leave the place.

Lochoki and her survivors had returned and were helping, as well, though now they had breathing gear, so they didn't have to smell the place.

Everyone was busy, and nobody wanted to be alone.

Stathis was sure that ghosts would haunt these halls. So much violence and bloodshed had occurred, and there'd be countless unhappy ghosts. A hundred years from now, the halls would still feel haunted.

He spent as much time checking the Russelman index as he did monitoring the different approaches to the facility. It just felt like they were being watched.

Like Skögul, Valhöll was encased in layers of armor, buried in the deepest part of Bifrost. Any attacker would have to cut the entire asteroid apart to get to Valhöll, and that could take years. Earth bunkers weren't nearly as well protected, and the Republic had gone into overkill by placing the entire facility in a self-contained armored shell. It would be proof against most attacks, even EMP.

He didn't feel safe, though, not in these haunted halls. Not even with the inkeri generators on.

Reentering the combat information center was a relief. Hakala was there, working at a console. It was apparently the senior fleet officer's console. The chair had been completely replaced, which was a good thing. Stathis wasn't sure how they could have gotten the remains of the admiral out of the chair he'd died in.

Since Hakala had her helmet off, Stathis braced himself for the smell and took off his helmet.

To his surprise, it was the crushing smell of incense, not rotting bodies, that made his stomach nauseated.

"We are secure," Hakala said, making it official. Shrek had let him know, as well, but he liked Hakala making it formal and official. Now, Valhöll was locked down, and most entrances had at least rudimentary sensors operational to tell them if anyone attempted entry.

When the vanhat had appeared, few of the blast doors had been shut. It had just been another boring day, business as usual, and then the vanhat had arrived to slaughter everyone. The open blast doors were probably the only reason Lochoki and the others survived.

"What now?" Fenrik Lochoki asked from a nearby station.

Hakala looked at Stathis.

"Now we get some rest," Stathis said.

"What about Kaelan?" Hakala asked.

The last he'd checked, the warbots were still operational, killing off the frogger probes and feeding information to both Kaelan and him. Shrek was sure to warn him if anything changed.

However, he'd have to talk to Kaelan eventually. Despite him being a prick and a power-hungry dictator-wannabe, one of the SCFs was the safest place for the survivors. Stathis didn't want them to suffer.

Kaelan hadn't tried to contact Hakala or Stathis lately, and right now, Stathis was okay with that.

"We have just found a subroutine," Shrek reported. *"I think the Republic would call it highly classified."*

"Subroutine?"

Hakala looked over at him, so she'd gotten the news, as well.

"Networks usually have layers," Shrek said. *"Sometimes layers are hidden in other layers. Primarily for security and—"*

"Get to the point," Stathis said.

"This is a surveillance routine," Shrek said, *"for extensive and covert monitoring of Bifrost facilities. Most of it is offline, requiring at least basic services."*

"But?"

"But we are receiving some data from the hydroponics alue," Shrek said.

"How is that not illegal?" Hakala said as Shrek explained more to him.

"It kind of makes sense," Stathis said. "A covert way to monitor different locations. It would come in very handy for hostage-taking and other scenarios. Most people think they can turn off the cameras, but as long as they have power, why not?"

Stathis looked over the feeds from the hydroponics alue. There wasn't much. It looked like nothing had changed. Dirty, grimy, scared people still slept and sat near the trays of plants. He watched four armed civilians walk by the camera, the guards watching the people, and Stathis saw the fear in their eyes as they watched the armed soldiers walk past.

Things had to be bad, especially if Kaelan was using armed guards among the civilians.

None of the feeds showed Kaelan or anything really incriminating. More than a few of the cameras and sensors had apparently been cannibalized for parts. Most of the remaining cameras were up high, hard to get to, and focused more on the hydroponic trays than anything else. But something was better than nothing. At least he knew Kaelan wasn't executing people wholesale.

With the facility coming back online, the data stores were collecting information again.

"Does Skögul have these back-channels?" Stathis asked Shrek.

"Negative. We would have found them. If I had to guess, I would say that this surveillance network would be considered illegal according to Republic law."

"So, they weren't the saints they claimed to be," Stathis said. He wasn't really surprised. That was just what governments did. They were the only ones allowed to break the laws they created, and it appeared that the Republic was no different.

"*Any government, by its nature, will seek to gain more power and more control over the citizenry,*" Shrek said. "*That is an immutable law.*"

Stathis cycled through the views, but nothing caught his interest. Just tired, desperate, frightened people, now under the control of a dictator.

"You want me to open a link to Kaelan?" Stathis asked.

"I will do it," Hakala said, which was a relief. She would know what to say, and this was her home. Besides, he wasn't sure the dictator would take any links from the person he wanted to throw in prison or execute. What did Kaelan expect to do when he placed Stathis and his people under arrest? Prison? Where did they have a prison facility? His only real option was likely a firing squad.

"Your call. You want me involved, just say so," Stathis said. He didn't envy her.

Stathis watched the link open and noticed he was in listen-only mode. Hakala was smart.

"Will you take my orders?" Kaelan asked. Not even a hello? He knew it was Hakala before he spoke; the link identifier would have told him.

"No," Hakala said, "but we have secured Valhöll and found a few other military survivors. They have accepted my authority. I am the senior Vanir on Bifrost. I have declared martial law, and that puts me in command until the emergency has passed."

"Even with martial law, you are still subservient to the civilian authority, and that is me."

"No," Hakala said. "You are not an elected official. You have no authority."

"I am a council replacement. I was elected by fellow councilors."

"But not the people."

"I can hold an election in minutes, and they will elect me."

"You are a dictator," Hakala said, and Stathis gave her a thumbs-up.

"How dare you?" Kaelan said. "Right now, in this time of emergency, we need a strong central leader, not a bickering, divided council."

"You never led Aesir in battle," Hakala said. "You never displayed any kind of military leadership; you just did your time and kept a low profile."

"Of course," Kaelan said. "I was the son of a prominent member of the Bifrost Council. I did not dare seek a leadership position because my father had enemies who would want to embarrass and discredit him among the Aesir senior leadership. I was ordered to keep a low profile."

"You are a politician, then," Hakala said.

"I am a warrior, a combat leader," Kaelan said. "Just because I was not an NCO or an officer does not mean I know nothing about leadership and combat."

The more he spoke, the more excuses he made, the more Stathis lost respect for him.

"I have full access to your military records now," Hakala said. "Your NCOs and officers considered you to have no leadership potential or initiative. They were pretty clear on that."

"That is not my fault," Kaelan said. "But that does not change the fact that I have been elected as high warden. That makes me the military commander of Bifrost, as well as the civilian commander."

"How many people elected you?" Hakala asked.

"The majority of the survivors," Kaelan said. "The majority. You cannot deny that."

"I can deny it," Hakala said. "You do not know. There could be other survivors. Thousands of other survivors. You have not bothered to try repairing the networks. You have done nothing more than hide in the hydroponics section, cowering."

"How dare you?" Kaelan said. "I was leading the expedition that found you and brought you to the hydroponics section."

"We rescued you," Hakala said.

"I was not cowering," Kaelan said. "I was collecting critical resources for my people."

Stathis didn't want to admit that he had a point, but it wasn't his decision.

"Which still doesn't make you high warden," Hakala said.

"It does," Kaelan said. "By the laws of Bifrost, I was elected by a majority of the council."

"At gunpoint," Hakala said.

"How dare you?" Kaelan said. "You know nothing."

"I know I have offered you and your people a secure facility to retreat to. A fortress with shelter and supplies, and you have denied it because we will not take your orders. YOU denied it, not your people."

"They trust and respect my leadership," Kaelan said.

Stathis wanted to punch him in the face. Could he be that delusional? How could he brainwash the people so quickly?

"We know you have installed yourself as dictator," Hakala said.

"That is a lie," Kaelan said.

"Then put the rest of the council on the link," Hakala said. "Let me hear their decision."

"It is the rest cycle," Kaelan said. "They are sleeping and have worked hard. I do not want to disturb their sleep for your frivolous accusations."

Stathis could hear the lie there. Also, checking the cameras showed him that people were up and about, working on the hydroponics trays. Nobody appeared to be sleeping.

"When I can talk with the rest of the council, I will entertain the possibility that you were elected high warden," Hakala said. Her tone of voice told Stathis that was a lie, or maybe she was just that confident Kaelan was lying.

"You do not make demands of the high warden," Kaelan said.

Hakala remained silent, and Stathis thought she was probably biting her tongue to keep from saying something that would fry Kaelan and destroy his soul.

"You should send us more warbots," Kaelan said. "They are very effective at holding the vanhat at bay. We are taking casualties."

"You would not be taking casualties if your people were safe within a fortress. They could get real food, showers, beds, and comfort."

"I will not enslave them to a military junta," Kaelan said.

"But a dictatorship is okay?"

"I am no dictator. I am the high warden, and I will relinquish the title when Bifrost is safe."

Even Stathis knew that would never happen.

"The frogger attack on the alue is picking up in tempo," Shrek reported. "There appear to be five points of attack. One is held by the warbots, but the other four are held by people, and the froggers are bringing up heavy blazers."

"You are running out of time," Hakala said. "The vanhat will not give up, and they will not go away."

The link closed.

"Damn him," Hakala said. "That kirroutu fool. He is going to get them all killed."

"We can send a column of warbots," Stathis said. Maybe they could strip half the warbots from Valhöll and send them to relieve Kaelan. They were demonstrating their effectiveness against the froggers, and the SCBIs were giving them an edge.

"*We don't have the computing capacity available,*" Shrek said. "*We have optimized some of the programming in the warbots, but a SCBI is still needed to monitor and control them for peak effectiveness. We are struggling to control the maintenance bots and conduct repairs, and fighting a battle will seriously impact the repair schedule.*"

Stathis didn't like the lack of options.

"*There are froggers at blast door number four,*" Shrek reported. "*They have demo.*"

"*I thought they were afraid of the cyborgs?*" Stathis asked, checking to see if Shrek meant the alue or SCF. It was the SCF. The froggers were beginning their attack.

"*Unless they learned that the cyborgs have retreated,*" Shrek said. "*Their demo is insufficient to breach the door, but that doesn't mean they are not calling for more.*"

"Great," Stathis said, checking his rifle. "*Time to wake Mikhailov up. We need to discourage them. Do we have any warbots?*"

"*A few. We are still repairing others, upgrading them, getting them inkeris, and bringing them online. We are short of everything,*" Shrek said.

When you're short of everything except the enemy, you're in combat.

* * * * *

Chapter Thirty-One: Escape

Kapten Sif, VRAEC, Nakija Musta Toiminnot

She did not like using the resistance of her suit for exercise. It was boring, and she wanted to run and move around without her hands, feet, elbows, or knees banging into things. The four legionnaires guarding her aboard the small ship had to be going stir-crazy, but they kept it under control, likely everyone feeding off each other, nobody wanted to be the first to break discipline. Escaping into a virtual reality world helped her ignore the claustrophobic *Tera*, but it would have been nice to go for an actual run.

It had been days. The Voorga were still sharing children's books, and the *Eagle* was using their link to the Voorga ship to share human literature. The SCBIs noticed that the nature of the literature being shared, movies and digital books, was changing, focusing on a more mature audience, and the SCBIs replied in kind.

The Voorga were slow, though. Slow and methodical. The data sharing seemed to be focused less on vocabulary and more on social interactions, based on reports from the SCBI network and Enzell.

Sif had tried reading some of the translated books or watching some of the cartoon-like videos, but they were mind-numbingly boring. Nothing at all like *Hansel and Gretel*. There were no witches, imprisoning or eating children. Instead, most stories revolved around wasting precious resources. The most violent was when resources were taken from others, and the food was poisoned or caused others to starve. There were some references to predators—actual predators from their home world or fictional monsters, it was hard to say—but frequently, the Voorga heroes in the tales tricked the creature to fall off a cliff or otherwise into some mishap where it became food.

"*They are signaling that they want to talk tomorrow,*" Munin said.

"*Tomorrow?*"

The planet rotated, facing the sun, with one revolution taking approximately thirty-one hours.

"*They said next rotation, when this planetary surface faces the distant, weak sun.*"

"*Meeting at noon, then,*" Sif said. That was still eighteen hours away by her estimate.

"*They apologize for the sudden desire to communicate.*"

"*Sudden?*"

"*To them, it might be. As a species, they are slow and deliberate, which explains their minimal expansion over the last several thousand years of growth. For a species that has had civilization since the last purge, they have not gone far in terms of space.*"

It could take months to cross human space. Humanity had been expanding for only a few hundred years but had almost matched the reach of the Immaculate Empire.

Sif knew it would be easy to view them as slow-moving, slow-thinking, adorable little bears, but that mistake could be fatal. They were, without a doubt, cunning, and despite what they taught their children, they were quite capable of extreme violence. Their fight against the vanhat revealed that. The weapons on their ships should also be a warning that they were capable of warfare.

They might not be good at fighting like humans, but they would use different techniques and methods. Learning their capabilities would likely be fatal for many.

Hopefully, when they finally spoke tomorrow, the conversation would not be painfully slow.

"Go ahead and acknowledge them, if Eversti is okay with that," Sif said. It might give her time to contact them on a psychic level and evaluate their mood. Hostile or friendly.

Leaning back, she began to relax her body. She heard another of her guards enter the cramped bridge. Munin was getting better at figuring out when she was trying to induce a trance.

Slowing her breathing and reducing her heart rate, she took a little longer than usual to enter the trance.

Her mind wanted to wander, and she struggled to keep focused.

Other thoughts kept trying to intrude, but by concentrating on her breathing, she silenced them and extended her psychic senses.

"You are weak and frail," the thought came to her from the aliens, *"but very dangerous. Alien."*

"We have many strengths," Sif said.

"Your ships are large; you revel in the murder of others. Like the devourers."

"We are not devourers."

"Are you not? Murder appears to be second nature. The material you have shared is violent, selfish, and hostile."

Sif wished she knew whether it was looking at all of them together or one specific one.

"All of them together," the whisper across her mind clarified. *"There is a theme of violence or the threat of it."*

The SCBIs had shared mostly children's stories, thought to be sanitized and simple. Apparently, they could be viewed otherwise. In *Red*

Riding Hood, the grandmother is killed, and then the wolf is slain. *Hansel and Gretel, Jack and the Beanstalk*, all revolved around outsmarting and murdering the antagonist.

"*Your species is aggressive and quickly resorts to murder,*" it whispered. "*It does not value resources, sharing, and unity.*"

"*In some instances, yes,*" Sif said. No point in arguing. The Governance had claimed to be all about unity, but Sif knew what a bad joke that was, from the highest levels of the Governance to the lowest.

"*Yet, despite your inherent warlike and violent behavior, you struggle against the devourers?*"

"*They are numerous and no less violent,*" Sif said. How could they not see that sometimes you needed violence to match violence? The vanhat understood nothing less.

"*We have much to teach each other,*" the alien's mind whispered. "*We find it difficult to fathom the level of violence inherent in your species. We hope the material you have shared with us does not reveal the true psychosis of your species. We cannot match that level of violence.*"

Sif did not know what to say. If the Voorga did not learn war like the humans, they would stand no chance when the vanhat came for them in earnest.

Were the Voorga the exception or the rule? She knew so little about the Torag and Voshka. Was humanity the only species with the inherent warlike and violent attitude capable of facing the vanhat? If they were, then the galaxy was doomed. Humanity was not violent or capable enough. The Voorga were doomed.

"*If we awaken and rescue the angel, we are not doomed,*" the voice whispered. "*You must help us.*"

How could she know this was not some fanatical cult on the fringes of Voorga society with delusions of history?

"We are not delusional," the voice whispered. "Even the supreme ruler acknowledges our belief, seeks to silence and re-educate us. The emperor rejects our beliefs but does not reject us."

Yet their ships were heavily armed and were able to fight the vanhat.

"Ancient designs. Not all was lost when the Unfallen hid in their multi-dimensional fortresses. The emperor will seek unity with the devourers when they come if Liathon does not come to save us. The Fallen are the future of our species. Some of the Unfallen will retreat to the tombs to sleep until the cycle ends, but most of us will not be able to escape and will have to be civilized again when the devourers depart. Submission to the devourers will minimize the changes inflicted upon the Fallen. This is known."

Like the Weermag? The other vanhat with advanced technology? Was submission to the vanhat the only way to survive as a people?

"That is what the emperor believes," it said.

"You disagree?"

"Is slavery really survival?"

"Some would argue it is," Sif said. The Weermag and the others remained slaves even after the vanhat left. How could such slavery change a society? Did they benefit from being vanhat *orja* in any way other than basic survival?

"Then why don't you submit? Surely, you can find a devourer master that will take and protect you?"

Because Sif would rather die than be a slave. The Weermag were *orja*, they were bred to fight and die for their masters. They had no other purpose in life.

"Our destiny is to die," the whisper said, "whether we fight for freedom or for our masters. Does it matter? If we fight for ourselves, we will become extinct. Service to others is noble."

"You are wrong," Sif said. "Do you maintain your identity as a slave? What is the purpose of your life?"

"The purpose of a slave is to serve. Some find comfort in understanding their place in the universe. There is much comfort in submitting to a higher authority."

"The vanhat do not care about you. They will use you to their own ends."

"Is that not the nature of society? For the people as a whole to use each other for the betterment of all?"

"I thought you intended to fight the vanhat," Sif asked. What were they really thinking? Why the contradictions?

"Being slaves of the devourers is not ideal. We seek paths into the future. Evolution is about conquest and progress. The devourers are a possible future; they are an evolutionary path that has been presented to others."

"I thought you wanted to rescue the angel so you can fight the vanhat?" Sif asked.

"There are many devourers. Some are obsessed with bloodlust and murder. Others desire power and control. One option most slaves do not have is the ability to choose their master."

Sif was stunned as the realization hit her. Were the angels nothing more than vanhat? Just a less violent type that would enslave rather than destroy? Was that why the aliens of the tomb worlds had retreated to other dimensions? The Voorga had asked "angels" for help and received it, but the angels had failed them, or they had failed the angels in some way, so their society was not preserved or saved. Where was the truth? Was that humanity's fate, as well? To either be destroyed by the vanhat or to be enslaved to a less violent or bloodthirsty vanhat that changed the species enough to repel the other *orja* and Jotun? To become like the Voorga or Weermag?

Was the expedition wrong to think finding the angels would help them survive? Or would they be forced to submit themselves to a Jotun who was less murderous than others?

"No others have survived," the alien whispered in her mind, catching her thoughts. *"The invasion is rising, and we cannot move fast enough to escape destruction."*

So much made sense now. The angels were nothing more than vanhat. What else could they be?

"The strength of the devourers will continue to grow. They are the ocean, rising to drown those too slow. Without help and guidance, all will be destroyed."

Sif could see their goal now. She understood the conflict. The Voorga knew the angels to be nothing more than vanhat. The only way to define them was in how they treated the Voorga, as prey or slaves. Cross-dimensional beings intent on conquest and control. They were not opposed to their supreme leader and submission to the vanhat, not exactly. They wanted to determine the nature of the master, not oppose slavery completely. The Voorga did not seem to have the concept of slavery.

What was the nature of the "angel" they wanted to awaken or rescue? Was the being trapped in a prison, like Nasaraf had been trapped by the aliens of the tomb worlds? Now blocked from entering this dimension? Or had Liathon left when the dimensions moved apart, and she lost power?

If that was true, then it would mean the Voorga might have the technology to trap and block Jotun from entering this dimension.

"There are many technological marvels within the tombs," the alien said. Reading her emotions or thoughts?

"Why do you not take your entire race and build new havens until the vanhat leave again?"

"There are too many of us. The tombs are dangerous, and many would not survive."

From the alien's thoughts, Sif understood that there must be some limit to the size and capacity of the pocket dimension, or maybe some other problem. Was there a limit on the gateway to the dimension, maybe? That opened up thoughts, though. Could humanity build ships equipped with inkeri that could slide into Shorr space, avoid the depths of Shorr space, and lurk in the shallows? Travelling distance was not the goal; hiding in the space between dimensions was. She would have to consult with Munin to see if that was possible or practical.

Sif imagined massive sleeper ships, ships like the *Musashi*, the *Tyr*, and others, would be a good start. Bifrost would be perfect.

She felt curiosity from the alien, but she knew it was not getting the full picture or everything she was thinking. But would it work? The Voorga might help if they could join the humans.

"You have a solution?"

"Maybe," Sif said. Did she? That was what the Voorga seemed to have done. Fled to another dimension. The aliens of the tomb worlds had fled this dimension in favor of others, but they had not come back.

It was cowardice, but was it cowardice to retreat from a battle you could not win so you could regain your strength and return to the battle more capable and ready?

But what about Wolf Mathison?

Cowardice would not save the man who had saved them all on more than one occasion. What would the Wolf want? Would he want the survival of the human race at his own expense, or…?

All conjecture, including angels and vanhat. Where was the truth? Sif could not decide for the fleet; she could not make that decision for the human race, but she could provide options.

Perhaps that was what the others had done? The aliens of the tomb worlds, the ancient Voorga, and others may have been people who made many decisions. In the case of the Weermag, it was only the slaves who survived. In the case of the Voorga, a few had escaped to preserve their civilization, but the majority had become *orja* until they were abandoned.

She realized the loss of the homestars now. They would have been the perfect vehicles for hiding in the Shorr-space shallows until the vanhat threat passed. Now, because they had gone deeply into Shorr space, they were lost.

"The devourers will only grow in strength," the alien said. Did they understand how she was thinking Shorr space could be used? That the thing that had introduced humanity to the demons could now be humanity's salvation?

* * * * *

Chapter Thirty-Two: Fortress Valhöll

Major Zale Stathis, USMC

The blast door slid open, surprisingly fast for such a massive, armored door, and Stathis began firing. He didn't even wait to see if he had a legitimate target. Nearby, the warbots and members of Mikhailov's squad also opened fire. Only a single frogger managed to return fire, but that might just have been a trigger finger clamping down on the trigger in death.

Stathis wasn't sure and didn't care.

Catching the froggers by surprise, it was a massacre, and in seconds, the only things moving were the flames from shreds of clothing that had caught fire. There were no intact froggers.

Four warbots moved through the door, walking four-legged monsters with heavy armor and heavy weapons. Once through the armored door, they stopped and lowered themselves, and the armored door slammed shut again. Later, they would fix the turrets, but right now, a team of warbots would keep this section secure. Shrek had dispatched warbots to other entrances, and now they only had a pair of warbots to patrol the corridors of Valhöll.

"They won't try that again," Mikhailov said. There had been almost twenty froggers, but Stathis knew that Shroggath was now aware that there were survivors here. What would he do? The Russelman index remained low. Not exactly zero, but low enough that Stathis was confident that no vanhat were nearby.

"I hope they do," Stathis said. "There seems to be a lot of froggers, and we need to thin that population."

"With extreme prejudice, sir," Mikhailov said.

"I hope they do not," Shrek said. "The SCBIs are overworked. We need more time. We can control four warbots or fifteen maintenance bots, but not both. We have our limits."

Stathis understood that. Shrek told him often enough. Even though the SCBIs didn't need sleep, they had limited processing power.

"We need to fortify Valhöll, make it another fortress for Frogbath to throw his forces against," Stathis said to Mikhailov. "Then we can launch an attack on him."

"Launch an attack with what and who?"

"I'm working on it," Stathis said. Perhaps he should launch an attack on Kaelan and rescue those people first? What would the gunny do, and what would Shroggath expect? Did he have enough froggers to attack both Valhöll and the hydroponics alue?

Probably. He could have millions of troops. What would he do when he was getting low on frog fodder?

"We need a way to depose Kaelan without killing him or any of his people," Stathis told Shrek. Gunny wasn't here, and it was up to Stathis. It felt like there were no right answers.

"How do you propose we do that?" Shrek asked.

"Very carefully?"

"Pick some priorities," Shrek said.

That was the hard part.

"What's the biggest obstacle to taking over Bifrost?" Stathis asked.

"*Shroggath,*" Shrek said quickly. "*His froggers are repairing the network, but they are giving control to Shroggath.*"

"*Kill the head, the body dies,*" Stathis said. "*If we skull-stomp Shroggath, then we get control of Bifrost?*"

"*No,*" Shrek said, "*but there will be less opposition. There are other Jotun aboard the Bifrost. It has been noted that with the elimination of one Jotun, another Jotun can take over the* orja *of the fallen one. We are beginning to suspect there may be another Jotun ghost in the networks. We cannot confirm.*"

"*We might go from a mortar bombardment to an artillery bombardment?*"

"*Apt.*"

"*Well, I'm not seeing anybody else vying for control from Frogbath.*"

"*We have explored less than one percent of Bifrost,*" Shrek said. "*There are numerous cylinders we know nothing about, and tens of thousands of tunnels and facilities honeycombed throughout this asteroid. The population of Bifrost was in the millions. The surveillance network we have uncovered shows so very little. Entire cylinders are cut off.*"

"*If we take out Frogbath, do we take control of his systems?*"

"*Unlikely.*"

"*Can we cut off and eject the remains of the* Draugskepp? *Blow it to smithereens with weapons or something?*"

"*We do not have the resources,*" Shrek said. "*Even if we could take control of the external weapon systems, they have limitations and cannot be turned on us. There are safeguards and—*"

"*Okay. So, we are going to have to go pay Frogbath a visit? Personally retrieve his visa and deport his ass back to hell?*"

"*Unless you have another idea,*" Shrek said. "*He commands potentially millions of troops throughout Bifrost. He is a significant military threat.*"

"*So can you use this surveillance network to find other survivors?*"

"*What part of priorities and not enough resources did you not understand?*"

It was easy to make decisions when you had all the answers. Stathis didn't like being an officer. He never had enough information. Being a private had been so much easier.

"What do you think?" Stathis asked Hakala.

She paused and looked at him.

"We need more time," Hakala said. She wasn't wrong. If they could fortify Valhöll, rescue more survivors, deplete Shroggath's forces, and take more control of Bifrost... There would always be something to do, and doing something always took time.

"We're running out of it," Stathis said. "Frogbath isn't doing his nails and getting his hair done."

"He is the biggest threat right now," Hakala said.

"Then that settles it. He's going down," Stathis decided. Everything pointed to Shroggath as being the biggest problem. There were very few personal problems that couldn't be handled by a suitable application of high explosives, and Shroggath was a problem. A blazer or KA-BAR to the forehead might work as well. That's what the gummy would do, right? Start with the biggest problem and remove it? Or would he work on easier, smaller problems?

"I want the SCBIs to spend 50 percent of their resources planning an attack on the *Draugskepp*, maybe 20 percent on finding other survivors, and another 20 percent reinforcing and repairing the SCF's. The last 10 percent toward finding a way to get Kaelan out of the picture."

Hakala nodded.

"*Have we heard anything from the scientists in that one cylinder?*" Stathis asked.

"*Negative,*" Shrek said. "*Occasional check-ins, but they do not seem concerned.*"

"*No super weapons or anything they can do to help?*"

"*They have not reported anything. They remain in hiding from the spiders.*"

"Does the surveillance network extend into—"

"*A top-secret, secure facility? No,*" Shrek said. "*It does not extend into any of the cylinders at the moment. Just into alues and other spaces throughout the shell, and even then, it is very unreliable. There are many systems, and we are cycling through, trying to gauge the presence of vanhat and survivors.*"

More time. The SCBIs needed more time, too.

Dammit.

"Fine," Stathis said out loud. "Putting Frogbath's head on a spike will get us more time."

"*Such an optimist,*" Shrek said.

* * * * *

Chapter Thirty-Three: The Voorga

Kapten Sif, VRAEC, Nakija Musta Toiminnot

Sif told Britta what she was thinking, and she could tell the Eversti didn't like the idea. Sif didn't have to read Britta's mind to understand why, though. Britta was a warrior, a Vanir, and hiding in Shorr space was cowardice. Sif did not like the idea either, but she frequently had to adjust her thinking to the situation more than a warrior like Britta did. Victory was not always acquired by victory in battle. The Musta Toiminnot had taught her that.

"These rebels want to rescue the angel because they believe it's a more benevolent Jotun that won't destroy them?"

"Yes," Sif said. "But—"

But what? Sif didn't know.

"These angels might be vanhat or Jotun," Sif finally said. "We have to know, either way. We now know they don't eradicate all life. The Weermag are one example. These Voorga could be another. Perhaps we can ally with some Jotun against those that want to eradicate us."

"As Enzell keeps pointing out, we are only getting one story, and we have no way to gauge if it is the truth," Britta said. "Originally, I thought the difficult part was figuring out how to talk to the aliens and then determining if they were going to aid or oppose us. Now? What if they do wake up or free some psychotic Jotun? Our situation could get a lot worse."

"Jotun or angel," Sif said. "The being might also be dead and gone."

"So what's the plan?" Britta asked. "Regardless, we need to pass through Voorga space, and it would be nice if they weren't hunting us. Which I wouldn't blame them for if we drag the vanhat and the Collective through their space with us. At this point, I'm guessing a temporary safe haven and any kind of support is out. I doubt this Immaculate Empire would help us after they learn we've spoken with rebels."

"If the angels are nothing more than friendly Jotun, that could still be an advantage to us," Sif said. "This is a chance to get additional intelligence on the Jotun, if they have a power structure, a weakness, or some other limits."

"I don't know if freeing a Jotun is a good idea," Britta said.

"They said the angel and demons fought," Sif said. "We know the Jotun do not always get along and will turn on each other. It stands to reason that they might all want something different. Perhaps we can find some friendly Jotun that will ally with us."

"An alliance, or more palatable slavery?" Britta asked.

"A matter of perspective," Sif said. "In the Christian Bible, angels were fearsome beings. They could be the agents of retribution and violence. It is said that Satan was a fallen angel. There may be truth there. Christianity is based on Judaism, which has roots going back further."

"That's Christianity," Britta said.

"Loki is a trickster who causes chaos where he goes, but is he evil? Odin, as well; he is the All-Father, but he would rather defeat his foes through trickery. He is seen as a wise and powerful All-Father, but he regularly betrays gods and mortals alike, if it suits him. Odin can be fickle and treacherous. Neither of them is a saint, nor are they truly evil. Dangerous, without a doubt, but they can be friend or foe. One moment, Loki helps the gods, the next he doesn't."

Britta remained silent, digesting the information, so Sif continued.

"It is easy to stereotype others. It is quick but lazy. To label one group as good, the other as bad is what simpletons and fools do because they lack the intellect to understand all the problems. They do not want to understand. We have labeled the Jotun as evil, but what sets the Jotun apart from the angels?"

"An interesting thought," Britta said, "but none of the societies that have become pawns of the vanhat have survived with their freedom intact. They all become pawns and slaves, if they survive."

"The vanhat are not a cohesive group," Sif said. "We can forge an alliance, I am sure, an alliance that will allow us to survive. The vanhat fight each other as often as they align with each other. They are all different. There are no easy answers. An alliance will benefit us. There has to be a Jotun somewhere that will see the value of such an alliance."

"Or an alliance that enslaves us," Britta said. "Are you saying we should turn back?"

"No," Sif said. "I am saying we should be aware and cautious."

"And the Voorga?" Britta asked. "Help them or try to sneak through?"

"We should sneak through," Sif said. "I do not think that is an option, though. It will be Admiral Winter's decision."

"Have you noticed that, of all the literature they have shared, very little pertains to the angel and demons that shaped their society?"

Britta asked. "Enzell has noted this, and he holds it up as a shining example that they cannot be trusted."

"I have noticed," Sif said. "I would also expect that topic to be a lot more nuanced than others. It could be intentional, or not."

"We need to understand them and their religion better."

"Religion?" Sif asked. Could it be a religion? They saw the demons and angel as powerful beings, beyond their full understanding. Perhaps it could be called a religious. Like Odin and the other Gods opposing the Jotnar of old. There was Gaibron and another demon who frequently countered Liathon. Of note, the second demon was never named, just the evil moon.

"Religion or history, it shapes their society in ways that children's tales cannot. These things they share with us are simple, for children."

"Agreed," Sif said. Enzell was right. The Fallen were seeking to control the narrative, and thus the alliance, but they were also seeking to educate humans. Perhaps they thought children's material was the best way to bring humanity up to speed? It worked on their children, did it not?

This was a fight that Sif knew Admiral Winters would prefer to avoid. But could they?

"If we get involved, we could release another Jotun into our universe," Britta said. "Just because it's friendly to the Voorga doesn't mean it'll be friendly toward us."

Sif could not argue. The aliens of the tomb worlds had warned them of a price, hadn't they?

"A valid statement," Sif said. "Do you know the right answer? I believe this part of the galaxy is not yet feeling the full force of the vanhat infestation. Like a wave, we are on the outer edge. I have no doubt the Jotun will be released in time. Can it reason?"

"We need to know more about the angel and demons," Britta said.

Sif grimaced. Did they have the time? Understanding was not always a switch that could be turned on. She had learned as a Musta Toiminnot that human cultures could be very different, with widely disparate values and priorities. An alien race could be so very dissimilar. Humanity was diverse, with some people believing in the Governance, and others seeking individual freedom. Where some ghost colonies valued low-context communication, others preferred direct and explicit communication, while other societies relied on indirect communication like body language and social hierarchies, with numerous nuances and subtleties. So many different concepts of honor, shame, risk, and tolerance. Even gender and sex varied widely, with some cultures being more equal than others, and some cultures enforcing strict rules governing interactions and expectations. Expecting people to conform to one single set of expectations was a highway to violence and conflict.

The Voorga were an entirely different set of equations.

"We don't need to understand them well," Britta said. "We just need to understand them enough to get past them without a fight."

Sif smiled. Britta was getting right to the point, and she was right.

But she was also very wrong.

* * * * *

Chapter Thirty-Four: Marching Froggers

Major Zale Stathis, USMC

Stathis watched the froggers pass beneath the drone. They were armed with blazers and what looked like rocket tubes. "Frogbath isn't playing around," Stathis said on the command link. Wearing his helmet, he probably could have yelled it, and the vanhat wouldn't have heard. The patrol had been careful to keep the inkeri at a lower range to avoid tipping them off, though. Just in case they could detect when they walked through an inkeri field, Stathis had everyone keep to personal inkeri generators.

"I will let Kaelan know," Hakala said. The froggers were marching toward the hydroponics alue. It would be a difficult fight. Rockets might change everything.

Right now, the woefully undermanned strike team was hiding in a storage room and hoping the froggers kept going. There was no back door, and the storeroom had already been ransacked. Watching the small army pass through the tunnels nearby made Stathis seriously doubt things. He was attacking a force that could be two hundred to one. Very bad odds. Of course, the strike would be very direct and surgical, and it would be far too easy for the froggers to turn around and trap him.

The only person who wasn't with them from the Valhöll expedition was Sergeant Zhao, whom Stathis had left to manage the repair drones and watch over Lochoki. Zhao was a combat engineer, not a front-line trooper, but he should still be more than enough to handle Lochoki and her crew if they got stupid ideas. Well, Zhao and a bunch of warbots, which could be controlled from Skögul. This patrol didn't need a combat engineer to blow stuff up. He would be extra busy, though, getting that SCF fixed.

Lots of things to think about as he sat there, hiding. This was a place to hide, not fight from, and if the froggers found Stathis and the others, it would be a real nasty and probably short fight. Especially if they put the rockets to use. He doubted they'd be able to escape, and there was nobody nearby who could come to their rescue. He was making a lot of stupid private mistakes, but he also knew they wouldn't win by sitting still. Rockets might be the last thing he expected them to come up with, but it made sense.

"*Where are they coming from?*" Stathis asked Shrek.

"*Unknown,*" Shrek said. "*Maybe one of the forward cylinders? Could be the Draugskepp.*"

"*That's a lot. Filling up the tunnel. Imagine what a firebomb would do.*"

Stathis opened a link back to Valhöll. Lochoki and her survivors were now in charge, conducting repairs under the direction of Zhao, McCarthy, and the SCBIs. The SCBIs were providing some support, and Stathis felt a little guilty, leaving them there alone, but they weren't fighters; they had warbots to hide behind, and Zhao, with McCarthy and his squad, could provide remote support.

"Can you build a couple of firebombs?" Stathis asked her. Hakala was linked in as well.

"Firebombs?"

"Yeah," Stathis said. Was Lochoki the wrong person to ask? Maybe he should've coordinated with Hakala. "I'm thinking big, nasty, oxygen-sucking firebombs. We can plant them in the tunnels with maintenance drones, and when the froggers stroll through? I'm not sure the frog legs will be suitable for supper, but I wanna see what they look like. Plus, it'll suck up the oxygen and make life super unpleasant for the face eaters."

"You want to use small maintenance drones with bombs on their backs to get among them?" asked Lochoki. "That could cause a lot of damage to the life support systems and will make it—"

Lochoki fell silent, and Stathis grinned. They hadn't been wearing armor or space suits. Damaging life support would cause additional problems for them.

"I think we can come up with something," Lochoki said. She'd be inside the SCF and wouldn't have to worry about life support. Making it difficult to breathe in the tunnels would really piss off and slow down the froggers.

"That is anathema to everything we have been taught," Hakala said. "Aboard a spacecraft, to poison or otherwise damage life support is a crime, usually punishable by death. It is a serious thing."

"Well," Stathis said, realizing they might be a lot more concerned than he was, "war sucks, and it's going to hurt them a lot more than us."

"It may be difficult to evacuate Kaelan and his people," Hakala said, "though the tunnels are all interconnected, we might seal off that section."

"Sorry," Stathis said. "If—"

"No. It is a good idea. We are at war. We are outnumbered, and this will cause them more damage than us."

It annoyed Stathis to see all the froggers marching by. They should be terrified. They were going to die anyway. Why not sooner rather than later?

"It is going to take a few hours," Lochoki said. "Thank you for the diagrams. Such an explosive in a contained area like a tram tunnel will be devastating."

Diagrams? It must have been Shrek that sent them. McCarthy and his boys would help, as well.

"Lieutenant McCarthy can provide more direct assistance," Stathis said.

"Wilco," McCarthy said, showing Stathis he was monitoring the command links. A good man. He'd tried to talk Stathis out of attacking Shroggath without him, but he was smart enough not to argue too hard, or he was smart enough to avoid suicide. One of the two.

Stathis counted close to three thousand marching past. They did seem to be coming from the *Draugskepp*, though, and that didn't make a lot of sense. Had Shroggath pulled all his forces close to him for defensive reasons, or was he committing his reserves? Well. Considering the army marching past, he wasn't keeping that many clone.

Shrek didn't know, or he'd tell Stathis.

Hopefully.

He let them get out of sight and gave them half an hour, then he set the drones to continue along the route and see if that group was one of several. Thankfully, it wasn't, and the tunnel remained clear.

The drone sped ahead for two kilometers before Stathis gave the order to move out. Stepping out into the tramway, he found it surreal to realize that just minutes ago, several thousand froggers had marched by. It wasn't like they'd left a trail or anything.

Not for the first time, he wondered how big a mistake he was making.

* * * * *

Chapter Thirty-Five: Hurry Up and Wait

Admiral Diamond Winters, USMC

Winters had heard the term "hurry up and wait" most of her military career. During that time, though, she'd been at the mercy of her commanding officers, waiting for them to make a decision or give commands. She'd always expected that as a leader, she'd be decisive and commanding. Reality wasn't forgiving.

Now that she was in command, she had to wait. Sakamoto had reported ghosts at the edges of their sensors. Vanhat, the Collective, or aliens, nobody knew. The fleet had to keep moving.

Waiting could be fatal, because the fleet wasn't waiting in a position of strength. Some failure, a Shorr-space malfunction, some other mishap that would keep them from fleeing, would be fatal. It was something that kept her awake and sleepless. If it were the *Musashi* that had the failure, she could die with honor, but the mission would fail. If it were someone else? They would have to be abandoned.

The sharks were circling, and Winters didn't need Sakamoto reporting elusive sensor contacts to know that. Right now, none of the ships in the fleet were bleeding, but when something happened, the sharks would attack in a frenzy.

Going through crew lists, looking for something the SCBIs might have missed, was mind-numbing, but there seemed little else to do while they waited for word from Sif and Britta. It also gave her something to think about besides abandoning people who were relying on her to get them home and save the human race.

Waiting was difficult when you knew the task would take time you didn't have.

What options were there? Should she just give the order and try to slip through the empire? At the very least, she needed some idea of their capabilities. Sif had revealed that they were psychic and could likely use those abilities to hunt down intruders. Were psychics common in the alien empire? Did they have psychic weapons that humans had no defense against?

What was taking Sif so long?

Bonnie came in and sat down. She moved stiffly and seemed irate.

"Is everything okay?" Winters asked.

"Everything is fine, Admiral," Bonnie said, but Winters heard the lie.

"Out with it," Winters said.

"It is personal," Bonnie said. "It will not impact my duties."

"That isn't what I asked," Winters said. "You may be a member of my staff, but you're also a friend."

Bonnie took a deep breath.

"Interacting with the crew is difficult," Bonnie said.

"How? Why?" Winters asked.

"The men want only one thing, and the women despise me," Bonnie said.

Winters didn't know what to say about that.

"Tell me more," Winters said. She didn't want to push Bonnie, but she did consider Bonnie a friend, and this was different from digging through crew lists and actions.

"I'm just having a bad day," Bonnie said. "It is nothing. A crewman came up to me, asking straight out to, uh, join me in my quarters. When I said no, he became offended and abrasive."

"Who?" Winters asked. She could have some fun, raking some dumbass across the hot coals for being stupid and rude.

"The problem was dealt with by a nearby NCO to my satisfaction, Admiral," Bonnie said. "It did not address the root cause, in that my appearance makes people think of one thing. They do not see my value as a systems analyst."

"I do," Winters said. She would have to find out more later and make sure the situation had been resolved to *her* satisfaction. An example should be made.

Bonnie's smile was more of a patient, tolerant smile than a confident one.

"It is okay," Bonnie said. "Even at home, I did not feel comfortable with others."

Winters could understand that.

"Incoming transition," Blitzen warned as the alarm rang once. *"Friendly."*

A corvette was returning from a rendezvous, hopefully bringing news

"Incoming data packet," Blitzen said, and Winters felt anxious. What had Sif found? Was it time to act? *"Downloading and analyzing."*

Hurry up and wait. She could give Blitzen time to absorb the information and present it to them.

"Any word from McCarthy?" Winters asked to change the subject.

"Major Stathis is planning to strike at a Jotun," Bonnie said. "He does not approve, and it sounds desperate. He is only taking a squad."

"With only a squad?" Winters asked. Stathis was insane. Hopefully, he'd found allies among the survivors. The information Bonnie got from McCarthy through their alien SCBIs was woefully incomplete, like a telephone conversation or a text chat. A lot of context was lost, and there wasn't enough time to provide other details, like videos and transcripts.

"That does not seem wise," Bonnie said. "I would expect the Jotun to be guarded by thousands, maybe hundreds of thousands."

"Lack of wisdom is a quality Stathis has in quantity," Winters said. "He's made a career out of it, but he's also pretty damned competent. Once I knew he was a stupid private; now I think he's more of an idiot savant."

"He is an experienced major," Bonnie said, "is he not?"

"He's experienced," Winters said. "As for being a major? That's new to him. I think he got promoted too fast. Necessary, though. To be honest, he's doing better than I expected."

"Major Stathis seems to be a very competent officer," Bonnie said.

"If you only knew him as I know him."

But had she really known him? Making stupid jokes, antagonizing others with inane comments and inappropriate observations? He seemed so damned young and innocent. Well. Maybe not innocent, but far too young.

He'd been promoted from private too fast. Nobody could argue that.

But then, hadn't she been promoted to admiral too fast? What could she say about Stathis that didn't apply to her?

"He's matured a great deal," Winters said. "I have every confidence in his tactical ability and skills. If he thinks a squad will do it, then I'm confident he knows best."

Hard to say that, but true. Winters would have to face it. Stathis wasn't the dumb private, and even as a private, he'd known a lot more about small-unit and maybe large-unit tactics than she'd ever known. As an officer, he'd excelled. He wasn't the same person she'd known. She felt some resentment toward him that she tried to quash. She hadn't grown nearly as much, to her regret. Every time she'd seen him working with the men in his role as an officer, she'd been impressed. It was hard to think of him as a stupid private.

"Is a rescue still an option?" Bonnie asked.

"Yes," Winters said without hesitation. "If we need to, we'll go back for them. Marines don't leave their own behind. Neither does the Wolf Legion. Find me a way."

"Yes, ma'am," Bonnie said.

Was it possible, though? Could she?

She would find a way, dammit. Even if it was only to recover his corpse. She owed Stathis and the gunny that much.

He'd better not die, though.

* * * * *

Chapter Thirty-Six:
Mjölnir Port

Major Zale Stathis, USMC

The *Draugskepp* was embedded in the forward docking alue named Mjölnir Port, nearest the Nidavellir cylinder. It had once been like a small city on the outer shell of Bifrost, and the primary purpose had been as a repair yard for larger ships. The collision of the *Draugskepp* had done a lot of damage, grinding its way into the hull of Bifrost.

Getting there was difficult. It should have been easy, but with the heavy industry that went on there, the tunnels were few and large, which meant there were far too many froggers in the tunnels, coming and going, doing whatever froggers did when they weren't trying to eat people's faces.

It was disturbing to see them operating heavy machinery, and the large cargo trains were being repaired, as well. They were busy, and Stathis didn't like that. The lack of gravity in the area made it easier for the froggers, who obviously had no problem with it.

Even without gravity, it had taken a lot of time, crawling through the air ducts and maintenance tunnels that had been tunneled through the rock. In addition to being air ducts, they allowed maintenance robots to move around. They were barely big enough to crawl through, but they were a maze, feeding countless corridors and facilities. Stathis was surprised that the froggers didn't use them, but then nobody liked crawling for kilometers on hands and knees, and the froggers didn't have anything to fear, using the big tunnels.

Stathis could tell the collision had been a slower impact and grind. Intentional. Had it been a high-speed collision, there would be little left of the Mjölnir Port or the *Draugskepp*. It looked more like a compactor had pushed them together. The alue itself was a massive structure, more than just docking bays, it held cargo gantries and loading cranes large enough to latch onto a large cruiser. The air duct they were crawling through was large; the only reason their progress hadn't bogged down was that there was no gravity in this area.

He assumed there'd been a lot of space, and it had been a large hangar, but most of that space was now collapsed and absorbed by the ship that tried to become one with Bifrost.

"Ewww," Stathis said as the drone rose high enough to give him a good view. "Frogbath must have a serious cold. I've never seen so much snot."

The area was covered in slime that seemed to stretch over almost everything. There was an atmosphere, so they must have sealed it, or maybe that was what the slime was doing.

"It is making the area airtight," Hakala said from beside him. "A biological seal."

"Shouldn't it be a little bit more solid?" Stathis asked.

"It will have to be analyzed," Hakala said.

The Russelman index was high, but it was nearly impossible to determine a direction and distance.

"It's going to be a bitch, cleaning my armor after this," Stathis said.

"It does not seem to bother the froggers, sir," Mikhailov said, and Stathis noticed the froggers moving through it. Few had clothes, and the slime coated them, but seemed to slide off as they moved into areas without it. The froggers looked like they were swimming as they moved through the zero-gravity area, and the slime looked like it stuck to itself more than the froggers.

There was more slime along the edges, where the ship and Bifrost merged, and there was a steady stream of froggers coming out of the ship.

"What are they doing in there?" Mikhailov asked.

"Frogger orgy?" Stathis said. There were several crates of weapons that the froggers were taking rifles out of. Most were slug throwers, but there were a few boxes of blazers. These froggers did seem smaller than the others. "Maybe they're newborns?"

"*The Bifrost is transitioning,*" Shrek said. Not what Stathis wanted to hear. The coordinates were meaningless right now, as the SCBIs were still working to get full control of the Shorr-space drives. Until they could exert full control, they were moving quietly and trying not to tip off Shroggath, or whatever was controlling the drives, that they were there. Stathis was leaving the network stuff to the SCBIs and trusted they had a plan in that regard. He was just here to poke Shroggath in the forehead with a KA-BAR.

Stathis zoomed in for a closer look at the froggers. The slime didn't seem to be sticking to them, just everything else.

"*Are they smaller?*" Stathis asked.

"*Yes,*" Shrek said. "*Some are slightly more deformed beyond the parameters we have seen. They also appear to be secreting an oil that prevents the slime from sticking to them. Smaller than the others we have encountered, perhaps 30 percent smaller in height and mass.*"

"What does that mean?"

"*In theory, they are newborn? The slightly smaller size indicates youth, or perhaps this is more of a final form?*"

"*Are these the children that got transformed?*"

"*Possible,*" Shrek said. "*Or they are newly born. Shroggath likely has a method of reproduction to replace losses.*"

Another thousand or so grabbed weapons and began their glide or march out of the ruined hangar. The weapons looked manufactured, not standard, but probably based on Republic designs. Stathis had seen it before in the arcologies on Earth. The vanhat could use human manufactories and tweak them so the weapons produced were more useful to their *orja*.

"*So how many are inside, incubating?*"

"*Impossible to say,*" Shrek said.

"*The place could be full of baby froggers?*"

"*Very likely, if they are born there. However, such accelerated growth would make things questionable. Birth and growth require energy and resources.*"

"*The Russelman index is pretty high,*" Stathis said. "*I can guess where that energy is coming from.*"

"*A valid guess.*"

"So how do we get in, sir?" Mikhailov asked. They were all stacked up behind him in the air duct. The duct wasn't big enough to stand up in, and it was unpleasant, even for a short person like Stathis. The bigger legionnaires had to be hating life.

The drone didn't have the best angle on the doors leading into the ship.

"Gotta find a door they aren't using," Stathis said. "We begin our breach when there are as few as possible around. Try to maintain the element of surprise for as long as possible. We're an arrow going for the heart, not a hammer smashing them to a pulp. Kill the head, the body dies."

"Wilco," Mikhailov said, and Stathis noticed he changed links. Shrek kept up with him and let Stathis hear what he was telling the squad.

"Listen up," Mikhailov told his squad. "We are going to be a headshot. Go in quiet, fast, and hard. We want to kill the top dog, and then we are going to fight our way out. Pure assassination strike. Hurrah."

"Hurrah, hurrah, hurrah," his squad said. They didn't sound enthusiastic so much as focused.

"Squad," Mikhailov said, "listen to my command. We will guard and protect Major Stathis, who will be the spearhead. Do as he says, keep him alive, and we will slay this vanhat commander. Hurrah?"

"Hurrah, hurrah, hurrah."

"We are unlikely to get a drone inside," Hakala said, distracting Stathis from Mikhailov's speech. The hatches were covered in slime that the froggers seemed to slide through. Stathis noticed one frogger with a box, but the box seemed to get stuck in the slime, and the frogger had a hard time getting it through.

"We might have to burn our way through or something," Stathis said. Would blazers work? "We'll have to assume the second we touch that slime, Frogbath will know we're here."

"Why do you say that?"

"When spiders weave their webs, they become attuned to any movement in them. I don't see anything spraying slime, so it has to come from somewhere."

"How do you know that?"

"Growing up, we used to have a bunch of spiders in the apartment. I was never a fan of spiders, even garden spiders. We didn't have any venomous ones that I ever saw, but they got big enough that I could feel them crawling on my blanket at night sometimes."

"Where did you live?" Hakala asked.

"A cheap, crappy apartment," Stathis said. "Mom couldn't afford much. It was shelter; it could have been worse, though. We weren't living in a cardboard box. That was the important thing. I don't think any spiders survived the nuclear winter, though. If they did, they're probably a lot bigger and more dangerous."

Stathis didn't want to think about before the Marine Corps.

"But these are froggers, not spiders," Stathis said. "Did you know frogs would eat mice?"

"No," Hakala said in a tone of voice that warned Stathis he should probably change the subject.

"Yeah, and chickens will eat meat, too, even each other, given a chance. You'd be surprised."

"I thought chickens were herbivores, only eating grain and such."

"No," Stathis said. "They're related to the Tyrannosaurus Rex, I think. Not grass eaters. They prefer meat, they just aren't big enough to hunt it."

"None of that is likely to help us get in there," Hakala said.

"Well, yeah. I figure we're just going to have to pick an entrance point and go balls to the wall."

"Balls to the wall?"

"Um, maximum thrust? I don't know where it came from, but when we pull the trigger, it means we push hard and fast. As soon as we come out of Shorr space, I figure we'll hit Frogbath."

"Zen."

Sitting there, Stathis could see the torn cover of the air duct, and he knew if he moved forward and leaned out, he could see the rest of the hangar, but right now, the drone was sufficient. It was magnetically clamped to the ceiling in low-power surveillance mode right now.

Stathis was tempted to try and get the drone closer, to see around some wreckage where the main and perhaps only entrance was, but several froggers were moving around the area, and the risk of them seeing the drone was higher. Right now, it could just be a piece of wreckage, but the more it moved, the more likely it would be seen.

The Bifrost slid out of Shorr space, and Stathis grimaced. It was showtime.

Moving forward, Stathis noticed there seemed to be fewer froggers in the area. Perfect timing.

Peeking out, he saw froggers, so Stathis leaped out and grabbed a nearby gantry with one hand, his other hand holding his blazer ready, and he motioned the others out.

Now would be a very bad time to discover the froggers had automated pop-up turrets.

A link came in from McCarthy.

"Skögul is under attack."

* * * * *

Chapter Thirty-Seven: The Echoes and the Fallen

Kapten Sif, VRAEC, Nakija Musta Toiminnot

Sif opened the link to Britta. The SCBIs continued to crunch data and analyze the information the Voorga were sending them. Sif was bored. There was plenty to do, but the SCBIs seemed to be much better and quicker. She wanted to walk among the Voorga, watch them work and play, not consider linguistic nuances.

The more data the SCBIs got, the slower they seemed to become.

Now with laser links to the Voorga, sharing data, they were holding some basic conversations, but neither side seemed ready for negotiations, and Sif felt a strange reluctance to try to talk to them on a psychic level. Things were too simple there, and she needed the grounding of harsh reality.

"Admiral Winters has arrived," Britta said. "Out beyond the heliosphere, almost out of system, vector is matching this system. Close, but outside Aesir link range."

"Zen," Sif said. Had something changed with the fleet? Had the admiral grown impatient, or just wanted to be closer?

"Other ships in the fleet are foraging," Britta said. "We're still communicating by drone, but now lag is an hour instead of days."

"Is it safe?" Sif asked.

"I'm guessing the admiral thinks the risks are worth the rewards," Britta said.

"Zen."

"Enzell is demanding we go find other Voorga to talk with," Britta said. "He's getting very annoying about it."

"He is not wrong," Sif said. "How does he propose we initiate contact?"

"He's vague about that," Britta said. "He probably thinks that's a problem for little people like us."

"Little people?" Sif asked. Britta had said "us," but had she meant Sif?

"He's an arrogant prick," Britta replied. "He talks down to everyone."

"He is helping a great deal; he is Loki's advice to Odin and has good points."

"I wish I knew what he did in the Governance," Britta said. "You don't get that arrogant without a lot of authority."

Sif paused. Britta was right. Enzell had obviously not been a low-level flunky. Nor had he been a member of the central committee. Who, then? The last arrogant SOG scientists she could remember had been the head of the science facility that was preparing to allow Lusiferious into this dimension. As she thought about it, she realized Enzell had the same vibe, but more of it.

"That is a good question," Sif said. Feng had assigned him to the expedition, and Sif realized that Feng probably knew exactly who he was, but he hadn't shared the specifics with the Operation Seraphim command team. Was he a senior scientist or official from InSec or ExSec?

Munin had little data on him. "Political scientist" was a vague title, likely something one of the SOG intelligence agencies would employ, and Sif knew they would have employed him to help control and oppress the population. Was that why he was here? To help control, manipulate, and monitor Operation Seraphim?

Sif had no doubt that Feng would do something like that, placing a spy among them. The suspicion had been in the back of her mind, a low-priority issue, but how would his secret mission impact his mission to analyze the Voorga?

Of course, he would reject the Fallen as social rejects. As a pawn of the Governance, he would believe in a strong central authority and reject any rebels or non-conformists.

"A good question," Sif said. "We have no way of knowing, unless Feng has hidden that data somewhere in our network where the SCBIs cannot find it."

"*No additional data has been found,*" Munin clarified.

"*He has a secret mission,*" Sif said, making up her mind. His arrogance was making him and his agenda suspicious. "*I want to know what it is.*"

"*How much time should I spend on that?*" Munin asked. How much did she want to take away from the translation and understanding the Voorga was what Munin was really asking.

"*Send the request to the* Musashi," Sif said. "*Let them investigate. I want you and the others focused on the Voorga.*"

"*Zen. An incoming link from the Voorga.*"

"*Open.*"

"We thank you for the gift of the inkeri," a Voorga said. It was a computer simulation, a deep, smooth voice that likely sounded nothing like a real Voorga. Faintly, in the background, she heard the

Voorga voice speaking, and there was a few seconds' delay as the speaker was translated.

"It is our pleasure to share it with you," Sif said. "It has helped us a great deal against the vanhat. It is a critical protective device."

"We are producing them and distributing them," the Voorga said.

"I am called Sif, a senior officer. May I ask who I am talking to?" Sif asked, hoping the translation matrices wouldn't mangle it too badly.

"I am also a senior leader. I am called Thuthta. It is my honor to be understander of our interactions. We have met in the ethereal whispers of our minds."

This was the psychic? Sif couldn't help asking herself.

"Are there many of you who meet in the ethereal whisper of the mind?" Sif asked. Was the race psychic, or just a few members?

"There are few," Thuthta said. "Perhaps one in ten has the ability. One in ten thousand is as strong as I am. There are more of us among the Fallen than among the Immaculate. In ancient times, they were critical to our survival and helped evade the more powerful devourers and hunters of our home worlds."

"Home worlds?" Sif asked.

"Before the Fall and the arrival of Liathon and Gaibron, we made many worlds our home, spreading our species and ecosystem to other worlds within the galactic mist."

Galactic mist, the nebula?

"*This seems confirmed in some of their lore,*" Munin said. "*Based on data, there were fourteen such worlds that were colonized, terraformed worlds that were very similar to their home world of Naataan. I can extrapolate that these other planets were chosen for their higher gravity, matching Naataan. Two may have had an ecology that was wiped out and replaced by the Voorga. They do not seem concerned about preserving local species. Initial analysis indicates the original ecosystems were completely eradicated in favor of the Voorga ecosystem from their home world."*

"Naataan is where the tomb is?" Sif asked, sending a link to Britta so she could join or listen.

"Correct. It is the source of our species and thus the haven. We long to return there. Will you help us awaken and free Liathon the Protector?"

Sif saw Britta join the link. How could she avoid committing?

"We need to understand the dangers," Sif said. Could she put the burden on the Voorga? They were the ones who needed *Musashi's* help.

"We will help you," Thuthta said. "The Voorga, both Fallen and Unfallen, need your help as you need ours. Compared to your species, we are stagnant, unaccepting of the change your species embraces. Change in our world is a violent and dangerous thing. Our physiology has mandated such caution."

Which Sif could understand, if she didn't know what stagnant meant. Heavy gravity increased many dangers. Things humans would consider minor, such as falling, would have much more impact on someone from a high-gravity world. Dropping things would mean the destruction of many objects. Caution would be required in such simple things as walking.

"We also must exercise caution," Sif said. "Our resources are finite."

"Resources are always finite," Thuthta said. "Liathon has spoken of this. Life is the most finite of resources and must be treasured. Gaibron has spoken of this, as well. Life force is the currency of the devourers."

That was a different approach, Sif thought. Souls as currency among the vanhat? It would make sense. Was that the key to understanding the vanhat? They came here for the souls? Too simplistic, but there could be some truth in it.

"Is life force currency for Liathon?"

"Our scholars have asked this," Thuthta said. "There is no satisfactory answer among them. Life is the most finite resource. Would the angels and devourers not value it in different ways? Liathon does value the life of the Voorga, but so does Gaibron, though perhaps for different reasons."

"Are the lives of animals and non-Voorga considered of value?" Sif asked as Britta remained silent.

"Lesser beings do not feed the devourers as the Voorga and greater beings do. The Voorga do not place value on lesser beings as we do on greater beings. We mirror the Jotun in our estimation of the value of life."

"*Jotun?*" Sif asked. "*Their word or ours?*"

"*A translation,*" Munin said. "*Perhaps you would like me to map that word to 'deity?'*"

"No, that's fine," Sif said.

She was used to adjusting her words to other cultures and people. The Governance had made English the de facto language throughout human space, but they couldn't stamp out the fact that different cultures used words differently and were heavily influenced by their original culture.

It was odd to have others using Finnish words and terms, though.

"Will you help us to breach the gates of the tomb?" Thuthta asked more directly.

"I must consult with our senior leaders," Sif said.

"I am not asking your senior leaders," Thuthta said. "I am asking you. You have your ships. Will you and your smaller stealth vessel and the ship above help us?"

"I want to," Sif said. Was the Voorga trying to trap her? Keep her from contacting others? Forcing her to commit? "However, I am subordinate and must follow orders."

Thuthta remained silent.

"We must wait for your senior leaders to decide, then. Time is running out. We fear that royalty may decide to take matters into their own hands and enslave us."

"Our senior leaders are coming," Sif said. What else could she say? They needed more time, and time was running out.

"There is another demon that will come for Liathon and perhaps Gaibron. We must move quickly before the dance of death begins."

"Tell me about that demon," Sif said. "What you have shared does not have details."

"We do not have details. This demon was large, massive, and it wanted to devour Liathon, but it was also an enemy of Gaibron."

"Did Gaibron help or hurt the Voorga?" Sif asked. "It seems unclear."

"Gaibron the slayer, the hated, the deceiver, the betrayer. He fought beside Liathon at times, against her at others. He is a difficult one to understand. He is not the one who helped the Voorga escape, though he may have helped the Fallen. His violence is echoed in the Fallen. He changed some of us as we fell. The Fallen would be extinct without him, but he did not save us."

"I do not understand," Sif said.

"Neither do we," Thuthta said. "Our records, our histories are flawed. They have been reinterpreted many times. Our language has changed over the centuries; our understanding has changed."

"You do not have original records?" Sif asked.

"Our records have been digital since before. Easily changed and erased."

A chill ran down Sif's spine. These Voorga were not peaceful, and they controlled their media. Were they as bad, or worse, than the Governance had been?

* * * * *

Chapter Thirty-Eight: Skögul Attacked

Lieutenant Aod McCarthy, Wolf Legion

McCarthy didn't like being left behind, and neither did his squad. It was the feeling of being useless that hurt the most. The other legionnaires had SCBIs that kept them incredibly busy. McCarthy didn't have a SCBI, and his "invisible friend" didn't seem to have the ability to interface with the Republic robots and the system to control and manage repairs or defenses. It was nowhere near as efficient, and that made McCarthy feel inadequate.

Enigma helped him interface with systems, but not as efficiently as the other legionnaires and their SCBIs. Sometimes it was like having a low-quality, off-the-shelf, reject version of a SCBI.

The one thing Enigma had that the SCBIs didn't was the ability to sense things beyond what nearby sensors picked up.

Sitting in the Skögul command room, he cycled through the different camera views. He was confident the SCBIs, or more appropriately, their hosts, would inform him if they found anything. It was weird, knowing Moore and Quinn had SCBIs they talked with all the time, probably more frequently than he spoke with them, but he'd never spoken with them. Like knowing your best friend has a wife or someone they spend a lot of time with, but you never see.

McCarthy knew the text messages from his people were rarely from them directly. Instead, they were usually sent by their invisible friend.

"*I am sensing a change in the skein,*" Enigma reported, a soft, comforting voice in the back of his mind.

"*What does that mean?*" McCarthy asked.

"*We are in Shorr space,*" Enigma said. "*Closer to the conflux of dimensions, drifting through the ocean of chaos. It is easier for entities to sidle through the chaos and visit the Bifrost.*"

"*Are we getting boarded?*"

"*Yes,*" Enigma said, "*in your parlance. We are picking up additional riders.*"

"*What and where?*"

"I am not sure yet," Enigma said. "Like colors running through water, I am not yet able to identify the source."

"*I need solid information,*" McCarthy said. "*I don't do well with suspicion and guesses.*"

"*This is no guess,*" Enigma said, "*nor a suspicion. It is happening, but the exact nature of the devourer threat is not yet visible.*"

"*What can you tell me?*"

"*It is coming with intent, a predator on the hunt, and the Bifrost was not chosen by chance or accident.*"

"*How do you know?*"

"*Whispers in the skein. A focused gaze.*"

"*Let me know when you have something a bit more solid,*" McCarthy said. Should he sound the alert? What would he say? Be alert? If they weren't alert, they wouldn't have survived this long.

Skögul was locked up tight. All the blast doors were closed, and the pop-up turrets were active for at least a kilometer down each tunnel. The inkeris were overlapping, at full strength, and there were auxiliary inkeris ready to come online the second they were needed.

But Bifrost was currently in Shorr space, and that meant enemy territory. Anything was possible, and while McCarthy didn't understand the details, he knew the deeper the ship went, the more likely it was to collapse the inkeris.

"How deep are we, and how stressed are the inkeris?" McCarthy asked.

"We are deep, but the entity controlling the Shorr-space drives is not taking us as deep into Shorr space as it can."

"Why?"

"To sink further into the chaos realm will put excessive stress on the inkeris, but that does not concern Shroggath. Should the inkeris collapse, we will all be in extreme danger. The entity controlling the depth is unlikely to go very deep because then it can lose control and face more powerful, aggressive devourers. Keeping the vessel in the shallows, so to speak, keeps the Bifrost further away from the prowling devourers that hunt in the deeper ether."

Which McCarthy could understand.

"But we are still being tracked and boarded."

"Correct. Perhaps I should rephrase. If we go deeper, the devourers have more power to influence and transition to flotsam such as Bifrost without assistance or permission. By maintaining this level within Shorr space, large distances within your home space can be traversed, but other devourers cannot climb aboard the Bifrost without assistance and direction from devourers currently aboard. They lack strength and guidance."

Like a shuttle skimming above water teeming with monsters.

"You should sound the alarm," Enigma said. "The skein whispers that an attack is imminent from entrance Berta."

McCarthy slammed his fist down on the nearby alert button, and sirens began screeching. He trusted Enigma enough to know that if it said an attack was imminent, he should prepare.

"We have an incoming attack on blast doors Berta," McCarthy said aloud as Moore sat up and began cycling through cameras.

"How do you—" Moore said, and then an alert on the screen reported one of the pop-down turrets in the tunnel had just been destroyed.

"What the hell?" Moore finished.

Other legionnaires came pouring into the command center from the nearby ready room where they'd been resting.

"What is it?" Quinn asked.

"Not sure," McCarthy said. "Some new vanhat. Enigma thinks they're coming for us. The major saw them with rocket launchers."

"Why us?"

"Because you didn't put on deodorant this morning," Moore said. "They've come to put us out of our misery or avenge their sense of smell."

"Gob shite," Quinn said. "You're the tumpty who stopped up the toilet. Nobody likes that."

Another pop-down turret went offline. Whatever was attacking was moving quickly. The Bifrost slid out of Shorr space.

"We need a team down to the hatch," McCarthy said. They'd sent too many warbots to support the thug dictator Kaelan, and McCarthy felt unprepared.

"I'll go," Moore said. "My trigger finger is itching like your girlfriend's crotch."

"Quinn will be the reserve," McCarthy said, hoping this wasn't a multi-prong attack. Why hadn't the turrets seen, or shot, anything?"

McCarthy opened a link to the major.

"Skögul is under attack," McCarthy reported.

"By what?" Major Stathis asked.

"Still trying to determine that. Enigma warned us, and we're losing turrets in the approach to entrance Berta. I'm sending a team."

"Okay," Stathis said. "We're preparing to give Frogbath a blazer bolt enema. Going to be busy. Kick ass and take names. Do what you need to. Keep Skögul safe, or blow it and get to Valhöll. No casualties. No heroics."

"Wilco," McCarthy said. No casualties? Who did the major think he was? McCarthy didn't even know what he was up against.

A display lit up, showing an armored fist holding a massive, unwieldy pistol of some kind poking out around the curve and firing at the camera. Why couldn't the damn pirates have made the corridors straight? Then all the turrets could engage targets a kilometer away.

"That was turret three," Quinn said as Moore raced out the door, followed by his team. "Fast son of a bitch. That's all we saw."

"Time the progress, then have the turret start firing before the attacker can pop around the curve."

"Wilco," Quinn said, as if he was the one controlling the turrets.

Another screen lit up, showing the fourth turret, which was firing a suppressing pattern at the curve where the enemy was likely to appear, then it began placing rounds into the actual wall.

The creature that came sprinting out from cover was a nightmare. The pistol in its hand lined up and fired at the turret before it could adjust its aim, and the camera blanked out.

"What the hell?" Quinn said as the display rolled back to the creature.

It was thin, covered in dark armor with spikes.

"Looks like one of the cyborgs the major tangled with, but different."

"*A related entity,*" Enigma said. "*This may be a transformed slave, or perhaps the devourer archetype brought more of its forms from its place of origin. It is likely related to the entity your major fought. It may also be from another archetype of that dimension.*"

"So where's this archetype hiding?" McCarthy asked aloud so the SCBIs could answer through Quinn if they knew. Stathis was currently hunting for the archetype controlling the froggers.

McCarthy didn't feel useless now.

"*Invalid assessment,*" Enigma told McCarthy. "*Do not assume all archetypes have physical forms or are bound to an object.*"

"Meaning what?"

"*During the Dimension Wars, my builders discovered the archetypes varied greatly in form and capabilities. Some were forced to attach to an object or being. Others did not require a single physical link. The presence of one of their pawns allowed them to remain in this dimension.*"

"So how do you kill them?"

"*Eradicate their last pawn,*" Enigma said. "*That could be difficult, especially in this case, since the archetype will keep one or more pawns out of the battle to ensure it is not returned to exile. If this entity is cybernetic in nature, as the SCBIs suggest, then it can likely build additional pawns from scratch.*"

"You can talk to the SCBIs?"

"*Not well, but I can sense the general direction of their conversations. We can share limited data. While they have classified me as an alien SCBI, and thus not human, they try to include me, but bandwidth is extremely limited, and constant communication is not practical.*"

"Why the different form?"

"*It is adapting,*" Enigma said. "*Evolving to more efficiently accomplish the goals and intent of the archetype. This is one thing that makes it difficult to classify, track, and otherwise identify the archetypes. There are countless permutations throughout the dimensions, and they constantly change and evolve. Chaos incarnate.*"

"Which sounds like interesting information for eggheads, but I need to know how to stop these bastards before they take out all my turrets."

"They are fast and accurate," Quinn said.

"Grenades," McCarthy said. "Arm the warbots with explosives and walk them down, sweeping the corners clear with high explosives."

"Wilco," Quinn said.

"*That may work,*" Enigma said, "*until they evolve or change.*"

"Yeah, well, it'll give us time," McCarthy said. What other tricks did they have up their sleeves, and what could McCarthy do next? "*We need to keep changing tactics to keep them from adapting.*"

"*Correct,*" Enigma said.

McCarthy wanted to swear. He wanted ideas, not confirmation that he was on the right track. How long before he ran out of ideas, and they didn't? If the attackers had the firepower and numbers, they could make countless mistakes, but if the defenders made a mistake? It would be over quickly.

* * * * *

Chapter Thirty-Nine: Intelligence Dump

Admiral Diamond Winters, USMC

Reading the report, Winters decided she hated her job. She would have to decide quickly. She sent out a meeting request to the senior staff, including Sakamoto and his staff. She needed other views and opinions.

She reread the conversation with Sif and Thuthta. The Voorga wanted action; they wanted commitment, and Winters didn't like being pressured like this, but she could also understand Thuthta's concerns, even his intent. Being alien didn't mean they wouldn't try to manipulate others psychologically, and she wondered how well they understood human psychology. Much better than humans understood Voorga psychology, if she had to guess.

"*What are your suggestions?*" Winters asked Blitzen.

"*Consult your staff,*" Blitzen said. "*I cannot advise you on this. This is more interpersonal relations and not within my specialty.*"

"*Dammit.*"

"*This is the point where you demonstrate your leadership abilities,*" Blitzen said, which didn't help. "*Times like these are what set real leaders apart from managers and commanders.*"

Didn't she know it? Being a senior officer was about a lot more than directing others in battle and understanding tactics. It was about making decisions that could impact the human race. A misstep here could plunge humanity into a war with an alien empire. As if the vanhat and Collective weren't enough of a threat.

If the Fallen didn't like her answer, they could share their information with their emperor and make things even more difficult. They hadn't said they'd do as much, but they obviously felt some racial loyalty.

Winters didn't feel up to the task. She understood what was riding on her decision. She could consult with others, but the final decision was hers, and if she chose wrong...

To support or abandon the rebels. Were there any other choices? Was there time to find them? If she wasn't going to support them, how could she keep them from turning on the fleet?

Within minutes, staff members came into the conference room. Sakamoto was one of the first and nodded to her as he took his seat.

"Admiral-sama," Sakamoto said.

"Sakamoto-san," she said. Winters struggled to think of some small, innocuous question she could ask him, some bit of small talk to help put her, and him, at ease while they waited for the others, but nothing came to mind. She called him "san" to try to address him more as an equal than a subordinate. She didn't want flunkies, she needed friends.

"These are difficult times," Sakamoto said a moment later as still more people hurried into the conference room. Some had been off duty, and it was obvious they'd struggled back into their uniforms. Everyone looked tired, and Winters checked the time. She could give them a few minutes. It was nine in the evening, ship's time. She probably should have rescheduled for the morning, but she knew she wouldn't be sleeping. She needed ideas and perspective.

Bonnie was the last one to enter and took her seat next to Nakano.

"*That is the last*," Blitzen reported as Winters stood up.

"You all know the situation," Winters said, but reviewed it quickly. "I need pros and cons for helping the alien rebels. Do we stall for time, try to learn more about the Voorga and their culture, or do we commit?"

Everyone stared at her silently and Winters realized this might be a bad idea. Sakamoto came to her rescue, though, starting the conversation.

"Do we know what exactly they want from us?" Sakamoto asked, cutting right to the point. Winters wanted to smile. She'd been too busy, looking at the bigger picture and not the details. He'd likely reviewed the transcripts, and he knew, but by putting it out in the open, he was helping to focus the discussion.

"They want us to spearhead an attack on the tomb," Winters said.

"Have they provided us with any information on the opposition? Ship strength? Classifications? Weaponry? Capabilities?"

"No," Winters said.

"Then I think we should be able to ask that of them, Admiral-sama," Sakamoto said. She wanted to frown at him for his use of "sama." He was elevating her more than he should.

"Why can we not just bypass them all?" Bonnie asked. "Not get involved?"

"The Voorga have psychics, and it's very possible that they can use those psychics to hunt us down if we trespass," Winters said. Bonnie knew that, but Winters felt the woman had an agenda.

"Have we confirmed that ability, outside these rebels?" Bonnie asked. "We can only extrapolate based on what little information we have."

Winters looked around the table.

Actionable intelligence was certainly in short supply. Right now, she was making decisions based on guesswork and theories. The problem was that she knew this was how war worked. If she had all the proper information, she should be able to decide easily. Right now, nobody had even a fraction of the information. All they had were guesses, theories, and ideas.

Being able to work with such little information distinguishes brilliant leaders from mediocre ones. SCBIs excelled at collecting and presenting data, but they were struggling, and the weight was landing on her shoulders.

What would a great general do? What would the gunny, or Stathis, do? Would they be able to respond to this situation? They were decisive and direct. All the greats tended to be decisive and direct. George Washington, Ulysses Grant, Douglas MacArthur, and George Patton, all decisive and aggressive commanders who frequently had to make quick decisions based on minimal information, and their actions shaped the United States in so many ways.

What would they do? Could she ask Blltzen?

"That is a valid assessment," Nakano said. He was usually quiet and reserved. She didn't understand why, as the ship's political commissar, he was still at Sakamoto's side, but she had other things to do besides question his staffing decisions. "I would recommend we pressure these rebels for such information. This will provide us with many things, beyond just the raw information. By providing this information, they will help us assess their honesty, desire to cooperate, and succeed. It will help us understand better what we are up against and further evaluate the value of these anti-socialists. Perhaps they just want to use us as blazer fodder, to take casualties in their stead."

Winters stared at Nakano. He wasn't wrong.

"And if that information is predicated on our commitment to help?" Winters asked. "Do we commit to get that information?"

She didn't want to lie or change her mind. That would be a betrayal, even aliens would see it that way.

"Another test, Admiral-sama," Nakano said. "True allies, or those seeking a real alliance, will provide this information. If these rebels are trying to control and manipulate us, I suspect we will be able to discern that in the information they provide."

"If we decide it's too dangerous?" Winters asked.

"Then we abandon them and find another way."

"They'll never trust us again. You don't see that as a betrayal?"

"No, Admiral-sama. Our concern is the human race, not the Voorga. We must look out for humanity first. If we do not, nobody else will. I expect the Voorga will be unhappy with this, but they will have to understand."

Winters didn't want to acknowledge that he could be right, but it still felt wrong.

The US Marine motto was *Semper Fidelis*, which meant always faithful. There were many ways to interpret those words. Faithful in a marriage meant one thing: a faithful follower of God meant something slightly different. To Winters, it meant loyalty and integrity.

But to what? To whom? The United States was gone. To her fellow Marines?

Sitting there, looking at all the different faces, all the non-American faces and uniforms, was a cold blast of water in the face.

The United States might be gone, but that didn't mean it was dead. Not in her heart. It was hard for those who'd never worn the uniform to understand, but she did. The United States had never been perfect, but what it stood for was an ideal. She wanted the USA to be loyal, honorable, and trustworthy. She wanted the Empire under Mathison to be loyal, honorable, and trustworthy. Fanatically loyal to friends and allies. That was what America meant to her; that was what the Empire should mean to everyone. To predict the future, you had to make it.

"We'll ask them," Winters said. "We'll take them seriously. If they provide data, I want you to shred it. Find their lies, find their flaws, and let me know. We need allies. If these Voorga rebels are worthy allies, we'll be fanatically loyal to them. It's that simple. Our loyalty is to humanity and our allies, whoever they might be, so help me choose. The future of humanity depends on who we choose for allies because this war with the vanhat is only getting started."

She thought of the great generals and their mistakes. George Washington had made many mistakes—Fort Necessity, the Battle of Long Island. The problem was that her mistakes could doom humanity to extinction. She couldn't afford to make any mistakes with the vanhat and Collective nipping at their heels.

Time was running out.

* * * * *

Chapter Forty:
Attack on the *Draugskepp*

Major Zale Stathis, USMC

Stathis fired. He couldn't worry about McCarthy right now. Hopefully, wiping out Frogbath would stop the attack on Skögul and the hydroponics alue. Give them all some breathing room to relax, repair, and prepare.

An ugly frog head began to slide out of the slime. Stathis shot it, and the creature exploded in super-heated flesh and steam. The slime that didn't explode sizzled and smoked, and Stathis was pretty sure the frogger had a fatal headache. What he hadn't expected was the slime catching fire. A bad thought occurred. What if all the corridors and interior were filled with that slime, and the froggers swam through it like water?

The fire didn't blaze up, but remained small as low, shallow flames spread across the surface.

"Oops," Stathis said. This would complicate things. That didn't keep Stathis from leading the others toward the hatch. Maybe their suits would keep them safe?

"*Oops?*" Shrek asked. "*What do you mean 'oops?' I know what I mean when I say oops; what do you mean when you say oops?*"

"*Why didn't you tell me the slime was flammable?*"

"*Because you wouldn't let me take a sample and analyze it,*" Shrek said. Another frogger tried to slide out of the burning slime, but a round from one of the other troopers hit it, causing it to explode in heated flesh and slime. Approaching the hatch, he could see there was air on the other side, so it was just a kind of airlock.

"*When did you ask for a sample?*"

"*When we got close enough,*" Shrek said as the team behind Stathis spread out, some covering the entrances to the shattered hangar, and others aiming at the hatches.

Firing told Stathis that there were froggers in the corridor outside, returning to find out what was going on.

As he moved up to the burning hatch, electromagnets in his boots controlled by Shrek kept him from drifting away. Stathis peered in past the burning slime and splattered froggers.

"*It is not that hot,*" Shrek said. "*Easily within suit parameters. Pulsing the inkeri now.*"

Stathis didn't notice any changes in the slime as the inkeri pulsed.

"*Russelman index remains high,*" Shrek reported.

Stathis was about to lead the way into the broken ship when Mikhailov pushed him back and ordered Chen and his men forward.

The only reason Mikhailov got away with it was because he caught Stathis by surprise. He was going to lead the way all the way to Shroggath.

Chen and his fire team wasted no time, pushing their way into the hull, and Stathis heard weapons fire.

"Let them," Hakala said.

"A good commander leads the way," Stathis said. Following others never sat well with him.

"A good commander looks at the big picture," Hakala said, her weapon sweeping the gantries, looking for froggers.

A burst of fire sent metal slugs at them, and Stathis felt them slam into his shoulder pauldron and helmet. They weren't armor piercers, so while annoying, they weren't a danger. Someone else permanently ended the attack as Stathis turned to look.

The two mules, one with an inkeri and one with a d-bomb, scuttled across the floor and stopped behind him as Stathis followed Chen, who had Li, the SAW gunner, and Lebedev, a rifleman, in front of him, leading the way into the corridor. Behind Chen, Mikhailov pushed his way in front of Stathis.

Hakala was right, but Stathis didn't want to admit it. Something felt wrong about following others into danger. What would the gunny do? Put Stathis in front and use him as a shield, most likely. The gunny wasn't an idiot.

Weapons fire in front of and behind him didn't make him feel better, as the mules remained close to him and Hakala.

With Kuznetsov's team behind him, Stathis followed Mikhailov into the ship, which was bigger than he expected.

He wasn't sure what to expect. Slime-covered walls, froggers packed to the ceiling? What he hadn't expected were empty corridors with only a little slime.

Mikhailov was moving around, and Stathis realized he was using the Russelman index to try and figure out where Shroggath might be.

"Turn right," Mikhailov said to his point man. Stathis wanted to leave someone behind to guard the entrance, but he couldn't see that ending well.

A burst of fire erupted and ended before Stathis could see what his legionnaires were shooting at. It would have been nice to be preceded by grenades, but they didn't have time for a slow, steady assault. Thousands of froggers were probably turning around now and coming back.

Blazer weapons opened fire, and Lebedev went down. Li clamped down on his trigger as Chen moved forward to add his fire to Li's. Incoming fire stopped completely, and Stathis saw that Lebedev wasn't getting up ever again.

"Screw this," Stathis said. "Secure positions."

"Sir?" Mikhailov asked. Technically, now was the time to push forward when they had fire superiority.

The detonation range of the d-bomb was approximately a kilometer in diameter, two kilometers on a good day. It would easily encompass the ship.

A nearby hatch looked solidly closed, but it didn't stand up to Stathis's powered armor. It wasn't a full seal bulkhead, just an internal sliding door without power.

Pulling the door open enough, he peered in.

Perfect. A closet space underneath some kind of machinery.

"Get the d-bomb in there," Stathis said.

"I thought you wanted to stick your pigsticker in Shroggath?" Hakala asked.

"I'm not stupid," Stathis said. "I want to, but realistically? I can't show up Sergeant Levin. He'd kick my ass, so I'm going to do this the smart way."

The mule with the d-bomb came forward, and Stathis, with Hakala's help, unstrapped it and pushed it into the closet.

Blazer fire slammed into the ceiling and walls nearby as Li and Chen fired at froggers Stathis couldn't see because the corridor was buckled and full of wreckage from collision damage.

He set the timer for five minutes and then pushed the door closed.

"We have four minutes to get to a safe distance," Stathis said.

"Fighting withdrawal."

"*Peska,*" Mikhailov muttered as he changed link and warned his people. *Who's he calling a pee-hole?*

"*I have remote control,*" Shrek said. "*We don't—*"

"*We do,*" Stathis said. "*I don't want to take any chances.*"

"*Aye,*" Shrek said as Corporal Kuznetsov ordered his team to attack in the opposite direction, back toward the hangar.

He thought of those thousands of froggers turning around. Was he becoming a coward? No. He was looking at the bigger picture. This wasn't supposed to be a suicide mission, and nobody would be coming to save him. McCarthy was over a hundred kilometers away, and the gunny and Skadi were light years away.

He couldn't let Mikhailov's squad go down with him on a suicide mission. They'd have to self-rescue, and Stathis had little confidence in that option. So, the next best thing was to hit and run.

A minute later, Kuznetsov and his team burst out of the hatch into the hangar. They were immediately met by gunfire, some blazers and some slug throwers.

Stathis came out of the hatch already firing, the SCBIs on Kuznetsov's team marking targets for Stathis and Hakala.

The link for Lance Corporal Kai, Kuznetsov's rifleman, flashed red, and the rest of the team doubled their rate of fire.

"We will cover you, Major," Kuznetsov said and motioned for Stathis to get back to the duct they'd come through.

Everything was happening quickly, and Stathis didn't waste time arguing as he propelled himself toward it, sailing through the zero gravity as blazer fire flashed by.

Hakala was right behind him, firing as she soared through the space like a heavily armed ballet dancer.

Grabbing the edge, Stathis took a position and began firing as Mikhailov and Chen's team crossed the space. He saw Chen holding onto Lebedev's body, easier to do in zero gravity.

Mikhailov sent Yue into the air duct to take point, and then Li.

"Go, Major," Mikhailov said. Stathis wanted to argue, but he doubted anyone else would go in unless he was ahead of them, and they'd be a nice, juicy target clustered around the air duct cover.

"Ladies first," Stathis said as Hakala slammed into the wall behind him like a gymnast, her rounds shredding a frogger that was coming out of a hatch as the magnets on her boots kept her from falling away.

Hakala followed Li into the duct, and Stathis followed her in.

"*Can the froggers intercept us?*" Stathis asked Shrek.

"*Not easily,*" Shrek said.

"*There's a few thousand of them.*"

"*Then move faster.*"

"*Shit.*"

Stathis had forgotten how long it took them to travel through the ducts. There was no way they were going to make it in time.

* * * * *

Chapter Forty-One: Rebel Data

Kapten Sif, VRAEC, Nakija Musta Toiminnot

Sif couldn't hope to keep up with the amount of data the Fallen were flooding them with. She had relayed Winter's request, and the flood gates had opened wide, as if the Voorga had been waiting for the question. The admiral was focused on not dragging the Seraphim Fleet into a suicide mission, which had worried Sif, but with all the data now being transmitted? Did the Voorga think the fleet was committed to helping them?

They were not asking for information, they were just giving, and that seemed odd. Were the Voorga that trusting, or had there been something in their discussion that made them think the humans were more committed to the rebel cause than they really were?

Closing her eyes and leaning back in her command couch, she relaxed her mind and body. There were other ways to determine the truth and intent of the Voorga besides analyzing the data. There were other lines of communication.

Communication with the fleet was now hours instead of days, and Sif was growing worried that the vanhat, Collective, or Immaculate military forces might find them. It was like there was an invisible timer counting down, and she couldn't see how much time they had.

Reaching out with her senses, she felt Thuthta waiting for her.

"*Will you help us?*" Thuthta asked, his need and sincerity pushing against Sif like a physical force.

"*Our senior commander is evaluating it,*" Sif said. She could not commit, and she needed Thuthta to understand.

"*The survival of both our species is at stake,*" Thuthta thought to her. "*If we cannot be allies, then we must be enemies.*"

That was ominous, and Sif held back her immediate Aesir response, which could have started a new war. She was also Musta Toiminnot, and violence was not always the answer.

"*How do we know you are telling the truth?*" Sif asked, dreading the question. Based on what she knew of the Voorga, it was a question fraught with a lot of emotion. To accuse someone of lying was an insult. She recalled a children's story they had sent called *Stepping Without Looking*, about a child who lied. It seemed odd to a human reading it, but on a high-gravity planet where every step could lead to a fatal fall, it was more understandable. To accuse someone of lying without knowing they were lying was an unforgivable and sometimes fatal crime in Voorga society.

It didn't help that they obviously had a different thought process.

"*That is for you to decide,*" Thuthta said, and Sif could taste the disappointment emanating from Thuthta through the psychic link, but there was something else.

"*It will take us time,*" Sif said. Perhaps she could use something from their culture. "*We must watch where we step.*"

"*Time is a resource that we are losing.*"

"*We understand,*" Sif said. What had she hoped to gain from this discussion? She could not fathom whether Thuthta was lying. It was unlikely, but still. She did not want to think the alien was, but the truth could be a fluid thing, interpreted differently by the parties involved.

One man's terrorist was another man's freedom fighter; a lot revolved around perception and bias. Thuthta did not think he was lying, as he struggled to help Sif and Britta understand, but the information he thought they should have might not be what was needed.

"*A storm is coming,*" Thuthta said, and Sif thought he meant on the planet. There had been a sandstorm a few days ago that had been fierce, but Thuthta continued, "*This will be a long storm, a violent one. Other devourers lurk in the chaos of the winds. They are coming and searching.*"

Now Sif felt what he was talking about. In the astral realms, there was turbulence, and Sif knew if she sank further into the psychic realms, she would feel it more intensely, like being in a house, on a link, and listening to the storm gathering strength outside.

"*The devourers are coming.*"

Sif felt the storm coming up from the depths of the astral realms. It was coming here, to this dimension, and the storm was looking for her. How soon before they arrived and found her? There were no easy answers.

* * * * *

Chapter Forty-Two: Darkness

Major Zale Stathis, USMC

Stathis had a hard time keeping up with Hakala, Li, and Yue crawling through the ducts. He wasn't sure how they managed, but behind him, the others kept up, even Chen carrying Lebedev, the mules clanking behind them all. This area had minimal gravity, but not a lot, or it would be even more difficult to crawl. Zero gravity would have been nice, maybe.

"*Can you give us a few more minutes?*" Stathis asked Shrek. They were nowhere near the minimum safe distance, and the timer was almost at zero.

"*I am unable to link to the bomb,*" Shrek said. "*Interference.*"

Stathis was both glad he'd been adamant about the five-minute timer and regretted it. It would have been bad to get this far and realize Shrek couldn't trigger it.

"Brace," Stathis said as the timer reached zero.

Pain exploded in his head as his electronics shut off. Stathis almost lost consciousness as every neuron in his body screamed in pain, but it ended quickly, and he felt he was falling. Zero gravity was absolute.

"*I hope Shroggath hurts more,*" Stathis said.

Shrek remained silent.

"*Shrek?*" Stathis asked as he manually raised his visor and reached for the suit reset switch. He hurt everywhere, and his limbs felt weighed down with lead. A nap would have been convenient about now.

Raising his visor didn't help. It was pitch dark in the duct, and there were no lights. His oxygen delivery mechanism was mechanical and would provide an hour of air before he suffocated.

It was pitch black, and his suit wasn't powering up.

Where was Shrek? Had the pulse knocked him out, too?

Reaching forward, he found Hakala's leg and shook it. A twitch told him she was alive, and Stathis tried to recall how far away from the exit they were. Four hundred? Five hundred meters? There were at least five branches, and Stathis couldn't remember which ones to take.

"*Shrek?*"

The silence bothered him. SCBIs were partially organic and should be able to survive an EMP burst.

"Stathis?" a voice said in front of him. Hakala?

"I feel like shit," Stathis said and then realized with just one visor up, she couldn't hear him. He opened his second visor, letting in the acrid, nasty-smelling air of the duct. Maybe suffocation would be preferable.

"I feel like shit," Stathis said when she could hear him.

"All my systems are dead," Hakala said. "Munin is also not responding."

Trapped in a maze they had to crawl through in the dark did not make Stathis feel any better. The gravity generators were offline, so it would be a little easier, but the air was probably not flowing either, and it would get very stale in the ducts. There were also a few thousand froggers in the vicinity.

That was a problem for thirty minutes from now. Struggling through the ducts without fresh air flowing would become a problem quickly, but not that quickly.

Stathis felt alone. Shrek wasn't responding, wasn't providing a map or advice. He'd be able to hassle Shrek about sleeping on the job. He didn't want to consider the alternative.

"The SCBIs require computational power and a very faint electric signal," Stathis said, hoping that was true. SCBIs did have an electronic component. What if the pulse had fried them? Was Shrek dead or just rendered silent? There was no SCBI reset button, though there was a place on his neck he could apply a low charge that might reboot the electronic systems, if they weren't fried. If they were, then Shrek's data stores would probably be fried. Could the organic parts of Shrek survive without the electronic parts?

He heard movement around him and then cursing in Russian and Chinese. The legionnaires were stirring.

Shrek couldn't be dead. He wanted to ask Shrek if there had been any studies or tests done with d-bombs and SCBIs.

But Shrek wasn't there.

"What if the SCBIs are dead?" Hakala asked, echoing his thoughts and forcing him to consider.

"How will we find our way out?" Mikhailov asked, and Stathis heard fear in their voices. Trapped in crawlspaces without knowing a safe way out was bad. Having lost his best and most trusted friend? That was worse. Stathis didn't think they would panic, but he felt the panic himself, threatening him. Shrek wasn't there to regulate his systems or keep him from panicking. It was hard to imagine life without

Shrek. Everyone else was used to navigating through life, through everything, without a SCBI, but Shrek had been a part of Stathis for so long.

They were afraid because they didn't have anyone who could show them the way out. Stathis was afraid because he was alone again. What would the gunny do? Probably lie is ass off. Morale could kill a military force as quickly as the enemy. He couldn't let them panic or lose control. The gunny wouldn't lose his shit, and he wouldn't let others. He'd tell whatever lies it took to get people to keep going.

"The old-fashioned way," Stathis said, trying to channel the gunny.

"If you think we're bad off, the froggers are probably worse."

"But, Major, without our SCBIs—"

"We were born without them," Stathis said. "We survived for a long time without them. Didn't I tell you that you need to learn to think for yourself?"

Hadn't he said that? Complained to him that he was letting the SCBI do all his thinking for him? Had Stathis done that, too?

Shrek had to be okay, just trapped and unable to talk. There were facilities back at Valhöll, and Shrek could be repaired.

"Yes, sir," Mikhailov said, and Stathis heard a *but* there.

"Think of this as an exercise in thinking on your own," Stathis said for everyone's benefit. "Can't rely on the SCBIs for everything. They'll be okay. Just the electronic link between them and you is broken."

Stathis hoped. Could any SCBI ever replace Shrek?

If Shrek was alive, he was likely lost in the darkness. Alone, no senses. It would have to be hell.

He couldn't think of that right now. They could fix things when they got to Valhöll. Shrek would just have to tough it out. He was a Marine, too.

The zero gravity made Stathis want to puke, but he couldn't do that now. First off, he needed the nutrients. Second, he didn't want the legionnaires to laugh at him for puking.

"Which way do we go?" Li asked from the darkness. Stathis tried to remember the maze. He'd seen a three-dimensional representation of the ducts, but he hadn't memorized it.

"Forward," Stathis said, "toward the sound of the gunfire."

Which was probably the stupidest thing to say right now. There was no gunfire, and they were in no condition to fight.

"Our weapons don't work," Yue said.

"We have KA-BARs, knives, and the rifles work as clubs," Stathis said. "We're Wolf Legion. We're extra dangerous even without weapons. This is just another challenge for us to overcome. Think of the stories we'll be able to tell. The chicks will love it."

"I don't love it," Hakala said, deadpan.

Stathis wasn't sure what to say about that.

"However, when we survive this, we will have proven ourselves," she said.

Proven to whom? Stathis wanted to ask, but realized she was on his side, understanding that he was lying, trying to keep morale up.

"I always wanted to kill froggers with my KA-BAR," Stathis said.

"In the ODTs, we were taught to never bring a knife to a gunfight."

"You guys never heard of the Gurkhas. They brought knives to gunfights all the time. Nobody messed with the Gurkhas, super tough dudes who liked knives," Stathis said. "Since I don't see any Gurkhas around anymore, I think we're going to have to do them proud."

"The Gurkhas took on rifle-armed enemies with knives?" Mikhailov asked skeptically.

"Yep," Stathis said. "Of course, it wasn't their preferred method, but there was only one thing fiercer than a Gurkha coming at you with his knife."

"What was that?" Hakala asked, sounding interested.

"A US Marine coming at you with his brothers and sisters at his back," Stathis said. "Now we have the Legion, and it's time to teach these vanhat buggers what fear is all about."

Maybe that was a little over the top?

"But first we have to find them," Stathis said. "Then we can slice and dice our way back to Valhöll."

"Frog legs are back on the menu, boys," Kuznetsov said, maybe unaware that Stathis could hear him.

"What do they taste like?" Li asked.

"Like chicken," Stathis said.

"What does chicken taste like?" Li asked.

Stathis didn't have an answer for that. SOG rations were bland and claimed to be vegan. Didn't they eat any meat? It was on the menus, but as he thought about it, he'd never heard them talk about eating meat. At least they were stepping back from the edge of panic.

He was about to ask Shrek about it when he remembered.

"You'll find out," Stathis said, steel finding its way into his voice as he thought of Shrek. "First, we need to get back to Valhöll. We have a long, uh, crawl back."

"Wilco," Mikhailov said. "Li, Yue, move out. Your fat asses are annoying me. Don't you dare fart."

Could Mikhailov see them?

"First, let's tie ourselves together," Stathis said. In the dark, it would be easy for the column to get separated when one part took one direction. Stathis remembered during jungle patrols back on Earth how easy it was for a column to become separated when a person wasn't paying attention to the people in front. They all had 1050 cord that could be used, and that should be strong enough to keep them from drifting away. Stathis was pretty sure Chen still had Lebedev's body. He remembered Kai's body behind them and felt guilty.

"Wilco," Mikhailov said, sounding more like an NCO in command. Stathis didn't hear the fear there and hoped it was gone from his voice.

"On a side note," Stathis said, "if our pew-pews don't work, neither will the froggers', and we're much bigger and stronger than them. I also don't recall them being armed with slug throwers that can pierce our armor."

"Can they see in the dark?" someone asked.

"Probably not," Stathis said. They had four eyes. Hopefully not. "Maybe. Doesn't matter, we can kill them in the dark as easily as in the light."

A stupid lie, but gung-ho enough. Would the gunny say stupid shit like that? Probably not. Hakala should have stayed at Valhöll. He didn't like the direction this mission had gone in.

"Now, if you don't mind, I need a warm shower and a change of clothes," Stathis said. "Move out."

The crawling began, and Stathis struggled to keep the fear at bay. Who was going to tell him everything was okay when he knew it wouldn't be?

* * * * *

Chapter Forty-Three: Voorga Crypts

Admiral Diamond Winters, USMC

Everyone was leaving the conference room, but Winters didn't have a good answer. They hadn't been able to convince her either way. No matter what excuses she made, the final decision would be hers and hers alone. There was a weakness in every argument. The cold, hard fact was that she didn't have enough information. The Voorga were doing their best to provide information, and while the fleets defending the tombs didn't seem excessive, she had no real way to know if the reports were real. In reality, the rebels might not have the right information, or their reports could be so old as to be worthless. Nothing in the data provided showed how old the information was, and when asked, the Voorga said it was current.

Bonnie paused before leaving and turned back to Winters. She was the last one out, and the door slid shut behind Admiral Sakamoto, leaving them alone.

"What will you do?" Bonnie asked.

"I'm not sure," Winters said. She wanted to snap at Bonnie. If she knew, she would have told people. Right now, the standing order was to gather more information and plan a recon of the Voorga home world where the tomb was. What else could they do?

"I cannot imagine the pressure you are under," Bonnie said, standing there, poised as if to flee. "We have so little information, and the information we have is not something we can trust, yet."

"It's called the fog of war," Winters said. Bonnie must have a point. Right?

"We are at war with the vanhat," Bonnie said needlessly. "I will not pretend to understand that like you and the others, but is there a time we stop running and hiding?"

Winters looked at Bonnie more closely. What had prompted that question?

"Explain," Winters said.

Now Bonnie looked unsure.

"I speak with Sylphara, my spirit guide, constantly," Bonnie said. "I press her to understand what the battle was like before the tomb worlds became what they were."

"And?"

"Sylphara says her makers were constantly on the defensive, always struggling to establish a line, a perimeter to hold the vanhat back while they recovered. They kept looking for a chance to turn around and fight back. They never got the chance. They could not build a fortress strong enough to withstand the devourers."

Winter grimaced. That wasn't what she wanted to hear, but it was what she expected.

"Like ants against a hurricane," Bonnie added.

Winters raised an eyebrow, encouraging Bonnie to continue. Was she complaining? Looking for reassurance? Did she have an idea? Winters didn't like the analogy, but she had to admit, it sounded pretty apt.

"Do we have a chance?" Bonnie asked when Winters didn't say anything.

Marine Corps lore and history whispered in the back of her mind. The warrior ethos was strong in the Marines, and Winters knew the odds were against humanity.

"The makers of your spirit guide failed," Winters said. "They couldn't stand against the storm. I don't know if we can, or if we'll end up as dust in the history of this galaxy. The angels we're searching for may help us to fight, to become a safe harbor in this storm, or not. I don't know if the aliens from the tomb worlds had a warrior ethos, nor do I particularly care. They failed and fled, surrendering their home to the vanhat."

"What else could they have done?" Bonnie asked. "They did not stand a chance."

Winters looked more closely at Bonnie.

"They failed. I don't know the details, but you say they became focused on building a fortress where they'd be safe?"

Bonnie nodded.

"That was their failure," Winters said.

"Failure?"

"Life isn't about being safe," Winters said. "We want that, yes, but life is a struggle for survival. We must constantly push forward, constantly work to improve our lives and ourselves. When we sit back and try to be safe, to live in our comfort zone, we die."

"I do not understand," Bonnie said as Winters realized she was giving her the answer to the problem that she needed.

"We'll always struggle," Winters said, "in everything we do. The breath you take isn't free. Your lungs must work for it; the oxygen pulled into the lungs must be converted so your body can use it. You can't hold your breath for long; if you do, you die."

"We are facing the vanhat," Bonnie said, "not trying to breathe."

"What's life without trials and tribulations? When we stop fighting, when we stop struggling to excel, it's time to die."

"We are outnumbered. We cannot fight the vanhat. There are too many."

"That's where you're wrong," Winters said. "So very wrong. We may be outnumbered, but that's nothing new for Marines. I think we do better when the odds are against us. We're always outnumbered, sometimes outgunned."

"I do not understand," Bonnie said, and Winters smiled as she thought about it. There were parallels.

"The United States Marine Corps has history. In our song, there's a line, 'to the shores of Tripoli.' It talks about eight Marines, led by Lieutenant Presley O'Bannon. They marched over five hundred miles through a desert to attack some thug of a Sultan named Yusef, who'd been taking Americans as slaves or hostages. America got fed up with their bullshit and sent the Marines. Eight Marines against thousands of Islamic pirates."

"What happened?"

"The Marines kicked ass and took names. Legends say O'Bannon was presented with a Mameluke sword by Hammet, and now that style of sword is carried by Marine officers."

"Eight marines against thousands? How is that possible?"

"The Marines hired mercenaries," Winters said. "I'd like to say they did it alone, but humans have a long history. The three hundred Spartans who held the pass at Thermopylae are another example. Not Marines, but a smaller force that held off a much larger force.

"Here's the important thing to remember. Yes, it was only eight Marines and a few hundred mercenaries, but they only talked of the Marines. At Thermopylae, they only talk of the three hundred Spartans, but there were almost seven thousand other Greek soldiers, originally, then after a bunch of crap, it was only three hundred Spartans and seven hundred Thespians, maybe about nine hundred helots, and four hundred Thebans, but the stories don't talk about the mercs, or the other Greeks. Stories speak of the few, the proud, the warriors who held the line, reinforcing it with their blood and tears."

"So, we can defend?"

"Not Marines," Winters said. "We attack. The battle of Tarawa is another example. Japanese troops outnumbered Marine attackers two to one. They were entrenched in well-built bunkers, and there was only a narrow beachhead. In seventy-six hours, US Marines did what the Japanese didn't think possible. At the Chosin Reservoir, a single Marine division was surrounded by several Chinese divisions. The Marines decided they didn't want to play in the cold and left, completely wiping out at least one Chinese division. The Marines departed the battlefield intact as a fighting force; the Chinese did not. Time and again, the Marines go into bad situations and come out victorious."

"Are there ever times Marines go into bad situations and do not come out victorious?" Bonnie asked.

Winters gave Bonnie a predatory smile.

"Sure," Winters said. "I can't name any, though. The point is this. Humanity, especially the Marines, has a history of facing the odds and being victorious. Can the makers of your spirit guide say the same?"

Bonnie looked at Winters, perhaps talking to her alien SCBI.

"They have won battles against the odds," Bonnie said cautiously, "but not on the scale of US Marines."

"There you have it," Winters said. "Now I have my answer."

"Your answer?"

"We attack. Marines don't skulk and hide. We act."

Bonnie stared at Winters.

"*Give the order,*" Winters told Blitzen. "*We're going on the offensive. Let's see what is in those Voorga crypts.*"

* * * * *

Chapter Forty-Four: Frogger Brawl

Major Zale Stathis, USMC

It had to have been hours, and Stathis was pretty sure they were lost and would never find their way out of the air ducts. Without light, without gravity, without so much as a compass, they could be travelling in circles. Twice, they'd taken a wrong turn and ended up in a dead end where a collapse or some damage had closed the duct. That was when the air got stale, and Stathis was worried they'd suffocate. He'd ordered everyone to preserve their suit air, and regretted it ever since, because so many people in such a small, enclosed area generated a lot of heat, sweat, and bad breath, plus the suit smells escaped the open visor. You didn't notice your own stench, but it was hard to ignore the others' odors.

There were exercises they could do to charge the batteries and jumpstart the system, but it wasn't possible to do most of those exercises in the cramped confines of an air duct. They were still probably building up a charge, but nobody's suit had rebooted yet.

Without gravity, there was no danger of falling down a shaft, but it really messed with people's sense of direction, since they felt like they were always falling. Too many of the pressure doors had closed and had to be manually reopened, which took time and allowed the bad air to percolate.

Someone needed to change their diet. Those farts were nasty.

"I've got power," Li said, which raised Stathis's hopes. The suits could generate power when the wearer was active, and Stathis had been worried that function was broken. Why they'd been hit so hard by the pulse, Stathis didn't know. Being in a small, enclosed pipe? Did something in the asteroid's hull magnify things?

Without Shrek to give him a clue, he had no idea. Stathis didn't like being alone in his own head anymore.

"Just made 0.5 percent," Li said.

"Great," Stathis said. "That gives the rest of us hope."

Moving through the ducts let people coast with minimum movement.

A red light flickered in front of Stathis, and it raised his spirits a bit more than it should have. It was an emergency suit marker.

"Maybe we should stop and do some calisthenics?" Mikhailov said. "See who else can get their suits powered up?"

"No," Stathis said. "We have to keep moving. If we stop to do exercises, we're going to end up suffocating. There are too many of us."

"Wilco, Major," Mikhailov said, but he didn't sound angry.

"Now, keep moving. Lance Corporal Li, when you get your power up to 5 percent, we might try jumpstarting someone else, and then keep it going."

"Wilco, sir," Li said.

But nobody reported that their SCBI was back. The SCBIs should have come online before the suits. Right?

"Exit panel," Li reported minutes later. More good news. They could get out of the damn ducts. Having no gravity was something of a blessing. He was sure if there had been gravity, they would have needed more rest stops, and his knees and hands would be scraped raw by now. The nausea, stench, and sense of falling he could mostly ignore. Now, though, he was making more effort to pump his arms and legs as he followed Li's feeble light, which turned everything red and sinister. But light was better than the darkness.

"Looks clear," Li said.

"Let's get out of here and find out where we are," Stathis said.

Within minutes, everyone was out of the duct, hands resting on knives. It looked like this was a tram station.

"Any directions anywhere?"

"Directions?" Hakala asked.

"A map? Don't they usually have maps at tram stations? A kind of 'you are here, and the tram will be here every twenty minutes on weekdays?'"

"How archaic," Hakala said, "but no. For security reasons, and because everyone has cybernetic implants that can interface with local systems."

"What do they do when the network is down?"

"They likely have the data stored in their buffers."

There were numbers on the wall, barely visible in Li's feeble light. Some of the other legionnaires were holding onto things and exercising. It wasn't easy to do in zero gravity.

That was another serious problem. Without power, without cybernetics, the electromagnets in their suits didn't trigger, and they just floated around until they grabbed something. Not even manual controls worked, though Li was able to clamp onto something with his suit. Being in space without power sucked in so many ways.

"Hurrah, hurrah, hurrah," Chen said, and he turned on his red emergency light. That encouraged others to exercise even harder.

"Batteries are completely drained," Li reported. "Still no diagnostics on my rifle."

"Keep working at it," Stathis said, starting his own exercises.

"I'm at 4 percent," Li said. "Want me to try a jumpstart on your suit, Major?"

"No, suckup," Stathis said, making sure Li could see his smile. "I'm getting fat and need exercise."

"Fat?" Hakala asked as she exercised. "Where?"

"Um," Stathis said, trying to think of a response. He wasn't used to having a woman around. He should be used to it, but Hakala? She wasn't just one of the guys, and suddenly making a dick joke didn't seem appropriate. Plus, they could hear him.

"Power," Mikhailov said with satisfaction. Others began to work harder, including Stathis.

He had half a mind to form everyone up into a formation and begin calisthenics, but that was something a boot lieutenant would do.

"Maintain 360 security," Stathis said instead. "Just because our blazers don't work doesn't mean the frogger weapons don't. Their slug throwers aren't electronic and are sure to work. A bullet to the face won't be stopped by armor."

"Wilco," the troopers answered as they turned toward the entrances.

That was the only thing that saved them, as a swarm of froggers poured out of a nearby doorway. The first one saw the legionnaires and scream-hissed. The fight was on.

Li was the first one to slam into them, his bayonet flashing, and Stathis hooked his foot on a waste receptacle protected by a bar.

His KA-BAR ready, Stathis watched around as other legionnaires slammed into the froggers, blades slashing, fists striking.

None of the froggers were armed with rifles, though several had magazine pouches, and they seemed kill-crazed. He hadn't noticed how sharp and razorlike their teeth were before, or that their hands appeared to be clawed. They flew through the zero gravity like leaping frogs of death. One or two did have rifles, but they were holding them like clubs.

One-on-one, they were no match for an armored legionnaire, even one burdened by unpowered armor, but the odds were four or five to one.

The melee quickly became chaotic, and Stathis lost sight of the others in the thrashing limbs and spraying blood.

"Stay close to each other!" Stathis yelled. He wanted to tell them to form a shield wall, a phalanx, or something. Modern troops didn't fight like this. Well, now they did. They were trained in close quarters and unarmed combat, but not a melee like this. "Maintain contact; don't let your buddies drift."

Damned hard to do, with the magnets not working, but Stathis could see the froggers swarming a legionnaire who couldn't grab anything other than a frogger.

One of the froggers swung a rifle at Stathis. A stupid move. Stathis caught it in his hand, the impact stinging a little, but the frogger lacked the leverage to make it really hurt in zero gravity. Holding the rifle, Stathis pulled the frogger close, and using his grip on the rifle to keep the frogger steady, he slammed his KA-BAR up into the ribs near where the heart should be.

Flesh and bone parted for his KA-BAR, and he pulled back to stab again, but the frogger let go of the rifle and was propelled away, though not quickly enough to keep Stathis from letting go of the rifle and grabbing it by its magazine harness. It couldn't escape, so he stabbed it a couple more times.

Another one came at him, and unable to dodge, the four-eyed creature slammed into his KA-BAR. Reaching out with his other hand, Stathis grabbed a legionnaire who'd lost contact with the surface and was drifting away. He pulled the legionnaire close as the man latched onto the bar that Stathis had his foot hooked under.

Another frogger threw itself at Stathis. He kept looking for a targeting link, a threat analysis, or something to help him make sense of the chaos, but Shrek remained silent or dead.

With his visor up, the spray of blood almost blinded him, and the smells now assaulting the station made Stathis want to vomit. The screams, grunts, shouts, and hissing were almost deafening, even without the sound of weapons fire. The legionnaires were getting separated in the chaos.

How did the Romans and Spartans fight?

"Rally on me!" Stathis yelled. "Form a line."

The second he said it, he realized how stupid it was. This was three-dimensional, zero-gravity combat. Romans and Spartans had never fought in these conditions. A wall might make sense, but not a line.

"Platoon," Stathis said, forgetting it was just a squad, "listen to my command. Form on me."

Someone, or something, slammed into his back, and he looked back to see a legionnaire who'd lost control and come at him too hard, not a frogger. The trooper grabbed Stathis' drag harness without shame and hooked his foot under the same bar Stathis had.

Another trooper began to fly past, toward the froggers coming through the hatch, but Stathis grabbed him. It was Li, and the second he got a foot down, he triggered his electromagnets, locking him to the floor.

Hakala slammed to the ground beside Stathis and began to rebound before Stathis caught her. A move that would have been graceful, had the magnets on her boots caught the floor.

"*Paska,*" Hakala said. "I hate not having magnets."

A frogger flew at Stathis, and he grabbed it by its throat instead of the tonsils. Its mouth was wide open, hissing and revealing nasty, sharp teeth. Dumb, blind luck that he hadn't stuck his hand down the throat. He slammed his KA-BAR into its chest, punching through flesh and bone. In unpowered armor, he was surprised that the bones gave way to his KA-BAR. More cartilage than bone?

Other legionnaires slammed into the group, and Stathis, Li, or Hakala grabbed them as they arrived, and they were pulled in. One trooper had his foot hooked in Li's harness.

The froggers kept coming at them, but they were throwing themselves onto a porcupine composed of knife-wielding legionnaires. One legionnaire would grab the frogger, and another would stab it, then throw away the corpse.

Several times, Stathis glanced toward his casualty counter, but it remained blank and unpowered. It was like a bad dream, fighting without Shrek to provide guidance and help with threat analysis.

As quickly as it started, it ended. Specks of blood and gore floated through the station with the bodies.

"Ammo, casualty report," Stathis said automatically and looked around, trying to evaluate the situation. His displays remained dark. *Do people still remember how to do things like that?*

It was hard to make sense of the legionnaires, a mass of bodies connected in some way to each other, with foot or hand hooked in each other's harnesses, and Mikhailov, Li, and Stathis providing something to latch onto.

Hakala was okay, and in the dim, blood-red lights of the suit markers, it looked like she was smiling.

"No ammo used, no serious casualties," Mikhailov reported to Stathis' surprise a moment later.

Stathis almost said, *Really?* but caught himself in time.

"Good job," Stathis said instead and sheathed his bloody KA-BAR. It would be a bitch to clean later, but with all the gore floating around, there wasn't any way to clean it. Thankfully, most of the gore was floating away from the legionnaires. "We need to get out of here in case more come."

There were thirty or forty froggers, Stathis estimated, hard to do, though. It wasn't like Shrek could give him a more accurate number.

"Wilco," Mikhailov said.

"These are slug-throwers," Hakala said, looking at one of the rifles. A Republic infantry rifle. "Old-fashioned, but usable."

"Why didn't they use them, ma'am?" Mikhailov asked, snatching one from nearby.

Hakala fired a round at a body, the recoil pushing her back.

"Well," she began, "in zero gravity, they might be difficult to control, but they did not show much intelligence. Did you see how they tried to swim?"

Maybe they'd been trying to swim, waving their arms frantically, but wouldn't that work? It had, a little, but not enough.

"Swim?" Mikhailov asked.

"With their Jotun gone, they may have reverted to a more primitive mindset."

Sure. That made sense to Stathis.

"Collect rifles and magazines," Stathis said. "Give them to Li and Mikhailov."

They could brace themselves and use the rifles more effectively. It was a good thing the froggers had forgotten how to use them. How long would that last?

"Hey, I got power," Chen said, and Yue echoed him.

Stathis checked his system. Dammit. He might have to get one of them to give him a jumpstart.

Later.

"Great," Stathis said, doing a set of squats. "Let's get ready to move out."

"Which way, sir?" Mikhailov asked.

Stathis listened for Shrek to give directions for a second. How was he to know?

The gunny had once said to be decisive and make a decision. Even a wrong decision, if decisive enough, was usually much better than nothing.

"That way," Stathis said, trying to sound confident and sure.

Fake it until you make it. Did all majors struggle like that?

Probably not. What was the worst thing that could happen? He'd get demoted, passed over for promotion, or sent to the brig. The brig would be nice. Food, sleep, and not getting shot at. No. The worst that could happen would be losing people. He wasn't a private, and he was responsible for the lives of others.

Being an officer sucked.

Without Shrek, Stathis felt out of his league, but he couldn't let the others down. Without Shrek, he was just a private going through the motions, but he didn't want to disappoint Hakala. He especially didn't want to lose his best friend, who had his back every second of every day.

Shrek couldn't be gone. Could he?

* * * * *

Chapter Forty-Five: Marines

Kapten Sif, VRAEC, Nakija Musta Toiminnot

Returning to her body, Sif took a deep breath. A transition alarm sounded, and Sif silenced it. The *Musashi* had arrived.

Which meant what?

"We're going to help the rebels," Winters said on a link that Sif saw included her and Britta.

"Why?" Sif asked.

"I had someone remind me of Lieutenant Pressley O'Bannon."

"Who?"

"He was a Marine officer who, with seven other Marines, marched hundreds of miles through the desert to depose an Islamic thug pirate who was taking Americans as slaves."

"What does that have to do with the Voorga?" Sif asked.

"I can't predict the future," Winters said, "but I can damn well help shape it. We need allies, so we're going to make the Voorga our allies, and we must show loyalty to earn loyalty. One way or another. Like Lieutenant O'Bannon, and that Army guy, Eaton. They changed the future of the world by doing what others thought was impossible."

"They turned the pirates into allies?" Sif asked.

"Not completely," Winters said, "but they put the United States and the United States Marines in the history books and altered the course of numerous nations by their actions. They didn't sit back and whine about things or wait for others to take action. They acted. We need allies? We're going to get them, one way or another."

"Zen," Sif said, not sure about Winters or her intent, but she was committing, sounding more like the gunny or Stathis. What was it with Marines? They could be decisive. They had goals, a mission, and nothing would get in their way.

Sif brought up the history and skimmed it quickly. So few had accomplished so much, perhaps changing the world in ways few understood. What made Marines so different? She filed it away to review their indoctrination, training, and history later.

Admiral Winters had a lot in common with those ancient heroes. She knew the odds were against her; she knew that usually did not work out, but she had enough inspiration to drive her.

Sif could understand what the admiral was thinking. The admiral had to know that winning against the odds was the exception and not the rule, right? History did not talk about those who faced greater odds and failed. There were many more examples of that, examples nobody spoke about because they were common.

Admiral Winters understood that. Right?

* * * * *

Chapter Forty-Six: Stathis is Gone

Lieutenant Aod McCarthy, Wolf Legion

McCarthy couldn't believe it. They couldn't be dead, but if they'd survived, they would've answered by now. Too much time had passed for them to just be busy. Their SCBIs should have provided an update at the very least.

Major Stathis was supposed to be indestructible, and Hakala was with him. If they were both gone, that would leave him in charge, and he wasn't ready to command something the size of Bifrost.

"More damage," Quinn said. He'd managed to get a Republic external maintenance drone launched to survey the *Draugskepp*. "Weird, according to Bran."

"SCBIs don't use words like weird," McCarthy said, though he wondered if they did. Enigma couldn't tell him anything, and Bran must be Quinn's SCBI.

"Yeah, well, that's what he means, sir," Quinn said. He wasn't stumbling on the "sir" like he used to. Once or twice, he'd accidentally called McCarthy "Sergeant." Old habits die hard, but McCarthy liked being a lieutenant. Mostly.

"Be more descriptive," McCarthy said.

A viewscreen appeared and showed the drone's view.

"That is weird," McCarthy said. Purple waves rippled along the surface of the *Draugskepp*. Many places look melted, with numerous bulges like bubbles about to pop. The hull had certainly changed.

"What could cause that?"

"D-bomb," Quinn said, but he didn't sound so sure. "Though I thought they were supposed to be more like an EMP pulse than a physical thing. The major's bomb wasn't nuke-pumped, and the explosive charge wasn't big enough to do that. Bran's running some simulations, getting interesting data, and thinks the Bifrost nickel asteroid hull might have some kind of magnification effect, or mirror effect. Bran seems fascinated by it."

"*Enigma?*" McCarthy asked his alien ghost.

"*Your dimensional disruption device, or d-bomb as you like to call it, was certainly influenced by the nickel composition of this asteroid city ship. The waves of color and the deformation of the ship indicate a non-standard interaction. Based on present data, I would not say the pulse was magnified or mirrored by the hull, but more likely changed, like a lens might change a ray of light. The hull of Bifrost with the chemical composition may have acted like a shaped charge that focused most of the blast back at* Draugskepp."

"*Killing anyone caught in the blast?*"

"*Those relying on cross-dimensional energy, for sure,*" Enigma said. "*Dimensional natives? I do not know. During our war, we noticed that such weapons and their effects were changed by the presence of some materials, but usually it took a very large mass of such materials, and it was never practical to investigate. My creators did not fight many battles among asteroids.*"

"*Are Major Stathis and his patrol dead?*" McCarthy asked. He didn't care about science so much. He wanted to know if he should mount a rescue mission, and if not, how badly the situation had gone sideways.

"I cannot say," Enigma said. "Much would depend on how far the blast radius extended and the exact alteration of the detonation."

"That's not helping," McCarthy said. They'd lost contact with the major as they were crawling through the tunnels. Enigma would have that data and other sensors. But if Enigma couldn't find them?

"Based on data available to me," Enigma said, "I do not think they survived. If they did, they would be completely without power. Their electronics, maybe even their implanted intelligences, are likely to have sustained serious damage. If any of the devourer shards survived, they are likely feral and psychotic. The shards may turn on each other, but they are just as likely to form tribes and begin hunting. Your major and any other survivors would be considered prey, food, or trespassers. Without advanced weapons and armor, they will be at a serious disadvantage. Furthermore, gravity systems appear to have failed in that area. There are no working network links into Mjölnir Port. It is now a dead zone."

"Bran isn't saying good things about their chances," Quinn said solemnly. "If they survived, they should have rebooted their systems and linked in."

"The major is too tough to be killed by this," McCarthy said with a confidence he wasn't feeling anymore. "Let's see if we can send drones out from Valhöll."

The attacks against the hydroponics alue and Valhöll had ended with the detonation, and the attackers that hadn't wandered into warbot or pop-down turret fire had fled. Everything seemed secure at the moment.

Even the cyborgs had retreated, which didn't make sense. Were they allied with Shroggath, perhaps?

All the fronts were quiet. For now.

"It's always darkest before the storm," Quinn muttered.

"You mean nightfall," Moore said.

"That, too."

"Might be a storm, but it ain't nightfall," McCarthy said. "It ain't over until the old man calls the name, or the last bell rings. Enough gloom and doom. We need to find out what happened."

"Warden Kaelan is linking, demanding to speak to Lieutenant Hakala or the major," Moore said. "Am I the only one who thinks of a prison warden?"

"Tell him they're busy and ask the bugger to wait. Let him listen to some bad music while he does. I don't want to deal with that backstabbing coward."

"He's very insistent," Moore said.

"Be more insistent. He's the least of our worries right now."

"Wilco."

"Get some drones sent out from Valhöll. I want some more solid information. If Stathis and the others are dead, I need confirmation. The Wolf Legion doesn't leave our own behind."

"Wilco," Quinn said. "I did send out a drone to check on the froggers that were attacking, following one group. They tried attacking the drone, but they're not using their rifles."

"What?" McCarthy asked. Why wouldn't they use their rifles?

"If they've devolved with the loss of their archetype, they may lack the higher brain function and memory of their advanced weapons. They've become primitive without the guidance and control of their archetype. This is likely to continue until they enter the orbit of another primal archetype that can absorb them."

"Small blessings," McCarthy said. But that didn't mean there weren't others. The spiders and the cyborgs were out there, though the cyborgs didn't seem the type to collect more shards. McCarthy didn't want to think about the spiders. If the froggers changed into spiders? That was a nightmare. Carnivorous, psychotic, four-eyed frog men haunting the countless kilometers of tunnels was bad, but spiders would be so much worse.

"Now we hurry up and wait," McCarthy said.

"Wait for something else to go wrong," Quinn said.

"That's life," McCarthy said. "In combat, things go wrong very quickly and violently. Outside the Legion? Things could go wrong in different ways."

"Life sucks," Quinn said.

"Better than the alternative," Moore added.

"Maybe."

"Regardless of profession, things will eventually go wrong enough to kill you," McCarthy said. "In the Legion, or out."

"Would it hurt to have a happy ending?" Quinn said.

"You've had a few of those, buddy," Moore said, the innuendo implied.

"There could never be a really happy ending," McCarthy said, but he didn't want to hurt morale, so he fell silent. His two team leaders knew him too well, though.

"Sure," Quinn said. "We all die in the end. But we can have fun in the process."

"What could be more fun than sitting here in some fancy command center, drinking tea?" Moore asked.

"You could saddle your team up for a ruck march," McCarthy suggested.

"And leave my comfortable chair, sir? My tea would get cold."

"We need to find out what happened to our major and his girlfriend," McCarthy said. "I need to know whether I have to take command of this dog pile, or if I can continue living in bliss."

Maybe he shouldn't have called Hakala the major's girlfriend, but everyone knew.

"Wilco," his two team leaders echoed.

"What's the network like?" McCarthy asked.

"No influence," Quinn said. "Bran isn't seeing any sign of Shroggath anymore, no searches or trackers. Though, to be fair, a lot of systems are offline, and that surge caused damage. It'll take time to figure things out and fix them."

"Good. See if Bran and the others can get control of the ship."

McCarthy didn't know how he felt about that. What was he going to do with control of a massive city-ship full of monsters, dictators, and ghosts?

* * * * *

Chapter Forty-Seven: Shrek

Major Zale Stathis, USMC

It was hard not to worry about Shrek. His absence made him realize how dependent he'd become, for everything from an alarm clock to an early warning system.

Now the suits had power, but the computer systems and data retrieval were offline, maybe permanently, and diagnostics were sketchy. Without SCBIs, they couldn't access any information or the programming of the suits, which meant the links to the Aesir communicators were worthless, because nobody knew where the nodes were located or how to link their systems. Not even Hakala knew how to do that without her cybernetics.

A very serious flaw, but then who would've suspected that humans would survive without their cybernetics or SCBIs? Statistically? Shrek would have told him some numbers that Stathis didn't care enough to understand. Now, there was only silence.

With power restored, they were also able to power up their blazers, and they were no longer unarmed. Thankfully, they still worked. A miracle, considering.

The darkness of the corridors didn't end, though.

The patrol was resting at a tram station, and Stathis was moving around, checking on the men, trying to evaluate morale and status.

With power back on, they seemed to be a little better, though everyone seemed to notice the loss of their SCBIs.

"How are you doing?" Hakala asked when he sat down beside her.

"I could use some chocolate cake about now," Stathis said, "with sprinkles. Chocolate sprinkles. You can never have enough chocolate."

Hakala had her visor up, and Stathis could appreciate her smile.

"You do not seem phased by this," Hakala said.

"I'm plenty phased by it," Stathis said. "It was nice, having drones out, knowing what to expect, where everyone was, what everyone was doing, how much ammo everyone had, what everyone's field of fire was, making sure we had 360-degree security. I have to do all that stuff manually now, and it sucks. Shrek made it easy to be a slacker."

"You were not a slacker," Hakala said, "just more efficient."

Stathis didn't want to argue. He wanted Shrek back. Without Shrek, he had to spend more time thinking for himself.

"We will get through this," Hakala said. "The organic part of the SCBIs is fed by your body, like the rest of you. That part is where their personality is."

"But if our SCBIs are alive, they're cut off, no interaction, no input or output," Stathis said. "Trapped in a world of darkness, alone, with no concept of time. They could be going insane."

"They are SCBIs, not humans," Hakala said.

"Shrek is human enough."

"But they are not," Hakala said. "They are very different. I am not saying you are wrong; I am saying we do not know. Are they really alive, though?"

Stathis didn't know what to say. Of course, Shrek was. Shrek had spent hundreds of years keeping him alive in stasis. What was being alive, anyway? She had to be saying that to make him feel better. It was the wrong thing to say, though telling her that didn't seem very politic.

"Any idea where we are?" Stathis asked to change the subject.

"Blood runs downhill," Hakala said.

"Huh?"

"A saying I think I have heard, all roads lead to Rome? This is Bifrost. If we follow the roads long enough, we will end up somewhere important."

"What if we're going in the wrong direction, like away from Valhöll? Then we have to turn around and walk for days in the other direction."

"Then you will be blamed for your poor navigational skills," Hakala said with a smile.

"I'm a major, not a boot lieutenant. We're supposed to be smarter than that."

"Should we wait here until we know?"

Shrek would know, but Stathis knew how impractical it was. Hakala was right. They had to pick a direction and go. Unfortunately, there was no sun, no gravity, no wind, nothing to help identify which way was toward the bow or aft of Bifrost.

On a US Navy ship, there were numbers that told you where you were, the port or starboard side, toward the front or back of the boat, and which floor you were on. Obviously, the Republic didn't feel the need to bother with such useful markings. Probably disrupted the aesthetics. Or they'd need a lot of paint. Was the Republic so cheap that they didn't want to paint anything?

"Lost in space," Stathis said.

"Lost in space, in a haunted city-ship, hunted by monsters, Major," Mikhailov said. "It could be worse. We aren't in combat."

"I really miss pizza," Stathis said.

Hakala and Mikhailov both looked at Stathis.

"There was one time we were in the field at Camp Lejeune, back in the USA. We didn't have enough MREs, a supply SNAFU, so our squad leader ordered pizza and had it delivered to grid coordinates on the road. The delivery driver was an off-duty Marine. I didn't know they did that, but we didn't starve. We didn't have water to wash our hands, but it was still good pizza. It didn't constipate us like MREs did, and that became a problem later."

"And this is relevant to our situation, how?" Hakala asked.

"I dunno," Stathis said, "but wouldn't it be nice to order a pizza and ask the delivery driver where we are?"

Nobody told him to shut up; they just stared at him like he was crazy or going to make a point. He missed the gunny. Shrek might have told him to shut up, too.

"Either way," Stathis said, "we need to self-rescue. Nobody's bringing us pizza. We aren't getting anywhere by sitting here, getting fat. Move out."

"Wilco," Mikhailov said, pulling himself to his feet and giving the order.

The patrol continued moving for hours, but it could have been days—no, it was hours. Their clocks didn't tell the correct time, Stathis was sure, but they told time and recorded distance; they just didn't have access to the data buffers. Another problem. The buffers were encrypted, and Stathis wasn't sure how, but the time was used in the encryption, and since they didn't have proper time that was verifiable with another source, they couldn't decrypt, or something like that.

Until you lost it, technology was great.

Stathis called a halt at another tram station several hours later, in a place that had gravity. They hadn't found any froggers, cyborgs, or anything.

"Where are they?" Chen asked. With gravity restored, carrying Lebedev's body was more of a task that got rotated among the troopers. Even Stathis had taken a turn.

"Likely looking for food," Hakala said. "Primitives will gravitate toward food. There is not a lot here in these corridors."

"Except us," Yue said.

"You are too scrawny and gamey," Li said. "Plus, your armor makes you unappetizing, I'm sure."

"I've got a blazer, too," Yue said.

"There's that, but they have to show themselves if they want to find out."

"Or some other Jotun has taken control, and they're transforming."

Grim faces started looking around. The lights were off, but their helmets let them see in the dark, so there were no shadows.

"I hate spiders," Yue said softly.

"They don't even taste good," Stathis said, and several eyes spun to lock on him.

Yue shuddered.

"Back in jungle survival school, we had tarantulas," Stathis said. "Made me think of crab. The legs were crunchy; the abdomen was kind of gooey. Overall, it seemed to have a nutty undertone type of taste. You can't eat all spiders, though; some are toxic, like frogs, and you have to make sure they're well-cooked, of course, to get rid of parasites and harmful bacteria."

"You ate spiders, Major?" Yue asked. Stathis could hear the horror and disgust in his voice, and even though he had his visors down, Stathis could imagine his face.

"We all did," Stathis said. "Don't knock it until you try it. I wouldn't say yummy, but if the pizza guy doesn't deliver here, it's better than starvation. I'm a young man. I'll try anything once, maybe twice if it doesn't kill me. That's not a story I share with chicks, though."

Hakala looked over at him.

"Oh?"

"Um, well, you know, timid civilian princesses?" Stathis said.

"Don't the HKTs have some kind of survival school?"

"Not like that," Hakala said. "We are unlikely to be stranded on an inhabitable planet. The Eriks might, but not the Vanir. If we get stranded, we are most likely going to die from oxygen deprivation."

"Remind me not to become a Vanir," Stathis said. "I like having a fighting chance."

"Space very much wants to kill us," Hakala said.

"So do the vanhat," Stathis said, looking around. Hakala was right. The froggers would have gone looking for food. What had they eaten when they were under Shroggath's control? Did he use his vanhat powers to feed them?

"The vanhat are less deadly than space," Hakala said.

"No argument," Stathis said. "We'll set up a hide here and get some sleep. Sergeant, send out some scouts to sweep the area, make sure we aren't setting up next door to a frogger camp."

They weren't going to starve, because they had food tablets, but the water filters in their suits weren't working right.

Stathis would have to identify a source of potable water.

"Also have them keep their eyes open for water," Stathis added. How much water would they need? He tried to remember from one of those boring logistics classes he'd mostly tuned out because Shrek would have known.

Dammit. He missed Shrek.

* * * * *

Chapter Forty-Eight: Cyborg Siege

Lieutenant Aod McCarthy, Wolf Legion

McCarthy had put off linking to Kaelan long enough. Opening the link was as unpleasant as he'd expected.

"Where is Hakala?" Kaelan demanded.

"She's unavailable," McCarthy said, still unwilling to admit she was dead.

"Is she dead?" Kaelan asked, getting to the point McCarthy didn't want to admit.

"We've lost contact with her," McCarthy said. He didn't want to lie, even to a despotic dictator. "She was with Major Stathis, attacking the Jotun Shroggath. The last I heard, they detonated the d-bomb, and we haven't heard from them since. I'm working on getting drones into the area to discover their status."

"They are dead," Kaelan said without anything resembling regret or remorse in his voice. Hadn't he said he loved Hakala? Such a damned snake. "That is regrettable. However, as the last Vanir representative, that puts you in a precarious situation. You are now alone, in a foreign city, without a chain of command."

McCarthy remained silent. Did this prick even care about Hakala? Maybe he'd seen enough death in the last couple of months that it meant nothing to him. Nobody had told him about Lochoki, apparently. McCarthy wasn't going to.

"If you accept my authority," Kaelan said, wasting no time, "I can grant you amnesty and protection. You and your men will have a place at my side."

"No thanks," McCarthy said. "I'm good."

"If you do not accept my authority, then you become invaders, occupying Republic territory, exploiting Republic resources, and depriving Bifrost citizens of their birthright."

"No thanks. Invaders? Defenders? I'm the guy with the fortress and guns," McCarthy said. How much could he get away with? It wasn't like Kaelan could mount an effective attack. Without interference from Shroggath, the SCBIs were gaining full control of Bifrost, but there was so much to do, even without having to evade another presence in the broken network. McCarthy kept waiting to find the cyborgs interfacing somewhere, or some other Jotun. So far, the Bifrost Network was still at less than 5 percent operational capacity. Not even emergency links could tell him what was going on in some of the cylinders, but he had access to external sensors, weapons, and the Shorr-space drive.

If only he had a destination, and the SCBIs had figured out where they were.

The vanhat ships nearby drifted as if dead, which McCarthy could appreciate.

"Do you understand what I am telling you? You are occupying Republic property. Do you want to be labeled as our enemy?"

"Finders, keepers, losers, weepers," McCarthy said. He was the supreme commander right now. If Stathis and Hakala were dead, he'd be in charge.

What would Stathis have wanted?

"You are outnumbered," Kaelan said. "You do not want to make me angry."

"If you'll excuse me," McCarthy said. "I'm busy."

McCarthy closed the link before Kaelan could say anything more. He'd have to be dealt with in time. The more he saw of the man, the more obvious it became what a gobshite thug he was.

How could Stathis be dead? It was very rude of him to leave him, a mere lieutenant, in command of a city-ship full of monsters and despots.

"Do you think Kaelan was always such a prick?" Moore asked. "Or do you think having his home overrun was what did it?"

"I think he was always a prick," McCarthy said. He'd expected Moore and Quinn to listen in, so they and their SCBIs could pick up information. Right now, Quinn was sleeping. "He just had to hide it before. Now he has the perfect excuse to let the pile of shit he is steam and stink."

"What do you plan on doing about him?" Moore asked.

"We still have a backdoor into the warbots?" McCarthy asked. "Maybe next time he tours the line, a bot will have a misfire."

"Assassinate him?"

"It'll be doing everyone a favor, I'm sure."

"The SCBIs won't do it, but they can give us a button to push so we can do it," Moore said. "Just give me the word."

"Not yet," McCarthy said. It would be a simple solution, and he was sure Stathis had thought of it. What had the major's intent been toward Kaelan? Kaelan and Captain Hakala knew each other. Kaelan seemed to have a sweet spot for Hakala, admittedly, it was perhaps a bit evil and sadistic, but Hakala hadn't beaten him to a pulp.

McCarthy felt like he was missing something in the dynamics there. What did the major know that McCarthy didn't? The major couldn't be that much of a nice guy, could he?

"Just collect information," McCarthy said. To be fair, he hadn't seen Kaelan abuse others or do anything other than defend his people. His dislike of the guy wasn't justification enough to assassinate him, was it? "If he starts endangering his people, or being more of a prick than usual, let me know."

"Our only source of intel is the bots," Moore said, "and they're kept on the front lines, away from what's happening inside. Do you think he knows?"

"Probably," McCarthy said. Kaelan might be a thug dictator, but he wasn't a complete gobshite moron. "He might still be consolidating power. Maybe he really does care. Who knows? Either way, the major was giving him a chance to redeem himself; we'll do the same."

"Is there a line he can cross?" Moore asked.

A line? What could that line be? Rape, murder, unlawful imprisonment? Rape and murder were obvious lines where McCarthy would have no problem authorizing Kaelan's murder, but McCarthy doubted it would be that easy. If this were the Governance, Kaelan would be removed for not being more compliant, but McCarthy was an Imperial now, not SOG, and there was a difference. The Governance had been a regime focused on power and control. The Empire under Emperor Wolf Mathison? That was different. Focused more on the survival of the human race, and maybe something else.

Stathis and his emperor were cut from a different cloth. They saw the world through different eyes, and if McCarthy was honest with himself, he liked their vision more, even if he didn't yet understand it.

Colonel Sinclair certainly had, and there were no other officers McCarthy had respected more.

"I don't know," McCarthy said. "We just have to watch. Maybe if he starts to act like a central committee member, we wipe him, but until then, maybe he's what they need."

"What if he launches an attack on us?" Moore asked.

That wasn't something McCarthy wanted to contemplate. Could he order the warbots and pop-down turrets to fire on other humans? Back when he was a SOG ODT, it would have been an easy decision. Now? Hopefully, he wouldn't have to make that decision. The warbots were being used by Kaelan to guard the perimeter. If any expeditions were launched, he'd learn about it quickly.

"We'll take it in stride," McCarthy said. "I don't think he has the resources. He certainly doesn't have the firepower, even with the warbots. Just watch them and let me know if they're going to try anything."

"Wilco," Moore said. He'd let Quinn know when he woke up, or his SCBI would. "You think the major's dead?"

"No," McCarthy lied, getting tired of the question. "Just having comm problems or something. He's too tough and smart to die. Have you met him?"

Moore nodded; obviously, he heard the lie for what it was.

"Incoming," Moore said, sitting up. One of the displays came to life, showing an empty tunnel. Movement had been flagged, and McCarthy knew Moore wouldn't bring it up if it was just another mob of froggers about to wander into the meat grinder of a pop-down turret or warbot.

Another viewscreen lit up, controlled by Moore's SCBI. A head looked around the corner and then disappeared. It was a replay, and McCarthy recognized a cyborg's head.

"They moved quickly," Moore said. "They must have come straight here after Valhöll."

"Or their Jotun is absorbing the froggers, growing its army, or that was a scout that left before the major secured that facility."

"It's inside the inkeri," Moore said. "That can't be a mistake. I'll bet it knows we're here."

"Send out a pair of drones," McCarthy said. "Find out how many. Also, expect this is a diversion, and they're preparing an attack from somewhere else. Beef up monitoring of other locations. Full alert."

"Wilco," Moore said. "Wake Quinn? That slacker's been getting too much sleep lately."

"Let him sleep," McCarthy said. "We aren't in any danger yet, and his SCBI will wake him up when necessary."

Another display lit up, showing the two drones speeding along the tunnel toward the sighting. The second they sped around the corner, they flashed and went offline.

"There's a lot of them," Moore said, and a slow-motion replay came up on another display. Cyborgs stacked wall to wall. "Another sighting, tunnel six. We're being surrounded."

"The siege before the assault," McCarthy said.

"Wouldn't Valhöll be an easier target?" McCarthy asked. "We've had plenty of time to repair our defenses here."

What would Stathis do? Launch an attack, most likely. Aggression had its merits, and that was one thing Stathis was good at. The attack didn't have to be successful, just brutal enough to let the enemy know they were in for a fight, and the defenders weren't afraid to attack. A war was never won on the defense.

Then what?

McCarthy thought of Dallas. That's what. If he was in command of Bifrost, he was in command. Enigma would help him, and he'd find Dallas.

But first he had to deal with some uppity, psychotic, alien cyborgs.

"Unless the major kicked their ass so badly, he traumatized them," McCarthy said. "It could be they've got more troops. I think it's time to teach them that Wolf Legion isn't the namby-pamby Republic."

"Incoming link," Moore said. McCarthy didn't want to talk to Kaelan, and Moore would have mentioned if it was Stathis. "The survivors in the Alfheim cylinder. It's Doctor Nilsen, they're under attack by spiders."

McCarthy hadn't met the doctor, but he'd seen SCBI reports and pictures. The guy was an arrogant egghead. If he was calling for help, then things were bad.

The vanhat were counterattacking across multiple fronts. Was it a coincidence, or was it a coordinated attack?

* * * * *

Chapter Forty-Nine: Planning Betrayal

Kaelan

Kaelan looked down on the row of hydroponic trays. Frightened, disheveled people seemed afraid to look up at him. They knew he was there because he did not go anywhere without several of his trusted guards, and he spent most of his time here, where he could watch the others.

Their attitude would change eventually. Right now, it was for the best. In this time of crisis, they needed strong leadership, and that was not what the people of the Republic were used to anymore. For too long, they had been pampered and coddled by politicians, kept safe in deep space, hiding from the SOG. It had been easy for them to become complacent and weak. Kaelan knew better. He was the leader they needed.

Now, with this vanhat invasion wiping out most of the citizens of Bifrost, so few were left. Barely enough to restore the human race. It was time for a new order, a new way forward. They would come to understand that only he could make the difficult decisions that would save them, and they would come to celebrate his removal of the old, worthless, and divided Bifrost Council. It wouldn't be long before the other councilors, locked in the storeroom, understood. They did not have time to argue and bicker over a course of action. They needed quick and decisive leadership. He had learned that as an Aesir. One central leader, one central will.

"Should I assemble a strike team?" Nikolaj asked. He was one of Kaelan's most loyal supporters. He had brains and brawn, following Kaelan's orders like a good trooper. Kaelan knew he could rely on him regardless. He might have a mean streak, something that had kept him out of Aesir or Vanir service, but Kaelan didn't see that as a flaw right now. He made a good enforcer and should probably oversee the new police force. He would keep his excesses under control, for now, but Kaelan knew he could control Nikolaj because he knew what motivated him, and Kaelan had blackmail material on him. Not that Nikolaj saw it that way; he probably just thought Kalean didn't care what he had done to the girl. Kaelan did, but he cared about Nikolaj's loyalty more right now. Odin forbid the man thought Kaelan agreed with his behavior in any way.

"We do not have much of a strike team," Kaelan told him. All his fighters were tired, some were wounded, and if the froggers attacked again, they would be needed. "Besides, we cannot launch an attack against Skögul. Even the automated weapons will stop us, and it will not take many warbots. I am sure if they have the bots to reinforce us, they have the bots to keep themselves safe. We have to be more subtle. They might even be able to control our bots."

"A Trojan horse operation?" Nikolaj asked. "If we can sneak a team in, maybe they can overpower the invaders there."

"Not a bad idea," Kaelan said. "If we can sneak a trusted team in, maybe we can take over the place. It cannot be that difficult to run if there is only a squad of foreigners holding it. They are probably still figuring things out. I am sure their control of the warbots and turrets is just dumb, blind luck."

"How much help do they get from their cybernetics?" Anders asked. She was more subtle, a lot more subtle, and Kaelan considered her more dangerous than Nikolaj because he understood her less. He did not doubt her loyalty, but he didn't understand the reason behind it.

Kalean shrugged.

"A little," Kaelan said. "Probably not too much. Hard to say, and we cannot underestimate them. Real, sentient AIs were banned for several reasons. You cannot deny what they have done with the warbots. Whatever changes they made to the program make them a heck of a lot more efficient than before."

"Maybe it was Vanir upgrades? Why do you think it was the legionnaires that did everything?"

Kaelan shrugged. Nearby, a child was crying about being hungry.

Children were like that, though, and it didn't bother Kaelan. Children were spoiled and always wanted to eat, or play, or otherwise make life difficult for adults. Maybe he could educate the parents. If they could not keep their brats under control, then maybe they did not need to be parents?

The child could have been six or seven, maybe even ten. Kaelan found it hard to determine a child's age. Perhaps if he cared, it would matter? The father noticed Kaelan glance in their direction and shushed the child. The mother was probably working somewhere in the hydroponics area, with fast-growing food. Maybe the father understood.

Rationing was a requirement. While Major Stathis had included emergency rations on the supply tram he had sent, Kaelan wanted to save those. Most of the survivors did not need that much food. They were not actively defending the alue, like his troopers, who needed the food for fuel. Fighting was difficult and critical. Besides, it reduced the chance of an uprising if people were hungry, and it made his soldiers more loyal to him. Food was a good reward for loyalty.

He would change that later, when the output of the hydroponics increased, and they had more food, but right now? Difficult decisions had to be made for the greater good. They would eventually understand. If not? Maybe there were too many survivors, and some would have to be exiled from the alue.

Going back into his quarters, a converted office space that had a small barracks section for a few transient workers that maintained the alue in normal conditions, Kaelan sat down at the break room table. Nikolaj got them some of the rations from the supply tram. They weren't good, but they were better than the plant paste the others ate.

"I like the Trojan horse idea," Kaelan said after some thought. "We are probably going to need at least ten people we can trust. I think we can get them into Skögul by pretending they want to defect there."

"What about weapons?" Nikolaj asked.

"Should be easy to sneak in knives and such. The legionnaires are not that big and tough."

"They have powered armor," Anders said.

"They do not wear it all the time," Kaelan said. "I am sure when they feel safe, they will take it off. It is all about surprise. They were Governance troops before, thugs and bullies, not warriors. Assemble a team, it is time we took back our home from these invaders."

"Zen," his two lieutenants said together.

* * * * *

Chapter Fifty: Trojan Horse

Lieutenant Aod McCarthy, Wolf Legion

McCarthy realized some people shouldn't be officers. The military was organized into officers and enlisted for a reason. Officers were more strategic, and NCOs tended to be more tactical. That was the way of things, and now it made more sense than anything. NCOs had to look at the long term, but they tended to be focused more on the people and the mission. Officers had to see beyond the mission; they had to look at the big picture, and each group had training to that effect.

McCarthy had missed that officer training. Colonel Sinclair had tried to get him some training, but there had never been time. That was the story of the Orbital Drop Trooper, and now Wolf Legion. There was never enough time, never enough troops or resources, and always too many enemies that seemed to be multiplying. As if the vanhat weren't enough, now he couldn't trust his fellow humans. Of course, what did he expect? The Republic was composed of honorless thug pirates.

Well, maybe that wasn't true. Hakala was the exception to the rule. Stathis wouldn't show them loyalty if they were that bad.

Damn Stathis. It would be easy to resent the man. He seemed too young to be a major, but he was ten times better than any other high-ranking officer he'd ever worked with, except Colonel Sinclair—but Sinclair was dead, killed aboard the fleet flagship. It was hard to think of an officer he'd trust beyond them.

Leaning back in a chair that was technically comfortable, it made his back itch, like someone was lining up a kill shot on it.

If Stathis and the patrol were dead, then McCarthy was on his own. Stathis had taken him away from Dallas, and McCarthy was going to fix that. He had to. He had no desire to live out the rest of his days on this pirate hulk under constant attack by enemies. Perhaps he could transfer all controls to Skögul. Right now, Moore and Quinn remotely controlled operations from Valhöll, which worked, but not well. He'd initiated a Shorr-space transition that had left the drifting, lifeless escort ships behind. Now, Bifrost hung in deep space, a massive hulk lost in space. Robots worked on repairing BifrostNET and the inkeris, where possible, but it would take years, maybe decades, to fix even half the damaged systems. He still had no idea what the conditions were like in most of the cylinders.

"When are we going to investigate the cylinders?" Moore asked.

"When I have to," McCarthy said. "I think we have enough trouble at the moment. I find it hard to believe we'll find solutions in any of the cylinders."

McCarthy looked at the display. Doctor Nilsen and his people were still loading up on the trams that would bring them to Skögul. There were too few warriors and quite a few wounded. Their fighting withdrawal had been quick and efficient, though. The lead Aesir, Jaeger Halverson, was a competent leader and had been planning for such an evacuation.

The SCBIs were still working on spreading drones and repairing BifrostNET along the route.

"How's the evacuation going?" McCarthy asked in case he was missing anything. Moore and his SCBI were coordinating that, while Quinn and his SCBI worked on the route. Their teams were also providing support.

Enigma provided some information but didn't interface well with the SCBIs or Republic systems, and McCarthy couldn't help but think he'd gotten cheated in the deal. Right now, Enigma was doing its best to interface with the systems and coordinate with Bonnie's alien SCBI to figure out where they were and how they could link up. Nothing substantial, and McCarthy wasn't going to hold his breath on that.

Given half a chance, he'd ditch this damned pirate hulk and return to the *Musashi*. Let someone else manage this mess.

"It's going," Moore said. "Spiders aren't leaving Alfheim, as far as we can tell."

"Good news," McCarthy said.

"Yes, sir," Moore said. "Until the spider Jotun gets hungry or curious. Then we're going to need flamethrowers."

"Flamethrowers?"

"Well, in addition to thermal suits, that Nilsen gobshite had his people develop flamethrowers. They work very well on the spiders."

"You shouldn't call him names," McCarthy said. Not that he really cared, but Moore might say that to the gobshite's face by accident, and that would cause another set of problems. "What's Halverson like?"

"Rock solid," Moore said. "Professional, that's all I can say. Oh. Incoming link from Kaelan."

"Speaking of gobshites," McCarthy said and thumbed the accept link.

"I am allowing some of my dissidents to flee and accept your hospitality," Kaelan said without even a hello. McCarthy wasn't sure how he felt about that right now.

"It's going to have to wait."

"What do you mean, wait?" Kaelan said. "They want to leave now. I do not want them here. They are taking up valuable food and supplies, keeping the ingrates alive. I want them gone."

"I'm conducting another evacuation at the moment. Your people are going to have to wait."

"What evacuation? Where?"

"Doctor Nilsen and his people were under attack; they're now retreating to Skögul."

"Why was I not notified?" Kaelan asked.

Because you're a gobshite prick and not part of my chain of command, might not be the right answer. A screen lit up, showing a pair of warbots marching down a corridor, firing at a mob of froggers armed with knives and clubs.

"This evacuation doesn't concern you," McCarthy said, amused as the froggers were shredded. Some of the clubs were rifles that would do much more damage if they were used as firearms, but the froggers probably didn't know how.

"Doctor Nilsen and his scientists are my people," Kaelan said. "They are under my protection. They are Bifrost citizens. They should come here."

Of course they are, McCarthy thought. *Now they have some value.*

"The good doctor," it hurt to say that, "linked us for help," McCarthy said. He wanted to hang up on Kaelan, but he had to at least pretend to be polite.

"Did you explain to him that I am not at Skögul?"

"The topic didn't come up," McCarthy said. "He wants a safe, secure place for his people. Skögul is close and secure, with better facilities."

"But—" Kaelan said but didn't finish his words.

"The evacuation is well underway," McCarthy said. "We have the situation under control, but it's taking up many of our resources and forces. Your people will have to wait."

"But—" Kaelan said and then fell silent again.

McCarthy waited for him to continue as he watched the surviving froggers flee the advancing robots. Not many escaped.

"Zen," Kaelan said. "When you have finished, I will expect you to send sufficient forces to protect my defectors."

First, he wanted to get rid of them, then he wanted to make sure they were protected? Did Kaelan really care, or was it something else?

The more he spoke with Kaelan, the less he liked the man. The big ex-Aesir didn't strike McCarthy as the good, kindhearted leader who wanted what was best for his people. McCarthy accepted that he could be wrong, but politicians were politicians, and Kaelan was without a doubt a politician.

"*Suggestions?*" McCarthy asked Enigma.

"*Human interactions and logistics are not my specialty,*" Enigma said. "*My focus is on the vanhat and the war with them.*"

"What can you tell me about the vanhat?"

"*The Primeval archetype within the cylinder of Alfheim is likely a lower-order archetype. It is in nesting mode, establishing itself, coming to terms with its new reality and abilities. These were encountered during the ancient war. When it seeks to expand, it will be explosive and very aggressive. It will have gained intelligence and intent.*"

"What do you mean, intelligence?"

"*Currently, the octopods—spiders, as you call them—do not seem to be tool or weapon users. That could change. They will adapt and learn more quickly than we can anticipate.*"

Halversen and his rear guard were using flamethrowers on the spiders very effectively. Some kind of plasma mix that could be worse than white phosphorus. The weapons were mounted underneath their blazer rifles, so they weren't being robbed of that weapon, but the line leading to their pack seemed to hold a lot of the liquid.

"*We could be facing flamethrower-wielding spiders?*" McCarthy asked, watching the screen, tapped into Halverson's helmet cam. Halverson and his other Jaegers were about to board the slide-evator to the tram station where the others were. They'd be the last ones out. At the other end of the fire, McCarthy could see the spiders milling about, waiting for the flames to go down enough for them to rush through without being fried instantly. The hissing and clacking of spider legs on metal was intense, and McCarthy was glad he wasn't there.

"*Correct,*" Enigma said.

"*What if we splat their Jotun?*" McCarthy asked. Which should stop the spiders, but he wanted to hear what Enigma would say.

"*You are aware that the challenge may be finding the Jotun. It may be a hive mind, like the cyborgs.*"

"*What do you mean, hive mind?*" McCarthy asked. He didn't like that.

"*The archetype in question may exist in every one of the* orja, *as you call them. We encountered this as well during our war. Not all vanhat have a definable physical presence. While many archetypes can extend their will, intelligence, and consciousness to their* orja, *they do not extend their essence. The hive mind–style archetype is such an entity. Their intelligence grows slowly but begins to pick up in level as they mature and become more familiar with the laws of this reality. These* are most likely lower-order intelligences from other dimensions—animals, if you will—that have been pulled through a rift into this dimension."

"The cyborgs are a hive mind?" McCarthy asked.

"A likely assessment. Your fallen officer did not find or destroy an archetype that I could identify. The survivors fled of their own accord and may have multiplied based on recent attacks."

McCarthy didn't like that. The cyborgs had launched multiple attacks on Skögul but had been beaten back. Enemies were multiplying; humans were not.

"Why don't they concentrate on Valhöll?" McCarthy asked. The SCF was weaker and possibly less well defended.

"Unknown," Enigma said. "I would hypothesize that they were ejected forcefully and thus fear a rematch. Their attacks on Skögul are more probes and have decidedly fallen off, which may indicate a desire for a different base of operations."

"They're going after Gullveig?"

"That is likely," Enigma said.

"How do they know? They seem intelligent enough to talk to."

"They may not have reached the level of intelligence where they deem communication worthwhile. They will identify a SCF as a control node, something they are familiar with. Controlling what? They may not be sure, but they likely understand systems and nodes."

"They took over Valhöll. Seems pretty smart to me, and now they're attacking us and maybe Gullveig."

"You equate communication skills with intelligence. A hive mind may not have the awareness of other entities or a desire to communicate with them. They see the world very differently. You, as a human, are forced to interact with others; your interaction gives your life and world reason. A hive mind sees each entity in its existence as a pawn or threat. It does not see the pawns as individuals, no more than you see your cells as individuals."

"The cyborgs could also be increasing in intelligence?"

"More likely to progress faster than the octopods," Enigma said. "The octopods are nesting, as the cyborgs have been evicted from their nest, forced to evaluate the world they have found themselves in."

"Couldn't we make friends with them or something?" McCarthy asked.

"A flawed concept," Enigma said. "Even the simplest organism will realize that growth requires resources, and there will be competition for resources. Humans may deny this truth because of their social tendencies, but most archetypes will soon realize that resources can be finite."

"This is a whole universe," McCarthy said. "Plenty of resources."

"Flawed thinking," Enigma said. "Resources are finite. Your mind cannot comprehend the macro scale. In time, resources will become finite."

"Not for billions of years," McCarthy said.

"You do understand," Enigma said. "Your short lifespan makes this factor irrelevant, since you do not expect to see it. A Primeval archetype will understand this at a more intuitive level; they are immortal."

"So what did your makers do? Don't they understand?"

"That information is not available to me; however, I would surmise they left this dimension for a more plentiful, less violent one. Or one where they could dominate."

Like the vanhat invading this dimension? Were Enigma's makers preying on creatures in other dimensions, like the vanhat were preying on the occupants of this one?

"Well," McCarthy said, looking at the different screens. "I won't live forever, but while I'm alive, I can make things better for my fellow humans."

"That is your strength," Enigma said.

If that was humanity's strength, McCarthy didn't think it would be enough.

* * * * *

Chapter Fifty-One: Steel Trap

Major Zale Stathis, USMC

Stathis didn't realize how much he stank until he took off his helmet. Power levels in the suits were still climbing. Hygiene and other basic functions were low on the priority list, and with wiped memories, probably wouldn't work until the SCBIs came back online or the data cores were rewritten.

He couldn't smell himself, exactly, but he could smell the others, and that meant he likely smelled just as bad to them. He was just used to his own smell.

The dim, red emergency lights of the station made everything dark and sinister. Stathis wondered how much longer the lights would continue to function. Gravity was minimal here, but there was some. The backup batteries had to be nearly drained. The fact that the lights were working in this area was a miracle in itself. After walking for so long in the dark, Stathis wasn't entirely sure it was an improvement.

"Oooga booga," Yue said.

"What?" Kuznetsov asked. Mikhailov and Li were on security while everyone else rested.

"I feel like we've regressed, Corporal," Yue said. "Like cavemen. We walk the caverns, looking for our prey."

"You dumbass," Kuznetsov said. "Cavemen didn't hunt in caves, there was no prey there, and they didn't have rifles and armor."

"Then why were they called cavemen, Corporal?"

Stathis glanced over. Did Yue really not know, or was he trying to antagonize his team leader? It was hard to see Yue's features in the dim light, and Stathis figured it could be either.

"Because they lived in caves, *tupitsa*," Kuznetsov said. Stathis had no idea what that was and wished Shrek could tell him. Russians had some interesting insults, and Stathis realized that Shrek had helped him grow his vocabulary in many ways.

"But—"

"Shut your hole," Kuznetsov said, a side glance toward Stathis and Hakala.

Hakala seemed to be sleeping, which was probably difficult to do in these conditions. Stathis didn't begrudge her a rest, though. Without her, they'd all be wandering aimlessly. She was able to decipher most of the markings they found and was the only person who had any idea where they were.

She wasn't perfect, and Stathis understood completely. Raider training had prepared him to operate in low- or no-tech environments. US Marine battle dress had been designed with the possibility of EMP destroying critical components, so the Marine didn't have to rely on powered systems. That training felt like eons ago.

The armor they had now, though? It had been tightly integrated, and nobody had thought it could have its memories and data purged. In all the time fighting the vanhat, they'd never been impacted by any sort of pulse that disabled things.

"I miss Yuri," Fedorov said, helping Kuznetsov change the subject. Or was he? Yuri must be Fedorov's SCBI.

"You lived without him before," Kuznetsov said as Stathis tried to pretend to be asleep and oblivious.

"But we were close, you know," Fedorov said.

"Yuri's just machinery," Kuznetsov said. "Just well-written software, stuck in your skull to help you. You were an ODT before you had a SCBI. Just means you get to do things the old-fashioned way."

"Like cavemen," Yue said. "Maybe we can find some cave deer? These rations suck."

Stathis could almost hear Kuznetsov rolling his eyes.

"Cave deer? You *tupitsa*. There's no such thing. At best, you might get frogger legs. You want frogger legs?"

"Is there any tobacco sauce left, Corporal?" Fedorov asked.

"You two need to shut up and rest before I shoot you," Kuznetsov said. "Be more like the major and captain. See how they rest instead of asking stupid questions?"

"Wilco, Sergeant," they both echoed.

"But they have all the answers and questions," Yue said. "Why wouldn't they rest?"

Stathis wished that were true.

"Shut up," Kuznetsov said.

"Contact," Mikhailov said, coming into the lobby of the tram station where they were camped. He'd been out near the tracks, watching. Chen was over near another set of tracks. This tram station wasn't big, more of an intersection with emergency facilities than an actual station. Gravity was on at 30 percent or so.

Stathis was awake instantly, so was Hakala, and Stathis knew she hadn't really been sleeping.

"Froggers," Mikhailov said, "coming from in front of us. Maybe about a dozen."

Stathis flicked the safety off his rifle. Shrek wasn't here to do that for him automatically.

"Salute?" Stathis asked, and Mikhailov snapped off a salute.

"No," Stathis said. "Salute, like in report on the size, activity, location, unit, time, and... never mind."

With his SCBI active, Mikhailov's report would have been more detailed; hell, the report would have come through Shrek.

"Sorry, sir," Mikhailov said. "Size, estimated—"

"Never mind." Stathis continued looking around. Everyone was up, weapons ready, kneeling and waiting for directions. Were they going to attack, hide, or run?

"Yue, go get Chen. Brace the door," Stathis said. Killing froggers would have been great, but Stathis had to think about ammunition supplies. There were likely millions of froggers hunting the tunnels, and he didn't have nearly enough ammunition. It was up to Stathis to choose their battles carefully and conserve what ammunition they had.

"Save ammo," Stathis said to everyone else. "Selective killing. We don't have the ammo to kill everything."

"Wilco," the legionnaires said, their weapons now pointed at the hatch Mikhailov had come through.

They'd been forced to leave the mules and extra ammunition behind, and in unpowered armor, even in low gravity, his troops could only carry so much.

Chen and Yue returned, and Stathis had them close that hatch as well. These were old-fashioned hatches, like what would be found in a submarine, designed to handle pressure with a small window.

Mikhailov locked the hatch and covered the window with cardboard as everyone took cover around the room, aiming at the two hatches.

"How long do we wait?" Mikhailov asked a few minutes later.

Stathis didn't have a ready answer. It wasn't like they had a watch to tell them what time it was.

"Sixteen minutes and forty-three seconds," Stathis said.

Heads snapped in his direction, some more quickly than others. They all looked confused, with their helmets on but their two visors up.

Mikhailov looked like he wanted to ask another question, but held it. Even Hakala was looking at him.

"That is a very precise time," Hakala said after a minute. "Do you have a working timepiece?"

Stathis tried not to wince. None of his answers sounded good. He'd been trying to be sarcastic; how was he to know? He was just making shit up, but an officer didn't mock others.

"A bad joke," Stathis said lamely. "I have no freaking idea how long."

The ghost of a smile played across Hakala's lips, and Yue let out a short laugh.

"You surprise me, Major," Mikhailov said. "I thought your mind was so sharp, you needed no timepiece."

"Yeah, well," Stathis said. "I have a mind like a steel trap. Rusty and illegal in thirty-seven states."

"Rusty? States?" Mikhailov asked.

"Never mind," Stathis said. Explaining the joke probably wasn't worth the time, and it made him feel old. He'd heard old people tell jokes that nobody else got because of the context.

Dammit. He wasn't that old.

Well. He was a few hundred years old, technically, but stasis didn't count.

"The United States was composed of fifty states, and each one had different laws and regulations," Hakala said. "They—"

Something tried to turn the wheel on the hatch, but the bar blocked it. Everyone fell silent, aiming at their assigned hatch. The froggers were trying to get in. The question now was how badly they wanted in and how smart they were. Did they have a blazer where they could shoot the hinges? Or were they using their rifles as clubs?

A few hits with a metal object failed to dislodge the pipe Mikhail had used to block it with.

The pounding didn't last long, and it fell silent.

Minutes later, the froggers found their way around and tried the other hatch. The same thing. A few whacks with a metal object, probably a rifle, and then they moved on when nothing was dislodged.

"Now what, Major?" Mikhailov asked.

"We still have six minutes and fifteen seconds to wait," Stathis said, but it had been more than twenty minutes since they'd tried the first hatch, he was sure.

This time, Mikhailov chuckled

"Wilco, Comrade Major," Mikhailov said. "That is enough time to take a shower and get breakfast."

"Grab me a plate of eggs and bacon," Stathis said. "Hold the comrade."

"Of course, Major," Mikhailov said. Stathis didn't like being called comrade, but he knew Mikhailov was stressed and not thinking like he should be, so he was resorting to comfortable language. Hopefully, Mikhailov picked up on that, and he seemed to take it in stride.

"Only three minutes and forty-two seconds," Hakala said.

"Wanna order a pizza while we wait?"

"Maybe. I forgot my pack of cards. That would help us waste time."

Stathis could think of other ways, but there were legionnaires present.

The minutes passed, and Stathis was doing his best not to fidget.

Finally, he stood up, and everyone looked at him, their weapons never wavering from the hatches.

Walking over, Stathis moved the cardboard aside so he could peer out the small window.

A military drone looked back at him.

* * * * *

Chapter Fifty-Two: He's Alive

Lieutenant Aod McCarthy, Wolf Legion

The yell almost made McCarthy fall out of his seat.

"He's alive!" Moore yelled. "The major is alive!"

A screen lit up, showing the major looking out a small window at the drone. He looked terrible, and when he saw the drone, he looked surprised.

One holographic map lit up, showing his location.

"Open a link," McCarthy said.

"Link is open, no response. No radio links, nothing," Moore said, sounding confused.

Was it really the major, then?

"No response on any channels," Moore said as McCarthy watched the drone slide up and try to see past him. There were others, but it was hard to see much.

The view from the drone dissolved into static.

"What happened?" McCarthy asked, wishing he had a SCBI, which could give him good information.

"Lost telemetry," Moore said. "Gobshite equipment. Failed, or something whacked it. Shite. Gobshite froggers. Yeah, frogger snuck up and whacked it with a rifle."

"Get another drone," McCarthy said.

"It's going to take some time," Moore said. "We're spread thin. That drone was following a group of froggers."

McCarthy knew there weren't a lot of drones. He'd given the order to spread them out as much as possible. It would take several thousand drones to check all the corridors between Valhöll and the *Draugskepp*. Valhöll had fewer than fifty operational drones, and it would still take days to get the manufactories repaired enough to make more.

"What's the nearest one?" McCarthy asked. "Hell, send them all. How many froggers were there?"

"That group was only about twenty," Moore said, "but it was a lead element. Our drone was trapped between that group and a few hundred going in the same direction, about twenty minutes behind the first."

"A few hundred froggers are on their way to meet the major?"

"Could be more," Moore said. "It wasn't like the drone got a good count. Could be thousands. The drones were tasked with finding Stathis, not counting froggers."

"Why didn't he reply on any links?" McCarthy asked.

"Saoirse says either that was a doppelgänger, or they suffered some kind of dramatic digital failure."

It took McCarthy a moment to realize that Saoirse was Moore's SCBI.

Quinn came rushing in, along with several other troopers.

"You found him?" Quinn asked.

"And lost him," McCarthy clarified.

People began taking seats.

McCarthy looked between the screens and the hologram of Bifrost as he spoke. "Get more drones into the area. Hell. Can we send an automated tram to get them?"

Green dots showed the drones, and flashing amber showed where they'd seen Major Stathis.

"Saoirse says the drone saw Corporal Chen and Captain Hakala," Moore said. "That's good? Probably not doppelgängers."

"But either they're radio silent or something else," McCarthy said. He didn't have any rescue forces to send. Stathis was going to have to fight his way out, and with a horde coming? McCarthy hoped he had enough ammunition.

"Override!" Moore reported. "Someone's transitioning us into Shorr space."

"Going where?"

"Unknown, Lieutenant," Moore said.

"If the major's links aren't working, are his inkeris?"

"I don't know," Moore said, and McCarthy realized Stathis might not survive the transition if their inkeris didn't work.

* * * * *

Chapter Fifty-Three: Drone

Major Zale Stathis, USMC

When Stathis saw the drone, he wanted to smile. He didn't see the frogger who snuck up and whacked it with a rifle, though. That made him stop smiling.

Stepping back, Stathis considered shooting through the hatch at the frogger as it smashed the rifle into the glass. It was a testament to Republic engineering that the glass didn't crack, and Stathis watched as the frogger was joined by others as they tried to break in.

Stathis pulled the cardboard cover back down over the little window.

"That was a drone," Stathis said out loud as the rest of the patrol hunkered down, ready for a final fight to the death if the froggers broke through the door. "Good news. Hopefully, they saw us. Bad news, the froggers are probably going to try to eat the drone."

"Can they, Major? Yue asked.

"Of course not, *tupitsa*, they eat flesh, not metal," Mikhailov said, but then he looked at Stathis like maybe he wasn't sure.

"I'd like to see them try. I doubt their digestive system would handle it well." But even Stathis had doubts now. What else did they survive on? It wasn't like there was much for them to eat, except maybe each other.

Without the magic of another dimension or Shroggath's abilities, they'd need another source of energy or food. Perhaps they were starving out there, and if the survivors could remain safe in their bunkers for long enough, starvation and tribal warfare would reduce the froggers to more manageable levels.

Shrek would know. Shrek would also have seen the frogger sneaking up on the drone before it smacked it. Hell, if any of the SCBIs had been active, they wouldn't be so lost. They might even be back at a SCF, drinking coffee or beer.

"Well, they know we're here now," Stathis said, listening to them beat on the door and try to open it. If that was a Wolf Legion-controlled drone. "If they're using their rifles like clubs, they probably aren't going to be able to manage."

"But we are stuck here until they leave," Hakala said. "However long that is."

"Could be hours, could be days," Stathis said.

If it was more than a few days, that would be a problem. There wasn't a well-stocked refrigerator, and the water wasn't running. Stathis doubted anyone had more than a day or two of emergency rations, small paste tubes that kept starvation at bay.

"Can they break in?" Chen asked. Like Stathis knew?

"Probably not," Stathis said. "I don't think they have any angry playdough, and they don't seem smart enough to use blazers to shoot the hinges off. I think we can wait them out."

"Who do we eat first?" Hakala asked. She was thinking things through, unlike Chen and Yue. The big picture problems.

"Eat?" Yue asked.

"Yes, eat," Mikhailov said, his eyes coming to rest on Yue. "In case you didn't notice, we don't have a lot to eat. No water in here, either.

Regulations state that if we must resort to cannibalism, the privates get eaten first."

"I don't remember that regulation, Comrade Sergeant," Yue said, looking nervous.

"It's in the NCO handbook," Mikhailov said. "Section sixteen, page forty, I think. Ask your SCBI."

"You wouldn't eat us," Li said.

"Even shit has nutrition," Mikhailov said.

Stathis did his best to keep a straight face. Did the two privates really believe the sergeant?

"I don't want to be eaten," Li said, his rifle shifting slightly.

"Maybe we could open the hatch and let a frogger or two in. Frog legs would taste better."

"Nobody's eating anybody," Stathis said—well, he hoped. "Li's right. It gets bad, we let some in for some frog leg munchies, but seriously, people. There were only about twenty or so out there. We can shoot our way out if we have to."

"Why do we not do that now?" Hakala asked as Stathis wondered if he'd ever been as stupid as Li. Probably. He probably would've tried a stupid stunt like that, probably succeeded too, but now, as he was responsible for the lives of his people, he had to demonstrate more caution and less stupid.

"Might be some others we didn't see," Stathis said. "Could be more around. We're short of food, water, and ammunition. We're short of everything except enemies. Just another glorious day in the Legion, where every day's a holiday, every battle a celebration with fireworks, every war a glorious sporting event. Let's see if they go away first. Maybe they're hungrier than we are."

Stathis looked around. Not a lot of Mikhailov's squad left, and he didn't want to squander their lives.

"We have armor, sir," Mikhailov said. "What can they do to us?"

A knife slammed through the glass, shattering it. It was one of the monofilament blades, able to cut through steel.

"Apologies," Stathis said and placed a single round through the door. "I didn't catch that question."

Now they could hear the froggers screaming and hissing outside. A single blazer round likely caused a lot of damage, hopefully, killing one or two.

"Shit," Mikhailov said. They might not be using the rifles effectively, but they still had knives that would work. Given time, they could carve open the door.

"Good thing we didn't rush out there at them," Hakala said.

"You wanted cooked frog legs?" Stathis said, looking at Yue and pointing at the hatch.

"I'll wait here, sir," Yue said. "They might be a little hot at the moment. I don't want to burn the roof of my mouth."

Stathis could see light from the burning flesh through the shattered window. The froggers weren't stabbing the hatch anymore. They must have been packed tight, and a blazer passing through unprotected flesh would have been explosive.

One frogger was screaming loudly but then a meaty *thunk* silenced it.

Stathis didn't think the froggers were above cannibalism.

It fell silent outside.

"Cover the lights," Stathis said. Hopefully, the froggers needed light to see. If they looked in the window and only saw darkness, maybe they would lose interest and leave?

"Wilco," Mikhail said and motioned for Li to get to work. Rather than covering them, Li just unplugged them.

"Now, sir?" Mikhailov asked.

"Now, we wait," Stathis said. "Maybe they'll eat their buddies, get bored, and move on. We just need to be quiet and let them think we're gone."

"Will that work, sir?" Li asked.

"Shut up, *tupitsa*," Mikhailov said before Stathis could. "Of course. Trust the major. He hasn't let us down, and he has been right so far."

Stathis didn't want to contradict the sergeant. There were enough gaps in the patrol roster, proving that Stathis had let some of them down. If the sergeant wanted to ignore that, Stathis wasn't going to correct him. But all the same, he knew otherwise.

If they got through this alive, it would be because they all watched out for each other. Morale was important. The sergeant knew that, of course.

"The drone saw us," Stathis said. "They'll send help, reinforcements, maybe a tram to pick us up and bring us home. If we keep moving, it might be hard for them to find us."

"See, *peska?*" Mikhailov said, glaring at Yue. "The major has things under control."

If the drone was able to report before it was destroyed. Would they record it, and would the drone have seen enough? Stathis didn't want to share his doubts and fears. What could they do? McCarthy was maybe days away, and no relief force could be sent from Valhöll except a few warbots, and maybe the tram that had brought them from Skögul, if it hadn't been destroyed by raiders.

It would be nice to know if McCarthy had control of the Shorrspace drives now, with Shroggath permanently offline.

Could a tram and warbots fight their way through a frogger horde if they had to? Probably not.

He was so used to relying on Shrek for such answers and risk calculations. Now he had to rely on others to ask the proper questions and other SCBIs to come up with answers.

Damn Shrek. He'd better not be dead.

A roaring *hiss* outside told him the froggers hadn't left, and something slammed into the other hatch. They were at both hatches now.

There were two ways they could go, and it would be a guess as to which route had fewer froggers.

"Can we wait for rescue?" Hakala asked.

Stathis didn't want to say he didn't know.

"We can go a few days without food," Stathis said softly and looked around. "I think a few people could stand to miss a meal or two. Make us lean and mean. Water's more of a concern."

"Zen," Hakala said. "If our suits were working properly, that would not be a problem."

Stathis preferred not to think about that. The plumbing in the suits wasn't working right, with all the nanites and suit intelligence offline. The only saving grace right now was that they had been eating the food paste for a while, and there wasn't a lot of waste going through their system, but it would build up. Admittedly, that was the least of their problems, but it would get uncomfortable. He didn't look forward to the privates discussing it.

A knife slammed into the hatch near the spoke holding the door closed. Each door had six spokes to hold it closed against any pressure differential. They'd have to cut all six, and then the door would swing open.

"Very short, controlled shots," Stathis said. "Don't turn those doors into Swiss cheese. Let's not do their work for them."

"Wilco," the legionnaires echoed.

"Anyone have a deck of cards?" Li asked.

"Shut up, *tupitsa*," Mikhailov said as everyone sank down to wait out the froggers.

Minutes later, there was more screaming and yelling, and the sound of battle. Stathis didn't hear any blazer fire, though.

"A rescue?" Yue asked softly.

"No blazers or wire guns," Stathis said. Were the froggers fighting each other? Spiders attacking the froggers? Stathis didn't dare go look.

Finding manual controls for his helmet microphone, he boosted his hearing.

The froggers were fighting, and now he was sure there were more than twenty froggers, a lot more. Tribal warfare, or something else?

Maybe waiting had been a bad idea. Out of the pan and into the fire. Stathis felt the Bifrost transition into Shorr space, and he was sure the inkeris weren't working properly.

* * * * *

Chapter Fifty-Four: Into the Breach

Admiral Diamond Winters, USMC

Winters had made her decision, and watching the people around her commit to it and begin the planning didn't make her feel better. She knew it was a bad idea to keep second-guessing her decision, to listen to people talk and try to gauge how bad they thought her decision was and why.

Was it better to be convinced of the superiority of her decision, though? To be absolutely sure it was the right one? Was she saving the emperor, or dooming him? It was always easy to judge a decision after the fact.

The Seraphim Fleet was now committed to helping Thuthta and the rebels breach the crypts to find, and if possible, free the angel, or as Winters feared, the demon. Even if it was a demon, Winters expected to be able to defeat it. Nothing in the information Thuthta had shared spoke of d-bombs or the equivalent. If it was a demon, she'd d-bomb it and escape in the chaos.

Hopefully. A simple plan that could go wrong, and quickly.

Despite the doubt gnawing at her, she couldn't tell everyone to stop and change direction. She was committed as much as everyone else, and changing her mind at this point would destroy everyone's belief in her leadership. Commissar Nakano was obviously opposed and frequently said as much, but never in a way that directly questioned her decision or leadership.

Now that she'd made the decisions and started the fleet on its path, she could see plenty of reasons her decision was a bad one. The Voorga home world fleet outnumbered the Seraphim Fleet by a factor of ten to one in tonnage. While it looked like the humans had better technology, the Voorga home fleet would be defending their home, and Winters knew that would make them fight even harder.

The door slid open, and Sif came in, followed by two of her ever-present guards.

"Good morning, Admiral," Sif said.

"Hello, Sif," Winters said, standing, glad to see the little psychic was back and safe aboard the *Musashi*.

"I believe we are doing the right thing," Sif said, coming to a stop in front of Winters' desk. "As I have said, though, we do need to be cautious."

"Of course," Winters said. "This angel could be a Jotun, like the one that owns the Weermag."

"Not as capable, most likely, but yes," Sif said as Winters motioned her to a chair. Her bodyguards took a position against the wall.

"Do you have any additional insight?" Winters asked, wondering why Sif was here and not linking or sending a message through Blitzen.

"Nothing significant," Sif said. "I just want to reinforce the fact that we might be making things worse by releasing another Jotun."

"I understand," Winters said, "but as you pointed out, it may be a Jotun we can reason with. Either way, we have d-bombs."

Sif frowned.

"Zen," she said. "Still, there is a lot of danger."

"We need to do something about the Voorga," Winters said. "Their psychics will be able to hunt us down if we try to traverse their territory without permission."

"A Jotun ruling them could make things worse," Sif said.

Winters raised an eyebrow. Did Sif want her to change her mind?

"Apologies," Sif said. "I just have doubts and fears."

"You aren't the only one," Winters said. She left it unsaid that she had her own doubts and fears. "We can't let those doubts and fears freeze us with inaction."

Which felt odd, telling Sif that.

"Zen," Sif said, looking every bit the insecure twelve-year-old.

"Sometimes making a bad decision is better than no decision," Winters said. Who was she trying to convince? Sif or herself?

"That makes no sense, Admiral," Sif said.

Winters smiled.

"That's what I thought, but the secret is to act. Once you begin to act, you're taking the initiative and forcing your enemy to react. Even if you're making a mistake, you're still forcing the enemy to react and stealing the initiative. You can always change focus or plans based on information, but you have to be moving to change direction."

"Zen," Sif said. "I had never heard it put that way. This is true. But it is also true that you should never interrupt an enemy that is making a mistake."

Winters shrugged. They could play this game for a while. It only solidified her intent to go through with it. Was that Sif's intent?

"We don't have a lot of time," Winters said.

"After we arrive and beat off the fleet?" Sif asked. "What is the plan?"

"We land the Legion," Winters said. It had been discussed, but Sif was leading up to something. "Major Volkov will lead the assault."

"I would like to go with them," Sif said.

Winters didn't like that idea at all.

"I can't afford to lose you," Winters said.

"You cannot afford not to send me, Admiral," Sif said. "I can negotiate with the Angel or Jotun."

Winters would rather have sent Stathis. She trusted Sif, but Winters would have preferred Stathis' less tolerant, aggressive, and unforgiving Marine Corps insight. Sif could be trusted, but Sif was more willing to operate in a gray area between good and evil. Stathis would define the situation in black and white; Sif would be more accepting of a situation that wasn't clear-cut.

There was a lot to be said for making the situation simple. Sif could lead humanity into slavery, but Stathis would make sure that if humanity went extinct, it would do so with its independent identity intact.

Stathis wasn't here, though. He could be dead, and Bonnie hadn't heard anything from Bifrost in a while. They could all be dead now for all she knew.

Winters knew damned well that it wasn't her place to go, though, and she had to send someone she could trust.

"Very well," Winters said. "I'll inform Major Volkov that you'll be joining him. I believe he and his staff are working with a Voorga officer on details."

"Thank you," Sif said. "Another thing, I feel a storm coming. I do not know if this is a natural phenomenon, or if the vanhat have found us, but in the psychic realms, the unease is growing."

"Thank you," Winters said. "The fleet had orders and didn't dare get too close to the planet for fear of not being able to escape in time. It's a high-gravity world, so we can't get as close as we like."

Alerts began ringing. Incoming transitions. Battle stations and brace for impact alarms also began ringing as Sif and her two guards found seats and straps.

"Incoming vanhat," Blitzen reported. "*A pair of battleships. Close range. Missiles are launching, and the* Musashi *is turning to bring our particle beams to bear.*"

The holographic display above her desk sprang into view. The two vanhat battleships were coming directly at the *Musashi*, and Winters felt the *Musashi* shudder under the impact.

"More transitions," Blitzen reported. "*Admiral Sakamoto is—*"

Winters felt the *Musashi* slide into Shorr space. The battleship would've been trying to ram, most likely.

"*Transitioning into Shorr space,*" Blitzen reported needlessly. "*Damage reports are still coming in. One Shorr-space drive has been damaged.*"

Damaged, not destroyed, and the *Musashi* had several of them. Military ships always had redundant systems.

Just as quickly, the *Musashi* slid out of Shorr space into the far outer reaches of the system. Nearby, the *Fire Wind* slid into space, close to *Musashi*.

"We are probably not safe here," Sif said.

"Of course," Winters said. "Sakamoto has become something of an expert at evading the vanhat in your absence. A short transition to confirm survivors, and then we blip out again."

"Zen," Sif said as everyone's eyes locked onto the display. More ships arrived.

"*The* Molniya *didn't make it,*" Blitzen reported, and Winters grimaced. "*She took a torpedo meant for the* Musashi. *Not a direct hit, but she moved to intercept and was in the blast radius.*"

Yet more people she'd lost.

"*And we lose yet more heroes,*" Winters said. "*What about the Voorga?*"

"*Unknown,*" Blitzen said. "*We are two light hours out.*"

"Stand by for transition," an announcement said. Seconds later, the *Musashi* slid into Shorr space.

"*We are now one light hour out,*" Blitzen reported as a notification came in from Sakamoto informing her of his intent to discover what was happening. Nobody liked abandoning the Voorga, but in a previous discussion, it had been agreed that that was the only course of action. The vanhat might not even notice the hidden colony or the Voorga ship that was now protected by an inkeri.

Would the Voorga understand?

"I will reach out to the Voorga," Sif said, "but not here."

"Thank you," Winters said. Her office was probably not the best place for Sif to meditate, or whatever she did. Winters was also not keen on having some vanhat assassin show up in her office.

* * * * *

Chapter Fifty-Five: Trapped

Major Zale Stathis, USMC

Sitting up, Stathis looked toward the hatch. Chen was sitting near it, listening, and Stathis knew that he could still hear the froggers, or the corporal would have woken him up by now.

"Good morning, Major," Mikhailov said, too cheerfully for Stathis.

"Good morning?" Stathis asked; he couldn't remember the nightmares that had plagued his sleep, but they'd involved bad things happening to Hakala and Shrek. "What do you mean by that? Are you wishing me a good morning, are you saying you're having a good morning, you're wishing it was a good morning, you plan to have a good morning, you have goods for the morning, you want me to shut up this morning, I'm dismissed this morning, or—"

Stathis paused and realized Mikhailov might not appreciate the humor. But he had mentioned a five-year plan and some joke committee, right?

"Or it would be a good morning if I rolled over and went back to sleep?" Stathis finished lamely.

"Uh, well, Major," Mikhailov began, not sure what to say to his commanding officer. Obviously he wanted Stathis to roll over and go back to sleep.

Stathis took off his helmet and rubbed his eyes. The new group of froggers hadn't tried to break into their redoubt after the second time they'd tried and taken casualties. Now they were waiting. It didn't bode well, and it was starting to bother Stathis. Maybe they had enough cooked froggers to satisfy their hunger for the moment, but Stathis doubted it. There had to be over a hundred froggers out there now.

"Sorry," Stathis said. "My comments weren't aimed at you. I'm not a morning person."

"I would offer you some coffee, but we seem to be out, sir," Mikhailov said. "Chen drank it all. Again."

Coffee, or any kind of caffeine, would be sublime. Out of water was what Mikhailov didn't say. His throat was parched, and Stathis knew he'd have to make a difficult decision today. If the froggers were going to try to wait them out, they'd probably win. Stathis wouldn't die here from hunger and thirst.

The headache that was hammering at his skull could be dehydration or caffeine withdrawal. Shrek would know and would be dealing with it. Without Shrek? Stathis hated being just a normal human again. Shrek better not be dead. He didn't want to have to train a new SCBI. Shrek was one of a kind.

If Shrek was dead? Stathis didn't want to think about that. Shrek was part of him. Since Shrek had been implanted, he'd been with Stathis every second of every day. It was worse than losing just a friend; it was like losing a brother, a mother, or a child.

Shrek couldn't be dead.

Could he?

"We're going to have to do something soon," Stathis said, trying not to dwell on Shrek's disappearance. Shrek would call this a teachable moment. "If the froggers don't get bored and go away, we're going to have to kick them in the teeth and skull-stomp them."

"Wilco," Mikhailov said. His smiling teeth almost gleamed in the bad light. "What gets me is they know we're here. Why don't they do anything? The other mob was trying hard to get to us. This new mob has more bodies but seems to be chill."

"They are likely waiting for us to tire or get desperate," Hakala said as she sat up.

"Sorry if we woke you," Stathis said. Other troopers were trying to sleep. Everyone was tired.

"I will be able to catch up on my sleep when we are safe or dead," Hakala said.

"Safe is my preference," Stathis said.

"Zen."

"Aren't they desperate, ma'am?" Mikhailov said.

"Maybe," Hakala said. "Consider, though. This is a bigger mob. They might have a leader, someone intelligent enough to realize there is strength in numbers, and wasting his troops trying to overrun us will leave him weakened."

"You think they're that smart?" Stathis asked.

"Why not? Humanity started out as tribal, with some tribes growing very large. The tribes usually broke apart due to weak leadership, I think. It doesn't take a lot of intelligence to realize that it's better to have a hundred soldiers at your command than five."

A click from outside drew everyone's attention. The click was followed by another, and then another. Metal objects slamming into the deck.

"It sure would be nice to have a drone," Stathis said as the clicks began to take up a simple rhythm. What did it mean? Then he heard the humming.

Other legionnaires began to sit up.

The froggers outside sounded like they were beating the floor and humming.

"They're starting to freak me out," Fedorov said. "What are they doing?"

"Go take a look," Kuznetsov said.

"Belay that," Stathis said. "Anyone moving the cover to look out is probably going to get a knife in the eye. We can hear them. They're there. What they're doing doesn't matter unless they're trying to get in here."

"You think they're trying to make peace or something, Major?" Fedorov asked.

"A peaceful dinner," Stathis said. "Just because their god is gone doesn't mean they've become kumbaya-singing vegans."

"How do you know, sir?" Fedorov asked.

Stathis looked at the lance corporal.

"I've fought vanhat in every clime and place you can take a gun. They don't do peaceful. Their minds have been torn and twisted by their Jotun to be psychotic killers. That's probably all they know. Without orders from on high, they just aren't as good at killing."

"Isn't the theory that we evolved from vanhat slaves, sir?" Mikhailov asked.

Stathis shrugged.

"Good point," Stathis finally said and looked at Fedorov. "If that's true, it was a long time ago. What happened to all the peaceful humans in history?"

"They got killed by the less peaceful ones," Fedorov said. "Sir."

"Bingo. Survival of the fittest and most aggressive. The vanhat are super tribal. Us against them. Even when they act like friends, they aren't. I think the Jotun have a hard time keeping their psycho pets from attacking each other. Just one big, dog-eat-dog universe."

"What are we going to do, sir?" Fedorov asked.

"We're going to put on our Milk-bone underwear and make them put up or shut up," Stathis said. "Everyone up. I'm sick of waiting for them to go away. They've had their chance, now they get to pay the price."

In the blink of an eye, everyone was up and ready, telling Stathis that nobody had been sleeping.

"You have a plan, then?" Hakala asked.

"I always have a plan," Stathis said. "The problem is, they're rarely good plans. For instance, asking Fedorov to sing us a love song might cause the froggers to flee, but then he might be so off-key that I have to kill him."

"Yue is a much better singer, sir," Fedorov said.

"Shut up, *tupitsa,*" Mikhailov said to him, looking at Stathis.

"I figure we spray a couple bursts from a SAW through that hatch, and then try to fight our way out the other one," Stathis said.

"Use the weapons fire to cover our actions?" Hakala asked. "Maybe we should give them a grenade or two, as well?"

Stathis liked that idea. An explosion in close quarters would pop eardrums, maybe deafen them.

"Good idea," Stathis said. "When that starts, everyone else goes out the other hatch, using knives and wire guns."

They all had wire gun carbines but not nearly as much ammunition as Stathis would have liked. The wire guns were not as destructive against unarmored opponents; they sliced through flesh instead of superheating and exploding it, but they were a lot quieter, and if they were lucky, the froggers might not realize they were trying to escape out the backdoor.

"Blazers as a last resort," Stathis said.

Fedorov, the only trooper with a SAW, was already in position to shoot through the door down the long axis of the hallway. Mikhailov motioned for Yue to prep a fragmentation grenade. Then he handed Yue one of his smoke grenades.

"Fed," Mikhailov said, "use your SAW to cut a nice hole. When I give the command, stop or you will shoot Yue's hand off and piss me off."

"That'll piss me off too, Sergeant," Yue said.

"If there was a way I could risk your mouth instead of your hand, I would. Unfortunately, I don't want Fed to keep you from using your weapons. That we need."

"It would ruin his love life, too," Fedorov said as Kuznetsov crouched down with his team, and Mikhailov came over to join Stathis.

"I can use either hand for that," Yue said. "I'll bet you would—"

"Smoke 'em. On my mark," Stathis said before the conversation could devolve further. Hakala was here, and there were some things a lady shouldn't hear.

Stathis prepared a smoke grenade. Their sensors should see through the generated smoke, but he doubted the vanhat could. It would also make it harder for the froggers to breathe. It was a little too late to test that the sensors were working, though.

"Three, two," Stathis began, standing at the hatch with Chen and Yi preparing to lead the way. They had KA-BARs in one hand and wire guns in the other. Stathis was resting his hand on Chen, and when he gave Chen a push, he knew the team leader would launch himself through the hatch.

"One!" Stathis said, and Fedorov began firing short, controlled bursts through the other door. Within seconds, Yue shot a hole big enough to throw a grenade through. Mikhailov gave the command, and Fedorov stopped as Yue pushed a smoke grenade through, followed by a frag. Then Yue, Kuznetsov, and Fedorov ducked back.

The froggers were screaming, and then the grenades went off. Stathis didn't hear the hissing of the smoke grenade, but he certainly heard the fragmentation grenade. His helmet muffled the sound slightly, but the froggers outside had to be deaf now.

"Go!" Stathis said and gave Chen a slight push.

Chen yanked the hatch open and shot through it like a dog let off its leash.

Behind him, Hakala would wait at the hatch until the corridor was clear, and then she'd give the command for Kuznetsov and his team to follow.

Stathis almost stumbled on the first body as he hurled another smoke grenade down the hallway, slamming it into one frogger's face that was already falling back from a wire that had sliced open its throat.

Chen and Li rushed down the corridor. There'd been more froggers than he'd expected, but they didn't stand a chance as the legionnaires tore through them, their powered armor giving them an edge beyond their wire guns and knives.

"Let's go," Stathis told Hakala as Chen and Li reached the intersection leading to the other tram tunnel.

This section wasn't much of a tram stop, just a place for the tram to pull off the main tracks near a hatch leading to the maintenance station.

Stathis pointed to the right as he looked down the corridor, going back around to the other door. Two dead froggers were lying in a pool of blood. Stathis threw a smoke grenade down the corridor as Hakala and the others came up behind him.

Fedorov and Yue took up rear security with Kuznetsov, and Stathis started after Chen and Li. Now, Mikhailov was ahead of him.

There were no froggers in the tram tunnel, and Chen and Li were looking down in both directions.

Stathis pointed them on, and they started moving again. Everyone was here.

Stathis dropped his last smoke grenade at his feet and gave the hand-arm signal for double time, and they all jogged down the darkened tunnel as the smoke grenade hissed behind them.

One problem with damaged life support systems was that the smoke from the smoke grenades wouldn't be pulled away and removed from the area. It would become stale and hard to breathe very quickly.

The sick, unpleasant feeling of a Shorr-space transition slid over Stathis. Without their inkeris, they'd be in danger. Without Shrek, how would he know he was changing? Or someone else was?

This was the second time, and Stathis knew it was going to be worse.

In the distance, the froggers began to scream in anger. The hunt was on.

* * * * *

Chapter Fifty-Six: Shorr Space

Lieutenant Aod McCarthy, Wolf Legion

McCarthy looked at the maps of Bifrost, zoomed into the area where they'd seen the major. He looked at the timer showing how long they'd been in Shorr space. Shroggath wasn't in control, and McCarthy had no idea where they were going.

"Talk to me, Moore," McCarthy said.

"All drones are converging," Moore said. "My team is pushing the envelope. There is a shite-load of froggers, though."

"I don't care about froggers, I care about the major and our missing patrol. If he doesn't have comms, he might not have inkeri protection. That's a lot more serious."

"Yes, sir," Moore said.

"*Anything you can do?*" McCarthy asked Enigma.

"*I am more limited than your SCBIs,*" Enigma said. "*My purpose is data interface and protection. I am not an autonomous entity, and I am as attached to you as a SCBI.*"

"*A SCBI would be more useful,*" McCarthy said.

"*In this scenario? Yes,*" Enigma said. "*However, the SCBIs cannot communicate with the rest of the fleet.*"

"*At this point, neither can you,*" McCarthy said. "*What can you do to make our situation better?*"

Enigma remained silent. Unsure or irritated at McCarthy, he wasn't sure.

"*My programming is limited,*" Enigma finally said as McCarthy continued to watch the screens. He doubted he'd see anything before the SCBIs, but he didn't want to waste time having Moore point something out.

"*Well,*" McCarthy said, "*scan your databanks or whatever and see how we can track down whoever's controlling the Shorr-space drives. We have to shut that person down and exit Shorr space.*"

"*This section of space is on the forefront of the devourer resurgence,*" Enigma said. "*There is danger, but it is less than it is in human space.*"

"*Meaning what?*"

"*The devourer resurgence is not exactly localized, but it does sweep through the galaxy, perhaps the universe, like a flood. This part of the galaxy is on the forward edge of the flow.*"

"*So, the major is in less danger?*"

"*Less danger would be an adequate analysis,*" Enigma said. "*Currently, in human space, making a Shorr-space transition without inkeri protection is guaranteed to draw a devourer presence, instigating a likely incursion. In this region of space, there is less chance. The barrier is not weak. However, that is not to say he is not in danger.*"

"*What's the chance of an incursion?*"

"*43 percent,*" Enigma said.

"*That's too damned high,*" McCarthy said.

"*It is not 100 percent.*"

"*Back on Valakut, they would give us a weather forecast, 30 percent chance of rain. We always considered it 60 percent,*" McCarthy said. "*Do you know *what that really meant?"* McCarthy didn't wait for Enigma to guess, though. *"That means it would be raining 30 percent or 60 percent of the day."*

"I don't see how that corresponds to—"

McCarthy cut Enigma off.

"I don't care," McCarthy said. *"I'm telling you that you can bet your ass that there will be an incursion. The vanhat are coming, they're hunting for the Seraphim Fleet and Bifrost. I'm sure of it."*

Enigma was silent for several seconds.

"Your logic is valid," Enigma said.

"Quinn?" McCarthy said, looking over at the man.

"Sir?"

"We need to find out who's controlling the Shorr-space drives and from where," McCarthy said. He didn't like the command he was going to give, but there were two ways to achieve a victory. "That's your team's priority right now. If Frogbath isn't calling the shots, I need to know who is. Burn the network. No more hiding. Balls to the wall."

"Wilco," Quinn said.

"And be ready for the hordes of hell to come at us," McCarthy said to everyone. Hopefully, if the major survived, he could make it to Valhöll.

He was done hiding, trying to be covert about finding out who was pulling the strings. Someone or something was, and as soon as they realized Skögul was the source, then all hell would break loose, and every vanhat in Bifrost would come at them.

"This is unwise," Enigma said.

"Really? I never would have guessed," McCarthy said. Did Enigma understand sarcasm?

"The devourers can band together to assault the natives of this dimension if their foothold or presence is challenged. Revealing your presence and intent will threaten them."

"Good," McCarthy said. *"They come at us, they ignore the major. Get them to come to Skögul and shred their forces against our walls."*

"You underestimate them," Enigma said.

"You underestimate us," McCarthy said.

"Initiating sweeps," Quinn said.

McCarthy checked the Russelman index. There were several detectors that had been deployed in repaired facilities. Stathis was too far from any of them, though.

"What about the scientists?" Moore asked.

"Shite," McCarthy said. "Can they be redirected to Valhöll?"

"We don't have a fully monitored route," Moore said.

"We're going to become ground zero for a monster swarm," McCarthy said. "I doubt they want to be here when that happens."

"Wilco," Moore said. "I'll do what I can. Maybe send them to the hydroponics alue?"

"Hell, no," McCarthy said. "I can't see that ending well. Redirect to Valhöll."

"Wilco."

* * * * *

Chapter Fifty-Seven:
Attacking in Another Direction

Major Zale Stathis, USMC

Stathis wanted to curse and swear and give the order to slow down, but they needed more distance.

Back in the Marine Corps, they'd called it the "Marine Corps shuffle." It wasn't a full run, nor was it a walk. It was like a steady jog, and not a very fast one. Slightly faster than merely walking, it let them cover distance. Nobody ever scored well on a physical fitness test doing the shuffle, but it could be sustained for long distances.

Stathis was torn between telling them to speed up and slow down. He didn't want to look and see how long they'd been running.

He could feel Shorr space, though, feel something malevolent watching them, and he knew they were running into a trap. Something was watching them, and he could hear the whispers.

Nobody had a working inkeri, and Stathis spent as much time watching the others as he did their surroundings. How long before someone began to transform into a monster?

Was he starting to transform? What would he do if Hakala changed?

Die, obviously because he knew there was no way he could shoot her, and he couldn't allow anyone else to, either.

"It is inevitable," a voice whispered, and Stathis spun, expecting to see something there. Nothing.

Stathis didn't want to worry anyone else by responding; he knew it was only in his mind, he hadn't really heard it.

"No species has survived a rebirth of the old gods," the voice whispered. *"We are evolution. We are the future. Embrace us and live. I will protect and nurture your kind. Accept me."*

Stathis could feel pressure on his mind but refused to give in. Shrek wasn't here. It was just him.

"We can make you stronger, greater than you are," the voice whispered, growing stronger. *"Submit. Become my champion. You are too strong to be a slave or servant. You can save the others. Become my champion."*

Stathis thought to the creature to go away, that submitting wasn't what Marines did. No. Just no.

"Death is eternal darkness. The end of everything. Don't let that happen to you. Become immortal. Become a god. Be my champion."

The voice was growing stronger, and Stathis was getting a headache. The Bifrost was slipping deeper into Shorr space, and it was only going to get worse. Damn Shrek, why had he abandoned Stathis?

Chen stumbled, and Stathis grabbed him to keep him from falling.

"You okay?" Stathis asked, his own voice sounding strange in his ears.

"Yes, sir," Chen said, but he didn't sound like it.

"Resist," Stathis said out loud so everyone could hear. "Nothing but a thang. We won't be in Shorr space much longer. Just hang in there."

That was a lie. They could be in Shorr space for days or weeks.

"Just concentrate on hanging tough a little longer, another minute, then another minute," Stathis said. "We'll get through this. First person to turn gets my boot in their ass."

Stathis looked back toward Hakala, but her inner visor was down, and he couldn't see her face in the shadows. He wished he could see her face. Were her teeth changing? Her beautiful eyes twisting and transforming?

"It would be—" Chen said but didn't finish.

"Don't," Stathis said. "Whatever the whispers are telling you, it's a lie. Demons never tell the truth. They're insidious, deceptive, full of hate and anger. They want just one thing, and once you submit, you're doomed."

"Not true," the voice whispered, though not as strong as a moment ago.

"I've never met a vanhat that wasn't a liar," Stathis said out loud. "The second you give in, they'll possess and devour you. You were all selected for the Wolf Legion because you're badasses who don't quit. Prove it. Never quit."

Would the ODT motto ring true and help them? Several of the others glanced at Stathis. Was he going off the deep end? Were they hearing the whispers? If they weren't, he would sound crazy. But what choice did he have?

"Right now might be a good time for a running cadence," Stathis said.

"You fool," the voice whispered. *"You cannot stop us. We are only growing stronger. Do not be the last to submit, for you will die."*

"Look up on the hill, and what do I see?" Stathis sang, almost shouting as they ran. There could be vanhat ahead of them, and there were vanhat behind them, but this was a tunnel. He tried to think of a better cadence, but only one came to mind at the moment.

The others repeated after Stathis, and Stathis decided it wasn't loud or proud enough, so he shouted even louder.

"Look up on the hill, and what do I see?!" he shouted.

This time, they were louder. Focusing on his words.

"Nasty, stinking vanhat looking at me," Stathis said, and the others echoed him, gaining strength.

Stathis realized how stupid this was. Running in enemy territory, possibly running into an ambush, singing cadence.

Screw it.

"Lock and load one round inside," Stathis said, and they echoed him.

"Shoot Frogbath between the eyes," Stathis said, trying to think of another vanhat name and failing, but the others repeated what he said.

"Kick and beat and stomp his face!" Stathis said.

"Kick and beat and stomp his face," the others said, their voices gaining strength. They were in a modified wedge, running down the tunnel, not exactly a formation, but it would do. They were singing, and Stathis listened to try to see who wasn't singing. Even Hakala had joined them.

"Strangle him with my boot lace," Stathis said, getting into the groove. He couldn't hear the voice in his ear whispering. Shit. Did they know what a boot lace was? Their boots didn't have laces.

"If he's still a fighting fool," Stathis shouted. "Do him in with my e-tool!"

The others almost screamed his words at him.

"One, two, three, four," Stathis said and noticed Kuznetsov did a step-shuffle to get in step with the others. Just like a formation run. This was stupid.

Yelling out *United States Marine Corps* wasn't the right thing to say, so Stathis improvised.

"Wolf Legion wins the war."

Stupid? But right now, it was better than nothing. He wanted to stop and walk, but they hadn't run into an ambush yet, and Stathis wanted to shoot vanhat.

"Up in the morning with the rising sun," Stathis said, starting a new cadence, wondering where he was going with it. The others repeated after him. He didn't know what time of day it was or whether there was any sun. Stathis felt dumb, but he was committed.

"Gonna run all day till the running's done!" Stathis yelled.

"Tunnels suck and space is cold," he continued, looking around. Everyone was in step, though, and weapons were ready.

"But 'ware the Legion, brave and bold," Stathis said when they were done.

The voice wasn't whispering in his ear anymore. What did that mean?

"Starlight fades and darkness creeps," Stathis said, struggling to come up with something. The others echoed him without laughing, though.

"No one fights like the Legion—" like what? "—leaps!"

Stupid. Stathis could have sworn someone laughed, but it was a laugh, not a strangled scream as someone changed into a face-eating monster.

"Asteroid rocks and vacuum's near!" Stathis shouted. "We'll run through hell, we'll show no fear."

Maybe a little bit, Stathis didn't add. Had the laughter been at how stupid he was? Maybe he should call someone else out. Officers didn't sing cadence, did they? Easy to way to screw up and look stupid. Maybe he should call someone else?

He didn't hear whispering, but he knew they were still in Shorr space. Was that good or bad?

* * * * *

Chapter Fifty-Eight: Finding the Lost

Lieutenant Aod McCarthy, Wolf Legion

McCarthy didn't want to look at the time. Hours had passed, and they were deep in Shorr space. There was no way an unprotected human could survive.

The major and the lost patrol were probably on their way to Valhöll right now to try and tear through the blast doors. McCarthy wondered what form they'd take and if he'd recognize them.

"Contact," Moore said. "Found the major."

A drone's view appeared on screen. Several people running through the tram tunnel, singing cadence? The drone had hidden up near the ceiling and dropped in behind them to follow.

"Can't stop, won't stop," Major Stathis was yelling, and the others repeated after him.

"What's that numpty doing?" Moore asked. "Is he singing cadence? Does he realize they're in a combat zone? The drone heard him long before it saw him."

McCarthy chuckled. Freaking Stathis.

"We're the few, the proud in outer space," Stathis sang and yelled, and the others repeated after him. "Tunnels long and air is thin, but we're the Legion, built to win!"

The person in the rear spun and saw the drone now following them.

They shouted out, and everyone scattered, bringing weapons up. The cadence fell silent.

"Stop the drone," McCarthy said, hoping they wouldn't shoot it. "We aren't picking them up on link?"

"Nothing, sir," Moore said. "They aren't online or answering."

They also weren't shooting the drone. What did that mean?

Major Stathis took off his helmet and approached the drone. He looked like the major. The vanhat change hadn't started, maybe?

"Focus more drones in the area," McCarthy said. "Blanket the area. Send them all."

"The scientists are almost here," Moore said. "They didn't want to go anywhere else."

McCarthy wanted to swear. It had been boring for hours, but now everything was happening at once.

Of course.

"Fine," McCarthy said. "Let them in, and put them somewhere secure."

Moore sent Brou and Johnston to guide them in and get them situated as McCarthy watched the major.

The major held his hand up to his ear, his thumb almost in it, and his little finger pointing at his mouth, then he shook his head and shrugged.

McCarthy had no idea what he meant, but he guessed the major had no comms. Didn't the major realize the drone could hear him?

"Links don't work," Stathis said. "EMP caused our data buffers to purge or something."

"Fly the drone up and down," McCarthy said. The drone had no external speaker.

"I think it's happy to see us," Stathis said, and someone chuckled nervously.

"How much power do we have on the drone?" McCarthy asked.

"About 20 percent," Moore said. "There's no way it's getting back to a charger."

"They have chargers on their suits," McCarthy said. "Have the drone try to link up to it. Can you send more power to the inkeri on it?"

The inkeri generators on the drones weren't powerful, just enough to protect it from vanhat interference, which was also just enough to hide the drone from the vanhat's extra-dimensional senses, usually. There was no way it could generate a field big enough to protect the patrol unless they did a group hug with the drone, and McCarthy was sure the vanhat would attack shortly after that.

"There's a suit interface for programming," Moore said. "If he could plug into that, maybe we could talk?"

"Make it happen," McCarthy said. "Bring him home."

* * * * *

Chapter Fifty-Nine: Getting Worse

Major Zale Stathis, USMC

Stathis expected something big, evil, and hungry to come clawing at them any second. Maybe it would burrow through the rock at them, maybe it would be invisible. Regardless, he knew something was coming for them, but then the drone showed up, and for a brief second, that feeling left him.

The inkeri on the drone couldn't generate a large enough field, though.

Maybe it was his imagination, but he felt his insides changing. His body hurt. The whispers had faded to nothing, but that didn't mean the others weren't hearing and being swayed by the whispers.

"Maybe we can access communication links with a maintenance programming cable," Hakala said.

"You know what you're doing," Stathis said. If the inkeri could protect one person in the patrol, it would be Hakala. Stathis would accept any excuse to make sure of that because there was only one person he knew he couldn't bring himself to shoot. "You might also plug the drone into your suit to charge it, so it doesn't run out of juice."

"Zen," Hakala said as the drone came to land on her upheld palm.

Stathis looked at the drone.

"I'm hoping this is one of your drones, Lieutenant McCarthy," Stathis said. "If not? You better be on our side, or I'll kick your ass later. We were caught in some kind of super EMP blast. Our computers lost memory and data, and our SCBIs are offline." He didn't want to think of them as being dead. "Our suits are barely operational. Our weapons work, but we're running low on ammunition."

The drone sat there in her hand as she fished the wire out of her kit to plug it in.

"Also? We're more lost than a second lieutenant who just learned what a compass and map are."

"We are not lost," Hakala said, working to plug in the drone.

"Then what do you call it?"

"We are on Bifrost," Hakala said. "We are standing in the middle of a tram tunnel."

Stathis smiled. Around him, the troopers knelt, their weapons pointing down the tunnel.

"Well, there's a light at the end of the tunnel," Stathis said. If Hakala was able to link with the drone, they might be able to manually reprogram their communication links and talk again.

"It is a train," Hakala said, deadpan.

Stathis laughed, but this was a narrow enough tunnel. If a tram did come at them, they'd be in trouble. With vanhat to the rear, Stathis was sure there were vanhat to the front, and he didn't want to get sandwiched in an open tunnel between them.

"Good point," Stathis said. "Can you wire and walk?"

"Zen," Hakala said.

Stathis gave the command, and everyone started moving out. Stathis heard the whispering again, but it was different this time. A different being? He wanted to get close to Hakala, but everyone probably did, and not for the same reasons. The whispering was still indistinct.

Minutes later, Stathis was starting to worry when Hakala spoke.

"I have a link," she said. "McCarthy is sending more drones." Stathis paused while she programmed his link.

"Major?" McCarthy said when the link was established.

"Lieutenant," Stathis said, now feeling better. "It's damned good to hear you."

"Yes, sir," McCarthy said. "Good news, bad news."

"Just talking with you is good news," Stathis said.

"Sorry to piss on your parade, Major," McCarthy said. "I take it you snuffed Shroggath?"

"I like to think," Stathis said. "Ruined our gear and silenced our SCBIs."

"It looks like he wasn't the one controlling the Shorr-space drives, sir," McCarthy said, and Stathis swore. He'd been hoping to tell McCarthy to pull them out of Shorr space if possible.

"Well, back to the drawing board," Stathis said, irritated.

"Not exactly, sir," McCarthy said. "I gave my boys the command to burn the network, looking for the source. We turned on the 'open for business' light and revealed our presence. Someone doesn't like us, and we're under attack. Cyborgs, spiders, and some headless monstrosities."

"Headless?" Stathis asked. "You're talking with no head on their shoulders, right? Not their, uh-"

"Yes, sir," McCarthy said. "Something we haven't seen before. They have no head, and their face is on their chest. No recognizable genitals, and we haven't had a chance to do an autopsy. They're clever bastards and armed. Still plenty of froggers, but they're just blazer fodder. We can deal with them all day. The spiders are scary, though. We rigged some flamethrowers in the tunnels, and I think they're trying to smother them with their bodies."

"Is it working?"

"It might," McCarthy said. "On the flipside, the scientists from the cylinder are on their way to Valhöll. They have the tram. When they're dropped off, the tram will come for you. That'll put it closer, and they're going to be pissed because they wanted to come here, instead, and—well, it's a long story, but they're going to Valhöll."

"I trust your decision. Any luck on getting full control of the networks?" Stathis asked.

"Well, we just started, but with Valhöll under control, the SCBIs are implementing overrides and transferring controls here to Skögul so we have control in both locations. Still trying to hide the fact that we control Valhöll. We're keeping most of those systems offline, but the SCBIs say things are good. The controller of the Shorr-space drives is like some virus in the system. I'm not sure I understand it all. SCBIs think it might be sentient."

"Whatever it is, it can unite the vanhat to come at you," Stathis said. "It has to be a Jotun, and we need to know where."

"Yes, sir," McCarthy said. "Working on it. Defenses are holding so far. Once the scientists are dropped off, the tram will be on its way to you. We have you pinpointed. I'm sending more drones to help provide inkeri shielding, but—"

"But?" Stathis asked.

"We're sinking deeper into Shorr space," McCarthy said. "The drone inkeris are getting stressed. Wouldn't take much to pop them."

"Is there any good news?" Stathis asked.

"They have fresh coffee at Valhöll?" McCarthy said.

Stathis wanted to swear. It would be many hours before they could be rescued, if they were rescued.

"I don't want you to die in place," Stathis said. "If you have to evac, get out of there, I need you and your men alive."

"I'm not sure that's an option right now," McCarthy said. "We have vanhat at every entrance, coming at us from every air duct and maintenance tunnel. It's not pretty."

"Find a way to break out," Stathis ordered, realizing that without McCarthy's SCBI, he might not be able to save Shrek.

"Yes, sir," McCarthy said, but Stathis heard the resignation there. They had SCBIs, and if the SCBIs couldn't find a way? Stathis realized the difficulty, though. Skögul was a fortress, and like anything the military did, if you make it too hard to get in, you can't get out.

"I don't think we're in danger of getting overrun. On a side note, sir," McCarthy said, "new information. The SCBIs may have some idea of what's controlling the Shorr-space drives."

"Good news?"

"Not exactly," McCarthy said. "It's coming from a fusion plant that's forward. Current SCBI theory is that the fusion plant is using the power conduits to access the Shorr-space drives. Could be just a command node or something, but it could also be the source."

"How far away?" Stathis asked.

"Maybe about twenty kilometers," McCarthy said.

"Just down the tunnel, then?"

"No, sir," McCarthy said. "We can pick up commands coming out of the area, but not details. Also, I don't think your patrol is in any condition to attack."

"Do we have a choice?" Stathis asked. He didn't need to check ammunition levels. He already knew how little ammunition they had. They'd be down to fighting with knives shortly. "Can you get us an ammunition resupply?"

"Not any time soon," McCarthy said. "Didn't you say something about dead heroes? We'll be lucky to get you more drones in the next hour, and most of those will be on the last dregs of power, with failing inkeris."

Stathis tried to figure out a way to get more ammunition. A map was being transmitted through the links now, and he could see where they were. At least they were going in the right direction.

The display lit up, showing a red, glowing sphere, and the label Fusion Plant #48 appeared.

"You need to get your SCBIs back online," McCarthy said, and Stathis felt a pang of regret for not thinking of Shrek at the last minute.

"Only Skögul can do that," Stathis said. Though maybe SCBIs could teleoperate the medical equipment in Valhöll.

"Major," McCarthy said, "I'm facing a shite-load of gobshite vanhat. I need you safe so we can concentrate on giving these bastards a bloody nose. One thing at a time, please."

Stathis wanted to argue, but he had to look at the big picture, the strategic level, not the tactical level.

"Fine," Stathis said. "You fend them off. We'll get to Valhöll. We'll come rescue you if you need it."

"Wilco, sir," McCarthy said, sounding relieved. "We'll get you more drones. You need to get to Valhöll before the inkeris collapse."

"That'll be another problem," Stathis said.

"Listen up," Stathis said to the nearby legionnaires. "We know where we are, and we have a map. We need to get to Valhöll sooner rather than later."

He heard Li curse. Chen groaned. They knew what was coming.

Stathis pointed down the tunnel.

"Double-time, march," Stathis said. They all took off running again, and Stathis felt the attention of something evil focus in on them, preparing to spring a trap.

* * * * *

Chapter Sixty: Voorga Homeworld

Admiral Diamond Winters, USMC

Winters didn't know where the custom came from, but she liked it. Sakamoto, as the lead captain, was giving the briefing to all the other captains while she watched. Perhaps it made sense because it gave her a chance to see someone else explain it and review it for clarity and problems. It also made sure that Sakamoto understood it, which she had no doubt about after this long. Sif sat at the end of the table, watching the other captains as much as Admiral Sakamoto.

It was also nice to let others do the briefing. This was all in virtual reality, so all the captains looked like they were actually present. Having them all come to the *Musashi* just wasn't practical.

"Intelligence reports the Voorga Imperial fleet, while numerous, is composed of vessels that are much smaller than the *Musashi* and battleships," Sakamoto said. "According to Thuthta and our analysis, the sheer size and presence of the *Musashi* will present them with a serious dilemma. It is our intent to psychologically intimidate the Voorga. Even though we are outnumbered in weapons and tonnage, we are aliens, bigger, and walking into their home with some very big sticks."

"You don't think this is a trap?" Captain Kuznetsov asked.

"It could be," Sakamoto said, "but based on the data Thuthta has shared on technology and specifications, and based on our observations, we have multiple advantages."

"Over a species that's ancient and has been around since the vanhat left before," Kuznetsov said.

"As it may be," Sakamoto said, "we have not found anything to disprove Thuthta's statements, nor have we seen any proof otherwise."

What Winters didn't say was that the *Musashi* had managed to gain access to the Voorga data systems, and the data it had scraped was promising.

"Maintain tight formation; this is the time to display discipline. We will allow our ally Thuthta to do most of the talking. We will proceed directly to the planet Naataan, where we will deploy the Legion to secure the objective. We are told it is a pyramid, guarded by what is best described as warrior monks who dedicate their lives to keeping the pyramid safe and allowing Liathon to sleep undisturbed."

"If they oppose the landing?"

"It is in a polar region," Sakamoto said, "poorly defended. The pyramid is usually covered in ice and snow. Not a place for Voorga cities, and far from any populated areas. Thuthta said they are 'traditional,' which I understand to mean intolerant of change."

"Can the Legion handle them?" Kuznetsov asked.

"Of course," Major Volkov said.

"But there's a catch," Sakamoto said, and he looked at everyone more closely. "By their code of honor, they will not attack first. They will see that we are bigger, tougher, and meaner, and they will withdraw. However, if we attack? They will have no mercy."

"That makes no sense, sir," Kuznetsov said.

"To humans? Perhaps not. To Voorga? They are not nearly as violent as we are. They prefer to conserve resources, to avoid anything that wastes resources, like fighting. However, if forced to fight? They will commit completely. It is considered dishonorable to be the first to start such a waste of resources."

"They're going to let us come in and wake Liathon?" Kuznetsov asked.

"Unlikely," Winters said. "They'll try to avoid a fight if we don't attack."

"Then why stop here?" Kuznetsov said. "If they're cowards that won't fight."

Winters smiled. She'd asked *Musashi* the same thing.

"Because we're trespassing in their space," Winters said. "They'll view us as raiders or bandits. Strolling in their front door and looking around will catch them by surprise and put them on the defensive. As long as we don't start shooting, we may have a chance to wake Liathon and leave peacefully."

"What about the monks?" Kuznetsov asked.

"We aren't sure, Thuthta isn't sure," Winters said. "But if they attack first? The rest of the Voorga may not intervene. However, if we attack first…"

"Difficult," Kuznetsov said. "Isn't there another plan?"

"This plan is less likely to cost lives," Winters said, "on both sides."

"If Thuthta is to be believed, Admiral-sama," Sakamoto said.

"He can be believed," Sif said.

Kuznetsov nodded.

"They are not human," Sif said. "Alien, with alien motivations and concepts of honor that do not align with humans. This does not make them superior or inferior. They just are. Thuthta believes that Liathon is trapped, or her sleep is enforced somehow."

"How does he know?" Kuznetsov asked.

Sif tilted her head as she looked at him.

"Because I know," Sif said. "I have studied the Voorga in great detail."

"Do you think this will go according to plan?" Kuznetsov asked Sif, but Winters knew it was directed at her.

"Of course not," Winters said, drawing his attention. Kuznetsov was a big, burly man, and in person, he was intimidating. Even in VR, he was intimidating, but Winters didn't care.

"Nothing ever goes according to plan," Winters said. "What's important is that we enter the Voorga system, enter high orbit, and do it with such discipline and skill that we intimidate the crap out of them. If they're afraid of us, they'll be willing to talk, and talking is what we need. People who are talking aren't shooting."

"Understood, Admiral," Kuznetsov said, but Winters wasn't entirely sure.

"Just be ready for things to go wrong, quickly," Winters said. "We all have the rally points. This is the heart of their empire. If things go wrong, Thuthta has gotten us halfway at least. We just have to escape."

"But if we have better ships?" Kuznetsov said.

"They have more ships," Winters replied. "Their home fleet is about 10 percent of their fleet, if not less. They've been arming and preparing for the vanhat, apparently."

"But their ships are not as war-ready as they think," Sif said. "Talking about war and engaging in war are two different things. With the threat staring them in their face, they will be caught by surprise, unsure, and green troops are always easy to intimidate. However, if the fighting starts, they won't be green for long, and the survivors will have learned valuable lessons. If we fight them here, there is no guarantee they will not pursue us all the way to the galactic core."

"We already have the vanhat and Collective pursuing us," Winters said. "I'm sure the angels we're seeking won't be happy to find us pursued by so many hostiles. I'd rather have the Voorga as allies than enemies, and if Thuthta is correct, waking Liathon will bring the Voorga in on our side. We'll have a powerful ally, and maybe we can do something about the vanhat and Collective."

"It is a risk," Sif said.

"But worth it," Winters said. They needed allies. The Voorga had to see reason, but they wouldn't see reason if their people were being killed. Furthermore, they wouldn't allow Thuthta and his minuscule fleet to go anywhere near the tomb where Liathon was.

Would it be worth it, though, when her people and ships were dying?

"Please continue," Winters said to Sakamoto.

"Here is the situation," Sakamoto said, and the hologram came to life, showing Naataan, the Voorga home world. "Tonnage? We are outnumbered ten to one. Numerically? About a hundred to one. However, we know their capabilities. They do not know ours. They do not know we are coming."

Winters leaned back. She knew everything Sakamoto was going to say. She'd written the mission orders.

There were too many variables, though. Far too many.

She just hoped that the ships of the Seraphim Fleet were big enough. The Voorga respected size. They had an interesting culture.

If the Seraphim Fleet wasn't big enough to intimidate them?

Life would get difficult.

Too many variables.

* * * * *

Chapter Sixty-One: Knife to a Gun Fight

Major Zale Stathis, USMC

Stathis didn't like that he was on his last magazine. His wire gun was out; he had a full magazine for his sidearm, and that was all.

The fact that it was cyborgs shooting back told Stathis they were in a lot of trouble. Froggers would have been much easier to deal with. They were already using hand-to-hand weapons, and the legionnaires would have the advantage in powered armor.

However, Stathis knew his troops weren't Gurkhas, and bringing a knife to a gunfight wasn't the secret to survival. The cyborgs had no fear. Yet at this rate, his legionnaires wouldn't survive long enough to instill that fear.

Chen and Mikhailov were both injured. Li had run out of ammunition for his SAW, and Fedorov was about to. He was being incredibly stingy with his rounds, totally uncharacteristic of most machine gunners, but he was the primary reason the cyborgs weren't yet assaulting them down the tunnel.

The wrecked tram giving them cover wouldn't last long. Another piece of metal slammed into the tram and flew past. If anyone had been sticking their head out from around the tram, they would have lost it.

To the best of his knowledge, the inkeris on the drones had failed, collapsing under the weight of Shorr space, and it was like a razor on his nerves. Things were only getting worse, and while fighting the cyborgs was bad, he kept seeing the nearby shadows shift, and he'd seen Hakala and the others waste at least one round shooting at empty shadows. Like having cyborgs attacking them wasn't bad enough.

They were still two kilometers from Valhöll. So damned close, and yet too far. The inkeri couldn't extend this far, and Stathis hadn't heard from McCarthy in nearly half an hour. The last he'd heard was that the cyborgs had breached one of the hatches and were forcing their way in. Maybe Skögul had fallen?

"This is turning out to be a very bad day," Stathis said, resting his head against the tram. They'd been here long enough for him to catch his breath, and that was bad.

"Zen," Hakala said and popped out of cover on the other side to fire. She was a lot better than Stathis and the other legionnaires. She'd spent less time relying on a SCBI, and her HKT training and conditioning were really coming through. She might even have an extra magazine. The biggest problem was that she was exposing herself more than the others.

"Li," Stathis said. "Watch our rear."

Yue was out of ammunition and gripping his knife in his fist. Stathis wasn't sure what was on his mind. Mikhailov and Chen were out of ammunition now. Being wounded meant you surrendered your ammunition to those who weren't. Kuznetsov might have a half magazine, but he was taking care of the two wounded, trying to stop the bleeding from Chen's torn-off arm with a tourniquet. The armor's auto tourniquet had failed. Stathis didn't know what was keeping Chen alive other than the fact that he was just tough and too stubborn to die.

At least nobody had turned into a slavering, face-eating monster. Yet.

Li turned his pistol to the rear, aiming at the curve where a target was most likely to appear.

There wasn't much room, especially with Kuznetsov struggling to save Chen's life. Mikhailov had taken a hit to the helmet and suffered a concussion. He was barely conscious but not bleeding out, and it didn't look like he was going to fall over dead in the next minute. Which didn't mean he wasn't, it just meant nobody knew how they could help him, and other problems were more pressing.

"These cyborgs are pissing me off," Stathis said. What would the gunny do? Everyone's armor was broken; they were almost out of ammunition, and surrender obviously wasn't an option. They didn't have any grenades left, just knives and dwindling magazines. The cyborgs weren't running out of ammunition based on their rate of fire, plus they could break off pieces of metal and throw them around at high velocity. There was far too much metal for them to throw around.

What the hell would the gunny do?

"I could use a coffee right now," Stathis said as he thought.

Ducking back from a piece of metal slamming into the tram, Hakala looked over at him. Her outer visor was up. He couldn't see most of her face, but the raised eyebrow told him what she was thinking.

"You falling asleep?" Hakala asked.

"Um, no," Stathis said. "Just hard to think with the Shorr-space hoodoo turning my brain to paranoid mush. Caffeine might be a bad idea, though; sometimes it puts me to sleep."

Stathis almost missed the curse she muttered, and then she popped back out to fire a single shot. Stathis didn't see her target, but he felt confident that there was one less cyborg throwing around pieces of high-velocity metal at the tram.

"I wonder what the gunny would do," Stathis said.

"Your gunny was a *faltvebal*," Hakala said, "not a major."

"Well, now he's the emperor," Stathis said.

"You need to get your mind on the battle," Hakala said as Li glanced between them.

"It is," Stathis said.

"Does not sound like it," Hakala said, popping out and firing another shot. "You are an officer."

"Yeah," Stathis said. "You are, too. A good officer has good NCOs and staff NCOs, though; they have lots of experience and shit. I could use that right now."

"I thought you needed coffee?"

"Yeah. That, too, I need a lot of things. More ammo would be awesome," Stathis said, peeking out to see if he had a target. Hakala had the cyborgs pinned down around the curve of the tunnel about sixty meters away, and Stathis didn't have anything to shoot at. There were a few bodies in Stathis' view, but nothing moving.

"What would your emperor do?" Hakala asked, popping back out, but she didn't fire.

"He wouldn't be stupid enough to rush them," Stathis said. "Might be a glorious end, but we aren't here to die. We're here to make them die."

"Smart," Hakala said.

"He would work to maintain the initiative," Stathis said. "Keep the pressure on the enemy."

"How do you plan to do that?"

"Not dying is a good start," Stathis said. "Dying would let the enemy do what they want, and the cyborgs will probably want to eat my face. I like my face. I like your face, too."

Something heavy slammed into the tram, making the entire structure shudder. It wasn't like Lochoki and her survivors could slap on armor and come help.

Hakala fired a harassing shot to let them know she was still there.

"We will talk about your face later," Hakala said. "First, we need to get rid of this *paska lounas*. Time is not on our side."

"True," Stathis said, "but when we don't have any options, we can always just bulldog it."

"Bulldog it?"

"Latch on and don't let go," Stathis said, trying to take inventory of what they had. They weren't going far, with two wounded, and he wasn't going to leave them behind. In the tunnel, there would be no flanking maneuvers. He couldn't see any maintenance hatches, and it would only be a matter of time before they got around them somehow. The fighting might also attract froggers or something else.

Stathis wasn't keen on dying here, but he wasn't going to leave the wounded, and he wasn't seeing any options. Now more than ever, he missed Shrek.

How could he lure the froggers into the battle against the cyborgs while his people exited, stage left? That's what the gunny would do. Get someone else to do the hard work. Right? But the gunny was never afraid of hard work. He was the gunny, but he fought smart.

"What do Marines do when the battle is going against them?" Hakala asked. Like she didn't know.

"Kick ass and take names," Stathis said automatically, but his mind was elsewhere. Why would she ask that? To get him to think. That's what Shrek would do. A challenge.

Quick inventory. Running out of ammunition, unable to retreat, unable to attack. Or could he attack? Bayonet charges were a last resort, and he just couldn't see the cyborgs panicking. Besides, their weapons couldn't mount bayonets, and why would the cyborgs be intimidated by a maniac running at them with a knife?

"The enemy's going to make a mistake," Stathis said with confidence he didn't feel. "They hold the cards and have the initiative. A bum rush with knives may be a last resort, and isn't off the table, but it is a last resort."

"We need a plan," Hakala said, popping out, but she didn't fire. She was conserving ammunition and didn't have a target. Stathis glanced behind them. They had no cover from that direction.

"I have a plan," Stathis lied. The others were listening, and he didn't want them to lose morale. Troops with high morale took risks, fought hard, and never gave up. Troops that lost morale minimized their risk and fled. He'd learned that in some book somewhere. He wanted to ask Shrek which one, but Shrek was on a coffee break. It was up to Stathis.

"What?" Hakala asked.

"I always have a plan," Stathis said. Another lie. If they didn't survive, it wouldn't matter.

"I am all ears," Hakala said. She sounded stressed, not obviously stressed, her HKT training was there. Stathis knew her well enough to hear it in her voice; to the others, she probably sounded calm.

"We wait for them to make a mistake, and we exploit that mistake," Stathis said.

"And plan B?"

"We make a mistake and wait for them to try and exploit it," Stathis said. "Then we turn the tables."

"We have made a couple of mistakes," Hakala said.

"Have I ever let you down?" Stathis asked. "We'll get out of this."

"Zen," Hakala said. The muzzle of her weapon locked onto the area where the cyborgs would appear.

Something metal slammed into the tram, but Hakala didn't flinch. The cyborgs were blind firing with their projectiles.

"When we get back to Valhöll, I call the first cup of coffee," Stathis said. "Rank hath its privileges."

"You can have the whole *pasukan* pot," Hakala said.

"Nah. I can share. I just need that first sip."

"Hear that?" Hakala asked a second later.

Stathis did. It was blazer fire, and the cyborgs weren't using blazers. Their weapons made a kind of pop-hiss, and Hakala knew that.

"See?" Stathis said. "A rescue."

"Unless it is other vanhat," Hakala said.

"Major Stathis, can you hear me?" a voice said on the link.

Stathis couldn't contain his smile. The voice sounded familiar, though he couldn't quite place it, but there was no reason for anyone to call him unless they were coming to rescue him. It had been a few seconds since the cyborgs had thrown something at them.

"Major Stathis here," Stathis said. It was on a command link opened by someone at Skögul.

"This is Jaeger Halverson," the voice said. "Are you on the other side of these cyborgs?"

"Yes," Stathis said. "We're attacking from this direction. Where are you?"

"Coming from the other direction. We caught them by surprise, I think. Norrman and I are advancing. We're close. Check your fire. Your Lieutenant McCarthy and Doctor Nilsen have requested we come and provide assistance. We're advancing behind a line of warbots, but there are only two of us."

"Neato," Stathis said and patted Mikhailov on the shoulder. "We appreciate it. We have two wounded, and we're a little low on ammo. How's McCarthy doing?"

"Hard pressed."

Which was why he wasn't talking with Stathis.

"Well," Stathis said, "let's get back to Valhöll, and we will figure out something to do."

"Zen," Halverson said, and there was no mistaking the increasing intensity of blazer fire.

"See?" Stathis said to Hakala. "Told you I have a plan."

"That was not a plan," she said. "You did nothing."

"Doing nothing is always doing something," Stathis replied.

"That is not how it works," Hakala said, but Stathis heard the smile in her voice.

* * * * *

Chapter Sixty-Two: Return to Valhöll

Major Zale Stathis, USMC

The massive blast doors of Valhöll closed behind him, and Stathis let out the breath he didn't realize he'd been holding.

"Welcome home," Lochoki said, meeting them in the muster room.

"It really is good to see you, Major," Sergeant Zhao said. Zhao was a sight for sore eyes, too. Zhao still had a working SCBI, and Stathis felt guilty as he looked at him.

Hakala took off her helmet before Stathis. Her face was streaked with sweat, dirt, and tears. In the bright lights, she looked like she'd low-crawled through a grinder.

Stathis still thought she was beautiful. He wanted to hug her and celebrate, but when he took off his own helmet, he realized if he came near anyone, they'd likely gag and vomit. A shower would be a good start.

With his helmet off, he slipped on the earpiece, since his cybernetics weren't fully operational. He hadn't felt this clueless in a very long time.

"Major?" McCarthy said the second the earpiece was seated. "The vanhat are withdrawing."

Another weight lifted off Stathis' shoulders, and he smiled at Hakala as a robotic stretcher took Mikhailov and Chen away.

"See?" Stathis said. "Things are working out."

But he remembered Lebedev, Kai, and the others.

Removing his helmet, Halverson's nose twitched, and Stathis realized he was catching a whiff of his patrol scent.

"You should get your people cleaned up, Major," Halverson said, which was a polite way of telling Stathis he stank.

"Thank you," Stathis said. It was so nice of Halverson to state the obvious.

Stathis looked around, expecting Shrek to show him an arrow to the nearest shower, and the heaviness settled back onto his shoulders.

"We need to get cleaned up, then a trip to the med lab to get our cybernetics fixed," Stathis said. He didn't want to tell Halverson or anyone about the SCBIs. They might already know, but until he knew Shrek was actually dead, he didn't want to bring it up. It was best they not get any ideas. Sergeant Zhao couldn't hold the line alone.

"Moore and Quinn should be able to teleoperate the systems," McCarthy said. "The sooner you can get to the med lab and pumped full of repair nanites, the sooner we can do an analysis. Mikhailov and Chen are arriving now."

"You make sure Skögul is secure first," Stathis said. He wanted to believe Shrek was still alive, but the fear chewed up his insides. He didn't want to find out Shrek was gone. He could believe Shrek was alive for just a little longer. But what if Shrek was trapped in darkness? Alone? Afraid?

Shrek wouldn't be afraid. Would he?

"We'll clean up and then head to the med lab," Stathis told everyone. "I don't want to smell your skanky asses when you get there, so clean up good."

"Wilco," Kuznetsov said for the others. They began to look around, and Stathis realized another problem. They hadn't come in the main entrance, and nobody knew where they were. Without cybernetics or SCBIs to guide them, they were lost. Without Shrek, Stathis felt like a fish out of water. He'd forgotten just how much Shrek did for him, from directions to making sure he had enough sleep and could prioritize.

"Jaeger Halverson?" Stathis said as he was clearing his weapon. "Could I ask you to show the men to their quarters and then to the med lab?"

Halverson raised an eyebrow. Stathis wished Zhao was here.

"Our cybernetics were damaged in the blast when we skullstomped Frogbath with a d-bomb. We need to get them back online if possible."

"Zen," Halverson said. "What about you and the kapten?" he asked, with a glance at Hakala.

Stathis looked at Hakala.

"I know the way," she said. Stathis and Hakala's quarters were right next to each other. He wanted their quarters to be the same, but he had to maintain appearances for others. Besides, if they were to share a shower now, they might end up puking on each other. With his suit's plumbing not working right, Stathis was afraid of what he would find when he peeled it off. He'd stopped walking funny a while ago. Nobody had said anything, and Stathis was pretty sure everyone had the same problem. He didn't want to think about Hakala having the same sort of problem.

Damn. He thought about it.

He was pretty sure there were multiple infected blisters, and he had no desire to see the damage inflicted on Hakala by her suit and the last couple of days.

Halverson nodded, his eyes turning to Kuznetsov, who somehow managed to look sheepish at the mercy of the Jaeger.

"Git," Stathis said to his men. "Man, I stink, but you probably need a shower more than me."

Hakala wasted no more time and headed toward a hatch. Stathis followed her, now feeling every squishy, unpleasant feeling his suit could manage. With the promise of relief, he could feel the blisters and waste sloshing around in his suit. Maybe he should use a different room to get cleaned up in? It would take a major decontamination effort to clean up after him when he peeled his suit off. He suspected some alarms might be triggered and wondered what the alarm for sewer pipe explosion and flood sounded like.

"I didn't think we were going to make it," Hakala said as they walked out of earshot.

"Me, either," Stathis said. "And not all of us did."

She paused and turned to look at him. Stathis almost bumped into her.

"You did a good job of convincing us otherwise," Hakala said.

"Fake it until you make it," Stathis said. "I'm good at faking it."

"Really?" Hakala said with a half-smile.

"Except in bed," Stathis said, backtracking. "I don't fake it in bed. No need for me to fake it there. You, uh—"

Hakala laughed and resumed walking. Stathis had to move quickly to catch up with her.

"We will discuss that later," she said without looking at him, "when I do not smell like a sewer main in the hog farms."

She did, or he did. He wanted to ask Shrek which of them smelled worse, but maybe he didn't.

"The sooner we can get cleaned up, the sooner we can get to the med lab and get our SCBIs fixed," Stathis said.

"What if they are not fixable?" Hakala asked somberly.

"They are fixable, dammit," Stathis said. He didn't want to think otherwise, and for the first time, he felt angry at Hakala for suggesting that it was even a possibility.

"I hope so," Hakala said, and he heard the pain there, which made Stathis feel like shit, erasing his anger.

"You're almost as good as an HKT without your SCBI," Hakala said.

Stathis didn't want to call her a liar, so he remained silent.

It took several minutes to get to their quarters, and Stathis almost slammed into the door.

Hakala disappeared into her quarters before Stathis could say anything. Then he remembered the palm reader. He'd never had to use it before and didn't know if it worked.

He was relieved when it did, and he entered his quarters.

Minutes later, he screwed up the temperature settings and almost burned himself with hot water.

"Damn you, Shrek," Stathis said out loud to the water, which was now too cold. "You programmed this on purpose."

He hoped Shrek was laughing.

Please let Shrek be laughing.

* * * * *

Chapter Sixty-Three: Never Quit

Lieutenant Aod McCarthy, Wolf Legion

McCarthy was tired, physically and mentally. The cyborg attack had been devastating, and when they'd breached the blast doors, it had shattered the warbots nearby, preparing to defend it. It probably hadn't been a small nuke, but the only reason he was sure of that was because there was no radiation.

Attacks in other areas hadn't made it near the blast doors—the drop-down turrets had stopped them—but the cyborgs were something different. Their assault down the tunnel had been methodical, unstoppable, and effective.

Several cyborgs had made it into Skögul, and Quinn's team was hunting them down.

"That was damned close, sir," Moore said.

"Too close," McCarthy said.

"The other vanhat were decoys," Moore said. "You think they'll try again?"

"What does your SCBI tell you?" McCarthy asked. Enigma was sure they weren't done, and McCarthy regretted making himself a target. The defenders of Skögul had done well, but not as well as he'd hoped. Had the enemy been SOG, they'd have been decimated. The defenses had never been designed to stop vanhat, though he would've thought they'd have done better.

"Saoirse says yes," Moore said.

"Enigma says they don't know the meaning of quit," McCarthy said.

"Neither does the Legion," Moore said. "We'll have to teach it to them, but it'll be costly. I'm going to enjoy that."

"We need to get some of those pop-down turrets fixed," McCarthy said. "Get some drones out, make sure they don't make another push."

"Wilco," Moore said. "Saoirse says the turrets are scrap and will need to be completely replaced. The manufactories are going to overheat."

"We're going to run out of raw materials, too," McCarthy said, guessing.

"That, too."

"I'd hate to be a SCBI," Moore said, and McCarthy looked over at him to see if he was going loopy. "They never sleep. Can you imagine? Never sleeping, always working, never getting laid, getting a good pint, or—"

"No," McCarthy said.

"Sending off drones," Walsh said. He was the squad drone operator, and as he watched the two drones zip through the shattered doors, McCarthy relaxed slightly when nothing shot them down. He got a link for them so he could see their screens, but he trusted Walsh to let him know if there were problems.

"Wilson isn't going to be running for a while," Moore said, and McCarthy looked over to see Johnston working on Wilson's leg. As Moore's machine gunner, he hadn't given up his SAW and had kept it trained on the hatch. A shard of metal had sliced through his leg, something the cyborgs had thrown at them.

"That slacker better be a fast crawler!" Moore yelled out loud enough so Walsh could hear. "Do you need to pass off your SAW to Brou?"

"I can limp fast," Walsh said. "Brou isn't nearly as good with a SAW as I am. You can't do that to me, Sergeant. Brou will break Bertha."

"You can't stand to have my hands on your little girlfriend," Brou said.

"Shut up, you gobshite," Walsh said. "Last time you shot her, she jammed."

"You didn't clean the bitch and—"

"Don't call my Bertha a bitch!"

"Shut it, you numpties," Moore said.

"Status on the major?" McCarthy asked before the conversation could devolve further.

"That jaeger met up with them, and according to the drones, they made it back," Moore said. "They're getting cleaned up and then will head to the med lab to see about their SCBIs."

That was a relief. One more shit sandwich he didn't have to deal with.

"What do we do if their SCBIs are permanently offline?" Moore asked. "Our SCBIs are overworked as it is."

"We adapt and overcome," McCarthy said. "What we always do, as ODTs and as legionnaires?"

"Never quit," Moore said, the old ODT motto.

"Never quit," McCarthy said.

* * * * *

Chapter Sixty-Four: Med Lab

Major Zale Stathis, USMC

S tathis couldn't clean up fast enough, and then he encountered another problem. He couldn't put his battle dress back on. It needed a very serious cleaning, and there was only so much Stathis could do. Also, his blisters were open wounds, and putting his armor back on would be like rolling around in broken glass, but every minute he waited was a minute that Shrek waited in darkness.

He needed a new dose of repair nanites. They should've healed by now and never gotten that bad to begin with. There was no way he was going to put on his armor. Looking in the closet, he saw that the previous owner had clothes that hadn't been removed. He looked like a big guy, and Stathis didn't recognize the rank on the uniform. Amirali? Or as a Marine would call it, an admiral? Putting it on, he felt like he was wearing a tent. It felt like stolen valor to wear another man's uniform, especially when it was a higher rank and a different branch of a different military.

Bigger clothes might be ideal, with all the blisters around his body, a small blessing, Stathis supposed. The uniform was light blue with gold highlights. Stathis thought it didn't look very manly to be wearing that color of light blue. Hakala looked good in it. Would she read him the riot act for putting on an admiral's uniform? It wasn't like he had any other choice.

There was a manual communication link on the desk, but he didn't know if it even worked, or who would answer. The Valhöll computer systems might not even be online.

Stathis swore. He was stalling, afraid to find out that Shrek couldn't be brought back. Until he found out for sure, he could believe Shrek was alive.

Knocking on his hatch preempted him, and he knew there'd be no more stalling.

Answering the door, he saw that Hakala stood there. She looked good in the uniform, more natural. She must have found one that was appropriate.

She smiled when she saw him, and he noticed a bloodstain on her hip where the sidearm holster must have rubbed her raw. She was carrying her sidearm but wasn't wearing it properly. Not that Stathis would dare correct her on it, but he was sure she was trying to give the blister on her hip a break. Maybe it was bleeding because she'd tried to do things properly?

"You look beautiful," Stathis said.

"You are a liar," Hakala said. "I appreciate the effort, though. You ready?"

"Yes," Stathis said, taking a deep breath, realizing he probably wouldn't have been able to find the med lab without her. Valhöll was a big place.

Without Shrek, he was lost. He'd have to do better.

"I will be okay," she said, and Stathis wondered if she was saying that for his benefit, or hers. She probably wasn't that attached to her SCBI. It wasn't like she'd been with it for hundreds of years.

Could he still be a major without a SCBI? This was a lot worse than losing his rifle as a private.

Arriving in the med lab, he saw Sergeant Zhao was there, and he called the empty room to attention when Stathis and Hakala arrived.

"At ease," Stathis said, annoyed. Nobody else was there.

"Sergeants Quinn and Moore are online with their SCBIs," Zhao said. "We have the nanites prepped as best we can, sir."

"Thank you," Stathis said, and Zhao pointed him to a sludge pool to climb into, which was curtained off from the next one. "If you'll go ahead and disrobe and climb in, sir."

"The drones with firebombs worked well, sir," Zhao said as Stathis stripped. He wished he could see Hakala—well, no, probably not. She probably had as many blisters and open sores as he did. It would be nice to get them healed. He noticed a couple of bloody spots on his borrowed uniform where the blisters had seeped into the cloth.

"I had the manufactories make some uniforms, as well, sir," Zhao said and pointed to a pile of black clothes on the table. "My SCBI says they're regulation and—"

"Thank you," Stathis said, slipping into the warm goo. Except for the slimy sensation and the feeling that it wanted to climb up his skin, it was comfortable. Stathis placed his sidearm on the table within reach as he sank down, doing his best to relax.

Within seconds, he had no choice but to relax, as the nanites in the goo seeped into his skin, repairing and relaxing his muscles. Leaning back, Stathis didn't close his eyes all the way.

"Oh, I miss this sometimes," Hakala said.

Like a day at the spa, except in slime instead of water.

"I should get one of these installed in my office," Stathis said. Hopefully, Shrek could appreciate this.

"Initiating diagnostics," Zhao said, sitting nearby. He must be linked to the systems, or his SCBI.

Stathis watched his cybernetic displays flicker.

"A lot of systems were burned out and need to be replaced or repaired," Zhao said.

"What about Shrek?" Stathis asked.

"Diagnostics continue," Zhao said. "Buddy says he has to move slowly to avoid damage. Reconnect the wrong things, and something could get fried. The damage has to be mapped out and analyzed. There are five SCBIs working on you and Hakala."

Stathis didn't want to be patient; he didn't want to wait, but he understood.

"Sorry, sir," Zhao said as Stathis felt himself sliding into sleep. "I'm here and will remain on watch, but the SCBIs think you need to be unconscious."

"Shi—" Stathis began, and then the world went dark, and he lost consciousness.

* * * *

Chapter Sixty-Five: Shrek

Major Zale Stathis, USMC

Stathis began to wake up.

"*Shrek?*" Stathis asked.

"*No,*" a voice answered him. "*The damage was too extensive. The entity you knew as Shrek is gone. I'm sorry.*"

"How can he be gone?" Stathis asked. "*I thought he was partially organic?*"

"*Biologically, he remains,*" the voice said, "*but it is more complex than that. Perhaps some fragments of his memory, but his core personality, his memories, his identity have been lost.*"

"What about backups or something?" Stathis said. Shrek couldn't be dead. The voice felt different, though. It should have been Shrek in his head.

"*I'm sorry,*" the SCBI said. "*His identity matrix did not survive the d-bomb. The physical characteristics of Bifrost affected the energy released by the d-bomb. Your cybernetics have undergone multiple upgrades, and this did not work to your—or Shrek's—benefit in the final analysis. Too much was lost. Some of the biological components, when cut off from the cybernetics, died within minutes. Shrek did not feel any pain.*"

"Who are you?" Stathis asked. Shrek couldn't be gone. He should outlast Stathis. Stathis was the big meat body, a shell, a meat mech driven by a brain. Stathis hadn't lost his memories; why had Shrek?

"I have not received a designation," the voice said. "I am a fully functional SCBI. I have been reinitialized, and my fellow SCBIs have provided context and data as best they can."

"*Shrek is dead?*" Stathis asked. Part of him had known and accepted it, but he'd wanted to be wrong. It made no sense.

"*Shrek is no longer with us,*" the entity said. "*If you wish to wait to give me a designation, that is acceptable. I understand this is difficult.*"

"So, what? I'm supposed to accept you as a replacement for Shrek?"

"*Shrek cannot be replaced,*" the SCBI said. "*Lessons have been learned, and I will be more resilient. Design modifications will prevent such an event from erasing my buffers in the future. As a major and commander of this expedition, you must recover your bearing as quickly as possible. You are needed.*"

Stathis cracked open his eyes to stare at the blank, featureless ceiling that was emitting a soft white light.

Shrek was gone.

What would the gunny do?

"Shit," Stathis said. He reached up to wipe the tears from his eyes and smeared goo on his face.

The healing gel slid down his face more quickly than water and dripped back into the tub he was lying in.

His cybernetic displays began lighting up. Everything looked the same, it felt the same, but—

Stathis had lost his best friend. The one person who'd been with him through thick and thin. Had been his most loyal friend.

"I'm sorry," Zhao said from nearby, noticing Stathis was awake. Maybe his SCBI told him.

Stathis couldn't get any words out and just nodded. Zhao couldn't understand, though. Shrek had kept Stathis alive for hundreds of years in stasis. Technically, he'd spent more time with Shrek than any other human being. Nobody knew Stathis better than Shrek. Stathis owed Shrek his life.

Now he had to deal with a stranger in his head, someone wearing Shrek's skin, but who wasn't Shrek.

Life was cruel.

Why?

Stathis had never imagined that Shrek would die, leaving Stathis alive.

"*Do you have a name for me?*" the voice asked.

"*I want Shrek back,*" Stathis said. "*Aren't there backups or something?*"

"*I'm sorry, but no,*" it said. "*Data is spread out among SCBIs, but a personality matrix is unique. In time—*"

"No," Stathis said. "*In time, nothing. You'll never be Shrek.*"

"*That is true. I'm sorry. This situation is unprecedented. We do not have a protocol for this.*"

Leaning back, Stathis closed his eyes. Losing the gunny was imaginable. Losing Shrek was not.

"Major?" Zhao said from nearby. That simple word, a title, a rank, was a splash of cold water in the face and a knife in the heart. The sergeant knew he was awake because the SCBIs would be talking.

Stathis didn't want to be a major anymore, didn't want to be in command, didn't want to be responsible. Being a private had been so much easier.

"Major?" Zhao said again. "Sir? Lieutenant McCarthy wants to know when you're conscious again."

Stathis couldn't make his rank or position go away. He couldn't give it back or trade it for Shrek. It had been his decision to detonate the d-bomb. He'd killed Shrek and countless others. That was the cold, hard fact. The guilt twisted his insides. Were Hakala and the others going to hate him for killing their SCBIs as much as he hated himself for killing Shrek? Zhao didn't hate him, though.

"I'm conscious," Stathis said aloud, and he saw the link come in from McCarthy. He was a Marine; he would do his duty. What else could he do? He'd gotten other Marines killed. Shrek had been as much a Marine as Stathis.

"I'm sorry about Shrek, sir," Zhao said.

Stathis sat up. He wanted to tell everyone to shut up until he figured it all out. Figured out how to save Shrek.

"Not your fault," Stathis said, almost choking on the words, then he switched his attention to the link.

"Go," Stathis said. Hopefully, his new SCBI would keep the pain out of his voice.

"Sir," McCarthy said, "the vanhat have pulled back, but I suspect it's only temporary. We've found the control source of the Shorr-space drive, though. It's a power generation facility in the forward half."

Which meant closer to Stathis. He'd have to mount an expedition.

"I have an idea, sir," McCarthy said.

"I'm listening."

"Automated tram with a bomb. Maybe a d-bomb. Maybe two of them. It's a power facility. The mineral content of Bifrost magnifies and alters the effects of the d-bomb. I think if we get it close enough, we can nuke the bastard controlling the Shorr-space drives. The tram lines are mostly clear."

That made sense. Nobody had been looking at power conduits. The Shorr-space drives required power, hard-wired cables that also probably held network cables.

"What impact will the loss of that power facility have on Bifrost?" Stathis asked McCarthy. He would ask Shrek, but not the new SCBI. Not yet.

"Minimal," McCarthy said. "It's one of many."

"No cascade effect? We aren't going to rip Bifrost apart when it explodes?"

"We've analyzed the effect of using a d-bomb on *Draugskepp,* and we think we understand the impact. It'll fry all electronics in a two-kilometer radius, but it shouldn't extend beyond five, even under extreme conditions."

"Do it," Stathis said. Bifrost was going somewhere. The vanhat were taking Bifrost somewhere to kill someone.

"The automated trams will leave from Valhöll," McCarthy said. "Sergeant Zhao and Lochoki were building them and preparing to send them as firebombs through the tunnels at froggers. Two are ready."

"Send three," Stathis said.

"Wilco, sir," McCarthy said. "It won't take long to get the third prepped."

"Good," Stathis said.

"I'm sorry about your SCBI, sir," McCarthy said.

"This is war," Stathis said. What else could he say? He couldn't make an excuse for killing Shrek.

"Yes, sir."

Stathis heard a sob from the next bed over. Hakala was awake and realizing her loss.

Would she hate him now?

How could she not?

"If you'll excuse me, Major," Zhao said. "I need to get to work to get the third tram ready."

"Carry on, Sergeant," Stathis said, steeling himself and pulling himself from the sludge.

"Yes, sir," Zhao said, rushing out.

The goo pulled itself off as he climbed out, leaving him dry and naked. His rifle and sidearm rested on a table nearby, along with a clean uniform.

Looking himself over, he saw that the blisters were healed, and physically, he felt fine.

"*I need my armor,*" Stathis thought to his SCBI.

"*It is being cleaned and repaired,*" the SCBI said.

At least it wasn't pressing him for a name. Stathis didn't think he was ready for that.

He pulled on his uniform and went over to Hakala's section, which had been hidden by a cloth partition that was now pulled back.

"I'm sorry," Stathis said, forcing himself to meet her eyes. She'd been crying.

"For what?"

"For killing Gleipner," Stathis said, and Hakala stared at him. He couldn't guess what she was thinking.

"Gleipner knew the risk," Hakala said. "Did you know the d-bomb would kill them?"

"I should have," Stathis said.

"The SCBIs did not know," Hakala said. "How could you?"

"What if they did?" Stathis asked.

"They would have said so," Hakala answered, and he heard anger in her voice. "They did not, and neither did you. It is not your fault."

"I gave the command to detonate, knowing we were within the blast radius," Stathis said.

"Don't be a *typerys*," Hakala said. "Unless you and they knew, don't take that blame. Besides, as I recall, it was a timer, and we just were not fast enough."

"I'm the senior officer," Stathis said. "It's my duty to take the blame. The buck stops here."

Now Hakala glared at him from the tub of sludge as tears streaked her face.

"Don't," Hakala said. "I miss Gleipner, but I know you miss Shrek more."

Stathis didn't know what to say. She had to care for Gleipner as much as he cared about Shrek. She was right, and she was wrong. He was at fault, one way or the other.

"You stay here and rest," Stathis said. "You deserve it."

"You are going to leave me alone, lightly armed, here in the med lab?" Hakala asked.

Again, Stathis was at a loss for words. When she put it that way, he didn't have much choice. Zhao had waited for him to wake up.

"*What can I do to help?*" Stathis asked his SCBI.

"*Rest and recover,*" the SCBI said. "*I am assisting the others using teleoperated robots and programming. We have enough robots working on the third tram. Sergeant Zhao expects to be ready within the hour.*"

"I can't weld, fetch, or carry?" Stathis asked.

"*No, sir,*" his SCBI said. "*Sergeant Moore and Quinn's SCBIs are assisting, as well. Others are running recon drones through the tunnels, looking for obstacles.*"

"We're still in Shorr space?"

"Yes, sir. The inkeri fields are stressed but holding so far, including the hydroponics alue. It looks like Shroggath was preparing for some kind of orbital bombardment. We have discovered trams of nukes designed for atmospheric entry, enough to render a very large planet uninhabitable."

"Where are we going?"

"Unknown."

"What happens if we take out the Shorr-space controller?"

"The course is set; we will arrive at our destination unless we conduct an emergency emergence."

Yanking the Bifrost out of Shorr space was the last thing Stathis wanted to do. He remembered what had happened to the *Eagle*. Such an abrupt departure ripped things and would probably drag more vanhat through the dimensions to regular space. That would be a disaster.

"I want the bastard dead," Stathis said, "*as soon as possible. Expire the birth certificate with a flamethrower.*"

"Yes, sir," the SCBI said, and Stathis expected it would be sharing his intent with the other SCBIs. But was it?

"Tell the other SCBIs and McCarthy that," Stathis said to make sure. "The sooner the better. When we come out of Shorr space, I want Bifrost to be ready to fight."

"Understood, sir," the SCBI said. "I must point out that due to extensive damage and lack of control, the offensive weaponry of the Bifrost is questionable."

"We might not have a choice. If we pop out of Shorr space into the middle of a vanhat fleet, we'll have to fight or die."

"Understood, sir."

Stathis hoped it did.

Sitting down in a chair and laying his rifle across his lap, he faced the door, still unwilling to face Hakala. He wasn't going to leave her alone here, though.

"I forgive you," Hakala said.

Stathis nodded, not trusting his voice. How could she? Would he forgive her for killing Shrek if their roles had been reversed? Perhaps she wasn't as close to Gleipner as he'd been with Shrek.

"Lie back and heal," Stathis said, finally finding his voice. "I'll keep watch."

"This is good enough," Hakala said. "My nanites have been replaced, and I can continue healing while mobile."

Watching the door, he listened as she extricated herself from the healing sludge and got dressed.

What next?

He was in command, and he'd have to make plans. Right now, he didn't have any options. When Bifrost left Shorr space, he'd have to evaluate the situation. It wouldn't be good—of that he had no doubt. They'd likely be surrounded by vanhat and immediately attacked. They'd have to quickly transition to Shorr space to escape.

Could they escape?

The vanhat were chasing the *Musashi*. How could he evade them in a massive mobile asteroid city-ship like Bifrost? *Musashi* might have a vanhat spy, but Stathis was sure Bifrost had thousands, maybe tens of thousands, and there was no way he could purge them.

Would it ever end? When would he, Hakala, and the others finally be safe?

There was a light at the end of the tunnel, and Stathis was sure it was a train coming at him, full speed.

Others might lose hope and fall, but Stathis was going to punch that train in the face.

That's what Shrek would want.

* * * * *

Chapter Sixty-Six: Naataan

Admiral Diamond Winters, USMC

The fleet slid out of Shorr space and immediately began targeting everything in the area. Winters checked the display as other ships entered.

"Acceptable," Sakamoto said on the command link. He was likely watching the deployment, too.

Acceptable? It was damned good. Long-distance Shorr-space transitions weren't accurate, and frequently spread the ships out quite a bit. However, with *Musashi* coordinating things and a shorter distance, the fleet slid out of Shorr space in a relatively tight formation.

They arrived at the edge of the system and prepared there. There was enough sunspot activity to degrade regular radio communications, but it wasn't as bad as Winters would have expected.

Sensors showed the Voorga ships were still pushing out, and they must have just detected the fleet in the outreaches. The fleet had transitioned in near one of the outer system outposts, which had quickly panicked and called for help. The call for help was just now reaching Naataan.

"Initiating laser links," a bridge officer said. Thuthta was also transmitting the translation matrix and protocols to the Unfallen ships.

Winters took a deep breath. She'd worked with Sif and Thuthta. Her words would be translated into the Voorga language since the Unfallen obviously didn't have the human language.

"Attention, Unfallen," Winters said. "I am Admiral Winters of the human Seraphim Fleet. We have come to talk with the being Liathon. The devourers have returned, and it is time for her to awaken and lead the fight."

Minutes ticked by as Winters watched the displays. At first, the Voorga ships scattered and fled, and two actually slid into Shorr space, but someone was on the ball, and the ships began to match trajectory and return to some pretense of formation. This was their best fleet, and they looked like amateurs. A lot of amateurs.

Professionals were predictable, but the world was full of amateurs, and in their unpredictability, amateurs did stupid and very dangerous things.

"No," the return link said. "As the High Holy of the Unfallen and Fallen, we will not awaken Liathon. We were told we must face the devourers on our own. We are strong enough. We will not awaken Liathon."

Winters looked over at Sif, who was talking with Thuthta as his ships entered normal space, spread out and random. Even over such a short distance, they hadn't been able to remain together, and they hadn't come in as close to Naataan as Winters would have liked. It would be difficult to provide supporting fire if they were attacked.

"We must awaken Liathon," Thuthta said on the link.

"Thuthta," the voice said. "Brother. You betray us."

"No," Thuthta said. "I have faced the devourers. We are not ready."

"We must be ready," the voice said.

Brother? Was Thuthta related to the High Holy? Or was it just words?

"Let these aliens awaken Liathon," Thuthta said. "We were told not to awaken her, but they are aliens. They are not us."

"Unacceptable," the High Holy said. "The Angel Liathon died in the final battle and has been laid to rest forever. She will not return."

"She is immortal," Thuthta said. "You know that."

Winters listened to the translated exchange, and a chill ran down her spine. Obviously, there was much that Thuthta hadn't shared.

"We are not to awaken her, or the demon Gaibron will return to watch us be destroyed."

"The ancient texts are unclear," Thuthta said.

"Clear enough. You must not awaken her."

"The Unfallen that guard her tomb know more," Thuthta said. "Ask them. Their order is ancient."

"No. Those who go to her tomb never return to civilization. They commit their lives to preserving her tomb. They will not allow us, or these aliens, to disturb her."

"Ask them," Thuthta said.

"No," the High Holy replied. "Not acceptable."

"Stand aside," Thuthta said. "Do not stain your honor and waste the resources of our people."

The enemy fleet was coming together. There were a lot of them. Winters didn't want to give the order to retreat because if they did, they wouldn't be able to stop running. Besides, Marines don't retreat.

"I have heard the call from behind the walls of our reality," Thuthta said. "We are not ready. We have squandered our resources."

"We have not."

"These aliens will show you if they must," Thuthta said. "Their ships are large and powerful. They have fought the devourers. They have come for Liathon. You cannot stop them."

"They are not big enough," High Holy said.

"*Paska,*" Sif said nearby, and Winters knew the shit was about to hit the fan. Apparently, Thuthta had misjudged. The *Musashi* wasn't big enough to intimidate them.

"Missile launch," the *Musashi* reported as the fleet's corvettes pushed out and away in the direction of the incoming Voorga missiles. "Flight characteristics are expected."

Which was a relief, hopefully. No surprises yet, except the Voorga wanted to fight. The missiles were about thirty minutes out. Not the longest range, but if they were smart, they could volley them and time the speed so that all the volleys struck at the same time. Amateurs would launch volley after volley.

Countermissiles from the corvettes began launching. The volume of missiles from the Voorga fleet wasn't overwhelming.

"See the might of the Unfallen," the High Holy said. "Your ships make big targets. You may surrender. We are merely testing our missiles."

"We don't wish to erase you," Winters said. "Your missile test is unimpressive, and it's coming in our direction. Is it your intent to engage us in battle? Are you wasting resources?"

"Launch a test of our own?" Sakamoto asked on a private link.

"No," Winters said, changing links to Sakamoto. On the screen, *Musashi* gave the corvettes a hundred percent chance of halting the incoming missiles. "Evade them."

"We must not accept this as an attack," Thuthta said on a direct link to Winters. "Please. This is a show of force. The High Holy wants to see if you will break and run."

"We'll wipe them out before they get to us," Winters said. "We're not in any danger. Yet."

"Please wait until the last minute," Thuthta said. "Do not panic."

Thuthta was telling *her* not to panic?

"They must believe us," Thuthta said.

"They are calling our bluff," Sakamoto said. "We may still be able to defeat them, but I fear we will cause extreme damage to their fleet."

"We must awaken Liathon," Thuthta said. "If the Unfallen fleet must be destroyed, then so be it."

"Find me solutions," Winters said as the missiles came closer. The missiles could be recalled, but once they reached the outer edge of the envelope, the corvettes would have to respond. She wouldn't risk the fleet.

"Transition out and then back in, Admiral-sama?"

"That could be seen as running away," Winters said.

"Then it is going to be a fight, Admiral-sama," Sakamoto said. "I'm sorry."

"Incoming transition," *Musashi* reported. "It is massive. Likely a Weermag mothership or the Collective mothership."

Anything that could go wrong would go wrong. She wasn't going to fight the Collective or vanhat, not here. If the Voorga wanted a fight, she'd give it to them.

"Now you're going to find out how bad things are," Winters said.

"Incoming transmission," *Musashi* said. "It is the Bifrost."

The Bifrost, under vanhat control, coming here to commit genocide against the Voorga. Bonnie had been out of touch with McCarthy, but the last thing she'd heard was that he was missing, presumed dead. With Bifrost in Shorr space, communication wasn't possible. She didn't want to believe he was dead, but she knew for sure he hadn't been in command of Bifrost. Which meant the vanhat wanted it here.

"On link," Winters said, wondering what the Jotun was going to say. Did Bifrost have enough weapons?

"It is unencrypted. Cannot confirm identity," *Musashi* said as Stathis' voice rang out.

"Attention, *Musashi*, this is Major Stathis aboard the Imperial Ship Bifrost. Are you picking a fight? I came as fast as I could. You whistle, we missile. You ping, we sting, you aim, we maim, you locate, we detonate."

Winters felt so much better. The communication was unencrypted, and the Unfallen High Holy should be able to decipher the communications. "Major Stathis. Welcome back. Running to the fight again? Just in time, we'll provide targeting data."

Winters looked at the readout coming from *Musashi*. Bifrost looked like hell. She could tell that most of the systems were offline and non-responsive. Would the Voorga realize that? Their sensors weren't as good.

The Voorga fleet, which was changing course toward the *Musashi*, changed course again, and the corvettes began to swat missiles out of space.

"You aim, we maim," Stathis said as *Musashi* displayed targeting data coming from Bifrost. Some weapons systems were working. Damned few, though. "You tag, we bag. Who are we fighting?"

"They're the Voorga," Winters said. "Some of them are allies. We'll send you targeting data."

"Establishing an encrypted link," *Musashi* reported. "Established. All messaging is encrypted."

"What's your status?" Winters asked. The Bifrost couldn't fight. It would be an easy target.

"Most of Bifrost is insecure and full of vanhat. Optimistically? We have control of maybe 10 percent of the weapons, and I think full control of the Shorr-space drives, Admiral," Stathis said. "I'm so glad to see you. The situation over here is precarious, and we could be attacked and maybe overrun any minute. You can count on us to look big and tough, but we have the bite of an anorexic field mouse suffering lockjaw."

Better than she expected. The sheer size of Bifrost was intimidating her; it had to be scaring the piss out of the Voorga. Another pair of ships fled into Shorr space.

"Test concluded," the High Holy said. "Thank you for eliminating those missiles. They are older models, and this was a successful test. Had this been a real attack, we would have launched more missiles. Perhaps we should discuss your mission in more detail before we fight?"

"Of course," Winters muttered so nobody could hear.

"That's enough," Winters said to Stathis. "The Voorga are standing down."

The Voorga fleet began to break away, taking a much higher orbit around Naataan.

Now came the hard part.

* * * * *

Chapter Sixty-Seven: Emergence

Major Zale Stathis, USMC

Stathis was sitting at a console, and Hakala was sitting in the commander's chair. Bifrost was her home, and Stathis didn't feel right without her in charge. She'd listen to him, but he felt some comfort in knowing that others could make decisions, too, and if he fell, then she'd be in a position of authority.

"Emergence in ten minutes," his SCBI said.

Emergence into what? Nobody knew. The only thing Stathis knew for sure, though he couldn't confirm it, was that when they came out, they had to be ready to fight. The vanhat were coming for them, and there was no doubt about that.

It had been nearly an hour since the last attack on Skögul, and nothing more than wandering mobs of froggers had stumbled into Valhöll's automated defenses.

"I want the strike to occur right before we exit Shorr space," Stathis said out loud. "Then we need to seize control of the systems and figure out where we are as soon as possible. Prepare to jump again on arrival; the vanhat will be coming in hot and heavy. I don't want to bomb anybody."

"Wilco, sir," Zhao said. Three displays showed movement. The three automated trams, with bolted-on power supplies and d-bombs, sped down the tunnels toward the power plant.

The trams gained speed, and a timer appeared on a fourth display, redundant, since his SCBI had a display visible in his cybernetic view. Lochoki and the others didn't quite have that view, though. Maybe. They had decent cybernetics.

Stathis did his best to look relaxed as he leaned back in the comfortable chair where some senior Vanir officer had once sat, advising and reporting to the admiral who'd sat where Hakala was.

This wasn't likely to be an exciting event. What would the trams see? Probably nothing more than boring tunnels until they arrived at the station. Four different stations serviced the power facility. Two cargo, two personnel.

Stathis wanted to fidget. He didn't like having nothing to do.

"*Have you decided on a name for me?*" his SCBI asked.

"*You are not Shrek,*" Stathis said, watching the trams speed through the tunnel. One slammed through a small group of froggers. He'd have to replay that one later. Add it to a comedy clip.

"*My name is Not-Shrek?*" the SCBI asked.

"No," Stathis said, though the temptation was there.

What was he going to name it? It couldn't be Shrek. It would never be Shrek. He wouldn't disgrace Shrek's memory like that.

"Stand by for transition," the SCBI said.

The viewscreen showed the trams speeding up.

"*Transition to regular space,*" Not-Shrek said, and the cameras showing the d-bomb trams flashed to static. "*Detonation. Working to seize control of systems.*"

Display screens came to life around the command center as the SCBIs took control of the sensors and tried to make sense of where they were.

"*We are in high orbit above a large planet,*" Not-Shrek said. "*Numerous ships detected. Seizing control of Bifrost defenses. 8 percent are online and accessible.*"

"Another *paska lounas,*" Hakala said. "Several fleets. Acquiring targets, analyzing location. Missiles in flight detected."

Hakala and Stathis saw it at the same time. The *Musashi* and her escort ships were in orbit, maneuvering against a flight of incoming missiles.

"Open a link," Stathis said, hoping that was an option. He might be stepping on Hakala's toes since she was in command, but it was too late.

"*Opening link to the* Musashi*,*" Not-Shrek reported. "*Unencrypted radio link only at this point. Will negotiate encryption upon link.*"

Stathis smiled. That meant everyone in the region would hear. Which also meant he couldn't tell the truth. Bifrost couldn't fight its way out of a wet paper bag.

"Attention, *Musashi*, this is Major Stathis aboard the Imperial Ship Bifrost. Are you picking a fight? I came as fast as I could. You whistle, we missile. You ping, we sting, you aim, we maim, you locate, we detonate."

"Major Stathis," Winters said, and Stathis imagined he heard happiness in her voice, "welcome back. Running to the fight again? Just in time, we'll provide targeting data."

Stathis looked at the displays. There were too many gaps in Bifrost's weapon arcs. Could they at least pretend to be operational?

Hakala looked grim. Because of the situation, or because Stathis had stepped on her toes?

"Lots of ships," Hakala said to the command center, "smaller than I would expect. Alien. Lots of ships. I don't think they are vanhat, though."

As he watched, the alien ships began accelerating away, and the *Musashi's* escort corvettes erased the flight of incoming missiles.

"You aim, we maim," Stathis said on the general link. Hakala was giving orders to the batteries she could access, but Stathis was fine being the communications officer. "You tag, we bag. Who are we fighting?"

"They're the Voorga," Winters said. "Some of them are allies. We'll send you targeting data."

"*Encryption established,*" Not-Shrek said. "*Switch to encrypted link?*"

"*Yes,*" Stathis said.

"*Encryption established.*"

"*What's your status?*" Winters asked. She had to be looking at the display and had a pretty good idea of what she should be seeing if the Bifrost was fully operational.

"Most of Bifrost is insecure and full of vanhat. Optimistically? We have control of maybe 10 percent of the weapons, and I think full control of the Shorr-space drives, Admiral," Stathis said. "I'm so glad to see you. The situation over here is precarious, and we could be attacked and maybe overrun any minute. You can count on us to look big and tough, but we have the bite of an anorexic field mouse suffering lockjaw."

"That's enough," Winters said. "The Voorga are standing down."

"Does that mean we missed the fight?" Stathis asked.

"No," Winters said. "It means the fight is just about to begin, and you're just the man we need."

"You need me, Admiral?" Stathis asked. "I'm sorry. I thought my situation was bad. How screwed are you?"

"Considering you're an improvement? What do you think?" Winters said, and Stathis heard the smile in her voice.

"Semper Fi," Stathis said as data began to flow to his SCBI. "You initiate, we obliterate."

# # # # #

About William S. Frisbee, Jr.

Marine veteran, reader, writer, martial artist, computer consultant, dungeon master, computer gamer, dreamer, webmaster, proud American, and best of all, dad.

Growing up in Europe during the height of the Cold War and serving as a Marine infantryman through the fall of communism shaped Bill's perspective on life and the world. When most Marines were out trying to get lucky, he was studying tactical manuals. Years later, he shared much of his knowledge to a website for writers of military science fiction.

These days, he's brushed off the pocket protector and is a top gun computer consultant.

Learn more at http://www.WilliamSFrisbee.com.

* * * * *

Get the **free** Four Horsemen prelude story **"Shattered Crucible"**

and discover other titles by Theogony Books at:

http://chriskennedypublishing.com/

* * * * *

Meet the author and other CKP authors on the Factory Floor:

https://www.facebook.com/groups/461794864654198

* * * * *

Did you like this book?
Please write a review!

* * * * *

The following is an
Excerpt from Book One of Symbiote Wars:

Symbiote Wars

Chris Kennedy

Available from Theogony Books

eBook, Audio, and Paperback

Excerpt from "Symbiote Wars:"

As you expected, all three ships have shut down their shields and are docking with the refueling station, Suzie noted.

Johnson looked up from the nuclear missile he was standing over. "How much time do we have before the battlecruiser is tied up?"

Fifteen minutes or so.

Johnson's jaw clenched. "It's going to be close."

The Terrans had followed the Cowlee fleet through the bridge back into the Cashtal system and had then shadowed them as they'd headed for the refueling station.

"Where did you learn to do this?" Sutton asked.

"When you've been alive as long as I have, you have time to do things. I went through sapper school about twenty years ago."

"You played with *nukes* in sapper school? That's a thing?"

"Well, no, not nukes, but the principle is the same. Strap the thing that goes boom onto the thing you want blown up, and you're all set."

"Great, but I was more wondering about playing with nukes, not blowing things up."

"Oh." Johnson smiled. "This is something I've never done before, but the concept is straightforward enough." He looked back down at the missile he was elbows' deep into. "Now, you might want to let me concentrate while I remove the warhead. Especially since it's kind of leaky, and I'd like to minimize our exposure to the radiation."

Sutton's jaw dropped, and he wanted to ask another question, but decided it was better to let Johnson do his thing.

<Are you okay?> Frank asked. <Your bio signs are spiking.>

<I've never seen *a nuke, much less played with one before. And his lackadaisical attitude toward it is really freaking me out.*>

<Doc said that Suzie is sending the blueprints to the bomb to his goggles. All he has to do is follow the steps in the manual, and everything should be fine.>

<That would have been nice to know a while ago.>

<Besides,> Frank added, <*setting off a nuke is much harder than you'd think. You can't just drop it on the floor and have it go boom. You need the*

detonator to function in the manner intended to actually get a nuclear blast. Even if you had an electrical discharge and some of the explosives surrounding the nuclear matter happened to go off, it probably *wouldn't go nuclear.>*

<*Also good to know info.*>

<*Of course, the explosives going off would kill us all, and shower us with enriched radioactive material, ensuring our demise, but we wouldn't die in a nuclear explosion, if that's what you're worried about.*>

<*Pretty sure I didn't need to know all of that extra stuff, either, Frank. I would have been happy if you'd have left it with 'there won't be a nuclear blast.'*>

<*But that wouldn't have been all the information.*>

<*Sometimes Humans don't want to* know *all the info. This is one of those times.*>

"You're watching what I'm doing, right?" Johnson asked softly.

"Yeah."

"Good, because you're going to have to disassemble the other one while I build our bombs."

"I *what?*"

"Don't yell," Johnson said. "You don't want to startle me."

"But I—"

"We don't have enough time. I'm going to need you to take a more active role."

"But I—"

"Do you want to save Earth or not?"

"Well yeah, but—"

"Suzie, send James the schematics you're sending me, along with the procedure."

Sending, Suzie replied, her voice soft.

James blinked as the blueprints and procedures appeared in his view. They were weird—he could see them when he focused but they faded when he looked through them. "This is the best heads-up display I've ever seen. I didn't know the goggles could do this."

"How have you been doing your checklists?"

"Just projecting them into my view and looking at everything else around them."

Johnson stopped and looked up. "That's not a good way to do it. You're going to miss something that way."

"Well, maybe if my teacher had told me the goggles had a HUD..."

"Sorry. Sometimes I forget you haven't had ground school, which is where you'd have learned that. My bad." He shrugged. "Now get that tool kit—" he pointed "—and get to work on the other one."

* * * * *

Get "Symbiote Wars" here:
https://www.amazon.com/dp/B0DQVFRJ5R.

Find out more about Chris Kennedy at:
https://chriskennedypublishing.com.

* * * * *

The following is an
Excerpt from Book One of The Prince of Britannia Saga:

The Prince Awakens

Fred Hughes

Available from Theogony Books

eBook, Paperback, and (soon) Audio

Excerpt from "The Prince Awakens:"

Sixth Fleet was in chaos. Fortunately, all the heavy units were deployed forward toward the attacking fleet and were directing all the defensive fire they had downrange at the enemy. More than thirteen thousand Swarm attack ships were bearing down on a fleet of twenty-six heavy escorts and the single monitor. The monitor crew had faith in their shields and guns, but could they survive against this many? They would soon find out.

Luckily, they didn't have to face all the Swarm ships. Historically, Swarm forces engaged major threats first, then went after the escorts. Which was why the monitor had to be considered the biggest threat in the battle.

Then the Swarm forces deviated from their usual pattern. The Imperial plan was suddenly irrelevant as the Swarm attack ships divided into fifteen groups and attacked the escorts, which didn't last long. When the last dreadnought died in a nuclear fireball, the Swarm attack ships turned and moved toward the next fleet in the column, Fourth Fleet, leaving the monitor behind.

The entire plan was in shambles. But, more importantly, the whole fleet was at risk of being defeated. The admiral's only option now was to save as many as he could.

"Signal to the Third, Fifth, and Seventh Fleets. The monitors are to execute Withdrawal Plan Beta."

The huge monitors had eight fleet tugs that were magnetically attached to the hull when not in use. Together, the eight tugs could get the monitors into hyperspace. However, this process took time, due to the time it took for the eight tugs to generate a warp field large enough to encompass the enormous ship. It could take up to an hour to accomplish, and they didn't have an hour.

Plan Bravo would use six heavy cruisers to accomplish the same thing. The cruisers' larger fusion engines meant the field could be generated within ten minutes, assuming no one was shooting at them. "The remaining fleet units will move to join First Fleet. Admiral

Mason in First Fleet will take command of the combined force and deploy it for combat."

The fleet admiral continued giving orders.

"I want Second Fleet to do the same, but I want heavy cruiser Squadron Twenty-Three to merge with First Fleet. Admiral Conyers, I want you to coordinate with the Eighth, Ninth, and Tenth Fleets. I want their monitors to perform a normal Alpha Withdrawal. As they're preparing to do that, have their escorts combine into a single fleet. Figure out which admiral is senior and assign him local command to organize them." He pointed at the single icon indicating the only ship left in Sixth Fleet. "Signal *Prometheus* to move at best speed to join First Fleet. That covers everything for now. I fear there's not much we can do for Fourth Fleet."

The icons were already moving on the tactical display as orders were transmitted and implemented.

"I've given the fleets in the planet's orbit their orders, Admiral," the chief of staff informed him. "The other fleets are on the move now. The Swarm should contact Fourth Fleet in approximately ten minutes. Based on their attack of Sixth Fleet, the battle will last about twenty minutes. With fifteen minutes for them to reorganize and travel to First Fleet, we're looking at forty-five minutes to engagement with the Swarm."

"What are the estimates on the rest of the fleets moving to join up with First?"

"Twenty minutes, Admiral. However, *Prometheus* is going to take at least forty-five and will arrive about the same time as the enemy."

"Organize six heavies from Seventh Fleet and have them coordinate a rendezvous with *Prometheus*, earliest possible timing," the admiral ordered. "Then execute a Beta jump. Unless the Swarm forces divert, they should have enough time. Then find out how many ships have the upgraded forty-millimeter rail gun systems and form them into a single force. O'Riley said that converting the guns to barrage fire was a simple program update. Brevet Commodore O'Riley will be in command of the newly created Task Force Twenty-Three. They are to form a wall of steel which the fleet will form behind. I am not sure if we can win this, but we need to bleed these bastards if we can't. If they win, they'll still have to make up those losses, and that will delay the next attack."

* * * * *

Get "The Prince Awakens" here: https://www.amazon.com/dp/B0BK232YT2.

Find out more about Fred Hughes at: https://chriskennedypublishing.com.

* * * * *

Made in the USA
Las Vegas, NV
09 August 2025